MW00810123

MURDER

on

HOLLYWOOD

BEACH

The Messy Girl Murder Series

PROPERTY OF
Waldorf Astoria Monarch
Beach Resort

MURDER

on

HOLLYWOOD

BEACH

The Messy Girl Murder Series

CAROL FINIZZA

Light Messages
Torchflame Books

Durham, NC

Copyright © 2022 Carol Finizza

Murder on Hollywood Beach: The Messy Girl Murder Series
Carol Finizza
www.carolfinizzaauthor.com
CarolFinizza@strandoc.com

Published 2022, by Torchflame Books
an Imprint of Light Messages
www.lightmessages.com
Durham, NC 27713 USA
SAN: 920-9298

Paperback ISBN: 978-1-61153-432-0
E-book ISBN: 978-1-61153-433-7
Library of Congress Control Number: 2021923343

ALL RIGHTS RESERVED
No part of this publication may be reproduced, stored in a retrieval system, or transmitted in any form or by any means, electronic, mechanical, photocopying, recording, scanning, or otherwise, except as permitted under Section 107 or 108 of the 1976 International Copyright Act, without the prior written permission except in brief quotations embodied in critical articles and reviews.

This book is a work of fiction. Names, characters, businesses, organizations, places, events, and incidents are the product of the author's imagination or are used fictitiously. Any resemblance to actual persons, living or dead, events, or locales is entirely coincidental.

With thanks for
the wonderful memories of my late husband Tony
the blessed friendship of my BFF Paul
the perpetual joy of my children Patrick, Kelly, and Billy

ACKNOWLEDGMENTS

SPECIAL THANKS TO MY FRIENDS AND FAMILY, Amy Brophy, Billy O'Connell, Chris Rush, Joan Thurman, Karen Boyd, Mindy Gullen, Nancy Boyarski, Paul Segal, Penny Rose, Rhonda O'Connor, and Torrey and Alana Mellgren who read early drafts of my book and provided valuable input. Thank you to Erin Haynes, the typo queen, who diligently edited my book. A big thank you to the team at Light Messages Publishing for helping me bring this story to life.

CHAPTER 1

FRIDAY, LATE DECEMBER. After midnight. I'm in my closet, buried in a pile of cashmere sweaters, wool crewnecks, and cotton pullovers, obsessively color-coding them into neat little summer, fall, winter, and spring stacks.

I step back, study my work.

Something's wrong.

Every article of clothing is either hanging straight on matching wooden hangers, or meticulously folded into well-organized sections, exactly the way it's done at J. Crew. To most people, my closet probably looks perfect. To me, it's a mess.

Seriously. In plain view, my Tod's rest in a clear box right next to my Nikes, which are next to Tory Burch flats. Totally out of alphabetical order. I grab the Nikes and quickly switch the silver flats in front of the Tod's. I step out of my bedroom closet, then walk back and linger at the threshold to take in the big picture.

Everything's in the wrong color sequence.

I pick up a couple shoe boxes, about ready to call it hopeless, when my next-door neighbor's dog erupts in a barking frenzy. I set the boxes back the way they were and step over to the window that looks out to the beach and gives me a glimpse of my neighbor's house. I pull up the bamboo shade and then crank open the window. Cold, damp air hits me.

During the day, I have a great view of the ocean and dunes behind my house. Sometimes, on one of those full-moon winter nights, the waves shimmer with phosphorescence, and the

1

crushed granite sand winks relentlessly at the star-studded sky. But on this moonless night, all I see is the ocean between dark mounds of sand. Through the mist, I can barely make out the blur of Christmas lights on the oil platforms off the coast in the distance. I search the beach for activity. None. At least, none that I can see. Daisy, my neighbor's dog, and the sweetest Lab in the world, is howling now. I can hear her pulling on her chain. But from this angle, I can't see her. Is she hurt?

Stepping back into the closet, I grab a sweatshirt from the ragbag, yank it over my T-shirt, then slip into a pair of Uggs.

Daisy yelps, loud and mournful. Goosebumps tickle my head.

An image of Nicole Simpson's dog Kato and the sound of his *plaintive wail* pops into my mind.

My heart thumps as I hurry back to the window and search outside for...I don't even know what I'm looking for.

Did I read that a young woman was found raped and murdered? Did it happen here on Hollywood Beach?

Was it before or after I moved here?

Crap. I hate living alone. Which is obviously one of the reasons I stayed married for as long as I did, even after everything started falling apart.

I search the endless stretch of beach houses for any sign of life. Not a light on in any of them. It's a ghost town. No wonder my grandmother gave me her house and moved to Santa Barbara.

After cranking the window closed, I drop the shade, then grab my iPhone off the nightstand. I scan the room for a weapon. The best I can come up with is a wooden hanger. My house is too damned organized. All the good stuff, like golf clubs and ski poles, are tucked away in the garage cabinets.

Standing in the middle of my room, a death grip on the hanger, I'm paralyzed. I'm not sure I really want to know why Daisy is barking—or at what.

Snapping out of my paralysis, I race to my bedroom door and shut it. The hinges screech. I quickly set the rusty old lock and lean against the door as if the Night Stalker is on the other side.

Stop it. There's no reason to panic.

Seriously, there are a million reasons why Daisy could be agitated. Clearly, I'm overreacting. *Dogs bark.* Except, when I think about it, Daisy's not much of a barker. And anyway, this doesn't sound like a *Get off my lawn* kind of a bark.

Daisy's growling now—a feral growl. *She sees something.* I feel it. Someone is out there.

Did I lock everything up before coming upstairs?

A snapshot of my downstairs pops into my mind: front door, back door, kitchen windows, bathroom window. Crap. Did I leave the bathroom window open? I hope not. It's just large enough for a Charles-Manson-sized mass murderer to crawl through.

I'll never get to sleep until I check the downstairs doors and windows. Phone and hanger in hand, I take a deep breath, open my bedroom door and tiptoe to the upstairs landing. I lean into the banister and stare into the dark, awful pit below.

Face your fears, right? I mean, that's the mantra my therapist gave me to help when I hit the panic button.

After taking a few moments to adjust to the dark, I tiptoe downstairs. I check the front door locks and latches, then the back porch door and windows. I creep through the living room, into the guest bathroom.

Sure enough, the window is open. I step in, trip over a paint can and grab the sink to catch myself before colliding with a step ladder. I painted the bathroom a couple days ago and obviously forgot to close the window.

I step around the new toilet yet to be installed and jam my phone into my pocket, then set the hanger on the counter. The window screen is in place—good news. But beads of rain are clinging to the inside of it and puddling on the sill. After wiping up the water, I reach up and force the old wood casement window down, then set the lock.

Next home improvement project is to replace all the doors, windows, and locks.

Once back in the living room, I press my face close to the window and cup my hands around my eyes to see outside. Everything looks fine...dark and spooky, but fine. Just the way it was when I got home from shopping tonight.

Even though it's windy, the patio chairs are positioned neatly around the table, the chaise lounges face out to sea.

But Daisy is still barking. This is crazy. Even though I can't see her, I can hear her chain clanging against whatever it's tethered to. I yank my phone out of my pocket and touch my neighbor's name on my iPhone. After six rings, her voice tells me to leave a message, someone will get back to me ASAP.

But what if my neighbor can't get back to me because something awful has happened to her? I hang up, then press her name and try again. No answer.

Okay. Be reasonable. It's after midnight. Maybe she's a really, *really* sound sleeper. She's probably not even home, which is another good reason not to go outside to check things out.

God, I'd really love to talk to someone right now. At least when I was married, I had Geoff to talk to. Even though he was hardly ever home, I could at least call him.

I scroll through my contacts list. A1 Self-Storage, AA (I never got a sponsor), Penny Abbott, Airbrush Tanning, Robin Andersen, Arbonne, etc. I finger down the list.

Seriously. I'm thirty-two years old, divorced, living alone, and at this point in my life, there's not a single person that I can call to commiserate with, or even message on Facebook. I know it's after late, but still...

It's my police record. That's why all my friends have kind of dropped me. My *police record.* I mean, if I can't even get my mind around it, how can I expect my friends to?

The thought makes me want to cry. I walk over to the couch and straighten the pillows for the second or third time tonight. Suddenly, I can't seem to carry the weight of my life. Halfway up the stairs, I sit.

My arrest wasn't even really my fault. I went out alone on July Fourth and drank way too much. Big deal. Everybody does stuff like that. On my way home, I was busted for riding my bike under the influence. *Riding my bike.* Not *driving my car.* The police are completely out of control. They said I almost ran into a pedestrian. The guy seriously came out of nowhere. Wasn't even in the crosswalk.

I spent a night in the slammer, and three months in DUI classes. My face suddenly feels hot just thinking about it.

Then a couple weeks after my classes ended, I was shopping for strawberries at Montecito Farmers Market and bumped into my ex-husband, Geoff Martin, and his new wife, Bree. Right in front of the melon cart, Geoff introduces Bree to me. Seriously. As if I didn't know her. For God's sake, she was the former massage therapist at Geoff's Center for Wellness and Rejuvenation. His A-list clients call it The Center. And Bree? Bree is The Center's new VP.

Geoff casually suggested that I go to The Center to lose some weight. He pointed out that I'd really bulked up since our divorce. I couldn't help myself. I smacked him on the head with a baguette and kneed him where it counts, sending him back into the melon cart. Bree called the cops while Geoff tripped and fell into a flower display. As I was led away, Geoff managed to blurt out a comment on the effect of carbs on BMI.

I spent the afternoon at the Santa Barbara jail, and a few weeks in anger management classes.

I'm not a criminal. Seriously. I'm a professional organizer. An anti-clutter expert. I write a weekly blog for the online version of the *Santa Barbara Tribune. Messy Girl.* That's the name of the blog. I know, *professional organizer* doesn't sound like a real job, right? But it's a growing industry. I actually served as publicity secretary for the Santa Barbara chapter of the National Association of Organizing Professionals.

I want to love it. I mean, who wouldn't love organizing Oprah's kitchen pantry, or Carol Burnett's sock drawer? Sock drawer. That's for real. Carol Burnett is a secret sock hoarder.

When I came on the scene, she had hundreds of pairs of socks in every imaginable color and pattern, jammed—*jammed*—into one big drawer. Most of them brand new. We donated the new socks to charity. Which was actually a really generous thing to do.

Stay positive, I tell myself. I mean, the job is definitely going to lead to some big opportunities. I know it will. But sometimes—okay, most of the time—I feel like something's missing. Like all my perfect life plans have steered me in the wrong direction.

I spent a year working these issues out in therapy. That same year, I tortured my friends and family with my sad story. For every smidgen of good advice they'd give me, I'd respond with a, "Yeah, but...." Even the door-to-door preachers stopped coming to my house. Honestly, I would never have been friends with me.

Finally, even I got bored with myself.

Now, with the exception of a few minor obsessions, I'm a new person. I'm getting my life back. I actually have a relatively decent relationship with my mother, two brothers, and a small contingent of friends and coworkers who have stood by me, more or less. I have no real love interest yet, but I've gone out on a few dates.

I feel myself starting to obsess on how pathetic I am to be reorganizing my closet on a Friday night, when everybody else I know, including my neighbor, is probably out celebrating the holidays with friends. It's just a week before Christmas, and I don't even have a tree yet.

It's not like I didn't have other options.

Kim, my best friend, sort of invited me out tonight. She zoomed right by me on my street when I was coming home from Target. Lucky for me, I made a U-turn and cut her off right before she left my neighborhood. She said she was happy to see me. She actually looked more shocked than happy. It's probably because I haven't seen her in months.

Anyway, I was thrilled to see her. She was in her brand-new

silver Range Rover. The big one. Love that car.

Kim didn't exactly invite me out. Did she say, "Let's do something?" or "Let's do something tonight?" I can't remember. But what I do remember is that she sped away before I had a chance to ask her why she was on Hollywood Beach in the first place.

I have that effect on people these days.

A metal-on-metal scraping sound wrenches me out of my funk. Did the sound come from next door or my patio? Crap, it sounds close. I sit ramrod straight. There it is again. My heart slams against my chest.

The wind picks up. A tree branch slaps a downstairs window. I stand and white-knuckle the banister. Daisy's bark is now a devilish rumble.

What do I do? Call the police? Tell them Freddie Krueger *and* OJ are outside my house, upsetting my neighbor's dog?

Seriously. I'm not thinking straight. I'm exhausted. My imagination's running wild. Maybe Daisy's just barking at moving branches and shadows. She could be. Right?

Right?

All I want to do is crawl under my duvet and sleep. I pocket my phone and run upstairs.

Halfway up, a sharp rap on the window stops me. I listen. Nothing. Then the gate at my side yard scrapes open. I lean toward the sound. Metal hinges scream. The gate bangs shut. My guts turn to ice. Is someone coming in or going out?

I swallow the lump in my throat. I don't care. I run upstairs, lock my bedroom door, and dial 911. My heart is pounding. Hands are shaking.

In a couple breathless seconds, an operator answers, "Nine-one-one. What's your emergency?"

"Amanda Beckwith." I'm breathing in spasms. "I live at 35625 Hollywood Beach Road. I-I'm all alone. I think someone's breaking into my house!"

"Have you seen an intruder? Is there someone inside your house now?"

Struggling to stay focused on the dispatcher's question, I peek out the window while listening for unusual sounds, like my downstairs picture window breaking, or the pop of a silencer shot through the lock of my front door.

"No, but my neighbor's dog is barking like crazy, and Jean isn't answering her phone." I realize immediately that this doesn't sound like a solid threat.

"Miss, who is Jean?" The dispatcher actually sounds bored.

"My gate opened and closed! I heard it!"

Someone—a man wearing dark clothes—darts across my line of vision. He's on my back patio. Did he come from Jean's yard, or from the beach? From up here, it's hard to see where he came from or what he looks like, but whoever it is, he's heading for my front door.

"I see someone!"

"Please hold," the dispatcher deadpans, "while I see if there is a patrolman near your house."

The line goes quiet. My legs are shaking so hard I can barely stand. Outside, the night seems to grow darker. Daisy is whining as seconds feel like minutes.

Bang! Did someone trip over one of my patio chairs? I can't believe this is happening.

"Ma'am? Are you still there?"

"What the heck's going on? I could be dead. Raped. Or... worse!"

Seriously, is there anything worse?

"I want you to stay inside your house. Do you understand? The sheriff is on his way," the dispatcher says in this no-nonsense tone that makes goosebumps rise on my arms.

The hair on the back of my neck is standing at attention.

"There *is* someone outside!" My voice is shrill, but I'm vindicated.

I'm going to buy a gun, or at least something more threatening than a hanger.

"I saw him!"

"Do not go downstairs."

"No, no, I promise. I'll never go downstairs again, ever!"

I'm blabbering now, but if I can keep the dispatcher talking, I won't feel so alone.

She ignores me. "Do you have guns, weapons in the house? A dog?"

"No guns. Nothing. I don't have a dog."

"Good. Open the door only when the officer identifies himself and shows you his badge."

I'm straining to hear a siren, but all I hear is Daisy.

"Is there any reason why the police are taking so long?"

"The sheriff should be there any moment."

"I'm scared." I sound more infantile than I have in years.

"You have every right to feel afraid."

CHAPTER 2

FEAR IS SENSITIZING EVERY NERVE in my body. My skin hurts. I'm freezing. I can't stop shivering. I think I'm developing restless body syndrome. *Breathe.*

"Stay on the line," the dispatcher says.

What else am I going to do? But I'm not good at waiting. Impatience runs in my family. If I didn't have my cell phone ground into my ear, amplifying the dispatcher's heavy breathing, I'd seriously be rearranging my sock drawer.

"How much longer?" I walk back to the window and fixate on Jean's house.

Daisy isn't making a peep, which is more disturbing than her bark and growl.

"Why's it taking so long?"

"There's an officer in your area," the dispatcher says.

I swear she's appeasing me. I can hear it in her monotone. She knows something but doesn't want to tell me.

"Are you holding back on me?" I say.

"Stay calm. I'll let you know when the sheriff has arrived."

A tree branch spanks the window. My stomach quakes. I retreat to my closet and tinker with the perfume bottles and picture frames on top of my dresser. Organizing things calms me down. By the time the back doorbell rings, I'm almost my normal, neurotic self.

"The sheriff is outside your house," the dispatcher says.

Daisy has started barking again.

"I'll stay on the line until you make contact."

l unlock my bedroom door and hurry downstairs, switching on lights as l go. At the front door, l look through the tiny window. It's the cop. Alone. His name tag reads *Young*. Another officer is in the distance, near the sand dunes. His back is to us. Officer Young is Alec-Baldwin-big. He's wearing a huge gun on his belt, along with a whole lot of other dangerous-looking equipment. The sight of him instantly restores my well-being. With one deep breath, my heartbeat returns to almost normal. l can't believe how scared l was.

"There's an officer here. Do l open the door now?"

"Yes, go ahead," the dispatcher tells me, and she might as well have said, *That's the idea.*

l can hear her drumming her fingers on a desk before the line goes dead.

l pocket my phone, then unlatch the chain and open the door. A blast of cold air hits me. Officer Young even *looks* like Alec Baldwin. Same full cheeks, same ruddy complexion and not-quite-pleasant blue eyes.

His uniform is dappled with raindrops. It's the same boring sheriff-green that cops have worn forever. Why hasn't anyone ever revamped the basic cop uniform?

If Isaac Mizrahi could completely revolutionize Target's style, imagine what another famous designer could do for people in public service. l could write the blog for the show. l'd invite—

"Please step outside," Young says in an official voice that makes me feel like I'm the one in trouble.

"l, um... where should l begin?" l say, without budging.

It's freezing outside and drizzling. Plus, there's something about this guy that makes me feel a little uncomfortable.

"l mean, should l start with the noises l heard, or when l saw the intruder? Or—"

Over Daisy's renewed barking, Young says, "Miss—"

"Daisy! We have to check on Daisy."

He narrows his eyes at me. His lips go unattractively slack. He moves closer to the door.

"Step outside, now!"

I jump, physically jump, at his words. "Sorry. Give me a second."

I grab a down jacket from the hall tree next to the door, and shrug into it. Then I step outside and shut the door behind me. Officer Young steps back, giving me some space.

Face-to-face, Young looks familiar. His eyes flash. *God, he knows me.* Is he one of the cops who arrested me for my DUI? He hands me his business card. Michael Young? His name doesn't ring any bells.

In a flurry of words, I explain to Officer Young that my neighbor, Jean Wilson, seems to be MIA. I tell him about poor Daisy's relentless barking, finishing with a hazy description of the intruder who came through my gate, by way of the beach or the street behind my house, and knocked over my patio chair. Did he come from Jean's house first?

"See?" I nod toward the upended chair, digging my hands into my coat pockets to quell my shivering. "I mean, my neighbor could be injured. Or dead. I think I heard Jean scream. And she didn't answer her phone."

I know I shouldn't lie about Jean screaming, but this guy doesn't seem to be taking me seriously. Really, he seems kind of distracted. I pull the cuffs of my jacket over my hands, fold my arms across my chest.

Young steps over to the chair, looks around, then bends down and rights the chair.

"You need to let me handle the investigation." He reaches into his jacket and takes out a small notebook and pen.

I don't think he's heard a word I've said.

For the next few minutes, Young jots down the who, what, where, and when of the incident. He's writing in slow motion. He keeps looking at me above the pad. If he doesn't hurry up, I'm going to have an anxiety attack.

"I'm going next door," I say.

I sound exactly like my mother, when she's bossing someone around at a charity event.

Daisy is still barking. The poor thing's got to be exhausted. I slip around Officer Young, angling for the Wilson's Cape Cod. The broad stretch of beach fronting our property reminds me how vulnerable we are, cut off from the rest of civilization.

I look over my shoulder. Young is rooted in place. He's talking on his shoulder radio. He's nodding, looking out toward the beach and then back at me.

When I reach the fence between my house and Jean's, Young catches up with me. I show him where I think the prowler came through the gate less than thirty minutes ago. Somewhere down the beach, voices thread into the sounds of distant traffic and crashing waves. Weird. Suddenly, I notice people and flashlights bobbing up and down on the sand. What's the deal?

Officer Young reaches for the gate, but before he opens it, I step in front of him. I mean, is he crazy or something? I watch *CSI*. I'm addicted to *Dexter*. I know all about the chain of evidence.

"Shouldn't we, um, have someone dust for fingerprints before we contaminate the crime scene?"

"I got this," Young snarls, shouldering between me and the gate.

He pushes the gate open and edges me out of the way. When I start to walk past him, he grabs me by the elbow, which is annoying beyond belief. It reminds me of being arrested. He walks me next door to Jean's yard. Daisy is under an awning, thankfully protected from the mist, tethered to a short metal pole near Jean's back door. But even though she sees me, she continues her relentless barking. She growls when I reach my palm-up hand her way. Weird.

"Don't move," Young cautions me, like I'm a ten-year-old, then turns on his flashlight to check around the outside of Jean's house, looking for foul play, I guess.

"It's okay, Daisy," I whisper.

I fill Daisy's bowl with water from a faucet in the garden and set it down within her reach.

"Everything's going to be okay."

"Locked up tight as a drum," Young says. "No sign of forced entry."

He steps over to the pathway that leads to Jean's back gate and turns his back toward me. He starts speaking into his shoulder radio again as his hands motion from the beach to the back of Jean's house. I can't hear a word he's saying, but something about his animated gestures causes my heart to beat hard and my hands to sweat.

"I need to ask you a few questions." Young takes me by the arm again. "Let's go inside where we can talk."

Back at my house, I yank off my Uggs and toss them in the basket next to the hall tree. I turn to find Officer Young right behind me, looking at me like I'd grown an extra head.

"I remember." He's smiling wide. "Figured it out."

"What?"

"Amanda Beckwith? Didn't recognize you at first. Didn't put two and two together. Amazing."

Oh God. He *is* one of the cops who arrested me. I knew it.

"You changed your hair? You look great."

"That's really sweet of you to say." My hand goes to my mop of semi-natural blonde curls.

I try to picture my mug shot. Was my hair longer then? Had I straightened it? I can't remember how I wore my hair on the night I was arrested.

I look at him again, taking in all his features at once. Maybe he's not the officer who arrested me. Maybe he's a friend of a friend. Impossible. He's such a dork.

In a nanosecond, I imagine Officer Young re-dressed for a reality show. You know, *What Not to Wear if You're a Public Servant,* or something like that. I see his blue eyes and full-lipped smile coming alive in trendier clothes. Maybe if he combed his hair differently. I try to picture him more Ben Affleck than Alec Baldwin.

Doesn't help. He looks familiar. I just can't place him.

1 lift the basket holding my shoes toward him. "Mind? I'm kind of picky about my wood floors. They're new. Sorry."

Young pushes the basket out of his way and takes a couple clumsy steps toward a table with family photos on it. He picks one up and studies it.

"Don't recognize me, do you?" His smile fades as he realizes 1 have no clue who he is.

He sets the photo down and looks back at me.

"Right, 1 know. 1 look different in uniform." He takes off his hat and runs his fingers through his hair. "Remember now?"

No, 1 want to reply, but choose diplomacy over honesty.

"Oh my God. I'm so embarrassed," 1 say, using as much enthusiasm as possible for someone who's been scared witless, and sleep deprived.

1 sneak a peek at his card. "Michael. Wow. It's been, um... forever."

"Mike. Everyone calls me Mike. No one except my bill collectors call me Michael," he says, deadpan, then bursts out laughing.

Actually, he's snorting, like he's told the funniest joke in the world.

Oh my God, the snorting. Now 1 remember him. We had one date, right after my divorce. One of my ex-husband's receptionists fixed me up with him—her older brother.

"A law enforcement professional," she'd said. He took me for pizza and a movie. Tried to hold my hand in the movies. 1 overreacted and pulled my hand away so quickly 1 knocked over his Coke. Soaked his pants.

For an instant, he looked mad enough to hit me. But he quickly covered his anger with some stupid joke and that God-awful snorting. 1 thought the people sitting around us were going to call the usher, 911, or both.

After the movie, he brought me back to my car and asked if he could see me again. 1 remember giving him some lame excuse about not being ready to date.

"Mike, of course. But you'll always be Michael to me." I collapse on the sofa. "Are we waiting for your partner so you can get my complete statement?"

"That was some date, huh?" He winks at me and is shaking his head like he's recalling the details. "You were something else."

"I...um, are we still talking about...me?"

I can't believe he's actually implying what I think he's implying.

"You know, the s-e-x."

I can't believe he just spelled out the word.

"You're joking, right?"

"Amanda, no worries. I get it. Hey, it'll be our secret."

He's confusing me with someone else, but I don't have the energy to set the record straight.

"Listen, I'd love to walk down memory lane with you, but my partner is out on the beach, waiting for the ME to arrive, and I need to sweep your house so I can get back to the crime scene."

I clutch a pillow to my chest. My stomach goes queasy.

"You mean ME, as in *medical examiner*?"

"Thought I told you?" Mike walks over to the door leading to the garage. He opens it and looks inside. "Can't go into the details, but when my partner was securing the area around your house, he found a body in the dunes. About a hundred feet from here."

A body? Jean? I'm icy. Mike's shoulder chirps to life. My heart skips a beat. He cups his hand over the gadget he's got clipped there, so the person on the receiving end can't hear.

He whispers, "Amanda. Neatest garage I've ever seen in my life."

Back to business, Mike speaks into the device.

"Young. Code Four. Copy. I'm wrapping things up. Be down there in a few minutes."

It's almost 2:30 a.m. I'm afraid again. I stand really straight and fold my arms across my chest. Mike and I are almost eye-to-eye.

"Is it Jean?" My voice trembles.

"I'm not at liberty to give out information."

Mike heads into the kitchen. I'm at his heels. He unlocks the back door, leans outside, and turns to me.

"How long did you say you've lived here?"

"I truthfully thought I was, um...just imagining the noises. My mother told me not to move here. It really is isolated. I think Jean and I are the only people who actually live here in the winter." I'm choked up and on the verge of tears. "Truthfully, I had to get out of Santa Barbara. I was...the thing is, people—people who used to be my friends—were, um...gossiping about me and my situation. I moved to Hollywood Beach for peace and quiet."

"Sorry, what'd you say?" Mike looks at me like I'm speaking pig Latin.

"A couple women were raped around here. I think there was a murder. This could be related."

"Closed cases," Mike says, dismissing me.

I'm seriously losing it.

I sniffle. "I thought maybe I was overreacting to Daisy's barking. When I was going through my divorce, my friends accused me of...you know, kind of expanding the truth. The point is, you found a body."

Mike's completely tuned me out. He's writing in his notebook, then turns his attention to the upstairs.

"I need to check the bedrooms. Wait here."

The bedrooms? Why? I mean, does Mike Young think the murderer is hiding upstairs?

When he reaches the landing and heads for the guestroom, I tiptoe upstairs.

I bump into him on his way out of the room.

"I told you to stay downstairs."

"Think someone's hiding up here?"

Mike rolls his eyes. "Could you get me a glass of water or something? Anything. I'm thirsty."

When I get back to him, a small bottle of San Pellegrino in hand, Mike's in my bedroom. It kind of creeps me out.

"Sparkling, okay?" I say, out of breath, and try to hand him the bottle.

"No offense, but I don't drink that foreign shit."

It's obvious why we never had a second date.

"Great view. Check it out." He walks over and looks out the window that faces the beach, then snorts a laugh. "Oh shit, the paparazzi."

I look down to the beach and see people setting up lights, taking pictures, and shifting through the sand for evidence. A helicopter is circling overhead, shining a light over the entire area.

Mike walks into my closet and stares into the mirror above my dresser. He takes off his hat and sets it down. A framed photograph of me, my mother and grandmother tips over. Perfume bottles scatter. I cringe.

Oblivious to the mess he's made, Mike runs his fingers through his hair and pinches color into his cheeks. He picks up his hat and turns to leave.

"The press'll want to talk to me, take my picture. You know the drill."

I don't know the drill, but I keep that to myself.

I follow Mike out of the closet and downstairs. At the front door, he lingers on the threshold as if he's formulating some brilliant observation.

"Amanda, you know, I'm willing to give it another shot." He hands me another business card. "Call me."

In your dreams. I can't believe law enforcement agencies aren't more careful with their screening process.

I pull on my Uggs and follow Mike outside. I really need to know what's going on.

"Whoa. Where do you think you're going?" Mike has

switched back to Officer Young. "Crime scene's strictly off-limits to the public."

"I'm not the public. I live here."

Mike takes me by the shoulders. "Amanda, no offense. A crime scene's no place for a woman."

I tug out of his grasp. "Don't manhandle me."

I have no idea where that comment came from, but it sounds like something my mother would say.

"By the way, we never had s-e-x."

"Jeez. Whatever." He throws his hands in the air and sulks off toward the beach.

Then, like he's forgotten something, he turns back to me.

"Hey, I got one for you. Question: Why did the blonde steal a police car? She saw nine-one-one on the back and thought it was a Porsche."

It's the stupidest joke I've ever heard. Mike tosses his head back and snorts. He actually looks like he's having some kind of seizure.

I stay back. As Mike ambles toward the beach where the crowd is gathering, his snorting fades away.

Once I see him merge into the small crowd, I hurry along the sand, toward the lights and activity. It takes me no more than a minute or two to reach the crime scene. No wonder Daisy was barking. The murder took place practically in my backyard.

I shoulder through about a dozen bystanders, too focused on the area marked by crime scene tape to notice me. Mike is nowhere in sight, but the blanketed body is in plain view, not far from where I'm standing.

The thought of someone murdered so close to my house is terrifying.

I walk around the cordoned-off area, hoping to overhear who the victim is and what exactly happened.

Someone taps me on my shoulder. I gasp. Loud. Loud enough to attract attention. I turn toward the source of the tap.

"You scared me!" I say to the guy in front of me.

He's taller than me, with messy, dark-blond hair and smooth, tan skin. He looks like he just posed for a Ralph Lauren ad in his leather jacket, pullover sweater, and no-brand jeans. He's cute.

I'm suddenly aware that I could be featured on a *Please Help* poster for the Salvation Army.

He smiles. Tiny lines web around his clear blue eyes. "Danny Starr." He takes my hand in a firm grip.

"Amanda Beckwith." I feel off-balance.

My stomach flutters. My heart skips a beat. What's wrong with me? I mean, this guy is *really* good looking, but so what? I'm around good-looking guys all the time. But my face feels hot. It's turning red. I should have obeyed Mike Young and stayed back at the house.

Danny gives me the once-over. I know I look like hell. I can't imagine looking worse. I mean, I'm wearing my oldest, most horrible baggy sweats, with a coffee-stained sweatshirt. My down jacket makes me look twenty pounds heavier than I am. I can feel the damp air turning my curls to frizz. I imagine dark circles under my eyes, and a piece of parsley stuck to my front tooth.

"Know how all this all came down?" Danny digs in his jeans to pull out what looks like a business card, and hands it to me.

Danny Starr. *Los Angeles Times.*

"Me?" I squeak, looking up from the card, then point to my house. "I, um...live here."

"Really?" Danny raises an eyebrow as he looks back toward my house, the only one with lights on. "So, what happened."

"I, um...moved here," I mumble, pulling my jacket collar up and digging my hands in the pockets. "From Santa Barbara. After, you know, my divorce. It was a seriously horrible time in my life. I was kind of desperate, ya know. My G-ma gave me her house and moved to a retirement home. She said she felt isolated here. I get it now. Believe me."

"G-ma?" Danny frowns. His face looks funny.

Oh God, I'm so embarrassed. He wasn't asking about me. He was asking about tonight.

"Can you help me out with some questions." Danny taps his note pad with a pen.

I didn't notice the pad and pen before.

"Do you know who called the police? What can you tell me about what happened here tonight?"

"Um...yes. I called the police. But I didn't—"

A photographer snaps my photo. The flash blinds me.

"I need a name," the photographer says.

Danny leans over the photographer's shoulder. "Amanda B-e-c-k-with. Spelled the way it sounds, right?"

Lots of pens are scratching across pads—scratching *my name* across pads. Where did all these pads come from? This is a nightmare.

"Holy crap." *This can't be happening.* I grab Danny's arm. "Seriously! You can't put my picture in the paper. I had nothing to do with any of this."

"Settle down." Danny struggles out of my grip.

Way too many faces turn in our direction. The reporters on the scene smell a *witness* making a *statement.* They start firing questions. I hear, "only witness."

I give Danny one hard look before I edge between a couple reporters to make my escape. I spot Mike Young and hurry over to where he's standing. I'm desperate for a diversion.

"Here you are." I loop my arm through his and pull him close—the damsel in distress. "I, um..."

He turns my way but doesn't look happy to see me. *If eyes are the window to the soul, Mike Young is the devil.* His face is ashen, which seems strange because cops see this kind of thing all the time.

Mike yanks his arm free. "I told you to stay back at your house. I meant it."

"Sorry. The reporters are asking for you."

He turns to a couple cameras and begins passing his cards

out to the press and everyone else standing around. I sink back into the crowd.

The reporters shift their attention to Mike. Out of the corner of my eye, I see Danny heading my way. So be it. I'm not moving. As long as the attention isn't on me, I don't care where Danny is.

I need to hear what Mike has to say. I need to know what happened out here.

"Trying to ditch me?" Danny tilts his head. "You were about to tell me about why you called the police."

Officer Young struts over to a couple guys with notebooks.

"Someone's going to scoop you," I say. "Better pay attention."

Danny's eyes meet mine. The butterflies are back.

"Call me." He hurries over to where Young is standing.

I work my way over to the reporters and duck behind a couple of lookie-loos.

Is Mike actually going to talk to the press? My heart is racing. God, please don't let it be Jean under the blanket.

The reporters fire questions at Officer Young. Does he know the identity of the victim? Have they apprehended a suspect? Are there other victims?

Young clears his throat, runs his fingers through his hair.

"You'll have to contact the Ventura County Sheriff's Department Public Information Office for further information."

Young gives the name and number of, presumably, the contact person.

"What I can tell you is that Ventura County Sheriff's Department received a nine-one-one call sometime after midnight. Officers responding to the call discovered the body of a Caucasian woman, approximately thirty to forty years old. So far, there are no other victims. The subject appears to be the victim of a homicide. But until we have the coroner's report, I can't confirm that."

Jean's in her sixties. Can't be her, thank God.

"The victim's name?" someone shouts.

"The, uh, victim's name?" Mike whispers.

He pauses. It seems to go on forever.

He coughs. "Her, uh, identity will be withheld pending family notification."

"Any suspects?" someone calls out.

"To be clear, people should be alert and take caution. There may be a killer, or killers, on the loose." Officer Young's brows pull together as he addresses the small crowd. "A tip line..."

A killer on the loose?

Could the murderer be someone in the crowd? Could he be connected to those other crimes I read about? Mike said those cases were closed. He could be wrong.

Did he hear Danny say something about me being the only witness? I'm not a witness. I didn't see anything. Seriously, I'm more victim than witness. Thank God Jean has a dog. Who knows what might have happened had I not called the sheriff? Someone came through my gate. Was it the same person who murdered the woman on the beach? Maybe it was his accomplice.

Was the murderer targeting my house? Targeting me? That doesn't make any sense.

I search the faces in the crowd around me. Everyone looks so normal. Ted Bundy normal. A shiver goes up my spine. Who are all of these people?

I spot a couple more reporters. Danny is among the throng. But there's something about him that distinguishes him from the crowd. Maybe it's the way he dresses, or that he just looks like the kind of person who belongs wherever he is.

I look toward the blanket-covered victim. There are a handful of medical professionals and law enforcement officers milling about in uniforms. Who else is here? It's still dark out, and the lights set up around the body make it difficult to see anyone very clearly.

In the distance, I see a pair of headlights bounce over the sand as a dark sedan pulls into the public parking lot that sits between the last house on Hollywood Beach—about twenty houses north of my house—and the Mandalay Bay Hotel. Even though it's a couple hundred yards from the crime scene, from where I'm standing, I can see two men in suits get out of the car.

Mike looks their way, nods toward the small crowd, and heads in that direction. They meet halfway to the crime scene on the beach. For a moment, they huddle in conversation. Then Mike turns to point toward me. Or more likely, toward the medical examiner and the body under the blanket.

It's time for me to go. I've heard all that I need to hear.

There may be a killer on the loose, and a bunch of reporters seem to think that I'm only witness to the possible murder. Perfect.

CHAPTER 3

I'M LOUNGING ON THE BOW of a Moody 66, leaving St. John, bound for St. Croix. The sky is a vivid Tiffany-box blue, and the warm breeze feels like tiny fingers massaging my skin. I'm incredibly relaxed, which is crazy because 99 percent of the time I'm a stress case. I mean, really tense.

Stress is part of my genetic makeup, Dr. Segal, my shrink, tells me from her lounge chair on the deck next to me. It's like blue eyes or long legs, she says. I extend my arms over my head and notice that I'm wearing my skimpiest black Italian bikini, and Isabella Fiore sandals. I hold my feet up to inspect them: the sandals are still really cute, even though they're last year's model. Anyway, recycling is *très chic,* and it's not even the season yet in the Virgin Islands.

The captain at the helm wears a midnight-blue uniform, heavy with medals from every war since World War I. Which is weird, since he looks about my age. I can't be sure, but I think I know him.

He smiles and waves. I happily wave back. The new me waves at everyone.

From behind the captain, the first mate emerges slowly through the cabin door. He's wearing a red Speedo. Nothing else. His bronze muscular body glimmers with sweat, but his face is shadowed by the giant mast. I hate Speedos. Plus, it's inappropriate for the crew to dress in a bathing suit instead of something more official.

What the hell? He's heading my way with a tray of Mai Tais.

Suddenly, I'm really, really thirsty. I can almost taste the rum and pineapple. I haven't had a drink since...well, since forever. I reach up to take the glass, but somewhere, a bell starts ringing. A barking dog shatters the tranquility. Are dogs allowed on yachts? I look past the first mate for the dog, and see a small crowd on the stern, talking and laughing. Where'd they come from? Why am I all by myself at the bow? I look next to me. Where's Dr. Segal?

My attention turns back to the Mai Tais. Amazingly, the shadow lifts from the first mate's face, and to my utter astonishment, it's that reporter from last night. He's hovering in front of me in a red Speedo, holding the dripping-wet glass.

I open my eyes. Where am I?

In my bed. My bed?

Sunshine fills the room. I grab the clock off my nightstand. It's after eleven. Shit. The phone's ringing. Someone's knocking on the door downstairs. Daisy's barking again.

My head is pounding. My eyes feel swollen. My mind scrambles to connect the dots.

Somewhere under my covers, my iPhone is vibrating. I throw off the duvet and dig through the sheets. When I finally find the damn cell, it's too late. Seventeen missed calls. My mailbox is not accepting any new messages. Crap. I had a 10 a.m. meeting with Lynette Jones. I'm already skating on thin ice with her—she's looking for a good reason to fire me. Late to another meeting might be her tipping point.

Last night comes back to me in a flash. The scary noises. Mike Young's moronic jokes. The murder victim. Oh, and the fact that a killer could be hellbent on silencing me—*me*—the only witness to the crime. Worst of all is that reporter. Danny something.

I can't believe he had one of his flunkies take my picture! Why take *my* picture? I had nothing to do with anything. This is truly the fake news in action. It'll probably end up on YouTube or TMZ.

For sure, Lynette will fire me. I'll never work again!

I bite my lip. I'm obsessing. *Get a grip.* Prioritize. Call Lynette. Take a shower. Get dressed. Return phone calls. Answer the door. No. *Do not* answer the door. I'll sneak out the back and return phone calls on my way to work. Or I'll take my time. Shower first. Look fabulous, confident. Ready for anything. I mean, I'm already late. Lynette's going to have a fit no matter what time I show up.

Throwing the duvet to the end of the bed, I force myself to get up. I feel groggy and off-balance. I turn on the shower and walk into my closet. It looks like Bloomingdale's after a sale. I don't have the time or energy to straighten things up right now. I choose a brand-new brown plaid Burberry mini skirt, coordinating cashmere turtleneck and brown tights, set them on my bed, then head for the shower.

I hit Lynette Jones on my phone and steady myself for my editor's wrath. It doesn't take much for Lynette to go from Athena, the wise, industrious mentor, to Medusa, who could turn you to stone with one look.

Lynette Jones is the publisher and editor-in-chief of the *Santa Barbara Tribune*. She is the owner of Jones Media Group. And besides the *Tribune*, she owns a radio station and a dozen trade publications. But the *Tribune* is her baby. She wouldn't be acting as my editor at all if most of her employees hadn't quit or gotten fired. For such a large operation, Lynette works with a skeleton crew.

Almost every former employee is suing Lynette for something—from wrongful termination to sexual harassment. She's practically created a cottage industry in pissing people off. Half the Santa Barbara lawyers would be struggling to make a living if it weren't for Lynette Jones.

Maybe I'm exaggerating a little bit, but in Santa Barbara, Lynette Jones is the person that people love to hate. In her defense, Lynette is not only beautiful in a Susan Sarandon sort of way, she's also one of the smartest people I've ever known. She can be your best friend, loyal to the end, or your worst enemy.

"Amanda! Where the hell are you? No, don't answer. Just get

your ass into the office. Do you know you're on the front page of the *Times*?" Lynette is saying it like she's holding the paper in front of her. "Amanda Beckwith, blogger for the *Tribune*. Are you out of your mind? No one with half a brain speaks to the press!"

Oh God. All I can think of is all the people I know who get the *Times*—including my mother, best friend, and ex-husband. Even my dad, in New York, reads it online.

"No—I mean, um...tell me." Beads of sweat are popping out on my forehead. "Is my picture really, really awful?"

"The *Times* scooped us on a story featuring you! Are you *trying* to get fired?"

But before I can say, *I'm on my way*, she clicks off the phone.

Well, I can just kiss my job goodbye. There's no way that Lynette *won't* fire me now. She has had a major grudge against the *Times* ever since they ran a tell-all feature story about her and the controversy surrounding the huge staff turnover at her paper, and the lawsuits that accompanied them.

I feel like crawling back to bed and sleeping off this nightmare. But as my mother would say, I'm going to have to face the music eventually, so I better get on with it.

I peek out my bedroom window, down to the small crowd of people gathering on the beach. I see reporters, people in official-looking uniforms, and the obvious lookie-loos. Danny Starr is among the group. Figures. He must have slept in his car, because he's wearing the same outfit he wore last night, and from my vantage point, he looks scruffy and exhausted. Good. He's wasting his time if he thinks he's going to get some kind of stupid statement from me.

The most important thing for me to do right now is to stay focused and positive. I am a professional, um...blogger, sort of, with a job to do. Out of crisis comes opportunity.

I'm a wreck.

I make my bed, reposition the clock on the nightstand, and smooth the wrinkles out of the shams and duvet. It's a beautiful morning. It's amazing what a little sunshine can do to transform a scary experience into something that feels almost normal. Almost.

I quickly dress and head downstairs.

Before leaving, I take a quick look in the mirror. Actually, I look semi-normal, considering. I reach for the front door like it's just an average day, when I remember that Danny Starr will be hanging around outside, waiting for me.

I can handle Danny.

Oh God, I can't believe I almost forgot another one of life's most basic rules: never discuss anything while under the influence of a new outfit. Everybody knows that.

I open the back door that leads to a pathway on the side of my house and then to the street. First, I poke my head outside to make sure no one is hanging around. Then I step outside and head toward my car on the street. I peek over the gate to make sure no one is on the street. All clear. I hurry next door to Jean Wilson's house and snatch the newspaper off the driveway and sneak toward my car. Sorry, Jean. Promise to return it as soon as I've had a chance to read what that reporter had to say about me.

I'm just about to press the fob to my two-year-old Mercedes wagon when voices stop me in my tracks. Jean and Danny Starr are in an animated discussion and heading my way. They don't see me yet. Thank God. I turn and concentrate on getting in the car and getting the hell out of here.

Maybe they won't notice me. But I'm so nervous, I end up accidentally squeezing the lock button on the fob, causing my car to chirp.

I'm busted.

Instead of just getting in my car and driving off, which is the smart thing to do, I turn to see if Danny and Jean are looking at me.

"Amanda, where did you come from?" Jean says, always cheery and oblivious. She's wearing pink fluffy slippers and a pink knock-off Juicy Couture sweat outfit. She actually looks cute.

"Jean, you're back." I feel trapped.

"Where'd I go?" She looks confused. "Oh, last night. I take that really good sleeping drug, Siesta, or something like that.

You could cut off my foot and I wouldn't wake up."

"Listen, I need to go. I'm really, really late for work," I say politely to Jean.

I shoot Danny a blistering don't-even-think-about-talking-to-me look.

"Amanda, you look nice. You okay?" He is obviously choosing to ignore that I'm in a big hurry. "Read the paper this morning?"

"I don't get the *Times*. And even if I did, I wouldn't read it."

I start to turn, but Danny hooks me back into the conversation. He nods toward Jean's paper in my hand.

"What's that you're holding?"

"Isn't it awful?" Jean says. "Amanda, you must have been terrified! I can't imagine what it would be like to witness a murder." She looks concerned, but her forehead refuses to wrinkle. Botox. "I heard you called the police. You saw the murderer. You're very brave."

I look from Jean to Danny and back to Jean. I know I'm being overly dramatic, but I can't help myself.

"Let me set the record straight." I clutch the paper to my chest. "Whoever told you I witnessed anything, quite frankly, got their facts completely wrong. I saw nothing. Nothing."

I edge to my car. Danny's smile makes me want to slap him.

"I wasn't a witness to anything. I heard a noise and called the police. End of story."

I pull my iPhone out of my pocket and look at the time. It's close to noon.

"Gotta run." I smile, lift my chin, and turn my attention to getting into my car and leaving with my dignity still intact.

"Amanda, dear. The *Times*?" Jean is pointing at me.

I follow her finger and see the white label with Jean's name and address on it, plastered next to the *Los Angeles Times* masthead on the paper.

"I think you must have taken my newspaper by accident."

"Accidentally on purpose." Danny smiles. "Thought you don't read the *Times*."

"Oh, Jean, I'm so sorry. I think, um...the paperboy must have, um, misplaced it."

l hand the paper to Jean. I'm so embarrassed, and l feel like such an idiot. l hate Danny Starr.

Danny steps closer to the car and rests his hand on the door.

"Hey, l had a great conversation with your ex. He's a nice guy. Very sensitive—emotional."

I'm stupefied. l can't believe that this guy would pad his stupid story with dirt from my ex.

"Why the hell would you talk to Geoff?" l say. "What does he have to do with anything?"

So, what does it matter that Danny spoke to Geoff? Big deal. What's Geoff going to tell him? That I'm a bad cook? That I'm a compulsive organizer? That l actually hate playing golf?

Seated behind the wheel, l reach for the door, but Danny leans against it, making the door impossible for me to close.

"FYl, there were two detectives here earlier this morning, looking for you."

l grab the door handle and try to jerk it toward me.

"Do you mind?"

"They're interested in talking to you."

"Right. Because you told them that l saw something."

"It wasn't me who told them anything."

"So?"

"Your ex. He talked to the police. The police ID'd the victim. Bree Martin."

"I'm sorry. What did you say?" l stare at Danny.

I'm finding it hard to breathe. I'm praying that l heard him wrong.

"Your ex-husband's wife. Bree."

My heart is pounding so hard, I'm afraid I'm going to start hyperventilating. My hands begin to shake.

Danny looks serious now. The arrogant smile is gone. His eyes are dark, his forehead creased.

"Bree Daniels Martin. Don't tell me you don't know your ex-husband's wife's name? Any comment?"

CHAPTER 4

I PULL INTO THE TRIBUNE PARKING LOT on State Street in Santa Barbara. I have no idea how I got here without having a major accident. I tap my horn to scatter a couple pedestrians chatting it up on the driveway, then angle into a space, shut off the engine, and sit paralyzed. Bree is dead.

I button my jacket and pull up the collar, but the cold is in my bones. Last night, my biggest problem was whether to color-code my shoes or arrange them alphabetically. And now I'm grappling with wearing black or plum to my ex-husband's wife's funeral.

But what's even worse than Bree being dead is that she died right in my backyard. What was Bree doing alone on the beach, a hundred feet from my house?

The point is that Bree *wasn't* alone. The man who tripped over the chair on my patio—did he kill Bree? Was he coming after me, too?

A million questions scream through my mind. What was Bree doing in Ventura on Hollywood Beach on a cold winter night, nearly an hour away from her home in Santa Barbara? Where was Geoff?

Was Bree's death a wrong-place-at-the-wrong-time kind of random act of violence? Did her killer coincidently end up on my patio? Were Bree and that man I saw connected?

How could it be anything else but that? Who was that man? Why would he want Bree dead? *How did she die?*

Geoff. *Geoff.*

CAROL FINIZZA

His name pops into my mind like a bad memory. Did Geoff kill Bree?

His biting sarcasm could bring tears to my eyes and bruise my feelings. He could definitely be below-the-belt mean, but he was never physically aggressive. He's not a yeller. At least, not when I was married to him. Geoff prides himself on discipline and self-control. But he has an icy, indifferent side that could hurt like a slap.

Could Geoff be a murderer? I don't think so. Murder is too messy for someone like Geoff. But since he married Bree, I've noticed changes in him. Subtle changes that most people might not notice. I remember that before he called the police on me at the farmer's market, he actually looked like he was going to slug me—it scared me. But is that evidence that Geoff killed Bree?

People might think I had something to do with her death because she died so close to my house. Or that I killed her because she stole Geoff from me. Even though Bree was the other woman in my marriage, I never even joked about wanting her dead.

I lean my head back against the seat and close my eyes. That's not exactly true. During the divorce, when Geoff put Bree in charge of the whole what's-mine-and-what's-yours process, I admit, I let my imagination run wild with thoughts of medieval torture resulting in something bad happening to both Bree and Geoff. Okay, death. But that was like a million years ago.

Anyway, the point is that even though I thought I was in love with Geoff when I married him, and was brokenhearted when we divorced, I realize now that we weren't really a match in the first place. For one thing, he's fifteen years older than me. Not a big of a deal, but he didn't want children. Wasn't *into* kids, as he put it. But in my heart of hearts, I thought he'd change his mind after we got married.

I was such an idiot.

The other thing is, all my friends were getting married. I was a bridesmaid at eight weddings before my twenty-seventh birthday. *Eight.* How could I not want a fairytale wedding?

I guess I fell in love with the idea of being a couple and doing the fun stuff that married couples do. Like buying a cottage near the beach, having two daughters who I could dress in adorable mommy-and-me outfits, organizing playdates, planning parties. The truth is, my all-time favorite movie is *Swiss Family Robinson*. Which, I know, isn't really about a cottage on the beach, but more about a treehouse on a deserted island with scary pirates. Still, there's that whole happy family thing that I really love.

Anyway, Geoff was all about flash and bling. He moved me into his eight thousand square foot *cottage* with a beach view, bought me a Mercedes station wagon and a membership at one of Santa Barbara's fanciest country clubs. For a while, we had this great life. Just minus, I don't know...joy.

My mother thought I'd scored big time when I married Geoff. *Dr. Geoff Martin*. Even though Geoff is a chiropractor and not an MD, my mom loved telling everyone that her daughter had married a doctor. Geoff didn't come from money, but he knew how to make a lot of it. In Southern California, that's just as good—or so my mother always said.

Seriously. Who was I to judge Geoff? I faked my way into Berkeley by checking the Native American box under nationality and wrote an unbelievably convincing essay about surviving a dysfunctional family. My bad, right? But I graduated with a BA in English, which is something, even though I never went to grad school like my two brothers.

What did I do with my expensive college degree? I used it to organize people's closets and blog about it.

So, I married Geoff in a cream-colored Armani gown. Geoff and his groomsmen wore khaki suits and Hermes ties. I dressed the flower girls and bridesmaids in eggshell, tea-length Vera Wang. I actually copied Lady Di's color palette.

Then, after a couple years of marriage, I discovered that Geoff and Bree, his massage therapist at The Center, were having an affair. Bree called our house and more or less told me. In her whispery voice, she left a message asking Geoff if he could stop by her house and pick up his clothes. Then came the giggle. After that, everything else was a blur. I heard *Bellagio* and *Las Vegas*, which is where Geoff held his wellness seminars.

I learned that *seminars* was code for their trysts.

Geoff held more than ten seminars the year we split up. My guess is that at least half of the *seminars* were a cover for his affairs. I'm pretty sure Bree wasn't his only affair he had during our marriage. But for whatever reason, Bree was the person he wanted to be with.

I got my Mercedes, my four-carat diamond wedding ring, and a fifty-thousand-dollar settlement. Geoff got the house (which, in all fairness, was his to begin with), his business, most of the cash in our bank account, and my stupid adolescent dreams.

I kept the car and hocked the ring. The ring plus the cash paid for two years of therapy, property taxes on the beach house my grandmother gave me and living expenses when I just couldn't face going back to work.

Maybe if I'd been a better wife, I'd still be married to Geoff, and Bree would be alive.

Stop it.

I sit up straight and blink against the glare bouncing off the windshield. The sun is struggling to break through the billowy, dark clouds. Looks like more rain.

What am I doing still sitting in the car? I'm just postponing the inevitable face-to-face with Lynette. I never did get to see the *LA Times* article that Lynette is so pissed off about. I could look the article up on my phone, but seriously, how bad could it be? What's she going to do, fire me for being in the wrong place at the wrong time? Seriously, it's not my fault that a *Times* reporter snapped my picture.

That's hardly the worst of my problems.

God, I hope Lynette doesn't fire me.

I take one quick look in the rearview mirror to make sure I don't have mascara running down my cheeks. I'm mortified to see the face looking back at me—my eyes look tired, my skin is pale, and my forehead is etched with worry. I pinch color into my cheeks and push the mirror away from me. Yank the band off my hair, then untangle it with my fingers. Sling my bag over my shoulder, lock my car, and head for the front of the building.

Just as I start up the stairs, Lynette barrels toward me like the building's on fire. She's gripping several pieces of red licorice. Her beautifully structured charcoal dress and jacket are a stark contrast to the frenzied expression on her face. Her copper-colored, shoulder-length hair is twisted up on her head and held in place by a number-two pencil. A frown is finding its way through her Botoxed forehead. And her lips, artificially plump, need a reapplication of lipstick. She's obviously been counting the seconds until I arrived.

Lynette grabs my arm.

I meet her ferocious stare and whisper, "Bree is dead."

"Amanda! Pay attention. I told you that this morning." She studies me as she chomps a licorice stick. "You never listen."

Lynette stocks her office with a Costco-sized container of Red Vines. God forbid should she catch you taking one.

"Pay attention. This isn't good. I'm telling you right now. Not good." She digs her acrylics into my arm. "There are two detectives upstairs. They're looking for *you*. This paper's going under. I can barely make payroll with the few reporters I have left. Now this. *You* on the front page of the *LA Times*. I hate that paper."

"Detectives?"

"Don't mess with these cops, Amanda. And don't try talking your way out of anything. I know your tactics."

"My tactics?" I sling my bag over my other shoulder and wait for Lynette to move.

"The cops have been pacing the floor, waiting for you. How'd they find out that you work here?

Geoff? "I seriously have no idea. Maybe that reporter from the *Times* told them."

I plant my feet. My mind's whirling. How would Danny Starr know where I work? Did I tell him? Probably. I practically blathered my bra size to him last night. I'm such a dope.

"Anyway, this has nothing to do with the *Tribune* or you, for God's sake," I say.

"Really? There's a stack of messages an inch thick waiting for you. Jeanine Pirro left three. Andersen Cooper called. This isn't going away."

"Fox News Judge Jeanine? That Jeanine?"

I follow Lynette through the heavy front doors, feeling like I'm in the wake of a Category 4 storm.

"Did the detectives say anything specific?"

"What happens to the *Tribune* when the advertisers get wind of this?" Lynette rages over her shoulder as pushes through a door that leads to the back staircase.

The back staircase. *Not* a good sign. She doesn't want to be seen with me.

"How will I keep the paper afloat? Nobody's going to trust someone with criminal ties. I'm finished!"

Criminal ties?

Lynette stops on the stairs and shoots me a suspicious look.

"That reporter made it sound like you're guilty of something. Did you actually see the murder happen? He said you saw a suspect leave the scene."

"This is all completely...completely wrong!" I stop. My voice sounds shrill. "Danny Starr is a big fat liar. Fake news. Don't believe a thing he says. I mean, he's making this stuff up. I never believed Trump when he accused the press of lying. Now, I actually get how he feels. I swear to God, I didn't see a thing!"

This is a mess. I feel sick to my stomach.

"Get a grip," Lynette barks, looking around like she's afraid someone might hear us.

Her hand is poised like she's going to slap me, like they do in old movies when someone's going off the deep end. Instead, she squeezes my arm.

"You don't want to look *crazy*, too."

Lynette drops my arm and hurries up the stairs, leaving me a couple yards behind her.

"Listen," I call after her. "I'm going to talk to the police. Set the record straight. All I need to do is tell the truth. Right?" Total honesty. That's all that really counts. Total honesty. Lynette turns toward me. "What you need to do is keep your mouth shut. Lawyer up."

Lawyer up? Why? Only guilty people hire a lawyer. I haven't done anything. I can't afford to hire a lawyer.

When I catch up with Lynette, she grabs my jacket.

"Listen, I told those detectives that you're just helping me temporarily. You know, like my personal organizer. You're a freelance blogger. As of today, you're on a leave of absence until further notice. Period. If anyone asks, tell them the same thing."

"Absolutely." I mean, there's no harm in telling a white lie.

At least Lynette didn't fire me. A leave of absence is like a vacation. When this whole mess blows over, everything will go back to normal.

Lynette shoulders the door in front of us and pushes it open, then drops the licorice in the trash can a few feet away. I see the detectives. My stomach does a somersault. I shouldn't feel nervous, but for whatever reason, I do. They're standing in the inner office outside Lynette's private office.

"I almost forgot." Lynette raises an eyebrow at me. "That friend of yours—Kim something? She wants you to get back to her ASAP. The *nerve* of her to talk to me like I'm somebody's secretary. And your mother called about a million times."

"The battery went dead on my cell," I lie, which isn't a real lie, since it's only to Lynette.

I know my mother and Kim were calling me, along with a bunch of other numbers that I've never heard of before.

"Nothing personal." Lynette digs in her pocket to pull out a couple Red Vines, then takes a bite and chews as she talks. "I don't want that woman in this building."

"Kim?"

"She's trouble."

Lynette doesn't even know Kim. She's only met her a couple times, at my bridal shower and wedding.

As we approach Lynette's office, I notice a couple reporters huddling next to the water cooler. They're whispering and looking over at us. It's such a cliché. They nod toward me. One of them covers her mouth to stifle a laugh. I'm glad I bring such joy to my coworker's lives. But there's nothing funny about what happened to Bree, or what's happening to me.

"Hey, back to work," Lynette snaps, waving the licorice at them like a fly swatter.

They jump at the sound of Lynette's voice. Her look says, *Now!*

But as we approach the door to the inner office where the detectives are waiting, her demeanor changes. She's morphed from the Bride of Frankenstein to Lady Di, all innocence and charm. Classic Lynette.

Just short of the door, Lynette stops and looks around like she's making sure the coast is clear, then whispers, "You really should consider calling a lawyer. Or at least call your father. He'll know how to advise you."

"I haven't done anything wrong. All I did was call the police. I heard a noise. This is just follow-up, right?"

Lynette gives me a disapproving frown as she pushes open her office door.

"Detectives, I'm very sorry we kept you waiting." Lynette's smile could light up a room. "This is Amanda. I know you'll want some privacy. You're welcome to use my office."

We follow Lynette into a glass-paneled room with twelve-foot ceilings. It's a corner office that looks out on one side to a beautiful courtyard landscaped with tall oak trees and benches. The other side showcases an ocean view just beyond the parking lot below.

She glides past me and the detectives, to her massive glass desk adorned with a large Mac and some kind of fancy, ergonomic caramel-colored leather desk chair.

"You should be comfortable here." She snaps several Post-its off her computer screen. "If you need anything, I'll be in one of the outer offices."

Lynette maneuvers past two creamy Kris sofas, and a large antique door imported from France that has been transformed into a coffee table. She motions for us to sit, before disappearing out the door.

The two detectives continue to stand, and so do I.

We're just about to sit when Lynette cracks open the door and leans into the room.

"Amanda's my little worker bee. Freelance worker bee." She beams a radiant smile. "Last night, when everyone else was out having fun, Amanda's slaving away, organizing the closets of one of Santa Barbara's most revered local celebrities. So selfless. By the way, Amanda, I want to remind you that you don't have a lot of time. Don't you have to be somewhere soon?"

"Absolutely. I have, um...a meeting."

Be somewhere? Seriously? I look over at her, then down at her white-knuckle grip on the door. God, she's trying to cover for me. She really is worried.

Lynette gives me a wink, waves the Red Vines at me, and gently closes the door.

I forgot that I lied to Lynette about where I was last night. Lynette had asked me a couple weeks ago to speak at a National Charity League mother-daughter dinner—*Getting Organized in the New Year*, or something like that. I hate public speaking. I'm horrible at it, so I begged off by telling her that I was meeting with Rob Lowe on Friday night to give him a bid on organizing his closets. Which was not completely true. I was at Target until about six or seven. Then I came home.

Lynette was thrilled about my meeting with Rob Lowe. I could blog about all the vendors we selected, and then blog about redoing his closet. That's how she attracts advertisers like California Clothes, The Container Store, Target, and so forth. But it's getting harder and harder to get advertisers to buy ad space in newspapers like the *Tribune*. The only reason Lynette hasn't fired me yet is because my silly blog attracts online advertisers.

But my meeting with Rob Lowe was actually on Thursday

afternoon, not Friday night, and with Rob Lowe's assistant, not Rob Lowe. It wasn't a complete lie. Just a minor expansion of the truth.

I bite my lower lip. I should tell the detectives now that I didn't actually meet anyone.

The window of opportunity to tell the truth is about to vanish. Both detectives hand me their cards. Detectives Alan Lynch and David Lee.

I squeeze the cards in my hand and look down at them. If I tell them the truth, Lynette is going to kill me for lying to her. I won't just be on leave, she'll fire me. Everyone is replaceable. At least, that's what she tells me.

If the police follow-up with the Rob Lowe meeting, I can just tell the detectives that I got my days mixed up. Seriously, why would they need to follow-up? All I did was hear a noise and call the police. Everything they need to know is in Mike Young's report.

"Which celebrity did you meet with?" Detective Lynch says.

"I'm sorry, what?" I feel sweat beading on my forehead.

"The celebrity's name, cupcake. We're establishing a timeline. I'll need the celeb's name."

Detective Lynch motions for me to take a seat, and as I do, Detective Lee sinks into the sofa opposite me. Detective Lynch continues standing.

"That m-makes complete sense," I say. "The truth is that I promise complete confidentiality for all my clients. And unless I'm being charged with something, I'm going to have to respectfully decline to give you that information."

I have no idea how I came up with that one, but it sounds right. I think I heard someone say something like that on *Law and Order*.

Detective Lynch, who gives me a hard-eyed, cut-the-BS look, is fortyish, string-bean tall, with shoulders that slump forward as if he's had to duck every time he walks through a doorway. His eyes are pinched too close to his nose, and his mouth is a grim, unforgiving line. Lee is my height, and probably my age, but his eyes look much older and kind of sad, like he wished he'd gone to law school instead of the police academy.

They're both wearing expensive-looking suits. Do civil servants earn decent salaries nowadays?

Both detectives could use a good haircut.

I wonder what a civil service job pays. Maybe I could get a civil service job. I make a mental note to check out civil service jobs after this blows over.

Detective Lynch says, "Miss Beckwith, my partner and I are here to ask you a few questions about last night. We're not here to rattle your cage."

"Don't be nervous." Detective Lee says in a voice that's matter of fact but kind.

He's probably considered the good cop of the two. Except, saying, *don't be nervous*, is exactly what cops say when there's a good reason to feel nervous. Which is exactly how I feel. Nervous.

Maybe I'm jumping to conclusions. Maybe the detectives are here to thank me for alerting them in the first place. Maybe my 911 call last night helped crack this case. Maybe Mike Young was wrong, and Bree's murder *is* connected to the cold cases I read about a while ago. They're here to thank me and tell me who murdered Bree and committed the other crimes.

"Miss Beckwith, we have a copy of the sheriff's report. We're still waiting on the cause of death, but it appears that Bree Martin was a victim of homicide."

I stay silent. God, I'm a wreck. I mean, I've rubbed one side of my sweater so hard that little brown wool balls are forming under my fingers.

Detective Lynch clears his throat. I quickly hide the fuzz under my skirt and look up.

"We just need to clarify a few things."

I slip my hands under my legs to keep them from shaking. I really don't like police. They're always so...I don't know, official. They don't have a sense of humor or any personality at all. When I was arrested for riding my bike under the influence, the cops were horrible to me.

I know the police have to act all serious and businesslike, but truthfully, it wouldn't hurt them to be a little nicer.

"Okay. I'm going to be a hundred percent honest. I'm here to help."

Why did I say that? Stupid. It's exactly what people say when they're about to tell a lie. Which I would *never* do. I mean, in any meaningful way.

"I'm going to tell you exactly what happened last night. Which, as you pointed out, is already in the sheriff's report."

Am I rambling? Completely.

"You're doing fine," Detective Lee says.

I take a closer look at him. He's actually kind of attractive, except for the bad haircut.

Suddenly, I remember something.

"Oh, by the way, do you think I could get a transcript of this conversation when we're done?"

I hope I don't sound too pushy. I know it's important to get everything in writing. Or at least, that's what my father always told me to do.

"Also, don't you need to read me my rights or something?"

"You're a witness, cupcake." Detective Lynch steps over and leans against the sofa across from me.

Cupcake? Honeybee? I'm a witness?

I bite my lip. "I guess the transcript can wait. I'm here to cooperate completely. But seriously, I didn't witness anything. I heard a noise, and my neighbor's dog was barking, and a man ran through my yard. That's it."

Detective Lee leans toward me, puts pencil to paper, and smiles.

"Let's start from the beginning. Everything you heard or saw last night."

I sit up straight in my chair and wipe my hands on my skirt. I feel like I'm taking an oral exam, which I was always good at, if I didn't psyche myself out first.

"To begin with, my bedroom closet was a total mess last

night when I got home from, you know, my meeting. You have no idea. I mean, I know I can be a little compulsive when it comes to—"

"Miss Beckwith." Detective Lynch is frowning. "We heard the nine-one-one tape, but we want to hear it from you. What prompted you to call the police?"

To the best of my ability, I repeat what I had told sheriff Young. I didn't actually see a suspect in my yard. I only saw the back of a black jacket. Maybe it was a man, but it could have been a woman. It was dark out.

What else did I see? What am I missing? I have this nagging suspicion I'm forgetting something important. My mind is blank. I can't remember.

For the next couple hours, instead of asking me about my neighbor's barking dog and the sound of the gate opening and shutting, both detectives grill me on my relationship with Bree.

"Okay, cookie," Detective Lynch says, for what seems like the hundredth time. "Let's take it from the top. When was the last time you spoke to Bree?"

Cookie? I look at my watch. It's after 3:00. I've been at this for what feels like forever. I'm completely exhausted.

"Okay, let's see...I know I told you before that I ran into Bree in September, at an art exhibit at the Wild Coyote Gallery in Montecito. Now that I think about it, I think I saw her again in November."

Actually, I saw her twice in November. But I can't tell the detectives about the second time. It ended with an ugly confrontation at Bree's house, which used to be my house when I was married to Geoff.

"As I, um...recall, I saw her at a Tory Burch trunk show at Wendy Foster's," I continue, matter-of-factly.

But when I look down at my hands, I realize that I've been twisting my sweater sleeve into a knot. I smooth the fabric down, then look up at the detectives.

"It was just an innocent coincidence that we were there at the same time." I smile.

But I feel guilty that I'm withholding something: Bree and I were both interested in the same little black dress. In the first place, Bree only wanted the dress because I had my eye on it. Bree is taller and, um...more voluptuous than me.

I wish I had Bree's body. Bree is Kim Kardashian. I'm more like...I don't know who I'm like. The point is, she has completely different taste in clothes than I do. She's all about glitz and glamour. I'm J. Crew boring.

The unfortunate thing is, I kind of yanked the dress out of her hand. It was an accident. But she got all dramatic about it. It wasn't a big deal. I handed it back to her after I tried it on. I never ended up buying the dress. It wasn't really my style.

"Tell me again about the gallery in Montecito." Detective Lee said. "You ran into her? Wait a minute. Who's Wendy Foster?" He is writing down absolutely everything I'm saying.

I shift my position in my seat. "Could I get a glass of water?"

"We're almost done," Detective Lynch says. "Okay. Back to the gallery? Wendy Foster?" He's tapping his pencil on his notebook, fast and hard.

"The gallery meeting was just a *hi, bye* sort of thing. Oh! You think Wendy Foster is a person. It's a boutique."

I can see that both detectives are losing their patience.

"The truth is, Wendy Foster is this darling boutique in Montecito. Anyway, they sell beautiful clothes and adorable gifts. Your wife would probably love—"

"I'm not married." Detective Lee's face is flushing.

Detective Lynch gives him a frustrated look. Lee adjusts his tie, clears his throat, and continues.

"You must be anxious to get this over with so—"

"So, what were you doing so far away from Ventura?" Lynch taps his pencil against his pad. "Montecito is what? Forty-five minutes? Aren't there shops and galleries around Ventura?"

For God's sake, do they think I'm stalking Bree?

"Santa Barbara was my home before I moved to Hollywood Beach. I've only lived here less than a year. I go to those shops because they're familiar. I guess it's been hard to give that up."

45

Lynch eyeballs me. "Miss Beckwith, we're going to cut to the chase. We had a long conversation with your ex, Geoff Martin, when we made the notification regarding Bree. We met him at the airport early this morning, when the first flight from Las Vegas landed."

"I'm thirsty. May I get a glass of water."

This entire meeting feels surreal. I stand and step toward the water cooler outside Lynette's office in the newsroom. Of course, the detectives would interview Geoff. I mean, his wife was murdered. Practically in my backyard. Two years after our divorce. What did I expect? But isn't the husband always the number one suspect?

Detective Lee stands and directs me back to couch. He does it gently, like I'm disabled or something.

"Just a few more questions."

Then Detective Lynch chimes in again, in a mean voice. It reminds me of my father and makes me feel small.

"We know about your assault charge, your DUI. We take these charges very seriously. We also know that you were somewhat obsessed with Missus Martin."

"Time out! Me? Obsessed with Bree? That's completely not true."

I stand. Walk to the window and fixate on raindrops that just started to splash on the roofs of the cars in the parking lot below. I want to run; escape from these hurtful questions and the bad memories they bring up. I close my eyes for one second then turn back to face Lynch and Lee. I take a deep breath and try to steady my voice, but my words sound brittle. I blink back tears.

"Bree Daniels Martin had an affair with my husband," I say, choking up. "I'm sorry if that's not a big deal to you guys. It was awful for me. But I'm over it. I've been over it for a long time. I'm okay now. The only person obsessed with Bree is my ex. Trust me, the further away I am from Bree and Geoff, the better."

"Miss Beckwith, please sit down." Detective Lee looks at his watch. "We're almost finished."

"I guess you don't have to worry about staying out of Bree's way anymore, do you?" Detective Lynch smiles for the first time, and it completely creeps me out.

His teeth are really crooked and need to be whitened by a dental professional.

"Honestly? If I had anything at all to do with Bree's death, why would I call the police in the first place? I heard one little noise, and I'm on the hot seat?" I look from one detective to the other.

"Back to the noise," Detective Lynch says. "A noise, or noises?"

This is getting ridiculous.

"Noises, I think."

"You think, or you know?" Detective Lynch fires back.

Detective Lee clears his throat. "Amanda, you had a meeting with a well-known celebrity last night. I believe Miss Jones told us that, and you confirmed it. What time did you meet?"

I was planning to tell the truth. Really. But I can't stop myself.

I say, "I think we met around seven."

"Uh-huh. What time did you return home?" Lee continues.

"Can you confirm the meeting?" Lynch says. "Did you stop anywhere after you left the meeting? Was it raining when you got home?"

"I, um, came right home. No. I actually popped into Target, then came home. I, um...what was the other question?"

"Was it raining?" Lynch sounds completely annoyed.

"Raining? I think so. Maybe. I'm not sure. When I went outside with Officer Young, it was drizzling, I think. Really damp."

"Did you use an umbrella?" Lynch looks over at Lee and raises his eyebrow.

"What does that have to do with anything? No. I didn't. I don't know if I even own an umbrella. I moved here in June. I left most of my stuff behind at Geoff's house."

Detective Lynch is jotting furiously. "We'll need the names

of the people you spoke to last night. Anyone who can confirm your whereabouts."

Oh God, I think I'm going to swoon. I'm starting to sweat again. My hand goes to my forehead.

I look from Lynch to Lee. Lynch is wearing a skeptical frown. Lee looks uncomfortable, like he wants to throw me a lifeline but can't. Lynch has the strident look of a middle school principal.

"People?" I say, forcing calm into my voice. "What I mean to say is that it wasn't actually an official meeting." I'm going for nonchalant, yet in control. "The truth is, I actually just jumped in, did my thing last night. Kind of spontaneous. Went to my client's home and took notes of what he needed. Organic. That's how I like to work. I, um, don't know if anyone even noticed me. I don't think anyone else was around."

Such incredible BS. No one's going to believe me. Even me.

Detective Lynch puts his pencil and pad down on the table.

"So, to answer my question—is that a no, as in, you *don't* have the names of anyone who saw or spoke to you last night?"

"Miss Beckwith," Detective Lee leans toward me, "it would be very, very helpful to our investigation, and to you, if you could come up with a few names of the people who saw you Friday night."

I stand and walk behind the couch. "Do I need to speak to a lawyer?"

"Hey, that's up to you," Detective Lynch says. "Personally, I don't like lawyers. Don't trust them."

I grip the back of the sofa. My fingers are squeezing little dents into the fabric.

"You know, this is completely nuts. Insane. There's a maniac killer on the loose, and you're grilling me about who I might've chatted with while I was surveying my client's closets!"

Detective Lynch is drumming his pencil on his pad again. He looks at me and sends Lee a knowing kind of look.

"I think it's best if you come down to the Ventura Station to give us a recorded statement."

"Now?" I'm feeling queasy. "Why? I haven't done anything wrong."

Lynch raises his eyebrow. "Let's move it, baby doll."

"Hold on a second." I take a step back from Lynch. "Seriously, I'm going to be completely honest. I didn't really have a meeting. I didn't go out at all last night. That's not exactly true. I ran to Target for some hangers and shoe boxes but left emptyhanded. That was around six. Maybe seven. I actually had a meeting with my client on Thursday afternoon, not Friday evening. I was confused. After Target, I came home. I was home, organizing my closet last night."

"Really? Organizing your closet at midnight." Lynch frowns at me. "All alone on Friday night. Doing housework."

"It's my job." I shift positions in my seat.

I suddenly remember what Lynette told me to say if anyone asked me about my employment.

"It actually isn't, like, a real job. I'm just a freelancer. I blog about it for the *Tribune*. Part-time. It's almost like a hobby."

"Save it for your statement," Lynch barks. "If you're telling the truth, you have nothing to worry about."

Lynch gives me directions to the station, which I pretend to listen to. He gestures to Lee.

They stand on each side of me, like they're afraid I'm going to bolt. Which is exactly what I'd love to do right now—bolt to LAX and hop a first-class Virgin Atlantic flight to London.

Then Detective Lee takes my arm and guides me toward the door. I push his hand away and stop.

"Wait a second. Statement? Like with a tape recorder? Why?"

Detective Lynch stretches his arms over his head, then cracks his neck with both hands. Which I personally find to be one of the most annoying sounds in the world.

"Amanda, murder victims almost always have a personal relationship with their killer. Like you and Bree Martin."

CHAPTER 5

I PULL INTO THE VENTURA COUNTY Sheriff's Department's parking lot, ahead of Detectives Lynch and Lee's black Ford Explorer. TV vans equipped with live-feed satellite dishes and antennas litter the parking lot. Fox, NBC, ABC, CNN, all here. Lynch said it: Victims almost always know their killer. He pointed his finger at me. Suspect? Person of interest?

This is not going to go away.

I spot Danny Starr in the mix of news people just as I quickly pop the glove compartment, grab my Tom Ford sunglasses, and plant them over my eyes. I pray nobody notices me.

I maneuver my Mercedes around the back of the building and into a space. I search the back lot for the detective's car. Not here. Must be an official parking area nearby.

I shift into park, turn off the car, and grab my handbag from the seat. My heart is pounding.

Outside the car, I take a moment to calm myself. I fluff my hair and reapply my lipstick. When I wipe the corners of my mouth, my hand is shaking.

I'll hurry through the crowd of reporters with my head down. Nobody will even notice me. I'll give my statement, go home, take a long, hot bath, make dinner, and go to bed.

The press must be here because of Geoff. He's the Zen 2 Slim guru. Owner of The Center, the home away from home for A-listers Oprah, Jennifer Aniston, Michael Douglas, Catherine Zeta-Jones, and yes, Rob Lowe. I mean, the list of famous people who belong to Geoff's club goes on and on. His beautiful wife,

Bree, was found murdered near my house, and reportedly witnessed by me, his ex-wife.

God. When you add in my father's status as one of New York's top ten hedge fund managers—I have no idea what he actually does—and my mother's job as one of California's well-known Democratic strategists and fundraisers, the story begins to grow from a tiny column on the back pages of the *Tribune,* to a front-page story in the *Times.*

Put it all together, and it equals tabloid heaven.

My poor parents are going to disown me. Check that—everyone I know will disown me. They gave me a pass for my DUI, and finally forgave me for my domestic violence charge. Now this.

I suddenly have the jitters so bad I can't get my feet to move. But if I don't get in there soon, the detectives will come looking for me. What a photo op that will be: Officers Lynch and Lee dragging me up the station steps. The video will stream right to Instagram, YouTube, and Facebook.

I take a deep breath, skirt a row of cars until I see the boxy cement gray and blue building that would make a great location site for a Russian prison movie.

This is where Lynch and Lee will re-interview me, this time with a tape recorder and a video camera running.

Routine, they said. *Routine for them.*

I hate this place. The shame of my prior two arrests creeps into my head like a migraine. The problem is that the press won't have to dig very deep to discover I've had a couple minor brushes with the law.

I wasn't totally honest with Lee and Lynch earlier. I didn't intend to lie, really. But I was nervous. All I must do is keep my story straight, even if I fudged it a little the first time. I mean, what's the worst that can happen? Could I go to jail for obstruction of justice or something?

I push these ridiculous negative thoughts from my mind and turn my attention to the pavement in front of me. God, I wish I wasn't alone. Maybe I really do need a lawyer. No. Getting a lawyer is like admitting I need one, which is also like admitting that I'm guilty of something. Right?

I look up at the huge, angry gray clouds. Any second it's going to start to rain, and I really don't have an umbrella. At least, not anymore.

The thought of my umbrella triggers this creepy feeling. Like I'm forgetting some important detail about last night. It'll come to me later, probably, when I'm driving home or taking a shower.

I round the corner of the building and make my way toward the milling crowd. Out of nowhere, someone yells, "Amanda Beckwith!" and like a pack of hungry dogs, the press is on me. Microphones are jammed in my face. A cacophony of voices smacks me from all sides. I squint against the blinding flashes and lights.

Shouldering through the throng of reporters, I head for the front of the building.

Not fast enough. A woman in an exquisitely tailored black jacket that looks like one featured in this month's *Vogue*, yells in an accusing tone, "Amanda, did you murder Bree Martin?"

Did I murder Bree? Those words, said out loud, in front of all these people, makes everything suddenly real. Like 3-D real. People think I did it! *Don't panic.* I mean, I'm in a crowd of reporters. They're not normal people, I remind myself. Don't say a word.

"Is your father going to help you?" someone else shouts.

I turn toward the voice. There's too many reporters shouting at me—I can't tell who's speaking.

"Will your mother resign from the Democratic National Committee?" a male voice calls from behind me.

I turn around. Lose my footing. My ankle buckles. I trip into the crowd. Strong hands clutch me from behind and break my fall. Danny Starr steadies me to my feet. I yank out of his grasp.

"Did *you* ask about my mother?" I snap.

God, if I'm not careful, I'm going to lose it in front of everyone. Imagine that front-page photo.

"You okay?" Danny says.

"Don't act like you care. It's insulting."

I manage to edge up a couple of the steps. Danny says something, but it's too noisy to hear. God, I hate him. His stupid Mr. Nice Guy tactics are so obvious. He's trying to disarm me. I'm just a headline.

I push a random microphone out of my way and take another step up the stairs.

Before going all the way up, a thought pops into my mind. Maybe I should hold a mini-press conference right here and now. That would stop Danny Starr in his tracks. Seriously, I'll proclaim my innocence, answer questions, and be done with it. The public has the right to know that I can be eliminated from the suspect list. Then the police can get on with finding the real murderer.

For a second, I consider the consequences of speaking candidly to the press. The woman in the black jacket presses something into my hand. I look down. It's her business card. Savannah Guthrie. NBC Morning Show.

"Call me," she shouts over the din of voices. "Your mother agreed to an interview. Let's do the two of you at the same time."

My mother has never been one to let a good crisis go to waste.

I pocket the card and turn away from the crowd. But a reporter follows me up the stairs. I cover my face with my bag, elbow past the woman, and rush up to the landing. I feel like Dorothy entering Oz. "Somewhere Over the Rainbow" starts to play in my mind.

Before going into the building, I take a last look at the crowd behind me. From the corner of my eye, I catch Danny standing with some people who I imagine are his so-called *team*. One of them is the photographer who snapped my picture at the crime scene last night. They're all sporting baggy jeans, flak-type jackets, and scruffy satchels. A couple are smoking cigarettes. *So unoriginal.*

Danny tries to catch my attention with a look of empathy

or something, but I swing my gaze past him, pretending to see someone I know nearby. *I'm a headline to you, buster, and we both know it.*

Even though I've been to the Ventura Sheriff's Department before, I've never been in this part of the building. When I was here for my DUI, I was brought through the back door. It was located really close to the place where the police fingerprinted me and took my picture.

I open the lobby door and spot my ex as he's being ushered into one of the offices or interrogation rooms. Geoff's wearing a black raincoat over black Nike warmups, and white trainers. He's carrying the Ghurka briefcase I gave him for Christmas, before I discovered that he and Bree were having an affair.

I swear, for whatever weird, sadistic reason, Geoff brought that bag here on purpose, hoping I would see him with it. Like he wants to remind me that we were married. I don't get it, but I know him like a book, and that's totally something he'd do to mess with my emotions.

I move toward a bank of orange plastic chairs and almost sit next to Jack O'Brien, Geoff's best friend and lawyer. Jack's taste in clothes is horrible. He's in an ill-fitting blue blazer, preppy blue and Kelly-green striped tie, blue shirt, khaki Dockers, and peanut-butter-brown slip-ons. Preppy, but not in a good way. Everything Jack is wearing is a size too small.

There are a number of other people milling around—several in The Center's signature purple polos embellished with its infinity logo on the left breast.

Why is Jack here? I know that Geoff is Jack's only client. Is Jack here officially? If he was, wouldn't he be in the interview with Geoff? Apparently, Jack is here for moral support, not legal counsel.

Jack is on his cell, but he looks up and nods in my direction. I look away, pretending that I don't see him. The whole time that Geoff and I were married, Jack and I never really connected. Jack is weird. I mean, weirder than Geoff's usual Las-Vegas–type friends that he hangs out with. The thing about Jack that really bugged me was that he was always whispering stuff to Geoff when I was right there. I never trusted him.

As I scan the room for another empty chair, I feel a chill go up my spine. The hair on the back of my neck springs to life. Geoff is walking toward me.

His eyes meet mine. His brows knit together in disapproving wrinkles. His stare makes me feel guilty, like I should have been the one murdered on the beach, not Bree. My stomach does a somersault, and my hands start to sweat. I feel ridiculously weepy and nervous at the same time. Even after being divorced from Geoff all this time, he still has the power to make me feel small and worthless.

Geoff continues to walk toward me. I freeze. His expression softens, but I don't trust it. I step back. God, he looks like he's going to hug me. *He really wants to hit me.*

I thrust my hand toward him in a sort of handshake gesture, offering my condolences. Before I realize what's happening, Geoff clutches my arm and pulls me into an embrace. I drop my bag on the floor. Stiffen. Goosebumps prickle my skin.

"Amanda, no matter what anyone says, I know you're not capable of murder," he whispers in my ear. "I'll never tell a soul how much you hated Bree."

I struggle out of his arms. He drops his umbrella. I reach down to pick it up and hand it to him. He's wearing gloves. I didn't notice them before. His lips are pinched, and his eyes feign misery. To anyone who doesn't know him, Geoff has the appearance of a grief-stricken man devastated by his wife's death. But I know him too well. I've seen that you-can-trust-me-Amanda look a million times. There's not an ounce of sincerity in it.

Somewhere nearby, a door opens and shuts. I look away from Geoff to see that Sheriff Young—the cop who showed up at my house last night—is heading in my direction. He waves me toward him, his expression as bland as cardboard.

"Amanda, you're up." He opens the gate leading to the offices. "This shouldn't be too painful."

I bend to pick up my bag, and out of the corner of my eye, I see Young wink and nod at Geoff.

What in the hell is that about?

CHAPTER 6

FINALLY, OUT OF INTERROGATION, Detectives Lynch and Lee escort me out of the police station through the back exit. It's dusk. It'll be dark soon. My iPhone registers a few minutes after 5:00. I've been here for about two hours.

Lynch pushes the door open. He steps to the side to give me some room. Detective Lee follows me outside. I breathe in the cool, fresh air. I search the lot for any lingering reporters. If there are any left, I don't see them.

"Let's walk." Lynch motions for Lee to follow. "Where'd you park?"

"Not far." I try to dig in my purse for my key fob.

I grab it, along with my Tom Fords. I sling the purse over my shoulder and clumsily plant the glasses over my eyes, more as a disguise then to block out the sun. The rain has stopped, but gray clouds blanket the sky.

I press the fob. My car responds with a loud chirp. My heart skips a beat. I'm a complete wreck.

"I can find my way. Thanks for everything."

"No problem, cupcake," Lynch says.

I head toward my car, with Lynch flanking me like I'm a criminal or something. I don't know where Lee went.

I open my car door, toss my purse on the passenger's seat, then ease myself behind the wheel. I feel Detective Lynch's gaze on me.

"Stay close," he says.

His gaze holds mine for a couple beats. He has one of those

mean-teacher-angry-father looks that's meant to scare you. It does.

"Miss Beckwith, don't even think about leaving the area. Keep your phone on. This is a serious investigation, and you need to be available immediately if we need to ask you additional questions."

"No. I mean, yes. What I'm trying to say is that I really think that you're wasting your time with me," I blurt out. "I know that I didn't...couldn't...wouldn't hurt anyone, so that means there is someone out there who did, right? Can I ask you a question?"

"Fire away." Lynch steps closer.

"I read about a rape or murder and some break-ins in my neighborhood a while ago. This could be related. Did they every catch the guy who did it?"

"What guy? Right now, we're talking about you."

"That's my point. You're focusing your attention on me and no one else."

Lynch's hand is on the inside of his jacket like he's going for his gun or something.

"You guys barely interviewed Geoff. You don't know him the way I do. He's not a nice person."

"Listen, Miss Scarlett, this is not a game of clue. Not being a nice guy isn't evidence of anything."

Lynch takes a step toward my car and rests his hand on the door.

"He's clever," I say. "Manipulative. You shouldn't trust him."

I have an empty pit in my stomach that has nothing to do with the fact that I haven't eaten since last night.

"Let us do our job," Lynch barks. "You just worry about you, cupcake."

He takes hold of the door handle, slams the door, and steps away from the car. I start the car and rev the engine a little. There's no one parked in front of me, so I ease down on the gas and pull forward. I look in the rearview mirror. Lynch is standing where I left him, arms folded across his chest, a grim expression on his face.

I'm scared. Gut instinct tells me that Geoff had something to do with Bree's death. The detectives aren't taking anything I say seriously.

The phantom image of the intruder that skirted through my yard last night has now morphed into the perfect likeness of Geoff.

But it couldn't have been Geoff that I saw last night. He has an alibi. He was in Las Vegas. Convenient, right? I was at home by myself, cleaning out my closet.

I didn't see a soul last night. Except Kim, I suddenly remember. She'll vouch for me.

But how's that going to help. I saw her in the early evening, not after midnight.

With Geoff off the suspect list, the detectives must believe that I murdered Bree.

Maybe Lynch and Lee believe that I somehow lured Bree to my house, murdered her on the beach, then covered up my tracks. Maybe they think I made up the intruder story.

I should never have lied to anyone about where I was last night. Even though I ended up telling the detectives the truth about my meeting with Rob Lowe, they probably didn't believe me. I mean, first I told them my meeting was with Rob Lowe on Friday evening. Then I told them it was on Thursday afternoon, with Rob Lowe's assistant, not Rob Lowe, and that I went to Target on Friday evening. I'm even having a hard time keeping everything straight. No wonder they think I murdered Bree.

It's hard to believe that anyone interrogated by the cops ever gets their story straight. Lynch kept asking me the same questions over and over again, like he didn't believe any of my answers in the first place.

I slowly maneuver the Mercedes around a lane of cars as I head for the exit. Out of the corner of my eye, I see Geoff and Jack standing next to an older model, white Lexus sedan two rows away. The car is probably Jack's, because Geoff drives a new black Range Rover. They're head-to-head, talking. Suddenly, they look my way. I avert my gaze.

A few reporters are still hovering around the front door, but their backs are to me. I don't see Danny Starr anywhere. Thank God.

Before I ease out of the lot and onto the street, I check my rearview mirror. Jack and Geoff are still talking.

I pull out into the flow of traffic and turn north on Main. Christmas lights twinkle on the storefronts. Even in bad weather, people are out shopping. I turn off of Main and onto Seaward, leaving the holiday shoppers behind me. Seaward is a long, lonely street flanked by flower fields on both sides of the road.

I try to focus on the road ahead, but my mind wanders back to the threatening way that Geoff grabbed me, and the things he said, and the creepy way Mike Young winked at Geoff, like they knew each other. Something feels wrong.

A horn honks, and I realize I'm driving slowly. I look in the rearview mirror. As cars pass under a streetlight, I see a white sedan three cars back. It looks like a Lexus. But every white sedan looks like a Lexus. Is Jack O'Brien following me? No. He lives in Ventura, but in the opposite direction of Hollywood Beach. Anyway, I left first. He and Geoff were still talking when I pulled out of the parking lot. Could he have caught up with me?

Maybe. I look in the mirror again, and the car I thought was a Lexus isn't behind me anymore. God, I'm losing my mind.

I need a drink. Somewhere in the back of my mind, a warning light goes off, but I quickly dismiss it and think how a sip of vodka would taste right now. *One little drink isn't going to hurt.* Actually, a drink will help me focus, clear my head, settle my nerves.

I hear the soft sound of my phone vibrating in my purse, on the passenger seat. I dig it out and wait a beat for it to go to Bluetooth. A horn honks. I pull over to the side of the road to avoid an accident. I look at my phone. My mother. God, I wish I had called her first. I touch the screen and answer the phone.

"Mandy?"

"Mom."

Her nickname for me brings tears to my eyes. I feel like I'm twelve years old, leaving the principal's office after getting caught for some prank I committed. *I'm in trouble—again.* But this isn't a prank, and I'm not twelve.

"Sweetie, how in God's name do you always seem to end up in the wrong place at the wrong time?" But she doesn't wait for my answer. "I spoke to your father. He's impossible. No wonder I left him. Want to know what he said?"

"I need your help, Mom."

"He said, 'California is what's wrong with Mandy.' California! According to him, you should've moved back East with him when he married that woman. Can you imagine? You know what he's getting at, don't you? He's blaming me for all your problems. Me! Anyway, I've got this under control."

I turn the volume down on the phone, but I can still hear my mother carrying on.

I cut her off. "I think I need to hire a lawyer."

I look in the rearview mirror and see the white Lexus. I sink down in my seat as it races by me. It's impossible to see who's driving.

"Have you spoken to Geoff?"

"Have you?" I sit up straight, my body tense.

My mom was more upset when I divorced Geoff than I was. She actually stays in contact with him.

"He's beside himself. I've organized meals with a few friends from the gym, but there's got to be something more we can do for him. Oh, before I forget—Samantha Guthrie called. From the morning show. She wants to interview us—together. I think we should go for it."

"I can't hear you," I say. "You're breaking up."

I click off before she can respond and rest the phone in my lap. When the traffic is clear, I pull back on the road. I've learned not to expect too much from my mom. She has a ton of stuff on her plate. Right now, she's fundraising for Gavin Newsom's re-election campaign while juggling the demands of three dating services. I wish I had her energy and optimism. I think I'm more like my father.

I turn on the radio. Dr. Laura's perky voice drones through the speakers. God, if there was ever a time when I needed to speak to someone about what I'm going through, it's now.

Keeping my eyes on the road, and one hand gripped on the steering wheel, I grab my phone and tap in Dr. Laura's 800 number. After a few rings, the phone picks up.

"Doctor Laura Show. This is Julie. The screener. What's your name? Age? Where do you live?"

"Amanda. I'm thirty-two. I, um…is it okay not to mention where I'm from?"

"No worries. So, what do you want to ask Doctor Laura?"

"My, um, ex-husband's wife was—no, scratch that. My mother, um—I mean, the police think—I'm alone—"

I choke up. Hang up and toss the phone on the passenger seat. My mind is racing. I quickly press the radio button to music. Jack Johnson is crooning "Someday at Christmas." I need to get focused. No. I need to let go. What I really need is a drink. Seriously.

That's the worst thing I could do. What I really need to do is make a note of all of the facts as I know them, then create a spreadsheet that shows exactly where I was every minute of the day, right up until the second I phoned the police. I'll cross-reference those details with everything I know about Bree's murder, including any crimes committed in my neighborhood in the last year. Then I'll confirm Mike Young's story that those cases are closed.

"The Christmas Song" is playing on the radio. I try to hum along with the tune, but I keep losing my place. I'm thinking about Bree again, her death, my ex-husband, my job, the detectives, and Danny Starr.

I switch channels in my mind from Danny Starr to Detectives Lynch and Lee.

They really didn't buy my reason for calling 911, or my account of the intruder in my backyard. I could tell by the way

Lynch rolled his eyes at Lee, that he thought I invented the noises and someone tripping over my patio furniture. The point is that I did nothing wrong, and I'm being treated like a criminal. Maybe I wasn't forthcoming with every single picky detail about my relationship with Bree. Maybe I stretched the truth a tiny bit. The important thing is that I wasn't anywhere near Bree last night—at least, not intentionally—and I had nothing whatsoever to do with her death.

The thing I can't figure out is what Bree was doing on Hollywood Beach last night? She lives an hour away, in Montecito. Maybe she went down to Hollywood Beach to escape Santa Barbara, where everybody knows her. Maybe she met someone for dinner at one of the beachfront hotels down the street from my house. Maybe she met an old friend for a drink at one of the local bars.

Even though Geoff was in Las Vegas for one of his seminars, surely Bree told him what she was up to on Friday night? Maybe Bree was fed up with Geoff's Las Vegas *seminars*.

God knows I know all about those seminars. I told the detectives that Geoff used his seminars to cover up his affair with Bree. That he probably used his seminars as a cover for a lot of things. They didn't seem interested.

I wonder how long it would take Geoff to drive from Las Vegas to Ventura, meet Bree, murder her, then get back to his Vegas hotel in time for the police to inform him that Bree was found dead.

But even if Geoff could have managed a roundtrip drive from Las Vegas to California and back, why would he want Bree dead? I hate to admit it, but they seemed really happy together. Bree was the nationally recognized face for Geoff's wildly successful Zen 2 Slim weight-loss program. Entrepreneur Magazine named Geoff Wellness Guru of the Year.

They seemed like the perfect couple. Since Bree came into the picture, Geoff's business has skyrocketed. His new, improved Zen 2 Slim supplements sell everywhere. I recently saw them at Target and Costco. Supposedly, the supplements are the number one rated weight-loss supplement on Amazon. I heard through the grapevine, that Geoff has big plans to franchise The Center.

Would Geoff kill Bree and jeopardize his success and his image? Would he risk going to jail?

A car horn honks. I look to my right. Whoops. I realize I'm drifting into the lane next to mine.

I glance in my rearview mirror as I ease back into my lane. Two car lengths back is what looks like the same white car that had been following me before. I grip the steering wheel and crank it to the right. Swerve through a lane of traffic. Up ahead, I see a side street. I step on the gas and fly around a corner. The light at the intersection changes to yellow. I press down hard on the gas and shoot through the intersection just as the light turns red.

I'm making myself crazy. I'm overreacting. White cars are a dime a dozen. They're the most common color cars on the road. It's a real statistic. I read that in *Forbes* or somewhere.

I take a deep breath and look over my shoulder. No one is following me.

I look up at the street signs. Only a few more miles and I'm home.

As I'm driving, bad memories about being married to Geoff take over my thoughts. The detectives kept telling me that Geoff was *helpful* and *cooperative*. The words I would use to describe Geoff are *duplicitous* and *diabolical*.

Unfortunately for me, most people think he's this charming, sincere, and professional guy.

He's not. He has a dark, sneaky, sadistic side. He constantly reinvented the truth to favor his own position on the dumbest stuff, just to make me feel crazy—everything from what he did with his free time to how much money he spent on things. He lied about things that nobody would question him about, like owning a baseball team, or being best friends with celebrities.

A horn honks. I look at the speedometer. I'm driving forty miles per hour in a fifty-five-mile-per-hour zone.

I look in the rearview mirror. A Volvo station wagon with a

Christmas tree on its roof is hugging my bumper. I step on the gas and move into another lane.

Maybe Geoff really was in Las Vegas. Maybe he had nothing to do with Bree's death. Maybe I'm just projecting my own hostile feelings about him because he dumped me.

I mean, Geoff did change a lot after he married Bree. At least, that's what people tell me. But I thought he'd changed for the worse. He was meaner to me after he married Bree.

I turn up the radio. Bing Crosby is singing "White Christmas." I maneuver around a couple cars just as my iPhone vibrates to life. My heart lurches. It's Kim.

"You heard the news, right?" I say. "I can't believe what a mess this is."

"Where've you been? I called your office, like, a million times. That woman you're working for is screening your calls. Where've you been?"

"I know. Lynette's just trying to help me," I say.

In her own way, I believe Lynette really is trying to help me.

"I had to give the police a statement."

There's no way in hell I'm going to tell Kim that two detectives just grilled me and consider me a person of interest. They never actually said that, but that was the vibe I got.

If I told Kim about my interrogation, it'd be all over Santa Barbara in a nanosecond. KNN—Kim's News Network. That's what everyone calls her. The truth is, Kim can't help herself. She means well. She really does. But even though we're more like sisters than friends, her good intentions to help me usually go sideways.

"I really need to talk to you," Kim begs. "Can I come over?"

My phone beeps. I look at the cell's screen. It's my mom again.

"Ten minutes," I say. "Dad's Liquor."

I switch calls.

"Don't hang up on me again," my mom says.

I can hear her take a deep, irritated breath.

In a razor-sharp voice that takes me back to when I was a

kid, she says, "You need to pack a bag and come stay with me before things really spin out of control."

"I didn't hang up on you."

"You're not listening. I'm watching the news."

I can hear Chris Cuomo's blustering voice on the TV in the background.

"Needless to say, Bree's death has hit the airwaves. I'd advise you to fix yourself up and do something with that hair of yours before you find yourself in front of a camera again. The *Today Show* has invited us on."

"You told me that. Mom, please don't speak to the press. Promise me?"

As if she doesn't know better. I mean, look what happened to me when I spoke to Danny Starr. I was such an idiot.

"I'm afraid it's too late for promises."

I think my mother just turned up the volume so she could hear the TV better over my talking.

"We have a live interview with Jeanine Pirro from Fox tomorrow evening, and a conference call with Andersen Cooper the following morning. A producer from *The View* called. You need public opinion in your corner right now. With a little hard work, I think I can turn this around."

"I'm going into a meeting," I say.

I feel myself losing it. I mean, as much as my mother demeans the entire newspaper industry, she thrives on being in the spotlight. I can almost hear the soundbites she'll use: *Valiant mother battles daughter's detractors.* Or *Elizabeth Beckwith kicks off daughter's defense fundraiser with a five-star gala at the Four Seasons Biltmore.*

"I'll call you when I'm done," I say. "Please don't speak with anyone about this."

I turn off the phone while my mother is still talking. She's impossible. There's no way I'm staying with her. I barely got through my childhood living with her. I couldn't wait to go away to college. No wonder my dad left us.

My heart is pounding, and I'm seriously afraid I'm going to

hyperventilate and pass out, going fifty miles per hour.

Everybody knows that *person of interest* means Scott Peterson, who was, in fact, the murderer. Why didn't I just tell the detectives the complete truth in the first place and be done with it? I mean, I have nothing to hide. I hate being a person of interest.

I have to calm down. No one said I was a person of interest. *Witness* is what Lynch actually said. Witness is so much better.

God, I need fresh air. I need to stand and walk around a bit. I need...

I need a drink. Up ahead, I see Dad's Liquor Store's neon sign flashing at me. I pull into a space furthest from the door, behind the building, and park. Kim will be here in a few minutes. I have just enough time to run into the store and make a few purchases.

Outside, I lean up against the car, close my eyes, and let the crisp, damp air wash over me. From this moment forward, I swear I'm not going to withhold or exaggerate one single thing ever again.

I already feel better. Empowered, actually. I'm going to be part of the solution instead of part of the problem, as my father always says. I can aid the police in their investigation. I'm really, really good at researching stuff and organizing details. For God's sake, that's what I do. Organize. I can turn this entire situation around.

The headlines will read: *Amanda Beckwith Cracks the Case of the Murder on Hollywood Beach*. I mean, Lynette will promote me to a real job, or make me a columnist in the paper instead of an online blogger!

I push myself away from the car, sling my bag over my shoulder, and head into the liquor store. Seriously, I deserve a drink. I've earned one.

Inside the store, I walk past racks of bagged peanuts, chips, candy, and gum, and head for the refrigerator section for tonic and orange juice. I look around and realize how utterly disorganized this store is, which is basically true for all convenience stores. In the first place, nothing feels very convenient, and there's no eye appeal whatsoever.

When I think about it, that's what's wrong with just about everything today. I mean, stores, people, the police department, transportation, movie theaters. They all lack a sense of style. The entire world needs a makeover.

I open one of the refrigerators and find the tonic in a sea of soda cans, milk, OJ, bologna, and cheese. It's all very unappetizing.

Maybe fixing up the entire world is a little out of my scope. But seriously, I love the idea of beautifully organized neighborhood stores with hardwood floors, gleaming chrome refrigerated bins stocked with imported cheese and crackers, with an entire section just for organic vegetables and fruits.

I picture Dad's staffed with really cute professional clerks wearing freshly starched white shirts, khaki pants, black aprons, and clean white Converse tennis shoes.

Wouldn't it be great to furnish the store with a hip European-style newsstand stacked with really great French and British magazines? A section for art and architecture?

Maybe I'll start my own business when this whole mess blows over. I'll quit my job and borrow money from my dad. No. My dad's new wife controls his money, so that's not an option.

I grab a six-pack of tonic and head for the cash register. How hard could it be to raise a little money? I'll start a Go Fund Me page, go on Shark Tank.

Behind the counter, the clerk raises an eyebrow when he sees me. Am I being paranoid, or is he looking at me funny, like he knows me?

"Excuse me. I'll take that little bottle of vodka," I point to a random pint of vodka, then set my stuff on the counter. "On second thought, I'll take that big bottle with, um...the pretty birds on it."

"Grey Goose?" The clerk bags the vodka and soda.

I dig in my purse for my wallet and take out two twenty-dollar bills.

"You're short." The clerk takes my money.

"Sorry." I dig another twenty out of my wallet and hand it to him.

He hands me the change as I pick up the bag and turn to go. It's been a long time since I bought alcohol.

"Miss, you're much prettier in person than you are on TV."

Great. I thought my mother was exaggerating.

I push the door open and walk outside. Kim is leaning against the door of her Range Rover, talking on her cell. She pockets her phone when she sees me.

"We need to talk. Why didn't you call me back? I had to read about Bree on Facebook! The *Times* article was at the gym."

Great. I look around. We're starting to attract attention. I pull her away from her car and around back toward my car.

"Kim. Shush. People are listening."

"Right." Kim looks around.

She's wearing a leopard-print T-shirt under a white Patagonia hoodie, AJ Jeans, and a pair of Nikes. She's chewing skin off her cuticles.

"Are you really the only witness? Did you see the murderer?"

"I wasn't a witness to anything." I open the back gate of my wagon to set my bag inside and slam the door. "Please don't spread that rumor."

"Why would you say something like that?" Kim whispers. "I would never say anything to anyone about you."

"That's a relief." I hope she doesn't detect the sarcasm in my voice. "Whatever you read in the paper is a lie. Tell your gym friends that. In a few days, this will all be over."

I push the fob and unlock my car. Kim goes around and gets in on the passenger side. I sit behind the wheel, shut the door, and turn to face Kim.

I have a sudden inspiration. "Can I stay with you and Brad for a couple days? Until things kind of blow over?"

Kim looks at me like I just asked her to lend me a million dollars.

"Forget it. I'll be fine." I force the disappointment out of my voice.

"Good. Listen, you can't tell the police, or anyone else, that you saw me yesterday. Promise me," Kim begs. "I've been seeing Sophia's teacher."

"Why? Is Sophia having problems?" I think I'm missing something.

"We met near your house yesterday," Kim continues. "Nothing's happened. We're just friends. Really. But if Brad finds out that we were together, it'll be the end of our marriage. You can't tell a soul."

I bite my lip. Brad and Kim have been having problems for years. She calls herself a golf widow. But rumor has it that they have money problems and he's verbally abusive.

"Are you okay?" I say. "You look really thin."

"I'm in the best shape I've ever been in my life," Kim snaps. "Just because you've gained some weight, you think I'm too thin."

"I have?" But I know I've put on a few pounds.

I didn't think anyone noticed except Geoff. I went from a size two to a size four, and I'm now squeezing into a size six. Seriously, only Kim tracks people's weight.

I press the ignition button and start the car. The engine roars to life.

"I really gotta go. Let's talk tomorrow."

"There's something else I need to tell you."

"What?" I set my hands on my lap and turn to face her.

"You have to promise not to say anything? I really don't want to get involved in this situation."

"What situation are we talking about now?"

A light rain tip-taps on the windshield. I look outside. Even in the dark night, I can see clouds knitting together in the sky. It's going to rain hard tonight.

"You sound angry," Kim says.

"No. Truthfully, I'm just tired. Tell me."

"Promise first."

"Promise."

"Okay. Early evening, after I dropped Sophia off for soccer

practice, 1 drove over to Hollywood Beach to see you-know-who, like 1 told you. Anyway, remember that creepy friend of Geoff's? That lawyer?"

"Jack O'Brien?" An alarm goes off in my head. "1 just saw him."

Kim continues like she didn't hear me. "You know the one I'm talking about. He's kind of portly. Fair skin. Older. He looks like Geoff, but not cute. He's always wears those really tacky mock turtleneck short-sleeve sweaters in pastel colors, over tight khaki shorts? We tried to fix him up with that girl at the gym a few years ago."

"You're talking about Jack O'Brien," 1 say.

Kim's favorite pastime, besides her children's sports activities, is playing yenta. 1 mean, truthfully, she'd fix Scott Peterson up with someone if she thought he was available and out of jail.

"For the record, 1 never tried to fix him up with anyone," 1 say.

"That's exactly who I'm talking about," Kim says.

"Listen to me. He was with Geoff at the sheriff's station." My body tenses when 1 mention Geoff's name.

"You saw him?" Kim's face goes white. "Did you talk to him?"

"Seriously, Kim. I've got to get home. I'm exhausted."

She probably wants to talk about who we can fix Geoff up with now that he's single.

"What was he doing at the police station?" Kim's voice sounds a little frantic.

"1 don't know. He was there with Geoff. 1 have to go."

"Wait. Listen." There's urgency in Kim's voice.

She grabs my hand away from the steering wheel and grips it.

"Hey, you're hurting me."

She finally let's go of my hand.

"When 1 was leaving Hollywood Beach, 1 saw Jack. At least, 1 thought 1 saw him. He was on the beach near your house. Before 1 saw you."

"Where? What time was it?" I can feel the fear in my voice.

I picture the white sedan three car lengths behind me on the freeway coming home. It looked like Jack's Lexus.

"What are you talking about?" I say.

"It was dark." Kim is fidgeting in her seat. "He was on the beach, not too far from your house. I think he was with someone."

"Jack lives somewhere around here," I say. "Did you say anything to him?"

"You don't listen, do you? I only got a glimpse of him. From a distance."

"You need to go to the police." I'm stunned. "This could be important."

"I can't tell the police," Kim snaps. "I can't get involved."

I could tell the police. But I already gave my statement. The police aren't going to believe a word I say ever again if I lay something like this on them now.

"Could you call the police anonymously?" I say.

"Let me think about it." Kim pauses, looking down at her hands for a thoughtful moment.

She opens the car and hops out and slams the door. She walks around to my side. I roll down the window.

"Wanna know the weirdest thing?" she whispers, then looks over her shoulder like someone is listening.

She pauses for effect.

"What?"

Truth is, I almost don't want to know. I feel myself holding my breath.

"The person Jack was with—she kind of looked like Bree."

CHAPTER 7

I LEAVE DAD'S LIQUOR, drive past Kim and wave goodbye. She's on her phone and doesn't notice me. I can't wait to get home. Maybe I'll put out my Christmas decorations or bake cookies for Jean. I really need to buy a tree.

I know it sounds strange, but a sense of utter relief washes through me with the news that Jack O'Brien was near my house on the same day Bree was murdered, and that Bree may have been with him.

Ten minutes ago, I'm standing on the edge of the black hole—all of my failed attempts at happiness, lack of purpose, and growing rap sheet are flashing before me. I'm an accused murderess. How am I ever going to live that one down?

This new development is a lifeline. I'm saved!

Maybe not until Kim spills what she knows to the police. It doesn't really matter that Kim isn't sure that the people she saw was Jack or Bree. She saw *someone*. That counts. Another person of interest. If nothing else, Kim proves my alibi.

Alibi really isn't the right word. Maybe it just proves that I wasn't the only person that was at the scene of the crime on Friday night.

I wonder if the police know that Jack, and maybe Bree, were on Hollywood Beach? Jack was at the police station when I got there. Maybe the detectives already interviewed Jack and have his statement.

That would be good news for Kim. Maybe she doesn't need to go to the police, after all.

Why was Jack on Hollywood Beach on Friday night? Was he really with Bree?

The one thing I do know, is that Bree was on Hollywood Beach. Was she with Jack, or someone who looked like Jack?

Whatever happened to Bree happened sometime between 6:00 p.m. on Friday night, when Kim thought she saw Jack and Bree, and after midnight, when her body was found on the beach near my house.

Why Hollywood Beach? If someone wanted to murder Bree, there were countless places to do it. There was something purposeful about that specific location. Bree's body was found more than fifty miles from her home in Montecito, and less than a hundred feet from my house.

Why?

To set me up?

That's the only reason. It wasn't a coincidence.

I swallow a lump, white-knuckle the steering wheel. That's exactly what happened. I'm being set up.

I flip on my turn signal, look left, then right, and wait for traffic to clear. I ease my car into the flow.

Set me up? Nobody's going to set me up. I'm not that girl anymore. I'm not. At least, not to me. Obviously, Geoff hasn't picked up on my transformation. They—whoever they are—have underestimated me.

But if the cops don't turn up any other suspects, then the detectives will eventually try to pin Bree's death on me. What else can they do?

Lynch and Lee are making me out to be a jealous, vengeful, obsessive-compulsive stalker who just happens to live on the beach where Bree was found dead. Do they think I lured Bree to the beach and killed her, then called the police?

It's plausible. But there's so much more to this story. Jack O'Brien, or someone that looks like him, was on the beach—my beach—with a woman who looked like Bree. Kim saw them.

She needs to tell the detectives what she knows.

Once Lynch and Lee get Kim's statement, they'll come to

their senses and turn their attention from me to Jack. Even if it wasn't Jack who Kim thought she saw, there was someone else on the beach close to my house, with a blonde woman who looked like Bree.

The only thing I know for sure is that Bree, alive or dead, was on Hollywood Beach, and I didn't kill her.

A horn blast behind me. I look at the speedometer. Ten miles per hour. Jeez. I step on the gas and look up at the street sign ahead. Damn. I overshot my street by four blocks.

I make a U-turn and head toward Hollywood Beach and my house.

I need to think like Bree, not Geoff or Jack. If I were Bree, would I go to Hollywood Beach on a cold, damp December night? Hell no. Maybe Bree didn't go to Hollywood Beach voluntarily. Maybe she didn't go there at all. Maybe she was brought there after she was murdered.

Maybe Jack killed her somewhere else—like his house, or his grimy Ventura office. He carried her body down to the beach and then left the beach through my yard, where he didn't think anyone would see him. Except Kim sees him with someone who looks like Bree.

That doesn't make sense. I didn't hear anything until after midnight. Kim thought she saw them sometime before 7:00 p.m. What happened in that five-hour gap?

When I saw someone dart across my patio, he was alone. I couldn't tell which direction he was coming from, but it looked like he was heading toward my house. He had to be returning to the crime scene, because by that time, Bree was already dead. Why would Jack—if it was Jack—leave through my yard and risk getting caught by me? The beach is full of unoccupied houses during the winter. Does Jack know that?

Okay, so Jack cruised my street, and when he didn't see my car, he dumped Bree's body. He wasn't counting on Kim being in the area. Kim thought she saw him. Did he see her?

Maybe he returned to the crime scene to retrieve some damaging piece of evidence—something smeared with his fingerprints and Bree's DNA.

I replay the scene when I first look out my window after I heard someone trip over my patio furniture. I see the back of a black jacket, but what else did I see? There's something I'm overlooking. I can't think about that right now. My head is pounding, and I'm starving.

I turn down my street, keeping a lookout for unfamiliar cars as I go. The street is pitch black. Two streetlamps are out. I try to remember if that's how they were last night. I can't remember.

I look at my watch. It's after 8:00. God, I wish I had left a light on.

The street is empty. Thankfully, the press hasn't found their way back to my house. It's the weather. No. Maybe they've lost interest in the story. Maybe my story has cycled out of the news, and some other juicy scandal is breaking somewhere else.

As I'm pulling up to my house, I see Jean standing in front of her garage. She turns toward me, shielding her eyes from my blinding headlights. There's a suitcase by her side.

I park my car and turn off the lights. Grab my purse, grocery bag, then step out onto the rain-drenched street.

"Jean! I'm so glad I caught you." I hurry over to her, hugging the bag to my chest. "What's going on? Where are you going? Where's Daisy?"

Jean's eyes are darting from her suitcase to the car. She scurries away from like I've just announced that I have the flu while punching her garage door opener. We both jump back from the door as it cranks open. Once open, she practically leaps toward her car, dragging her suitcase with her. She digs into her purse and pulls out her keys.

I follow her into the garage. "Wait."

She faces me but darts her gaze away from mine.

"Sweetie, I'm on my way to LA. To stay with my son. Daisy is at a friend's house."

"Why?" Now I'm really alone. "Did something else happen?"

Jean opens the trunk and tries to lug her suitcase up and over the edge of the bumper, but it's too heavy.

I set my stuff down, grab hold of her luggage and pull it into the trunk, with a thud. Jean slams the trunk, then hurries over to the car door and scoots behind the steering wheel.

I walk around so I can see her.

"My kids are expecting me." She grabs hold of the door handle. "I need to dash."

"Did the police tell you that you should leave?"

"Not specifically," she says, but I can hear the lie in her voice. Jean lives next door to the one and only *person of interest*. No wonder she's leaving.

"Please give me a second." I hold her car door open with my hip. "Did you see anyone on the beach last night? Before you went to bed?" I sound desperate.

I mean, if Kim saw someone, maybe Jean did, too.

"Anyone?"

"The only person I saw yesterday was you," There's an accusatory edge in her voice. "Now, please. I really do have to go."

She yanks the door shut and revs the engine. I step away from the car, pick up my things, and walk out onto the street. I watch Jean back up as the garage door closes. She makes a U-turn, almost hitting me, and speeds away.

I jump back, clutching my purse and bag. Jean's afraid of me.

It's drizzling. The wet asphalt streets soak up the multicolored Christmas lights on Jean's house. I wonder what the detectives said to Jean to cause her to leave? I wonder what Jean said to the detectives?

I look up at the darkened windows in my bedroom. My body tenses. My heart's pounding. I swear I'm going to have an asthma attack. Chills wrack my body, and I have a creepy feeling of déjà vu.

I hurry around to the front of the house, pushing memories of last night to the back of my mind. I steady the grocery bag on my hip and dig my keys out of my purse. I fumble with the front door lock until I hear it click.

Once inside, I lock the door and latch the chain behind

me and turn on the lights. I step out of my shoes and enter the kitchen and set the grocery bag on the counter, then hang my purse on the back of the kitchen chair. Back into the living room, I hurry to the thermostat on the wall and turn up the heat. It feels like a meat wagon in here.

Back in the kitchen, I pour myself a bowl of cereal and sit at the kitchen table. I'm not hungry. Just cold and exhausted. I can't believe it's been almost twenty-four hours since I called the police.

I wiggle my toes and wince as pins and needles prickle my feet. Stretch my arms over my head and yawn deeply. My gaze rests on the grocery bag. The Grey Goose is inside. I really want a drink. After what I've been through, I deserve one.

I set my spoon down and push away from the table. Take the bottle out of the bag and grab the soda.

This is crazy. I can't drink. I have no interest in drinking. I like being sober.

I whisk the vodka off the counter and shove it into the back of a cupboard. Stick the tonic into the fridge, then wad up the damp bag and toss it in the trash under the sink. Rinse the bowl and spoon, then grab a dishtowel, wipe them dry and put them away.

The drizzle has turned to rain, and it pounds the roof in long, noisy bursts. Wind whistles through the trees. I pull the curtain away from the window above the sink. The rain is really coming down.

Kim enters my line of vision.

"Let me in. It's freezing out here!"

My heart jumps.

"Go to front door," I yell, and point toward the door.

After grabbing a handful of towels from a kitchen drawer, I hurry to meet her at the front door.

"I forgot you've never been here before."

Kim grabs the towels out of my hand and pushes past me, into the house.

"I'm drenched." She wipes her face with one of the towels.

"What's going on." I pull her into the kitchen. She's dripping wet.

"You scared the crap out of me," I say.

"You didn't answer your phone," Kim grumbles, struggling out of her wet jacket.

She hangs it over one of the kitchen chairs. Water puddles on the floor.

"I parked in the lot next to the hotel and came up from the beach. I didn't want the reporters to see me."

The Mandalay Bay Hotel is a few long blocks north of my house. No wonder Kim is soaked.

I take the wet towels from Kim and throw them in the sink and hand her a couple dry ones. She wipes her neck, then wraps a towel around her hair.

I get down on my knees and wipe up the rain, sand, and dirt from the floor. I toss the towels in the sink.

"Sit down." My heart is still pounding. "What's happened. You look horrible."

"I need coffee." She shakes her hands, then blows heat into them. "I'm okay. I came back to tell you that you can stay at my house. I'll help you pack."

"Really? Thanks. One or two nights, max. Come on, let's get you into something dry while I pack."

"Great house. It's bigger than I thought it would be. Quaint. I like your furniture." Kim wraps the ends of her hair in a towel. "Do you have anything smaller than a medium?"

I ignore her jab. "I redid the floors. White oak."

I fill the Nespresso canister with water, add a pod, then push the *on* button. I wait for the coffee to fill Kim's mug, then repeat the process for me. I set the mugs and sugar on a tray and go to the fridge and grab the cream.

"You didn't have to drive to my house to tell me. You could've called or texted me."

"I just told you I've been trying to call you. If you answered your phone once in a while, I wouldn't have had to drive all the way here. Anyway, I haven't been a very good friend lately."

"Ditto," I say.

I rest the tray on the kitchen table and sit next to Kim. Hand her a mug and take a sip out of mine.

"I'm glad you came by. I really need to talk to you."

"Now what? I said you can stay with us."

She doesn't even know what I want to talk to her about.

Kim repositions herself in the chair.

"I'm just trying to figure out a few things," I say. "I'm confused. I saw you yesterday, around seven. Did you see Jack and Bree before or after you saw me?"

"It was around six-thirty p.m., not seven. I don't even know for sure if it was Jack and Bree. I barely know Jack. All I saw was a guy that kind of looked like Jack, and a woman with blonde hair. I was too far away to really see anything for sure. I told you that."

Is Kim changing her story?

"Let's just say you saw one or two people on the beach near my house. How close were they to my house?"

"I don't know. Maybe half a football field away. Maybe closer. It was dark, okay?"

"Did Sophia's teacher see them?" I take another sip of coffee.

Kim huffs as she scoots the chair back and stands. She takes her coffee and walks over and sets it in the sink.

"I gotta go. Are you going to stay with us or not?"

Her phone chimes. She digs it out of her pocket and looks at the screen.

"I need to take this. Is your bedroom upstairs? I need privacy."

"We need to go to the police together." I grab my phone off the counter, then follow her upstairs to my room. "You need to tell them what you saw."

Kim covers the mouthpiece of the phone. "You promised you wouldn't say anything to anyone."

"You don't get it. The police think I killed Bree," I blubber, on the verge of tears. "But even if they don't think I murdered Bree, they think I saw who did. I'm supposedly the only witness.

Which could also make me the next victim."

"Don't try to make this about you, Amanda." Kim turns her back to me and whispers into the phone. "You're always doing stuff like that."

"What are you saying?"

"I'll call you back." Kim pockets the phone and turns back to me. "I wasn't even going to tell you about seeing Jack and Bree. I knew this would happen. I knew I couldn't trust you."

"Couldn't trust me? What are you talking about? I can't believe you don't see how important your information is. You saw Jack and Bree together on the beach where she was murdered!"

"Maybe I just imagined seeing people on the beach. I told you, it was really dark."

I squeeze back the tears. I've brought this all on myself. I can hear my mother saying something like that. I can't blame Kim for not stepping up. Why should she?

Kim's phone chimes again. She walks out of the room.

Kim will help me. We've been friends our entire life.

The truth is that all the bad stuff I've done over my life is culminating with Bree's death. I run down the list, from copying the correct spelling words off Esther Freelander's paper in second grade, to making phony phone calls with Kim in junior high, to lying to my parents, fighting with my parents, secretly going out on a date with Kim's ex-boyfriend in college, my divorce, my DUI. Where does it end?

My karma bank is completely empty.

I'm on my own. Nobody's coming to my rescue. I can figure this out. I don't need Kim. I don't need anyone.

I need time. Maybe I'm being overly dramatic. Maybe things aren't really as bad as I think. They can always be worse, right? At least I know that Kim saw someone on the beach. Which is huge. I'll tell the police about Jack. Let them investigate the lead and try to connect the dots. It's their job.

"Don't be mad. If you want me to go the police, I'll go. Tomorrow. I promise." Kim walks back into my bedroom. "Do you have an old pair of sweats I can borrow?"

"Sure. It's all going to work out. Right?"

"Exactly." Kim pulls her long blonde wet hair into a knot on her head and wipes her hands on her jeans as she follows me into my closet.

She pulls her wet sweater over her head, then wiggles out of her jeans and wads them up before dropping them on the wood floors.

"Do you have a bag?"

I grab a plastic Gap bag from a stash in one of the closet drawers and hand it to her. Then go to the *size small* section in my closet and find my best pair of Lululemon sweatpants, and a matching sweatshirt.

"Will this work?"

"Cute." Kim takes the outfit out of my hands. "Jack *is* really creepy."

"I agree. Do you think he could have killed Bree?"

"How would I know? I only knew Jack and Bree because you introduced me to them." Kim pulls on the pants, then yanks the sweatshirt over her head. "So, what exactly happened last night? What did you see?"

"You really want to know?"

"Of course."

"Come on." I walk Kim out of the closet and step to the window that looks out to the beach.

I give her the CliffsNotes of what I heard and saw on Friday night.

"That's it?"

"In a nutshell."

We turn from the window.

Kim sits on my bed. "No big deal."

"Hey, let me drive you to your car. I'm going to sleep here tonight and go to my mother's tomorrow. You must be exhausted, too."

"Thanks. You're right. I'll meet you downstairs. I have to call my friend back."

I go into my closet and yank off my tights and Burberry skirt. After putting them away, I put on a pair of wool argyle socks, AG jeans, and a black cashmere turtleneck.

The house is suddenly quiet.

Something feels wrong.

The sound of a door slams shut downstairs.

Did Kim leave?

I think about the two broken lights on the street, the white sedan I thought was following me.

Jack O'Brien.

I pull my cell out of my pocket.

I hear footsteps downstairs.

Outside, the rain is pounding on the roof. I hold my breath. The footsteps are heavy. *Work boots?* The wood floors downstairs creak.

"Kim," I call, but my voice falters and fades.

The footfalls move to the stairs.

CHAPTER 8

KIM SCREAMS.

I run out of my bedroom, to the stairs. Halfway down, my ankle buckles. I fall against the banister. My phone flies out of my hand and tumbles to the floor. It skids out of sight.

"Kim...!"

I shift my weight to the railing and limp the rest of the way down.

I pause at the landing and listen.

Nothing.

I'm out of breath. My heart is racing. God, I'm having an anxiety attack. I need a paper bag, a glass of water, a .357 Magnum.

"Kim?" I whisper, which is obviously ridiculous because I want Kim to hear me.

At the bottom of the stairs, I stop to catch my breath.

It's Jack. He followed me home. He's got Kim. She needs help.

I stumble into the kitchen, grab the landline and punch 911. The dispatcher answers and asks me to state my emergency.

"It's me again," I whisper.

"Ma'am, I have no idea who *me* is," the dispatcher says in bored voice. "Please state your name and emergency."

In a rush of words, I tell the operator my name and address.

"Oh. You again."

Seriously? I'm feeling a little insulted.

"There's a murderer in my house." I force calm into my voice.

I step over to the opening to the kitchen and peek around the wall toward the back porch and garage. It's dark. I hear voices, but I can't make out what they're saying.

"Help." I keep my voice low and steady.

The dispatcher is talking, but I'm not listening. All I hear is that the sheriff is on his way.

I tiptoe to the wall between the kitchen and hallway and try to listen. Kim is talking to someone. Her voice sounds terrified. I can't make out what she's saying, but now that I think about it, she actually sounds more angry than afraid.

I flatten myself against the wall like they do in the cop movies and try to listen.

I hear footfalls in the hall. A shadow falls across the wood floor.

I clamp my eyes shut. I don't know what to do. I can't move. My thoughts are chaos. I hold my breath. I want to run, but I can't desert Kim.

I crack open one eye. All I can see is the toe of a big brown boot stepping toward me.

"Jack. Let Kim go. Don't kill her. She has nothing to do with anything. I promise—"

"What are you talking about?"

I can't believe my ears. It's Danny Starr, not Jack O'Brien.

I open my eyes. What the hell? Danny is standing in the middle of my hallway. He's frowning at me like I'm the biggest idiot in the world.

I don't care. I'm so relieved that it's Danny and not Jack that I want to rush over and throw my arms around him. Instead, I stand my ground.

Danny steps closer. "You look like you've seen a ghost. You're shivering."

He takes off his jacket to place it over my shoulders and pulls it tight around me.

Time slows. My chest is almost touching his. I feel Danny's

heart beating. He smells like Ivory soap. The warmth of his hands radiates through his jacket. His arms are strong and protective. I'm totally overwhelmed.

I bury my face in his shoulder. A sob turns to embarrassing hiccups.

God, I'm acting like a character from a Danielle Steel novel.

I stifle another hiccup. Open my eyes. Black mascara has smudged his white pinpoint cotton shirt.

I look up at him. His eyes are prisms of deep blue. He's looking down at me. There's compassion in his eyes. Seriously, who am I kidding? It's not compassion, it's amusement. Even I can tell the difference.

"Where's Kim?" I hiccup.

"Say *one* fast, without thinking. Which shouldn't be hard for you." Danny works his way out of my arms and steps away from me. "Gets rid of the hiccups."

I'm standing in the middle of the hallway, unsteady, like I've had one too many glasses of wine. My knees are shaky, but my mind finally starts to clear. My face feels hot. I can't believe I threw myself on Danny like I did. I'm so humiliated.

"Say what? One? You're joking, right?" I push him out of my way. "How'd you get into my house?"

"If you could have seen your face a minute ago." Danny smiles. "I wish I had a camera."

I freeze. He's making fun of me. My entire body tenses. I clench my fist and take a swipe at him. God, maybe I do have homicidal tendencies.

"That is so rude. You wish you had a camera! I wish I had—"

I'm about to say, *a gun*, but even I know that's completely inappropriate, given the circumstances, and that Danny is a reporter.

He takes a couple steps back, toward the living room, and raises his hands defensively.

"You really *do* have a bad temper."

"What the hell are you talking about? Who told you that?"

"Public record. Anger management classes. Remember?"

"You're a menace." I say as I head into the kitchen, a safe distance away from him. "You broke into my house. I could have you arrested."

"Was Bree a menace?" Danny says in his reporter's voice.

I turn and look back at him. His face is serious.

I can't believe he just said that. Danny thinks I killed Bree, and he's fishing for quotes for his next story. God, I'm such a dope. I mean, why else would he be here?

"Out. Leave." I storm over and grab him by his cheesy Gap jacket, and pull him toward the front door. "The police are on their way. You're in big trouble."

"Your door was wide open."

"Open? No, it's not. It's chained and bolted."

"Your side door."

"So, what does that have to do with anything? You can't just walk into someone's house. You broke the law."

My door wasn't open. Danny broke into my house.

I'm on the verge of tears, but I won't let him see me cry.

"I'm going to report you. I'm a witness to a crime. It's illegal to, um...intimidate me."

"You mean *suspect*." Danny walks toward the top of the stairs. "Who's Jack?"

"None of your business." I give him a little shove. "Who told you I'm a suspect? I'll sue the *Times* if you report that. I'm *a person of interest*. There's a huge difference. Don't change the subject. You broke into my house. You were snooping? What the hell were you looking for?"

"Your garage is, like, serial killer organized."

"You went into my garage? Seriously, I've had it with you. Go." I square my shoulders and head to the front door.

Danny Starr is crazy, untrustworthy, and mercenary.

Suddenly, I remember Kim.

"Where's Kim?"

"Your friend is in the garage, on the phone. If I were you, I wouldn't disturb her. She's got *real* problems. Kids, husband, boyfriend ...soccer schedules."

As if on cue, Kim opens the garage door and walks into the hall, her phone glued to her ear.

"So, who's Jack?" Danny says again.

Kim shoots me a sharp you-promised-not-to-tell-anybody look as she holds the phone to her chest for a second, and then punches in God only knows whose number.

She covers the mouthpiece of her phone and says to Danny, "You're an asshole. You really freaked me out."

"He's dangerous," I say to Kim, then look at Danny. "You're a witness. Breaking and entering is a serious crime."

"I didn't break into your house," Danny says in an exasperated tone.

He runs his fingers through his hair. I turn my back on him and open the front door. A rush of cold air chills me. The beach is dark and empty.

"You left your side door unlocked. You don't answer your phone. I've been calling you. Believe it or not, I'm worried about you."

"My phone's been ringing off the hook. Numbers I don't recognize. The truth is, Danny Starr, I've been traumatized. I probably have PTSD, or whatever it's called."

"Give me a break." Danny huffs.

"Someone obviously jimmied my back door lock. I always lock my door. It's automatic, like brushing my teeth." My voice starts to quiver.

I bite down on my lower lip, then take a deep breath.

"You should follow-up on other leads instead of harassing me."

"Amanda! Are you staying with me or not?" Kim says. "I really need to get home—now. Could someone walk me to my car."

"Which one is Brad? Your husband or your boyfriend?" Danny says to Kim, as she brushes past us and walks to the front door. "Amanda and I will walk you to your car."

"We? No. We aren't doing anything," I tell Danny. "Kim, don't give him your last name, or you'll be the lead story in tomorrow's *LA Times*—and it won't be good. You should be working for the *National Enquirer*, not the *LA Times*."

"I need to go home without getting murdered on the way to my car," Kim says.

For one seemingly endless moment, Danny, Kim, and I stand outside, next to the front door, completely speechless. Kim eyes her phone, looking like she's willing it to ring. Danny stares out at the night sky, looking frustrated. I study the intricate scroll design on the back of my patio chairs.

A breeze sweeps the hair away from my face, and with it, the fear returns. The breeze dies. The air feels flat. A sense of emptiness settles on me.

"Amanda, I'll walk your friend to her car." Danny steps away from the door and gallantly bows. "Sorry for the fright."

Not sorry enough. I walk inside and slam the door shut. Engage the lock and fasten the security chain. I'm freezing, exhausted, and yes, frightened.

I lean against the closed door and hesitate to move. Several minutes go by. What am I waiting for? Danny to come back and babysit me?

The point is, I know with absolute certainty that I didn't leave the back door unlocked. If I weren't so exhausted, I'd go to my mom's house or check into a hotel. First thing in the morning, I'm getting out of here.

I go into the kitchen and grab a dinette chair to carry it to the back porch. I shove the chair under the back doorknob.

Back in the living room, I sit and rest my head on the back of the sofa and try to think.

Would Danny Starr stoop that low to break into my house to steal information? Is he that desperate for a scoop? Why wait around for me to get home? It doesn't make sense.

What if Danny did find the side door open? Could someone have come into my house earlier today? Why?

I can't think anymore. I look up at my grandmother's old clock. It's already half-past eleven. Rain is coming down hard. I watch the clock's second-hand tick by, one second at a time.

Day two of this nightmare, and I'm still a mess.

I flip the lights off in the living room. I'm alone. It's a horrible feeling.

Not for long. A solid rap at the front door breaks the silence.

CHAPTER 9

MY HEART SKIPS A BEAT. I turn and look through the window in the door. Mike Young. God, I completely forgot that I called the police.

Is he on duty 24/7? I unlock the door but keep the security chain latched. Crack it open and peer out. The last person I want to see is Mike Young.

"False alarm." I force a smile. "Sorry. I, um...thought I heard something. Actually, I accidentally left the back door unlocked. The wind blew it open. I overreacted."

"Open the door, Amanda," Young says in a strident voice. "Stop playing games. Gotta make a report."

I push the door shut and disengage the chain. Before I open the door, Young shoves it open and steps into the room. I stumble back. He kicks the door shut with his boot.

"False alarm?" Young takes a step closer to me, grabs my arm. "You working us, Amanda? Cops don't like people messing with them."

"I'm not working anyone. I mean, not on purpose, Mike. I mean, Officer Young. Hey, you're hurting me."

I try to pull out of his grasp, but he doesn't let go.

"I'm cooperating. I want to help find whoever killed Bree."

"Not according to the detectives," Mike says.

He eases up on his grip, and as he does, I slip my arm away and take a couple steps back toward the front door.

"Is your partner outside?" I say.

The thought of being alone with Mike Young makes me

nervous. He's creeping me out.

For the first time, I notice that he's wearing street clothes, not his uniform. But his gun is clearly visible on his belt.

"You wanna help?" Mike growls. "Confess."

"Me? Confess? To what?" I choke.

I want to tell him about Jack O'Brien, but I promised Kim I wouldn't say anything. At least, not until she's able to sort things out.

"Bree was, um...my friend. I mean, she wasn't actually, like, a real friend. More like a former coworker. I would never hurt her."

"Everyone knows you had it in for Bree." Mike is pacing around the living room, picking up things and putting them back down in the wrong place.

My grandmother's sterling box sits haphazardly on the edge of a table. I step over and pick it up, polishing the top of it with my sweater as I move over to the shelf to place it back where it belongs.

"You need to leave." I keep my voice strong and steady. "I haven't done anything wrong."

"You had motive. Opportunity. The crime fits your MO. Slam dunk." Mike chuckles out a string of clichés. "Over and out. Done deal. Admit it. Make it easy on yourself."

"My MO? Did Lynch, or Lee, tell you that?"

My heart's pounding. What MO? My knees feel weak. The cops can't possibly pin this crime on me. First of all, I didn't do it. Second of all, they don't have evidence that I did. How could they?

"I mean, just because Bree was murdered near my house doesn't mean I did it. I'm the one who called the police. Why would I call the them if I'm the one who killed Bree?"

Mike flops down on my white down sofa. Puts his boots on my almost new Restoration Hardware coffee table.

"Please leave. It's late."

"Actually, I knew Bree. She treated some of my old football injuries. Massaged the hell out of the kinks, if you know what

I mean. That woman had really strong hands. Always told her she would've made a great wide receiver." He snorts a laugh and winks at me as if he's remembering Bree's therapeutic treatments.

Mike stretches his arms behind his head and cracks his neck.

"I miss her."

"You do?" I step over to the chair across from Mike and sink into it.

I stifle a yawn with the back of my hand.

"We were friends. That's how I know that you had it in for her."

"Bree told you that?" I straighten.

I'm suddenly wide awake, alert. Mike is going on and on about Bree's great body, her beautiful hair, great personality, their incredible connection. He's edgy, hyper. Maybe he's on drugs. He could be drunk.

He continues his rant for what seems like hours. Maybe he'll wear himself out.

"Your ex never appreciated Bree."

I open my eyes with a start. Must have dosed off. I look up at the clock. It's 4:30 a.m.

"He used her."

"You may be on to something, Mike. Did you share this information with Detectives Lee and Lynch?"

Mike's eyes flash. Great. I've made him angry.

"Tweedle Dee and Tweedle Dum don't need to know jack about my relationship with Bree. That's private..."

Crap. The guy is nuts. Dangerous nuts.

I stand and stretch, casually inching closer to the front door. I really need to get out of here before I set Mike off and something bad happens.

"Amanda, I don't blame you," he continues, slurring. "Once your ex hired Bree, you didn't have a chance. Your ex fell for her like a ton of bricks. Truth is, she wasn't that into him."

This is insane. He's insane. He's scaring me. I want to tell him to get his stupid boots off my table and get the heck out of my house. But Mike Young knows something. I have to keep him talking.

"Sounds like you two were really, um...close." I stretch. "You really seem like her type."

Tall, dark, and stupid.

"Yeah. Bree and I...we had something special."

"So, um, you and Bree were seeing each other? Like, romantically?"

"Our little secret."

"Were you and Bree going to run away together? I mean, was she planning to leave Geoff?"

I lean toward Mike, eyeing him with interest. It's a technique I learned in journalism class. I realize that I have to be careful. Mike could turn on me in an instant.

I spot my cell on the floor near the hall tree, where it fell earlier. I walk over and pocket it. Mike doesn't miss a beat. He seems oblivious to me.

"We were tight. Wanted to start a family. The whole ball of wax. But..."

"But...?"

We could be here all night. He obviously needs to get this off his chest. But why tell me? Because he doesn't have any friends? Because I have to listen to him, like it or not?

No. Mike knows something. Some inside information. *He doesn't care what he says to me, because he believes I'm going down for Bree's murder.*

"But Geoff has money," he says.

"I've been there."

"Thing is, I don't care about money. It was never about the money for me."

But it was always about the money for Bree. God, just when I think that Jack O'Brien murdered Bree, case closed, this big dope presents himself as a possible suspect. He wants me to confess so he can get himself off the hook. Maybe I can rule out Jack O'Brien and Geoff as suspects. Still, if Jack didn't kill

Bree, what was he doing on Hollywood Beach the night she was murdered?

I may be asking for trouble, but I take a shot at it anyway.

"I heard that Bree was, um...seeing Jack O'Brien, too."

"Jack was Bree's boy toy. She was a lot of woman for one man. She dumped him for me."

Jack O'Brien, a boy toy? Really? The idea is completely and utterly gross. Yeah, well there's no accounting for taste. God, who else was Bree seeing?

"I heard Bree and Jack were still seeing each other," I say.

Mike's eyes narrow, his brows knot.

"You're a liar!" He kicks the table out of his way, sending a thick volume of *Monet's Garden* to the floor with a *bang!*

"That's the word on the street." I grip the hall tree next to the front door.

Mike eyes me with suspicion. His face turns red and pinched like he has bad gas.

I'm asking too many questions. I'm hitting a nerve.

"You messing with me, Amanda?" Mike barks.

He sets his feet on the floor with a *clomp*, then pushes up from the couch. He takes a step toward me.

Did Mike Young kill Bree?

I'm exhausted and scared. I can't think. Maybe I should just confess. Let Mike arrest me. At least I'd be safely locked behind bars. At least I'd finally get a good night's sleep.

I step around the hall tree to the front door.

"Mike, I'm truthfully sorry that, um...you and Bree never had a chance to tie the knot. But I want you to know that I think you would have made a lovely couple," I say in my best Dr. Laura voice.

"You're working me, aren't you? Bitch," Mike spits, and lunges toward me.

Crap. I reach for the door and look back. His boot catches on the jute rug. He trips and stumbles to his knees. I don't look to see what happens next.

I open the door and run around the side of the house to the street. I look behind me. Mike Young is on my heels. His hand is on his gun. I turn and run smack into Detective Lynch. Lee is close behind him.

"Whoa!" Lynch grips my arm. "Where ya think you're goin', cupcake?"

I realize it's dawn.

Lynch and Lee aren't the only ones waiting for me on the street. The press is here, milling around. I spot Danny Starr. He's standing on the periphery of the small crowd. Someone tries to shove a microphone in my face. A large TV camera is rolling.

Mike steps between the press and me. He takes hold of my arm and squeezes.

Out of earshot from the detectives, he whispers, "Watch your back, Amanda. Remember what happened to Bree."

"Thanks for taking the call, Mike. I know it's your night off." Detective Lee takes my arm. "We'll take it from here."

"Glad to help." Mike is digging his fingers into my arm.

I push him away and take a step closer to Detective Lee. I've never been so glad to see anyone in my life.

I turn my back to the press. "What's going on? What's happened? I called nine-one-one a few hours ago, but it was a false alarm. That's what I told Sheriff Young. But he—"

Mike gives me a don't-you-dare look. I bite my lip and turn back to Detective Lee just as the clouds break to a beautiful sunrise. It somehow feels divinely inspired.

I look up at Detective Lee. He looks stricken. Something *has* happened.

Lynch looks smug. "Cookie, this isn't a social call. We're here on official business. We have a warrant to search your house. Bring you in."

"I don't understand." I step away from Lee.

He's holding a pair of handcuffs.

"I'm sorry, Amanda." He takes my right hand, then my left, and clamps the metal cuffs around my wrists.

Lynch drones, "Amanda Beckwith, you are under arrest for making false statements to the police..."

"No! I mean, I didn't mean to lie."

The press is snapping photos like crazy and talking into their mikes.

"You're jumping to conclusions. I haven't done anything wrong."

Lynch continues, "... obstruction of justice, and violating probation. You have the right to remain silent. Anything you say can and will be used against you. You have a right to an attorney. If you can't afford an attorney..."

I don't hear the rest. My knees buckle. Everything goes black. The next thing I know, I'm in the back of an unmarked police car with Detective Lynch at the wheel. A pair of shoes are sitting on my lap, courtesy of Detective Lee. He was decent enough to go back into the house and grab a pair out of the basket next to the front.

I don't know if I'm more upset that I'm going to jail for a crime I didn't commit, or that Mike Young just threatened to murder me.

CHAPTER 10

THE TWENTY-MINUTE RIDE TO JAIL IS A BLUR. All I know is that Detective Lee hasn't made a peep since he gently helped me into the back of the squad car. At least Officer Lee treats me with a little respect.

In the rearview mirror, I catch Lynch glaring at me. For what seems like the millionth time, he shoots me a you're-in-big-trouble look. Seriously, I get it. He doesn't have to rub it in.

I try to shift my rear into a more comfortable position and out of Lynch's line of vision, but because my hands are cuffed behind my back, I'm kind of stuck in a forward, hunchback pose that makes me look like I'm searching for a stray contact lens. My wrists are burning. I'm scared.

Lynch careens around a couple more corners until he finally whips into a parking lot and comes to a bumpy stop. The back door flies open, and a burly lady guard grabs my upper arm and drags me out of the backseat.

"Stop. You're hurting me." I lean away from her.

The handcuffs dig into my wrists. I mean, I'm innocent until proven guilty, right? She's treating me like I'm a convicted killer.

Detective Lee steps between us. "I'll take it from here, ma'am."

One hand gently grips my arm, while he places his other hand on the small of my back and starts to guide me forward.

The guard steps back, barely giving Lee and I enough room to move.

"I can handle this," she barks.

I think I hear, *asshole,* under her breath, but it's hard to tell. The reporters who followed us here are firing questions at me.

"Okay. Hang tight," Lee says under his breath, maybe so Lynch won't hear him.

He whisks me through the big glass doors, into a room where a giant sign identifies the place as the county jail. My heart sinks.

Lee elbows past the guard as he guides me through another door and into a large, windowless, gray-walled room. Who is the interior designer for these places? Several rows of gray plastic and metal chairs decorate the space. Someone stuck at a hapless desk in one corner, a bank of pay phones in another. A bulletin board, littered with bail bondsmen's cards, hangs on one wall. Another wall features a monitor. This place makes the Santa Barbara Police Department look like the Ritz Carlton.

Lee guides me to one of the uniformed officers.

He turns to me and whispers, "Don't say a word. Ask to make a call. Period."

Lynch shows up wearing his usual mean-cop look and holding a thick file.

"Hey, buddy boy, no fraternizing with the perp," he says to Lee. "You can't be that hard up."

Lee drops his hand from my back and shoves Lynch out of the way. They walk to a corner of the room and go at it, head-to-head. I can't hear a word they're saying, but they keep looking back at me. Lynch shoots me a smug look, then disappears out the way we came in.

When Lee returns, his expression is unreadable, but he doesn't look happy. He gently grips my arm and turns me toward an interior door.

"Let's get this over with."

"Okay."

I'm not sure I know what he's talking about, but I can guess. I'm going to be booked, fingerprinted, and placed in custody.

A couple reporters yell questions, but Lynch slams the door, and the clamor of voices dies. At least I didn't see Danny Starr.

That's one positive thing.

"I don't belong here," I say, as Lee pulls me along a dank hallway that ends at a metal door with a small chicken-wired window.

This is it. He presses a button next to the door and speaks into an intercom. He gives both our names. Someone on the other side buzzes us through. Lee pushes the door open. Inside, a very large female guard with short-cropped brown hair and a lewd smirk greets me.

"I really, really don't belong here. Please believe me. I didn't hurt anyone. Can't you do something?" I'm looking up at Lee.

"Right." The guard says sarcastically, as she eyes me from head-to-toe.

Her name tag reads *Alacata*. The woman is over six-feet tall. Her girth is stretching her tan standard-issued uniform to the max. The buttons on her shirt are pulling against her chest, and the zipper teeth on her slacks are screaming, *Open me!* She has an expressionless face, but her eyes look mean.

She stretches a wad of keys attached to her belt and unlocks a door.

Lee takes a step back. "Remember what I said."

He squeezes my cuffed hand, turns and leaves.

Deputy Alacata yanks me by my elbow and pulls me into a brightly lit room. This is where I get fingerprinted and booked. I remember this part from the last time I was arrested. There are a couple other guards milling around, but nobody's paying attention to us.

She uncuffs me and pats me down. I rub my wrists. Welts mark where the cuffs chafed my skin raw.

"No jewelry inside," Alacata barks, and nods at my gold signet ring passed down from my grandmother.

I take it off and hand it to her. She puts it in a plastic bag, along with my shoes.

She fingerprints me and takes my picture, which will probably end up on Facebook, Instagram, and featured in the *LA Times.*

Alacata pushes me into a holding cell and slams the cell door shut. I sit on a cold cement bench and look around. A steel toilet without a toilet seat, and a rust-stained sink that's dripping monotonously, decorate the room.

"Excuse me, I need to make a call," I call out through the cell bars.

It's freezing in here.

"I need to phone my lawyer?"

"Gonna call Daddy? Get Daddy's lawyer to bail you out?" Alacata says. "Saw him on CNN. He's a real kick in the pants. Saw you on TV, too. You're a celebrity."

"I'm allowed a phone call." I force the whine out of my voice.

I take a deep breath. I have to stay strong, but tears burn my eyes.

"I have, um...rights."

"Think you're Paris Hilton or something? Daddy's just gonna come to your rescue." Alacata turns her back on me and goes back to her paperwork.

Tears start to flow. "My dad is very busy. I'm going to use the public defender." I sniffle lamely.

"You can't be as dumb as you look."

"Truthfully." I wipe the tears off my cheeks with the sleeve of my sweater. "I am."

Alacata stifles a laugh. "Crybabies get their asses kicked inside."

"Thanks for the heads-up." I sniffle.

I stare down at my filthy sweater and stained jeans. I can't believe it's only been two days since I first learned about Bree's death. It seems like a year.

"Anything else I should know?"

"Save the Q and A for the public defender." Alacata cackles.

"I didn't do it." I rub the snot off my nose with the back of my hand.

"Yeah, yeah, yeah." Alacata snorts.

"I really am innocent." I look at her. "This is a huge mistake."

"Well, get in line with all the other losers who say that."

"Seriously, I could never ever murder anyone, no matter what they did to me."

I suddenly remember that Officer Lee told me not to speak to anyone. I bite my lip before I dig my hole any deeper.

"Who said anything about murder?" Alacata perks up. "Is that what you're in for?"

She's right. I mean, I wasn't really charged with murder.

I look at the big round industrial-style clock on the wall: 8:15 a.m. Any second, I'll get to make my call, and I'll get out of here. I have to be patient. Maybe it'll be one of those times that I look back on and think how grateful I am to have been here because it taught me patience.

I curl up on the icy cement bench and close my eyes. I try to remember the words to the Serenity Prayer—a prayer I learned in the mandatory AA classes I attended after my DUI last year. The words come in snippets.

The bright lights and freezing temperature in this God-awful hellhole make nodding off impossible. I'm exhausted. I pull my sweater down over my hands and shift my body into a more comfortable position. I slip one arm beneath my head and use the other one to cover my eyes.

I'm going to organize my thoughts just like I organize my closet. Kind of like counting sheep.

I line up everything I know about Bree's murder. Bits and pieces from the last two days trip into my memory bank, one at a time. Scary noises, the shadowy figure moving across my backyard, a body under a blanket, my umbrella, Mike Young, Jack O'Brien, and Geoff.

I wonder if Bree's death is just a simple crime of opportunity, passion. Or is it something more sinister? Bree was having an affair with Jack O'Brien and Mike Young. Geoff found out and killed her. But Geoff was in Las Vegas, and Kim thought she spotted Jack O'Brien and Bree near the crime scene.

Maybe it was Geoff she saw. Jack and Geoff look a little bit alike. They're sort of the same height, have the same basic hair color. Geoff is in better shape, but in the dark night, it would be hard to tell.

Geoff was in Las Vegas; I remind myself for the hundredth time. He has a solid alibi.

My memories of that night are all over the place. Should I begin with who, what, where, and when? Or when, who, and why? Or what, when, why, and who? I like *when, who, and why.*

When did all of this start? Friday night? No. Something tells me that someone had plans for Bree to go to Hollywood Beach long before Friday night.

I try to imagine how it unfolded. I mean, why would Bree agree to go out alone on a cold, drizzly December evening? Why Hollywood Beach? She knew I lived there. Was she coming to see me, and was ambushed by her assailant on the way? Bree alone, walking on the beach on a Friday night? Doesn't sound like Bree. At least, not the Bree I knew. She seemed like too much of a glamour girl to hike around on the beach on a cold, rainy night.

If Bree came to Hollywood Beach by herself, then where did she leave her car? Have the police recovered it?

What if Bree and her assailant came to Hollywood Beach together? Did Bree and her assailant come to Hollywood Beach to see me? Maybe I have something they wanted? What would Bree want from me?

Did they come to hurt me? Kill me? Or set me up?

Set me up. For real. I mean, there's not a chance in hell that Bree Martin just happened to get murdered in front of my house, either by coincidence or accident. No way.

Something triggered Bree's assailant to plot her murder. Bree's assailant—Geoff, Jack O'Brien, or someone else—specifically chose Hollywood Beach because I lived there. There's no other plausible reason.

The question is, why? Motive is super important. I think about all the episodes of *Law and Order* that I've watched over the years, and motive seems to be the key to cracking a case.

What was the murderer's motive? Was he a scorned lover? Did Bree have something he wanted, and she wouldn't give it to him. What? Sex? Money? Drugs? Why set me up? Because I'm a really good suspect. I have a bad history with Bree, and a police record.

My chest heaves. I'm the perfect patsy—a real loser.

I try to shut off the negative voice in my head, but it's kind of hard when you're lying on a cement bed in jail.

But when I think about it, this isn't about me.

Maybe if I knew why Bree was murdered, I could figure out who murdered her.

Each question and possible answer lead to a whole new set of questions.

What I do know is that Bree was murdered by a blunt-force injury, sometime between 6:00 p.m. on Friday night, when I got home from shopping, and sometime after midnight on Saturday morning, when I first heard noises on the beach outside my house.

At least I finally told Lynch and Lee that I went shopping on Friday night. Even though I didn't buy anything, there are security cameras. Maybe someone saw me and can help place me somewhere else besides Hollywood Beach. But that doesn't exactly clear me. I could have arranged to meet Bree after I got home from Target.

I've got to face it. I don't really have much of an alibi. Even that I'm the one who called the police doesn't prove anything.

That I have a lot of negatives stacked against me can't be ignored. In the first place, I lied to the police, which is why I'm in jail. Jean, who could have been a great witness for me, told the police that the only person she saw on Friday was me, placing me at the scene of the crime. I also know that the press, especially Danny Starr, are going to look for every opportunity to throw me under the bus.

The one thing I've got going for me is that Kim saw two people on the beach Friday night who looked like Jack O'Brien and Bree.

Kim is key. She's going have to tell the police everything she knows. Her friendship with Sophia's teacher is completely innocent. I know Kim. She'd never do anything to hurt her family.

Lynch and Lee will have another potential *person of interest*: Jack.

At the very least, they'll have a new lead.

Once I get out of here, I also need to go online and research cold cases in Oxnard, Ventura, and Santa Barbara. Mike Young said those cases were closed, but I don't believe him. There could be a lot more to Bree's murder than what I've learned so far. I mean, maybe Jack and Geoff had nothing to do with Bree's death.

I'm going in circles. I wish I had someone who could help me with this.

Truth is, I have very few allies, including my family. Which is not to say that they don't care about me. It's just that they've had a lot of stuff going on in their own lives, and...

Tears burn my eyes again. I wipe my nose. Pull my knees up closer to my chest for warmth.

Everyone's been through a lot in the last few years because of me.

Getting down on myself isn't helping. I have to stay focused.

I create a to-do list in my mind. Find out what hard evidence the police have collected in general, and what evidence is directly related to me? Who was the last person to see Bree alive? It wasn't me, that's for sure.

Who were Bree's enemies? What was Bree's financial situation? Why did the police search my house? What were they looking for? What was Bree wearing the night of the murder? That could be important. I mean, if she was wearing those silly four-inch stilettos she always wore, it's obvious she wasn't planning a walk on the beach. It could mean that someone forced her to go to the beach, or that she was murdered somewhere else, and her body was moved.

But if she was wearing—

A screech of metal hinges startles me. I sit straight and rub my eyes to clear my vision.

Detective Lynch. He's looking down at me. God, Lynch is wearing one of his goofy, smarmy smiles.

"Hey, cupcake, this isn't the Bacara Resort." Lynch reaches down and grabs my arm. "Up. Time for your strip search."

CHAPTER 11

LYNCH DRAGS ME OUT OF MY CELL, down another dismal hallway, and into the shower room. I clutch a chair.

"No!" I'm holding onto it for dear life. "Deputy Alacata, help! I want Detective Lee." God, this can't be happening. "Men aren't allowed to search women. This is crazy! I know my rights."

"Settle down, fruit loop. Don't flatter yourself." Lynch walks out of the room. "It's Alacata's job. She likes girls. A lot."

Deputy Alacata enters the room. She's wearing surgical gloves and a smile.

"Take off your clothes."

Time slows. I feel lightheaded. Nauseated. The room starts to spin. I let go of the chair. Feel myself falling. Alacata grabs me by the arm to break my fall.

"Stop!" I pull my arm away and stumble into a corner and hug my knees.

I'm shaking like a leaf.

"For Christ's sake, Beckwith. Don't go having some kind of seizure on me," Alacata says.

"I need to speak to a lawyer. I never got my phone call."

"You need to get up, drop your drawers, and hop into the shower, pronto." Alacata steps toward me. "You don't want me to call for backup, do you?"

"I want backup! Seriously. Call for backup. Please!"

"I'm gonna do you a favor, girl." Alacata bends to the downed chair, then stalks over to the corner, where she looms above me. "I'm gonna tell you a couple of dos and don'ts about

107

incarceration in the Ventura County Jail."

"I'm not taking off my clothes."

"Number one, do what you're told." Alacata steps closer to me and squats so we're eye-to-eye. "Two, keep your yap shut unless you're spoken to directly. Three, don't make eye contact. Four, don't get sick. You get sick, you get sorry. Five, don't whine. Whine, no dine."

"I'm not taking a shower." I unwittingly look Deputy Alacata directly in the eye.

Suddenly, I feel queasy.

"I, um…I, um…feel sick…"

Before Alacata can jump out of the way, I barf what little food I had in my stomach, all over her regulation boots and pants.

"Shit!" She grabs a walkie-talkie off her belt. "Alacata in holding cell one. I need backup. ASAP."

Everything unfolds in light speed.

Two very strong lady guards yank me from my corner without saying a single word to me, or even asking if I need to go to the infirmary, or whatever it's called.

They deftly help Alacata yank off my clothes, and, push me into the most miserable freezing shower I've ever taken in my life. I reach for the Motel-6–sized bar of soap but drop it when I see that it's embedded with a pubic hair.

The shower seems like it takes forever, but it probably only lasted a few minutes.

"Out!" Alacata yells and throws me a frayed white terrycloth bath towel that is not much bigger than a dish towel.

I clinch the towel under my chin. I am shivering so hard I can barely stand.

"Beckwith!" She hands me a bundle of stuff. "Get dressed and get your ass over to the phone and make your call. Make it snappy."

I timidly take the bundle of stuff that Deputy Alacata hands me. I'm issued two pairs of grandma-sized underwear, grayish sports bra with faded yellow perspiration stains in the arm pits, a set of faded navy-blue scrub-like pants and top, orange slip-on tennis shoes that look too big for me, a shapeless nightgown, and an ID bracelet. My ID number is 52756. I'm also given a tired-looking set of sheets, a mattress pad, and a blanket. No pillow.

I set my stuff down on the floor and turn my back to the guards. I drop the towel and quickly dress. The clothes hang on me.

"Beckwith!" Alacata barks. "Make your call."

She nods at an old-fashioned black wall phone that I remember from the last time I was here. Calls must be made collect.

I plod over and stare at the phone. I don't know who to call. Don't know what time it is, but something tells me that I must have slept through half the day. I can't call my dad. He's on the east coast.

I can feel Deputy Alacata's gaze on me. There's an any-day-now expression in her eyes.

A lump forms in my throat. Tears burn my eyes. Who'll be home? Calling a cell phone isn't allowed. I pick up the receiver and dial my mother's number. Maybe she can get in touch with the public defender.

Four rings later, I hear my mom's voice, but it's a recording telling whoever calls to leave their name, number, and a brief message, and to have a fabulous day. I hang up.

"What? Daddy won't take your call?" Alacata says.

I pick up my stuff and wait for her instructions. I look up at the clock. It's almost 9:00. This is truly like hell. I have no concept of time. There's no natural light, so you can't tell if it's day or night.

"Upstairs, princess. Your suite awaits you."

On my way upstairs, I keep my gaze focused on the floor in front of me. I feel sick.

I must look hideous with my face scrubbed and my eyes swollen from crying. My hair is soaking and plastered to my head.

As we head up the stairs, I roll up the waist of my prison-issued outfit to keep from tripping on the pant cuffs. Truthfully, no amount of imagination can make this get-up look even halfway decent. I wonder what it would look like if Tory Burch got her hands on it. She'd embellish it with her famous monogram, rhinestones, and gold braid.

There's no way the Board of Prisons would redesign their prison garb. These clothes are part of the punishment.

No wonder recidivism is so high! I thought jail was supposed to be all about rehabilitation. I mean, these women's self-esteem must be seriously non-existent. How can anyone even think about changing their life when they're forced to wear clothes that make them feel like a prisoner?

I can't believe I'm thinking about this. I'm demoralized. This is hopeless.

Alacata jerks my arm and directs me into what looks like a dorm, through a sliding gate made of steel bars. The doors slams shut behind us as we enter.

"This is home for the next forty-eight hours." Alacata says something else, but I'm not listening. "You're bunk twelve. Make your bed and wait for the next instructions."

She slams the gate closed and leaves.

Crap. If anyone was asleep before I walked in here, they've got to be awake now.

My dorm for the next forty-eight hours. The look of it is shocking. This isn't like any dorm I've ever stayed in. This is what hell looks like. The walls are painted dirty gray to match the chipped and cracked cement floor. There are more than a dozen military-style bunks, and no windows or decoration. This will be home until someone bails me out. Who's going to bail me out?

I look up. At least twenty female inmates are staring at me.

"Bitch." The voice comes from across the room, but I can't tell who said it.

"We saw you on TV, girl," someone else says. "You gonna fry."

I keep walking with my head down, and try my best to look at the bunk numbers without making eye contact. I won't last forty-eight hours.

My bunk is on the bottom, close to the back of the room. I match my bunk number to the number on a small locker where I store my extra stuff. I ignore the snickers and whispers from my dormmates and make my bed. I roll the mattress pad into a makeshift pillow and get under the covers.

The girl in the top bunk pops over the edge of her bed. All I can see from this angle is her dark-brown dreadlocks hanging down into my view.

She whispers, "Hey. You're that girl on TV. You offed that blonde bitch—Bree something. See you in the morning."

"No talking!" a guard yells from outside the room.

Perfect. I'm on TV. I always dreamed of being famous, but not like this. Everybody is jumping to the conclusion that I murdered Bree. What am I going to do?

I pull the scratchy blanket up under my chin and close my eyes. The tears start to flow again. I really am going to fry—one way or the other.

CHAPTER 12

IT'S EARLY MORNING. I'm guessing around 4:00 a.m. It's quiet. Feels like I've slept forever. There are no clocks *inside*, so it's impossible to tell what time it is. I can hear blankets rustling, and snoring. Hope I didn't snore.

Truth is, I had an absolutely wonderful sleep last night. I mean, Ritz Carlton wonderful. As soon as I closed my eyes, I was out. I actually slept through the night without having a bad dream. It's hard to believe, but I feel safe. Which is huge, because right now I don't trust anyone or anything. I mean, for all I know, Danny Starr could have murdered Bree. I know that's a crazy, out-of-the-question stretch of the imagination, but how the hell did he get into my house last night. Was the back door really open? I don't think so.

Why did he think it was okay to sneak into my house without knocking? Thank God Kim was downstairs to intercept him.

I stretch my arms over my head and let out a noisy yawn. Whoops.

"Shut the hell up," someone grumbles. "I'm trying to sleep."

"You snore like a freight train," someone else barks.

Is she talking to me? Crap. I do snore. It's not the first time someone has told me that.

"I'll turn your face into a Big Mac if you don't shut up," gripes the woman in the bunk next to me, as she pulls the blanket over her head.

The other inmates start to stir. God, what if I'm starting a jailhouse riot?

I close my eyes and pretend to sleep.

My situation is utterly hopeless. I'm in jail. Again. No one's going to rescue me. I'm completely alone.

No. I can't—I won't—think like that. I am a victor, not a victim. Victor, not victim. I say it to myself a couple more times. Stay positive. *Remember the law of attraction.*

I roll over and pull the blanket up under my chin and open my eyes. My eyes finally adjust to the dark, cheerless surroundings. God, I wonder who decorated this place. Probably someone like Eva Braun. Metal-on-metal on cement with razor-wire accents and lock-and-key accessories. Whoever thought up this miserable color palette and materials wasn't thinking rehabilitation. They were thinking Dante's *Inferno.*

This isn't the Ritz, but I really do have to stay positive. What else can I do?

I turn on my stomach and bunch up my makeshift pillow. The point is, I haven't been charged with murder. Which obviously means that I'm in here for completely bogus reasons. I can post bail. I have money saved. I'll hire a lawyer, mount a defense.

All I have to do is figure out how to get money from my bank to a bail bondsman. Once I'm out of here, I'll get a lawyer.

Kim. I'll call Kim. I'll borrow some money from her to give to the bail bondsman. She knows I'm good for it.

When you reduce things to their lowest common denominator, everything is so simple.

At least I have a plan.

Then a disturbing thought dances into my mind. What if Kim won't loan me the money? I'll have to come up with plan B.

I can't go to my mom or dad for bail. I think about how much I've already disappointed them, and how much money they've spent on getting me out of trouble. I won't do it to them again.

No. Kim will loan me the money for bail. Then she'll tell the cops everything she knows about Friday night. Kim's statement may not solve all my problems, but it'll help.

Another yawn escapes my mouth as I close my eyes. I'm going back to sleep. But my mind's spinning with more questions. I can't think anymore.

I repeat my victor-not-victim mantra over and over in my head, like a prayer, until I feel myself relax, and fade.

My mind drifts to Martha Stewart. God, Martha got a bum rap, just like me. Truth is, we have a lot in common. I mean, we're both women. We're both blonde. We both went to jail on trumped-up charges.

Maybe someone will knit me a poncho like they did for Martha. Maybe the other female inmates will have a really fun going away party for me when I leave. I'll become their advocate on the outside.

We'll exchange emails, and I'll write a really great blog about prison life. I'll call it something like, *First Person: Survival on the Inside*. Or, *Falsely Accused: An Exposé*.

Maybe I'll win a Pulitzer, or some other award, for best investigative reporting.

Or maybe I'll produce a reality show: *What Not to Wear...In Jail*. That's a non-starter.

Maybe I could write a how-to guide on decorating small spaces. I could—

"Up! Get dressed. Line up for count," booms a voice somewhere on the edge of my consciousness.

I pull the blanket up over my head and turn away from the intrusive voice.

The blanket is ripped off me. I open my eyes against bright fluorescent lights. God, what's happening? I rub my eyes and struggle into a sitting position.

A stocky woman in a uniform is staring at me. She doesn't look happy. Now I remember where I am. I shudder.

"Are you deaf?" The guard yells at me. "Up!"

"No." My voice squeaks. "I mean, I'm sorry, I—"

"Get your skinny ass dressed and into the cafeteria for breakfast."

My dormmates are lined up against the wall, staring at me. They're actually snickering.

They're whispering Bree's name. I hear my name in the mix of conversation. They obviously have television privileges. They all probably know a lot more about my situation than I do.

I dress, make my bed, and fold my PJs in less than a minute. I hurry to catch up to the end of the line. Once in line, I hear snippets of their gossip. I try to tune out their voices, but I can't help listening. I hear Bree's name mentioned repeatedly, along with the word *murder*.

In the cafeteria, I plod along in line, keeping my gaze down. I grab a gray plastic tray like the woman in front of me did, and a plastic spoon.

I try hard not to be grossed out by the food selections. Seriously, I'm practically faint with hunger, so it doesn't really matter what the food looks like.

The chef's breakfast includes grits, hash, watery eggs, bread, canned fruit cocktail, apples, and a carton of milk. Everything looks gray, even the bread. Food is food, I tell myself. Be grateful. Think of the starving people all over the world.

I take the offered milk, a scoop of scrambled eggs, a green apple, and a piece of whole-wheat bread. With my tray in hand, I stand in the back of the room to search for an empty place to sit.

God, this cafeteria is a joyless place. I mean, staying consistent with the decorator's vision, the floors are cement, the walls are a grayish, pale-green plaster begging for fresh paint, and the tables metal. There are four metal stools attached to each table. The room is completely devoid of color or imagination.

I make eye contact with a woman with dark-brown dreads. She enthusiastically motions for me to join her and another woman. Just as I'm about to take a seat, a tall, thin woman with beautiful reddish-brown hair sets her tray on the table and sits.

She fist-bumps the two other women at the table.

"Here." The woman with the dreads pats the spot on her left.

She has a cross tattooed on her cheek, and a weird symbol etched below her right eye.

"Sit next to me. I'm Jody. I sleep in the bunk above you."

"Thanks. I, um...love your tattoos." I set my tray down next to hers, then maneuver around the bench and sit. "They're totally cool."

I notice the skull and crossbones on her arm, and her neck is covered with a biblical quote. My rule of thumb is, always compliment someone when you first meet them.

"Saw you on TV last night. You're Amanda, right," Jody says. "We all watched when the police cuffed you. You killed that Bree chick who stole your old man? You can tell us. We're your friends. You can trust us."

"Damn straight. Hey, you want a tattoo?" whispers the bleached blonde with black roots sitting across from me, leaning forward. "I got me some tools. Hid 'em under my mattress. Name's Juanita. My friends call me Nita. I'm Juanita to you."

The three women laugh.

This is a freaking nightmare. Do I look like an idiot? Probably. Like I'm really going let someone in jail give me a tattoo.

I look down at my food. "Seriously, I didn't kill anyone. That's the truth. I was in the wrong place at the wrong time."

Detective Lee told me not to talk to anyone. But claiming my innocence can't hurt me.

"You go, girl," Juanita says.

The three women break into laughter again.

Truth is, I don't really care if they believe me or not, because I'm getting out of here soon.

I take a bite of eggs. They're delicious. They're hot and salty and remind me of the eggs that were served at UC Berkeley's cafeteria.

Juanita raises her hand. "Some chick tries to steal my old man, I'll beat the living daylights out of her." She flips her hair side to side as she talks. "I don't put up with that kinda crap. You stick with us, girl, and you won't have no problems on the inside."

The woman sitting on my right turns to me. "I'm Audrey. Looks like you're in a lot of trouble."

"Is that what people are saying on TV?" I notice Audrey's beautiful reddish-brown hair.

I want to ask her who her stylist is, but instead I stay quiet and take another bite of my eggs.

"That I murdered Bree because she stole my husband?"

"My old man cheated on me like that," Jody says, "I do a Lorena Bobbitt on him."

"T-thanks," I say." I appreciate everything you guys are saying. I mean, I'd feel the same exact way about my old man, if I, um...had an old man."

I pick up the waxed milk carton and take a sip. Haven't done that since junior high.

"I didn't kill Bree. Someone is trying to frame me, set me up. I've got to get out of here so I can find out who really murdered Bree."

"Framed?" Jody raises her hand in a high-five gesture.

I slap her hand. Crap. I don't know what the hell else to do.

"So was I," Juanita says through a mouthful of scrambled eggs.

"Me, too. I never sold no drugs," Jody says. "My old man put a couple ounces in my purse. I had no idea the drugs were in there."

"What about you, Audrey?" Jody says, grits sticking to her lips. "Someone set you up?"

"Damn straight. I got thirty days for trickin' to an undercover cop. He was pretty hot. Should've just given him a freebie. I'm getting out of this hellhole tomorrow."

Juanita laughs as she turns her attention back to me.

"You got screwed, girl."

"Damn straight. 1 did, too." Audrey shoves her tray away. "That Bree chick had it coming to her."

"Thank you, Audrey," 1 say in my most diplomatic voice, trying to join the conversation without offending anyone. "But nobody, um...deserves to be murdered."

"Screw you, Amanda Rich Bitch." Audrey's eyes flash, and her voice goes up a couple notches.

We're attracting attention.

"Don't act all innocent. 1 know all about you."

"Amanda." Juanita swivels on her rear to look directly at me as she gestures for effect. "Audrey's just saying that you probably know more than you're telling. Right, Audrey?"

"Fuck you, Nita?"

The two guards standing over by the gate turn their attention our way. Deputy Alacata walks over and joins the guards. God, 1 know I'm going to get in trouble. If 1 get in trouble, I'll never get out of here.

"1 knew Bree," Audrey continues. "Her name wasn't Bree when 1 knew her. It was Barbara. Babs. She stole my old man."

"Bree is Babs?" 1 say. "Are we talking about the same person?"

1 can't believe this. Bree stole Geoff from me, married him, then started dating Jack O'Brien and Michael Young when she was still married to Geoff. But Bree wasn't always Bree? She was Barbara first?

"I'm confused. You and Bree...1 mean, Babs—Barbara—knew each other in Santa Barbara?"

"Not Santa Barbara, you dumbass," Audrey whispers, but looks nervous. "We worked the streets in Vegas."

"Truthfully, Audrey, 1'm not trying to argue with you. But you must be thinking of someone else," 1 glance over my shoulder.

Deputy Alacata and the two guards are moving toward us.

"You calling me a liar?" Audrey growls, her voice cutting through the chatter in the room. "1 ain't no liar!"

The guards are twenty steps away.

1 say, "No. 1 mean, maybe the girl you're talking about just

looks like Bree. Seriously, I know for a fact that Bree was a very successful massage therapist at the Bellagio. She, um, massaged, um...all the movie stars. Celine Dion. Wayne Newton. She told me that herself when she started working for my ex-husband. You know, before she, um, stole him from me."

"Babs and me worked side-by-side on the strip for five or six years. Massage therapist to the stars my ass," Audrey barks, shoving her tray for emphasis, and sending it to the floor.

Hash and grits are everywhere.

I can't believe what I'm hearing.

"But maybe—"

The guards are on us. Alacata yanks me up by the arm and pulls me out of my seat. The other guard grabs Audrey.

"Breakfast is over, Beckwith," Alacata barks.

"Maybe nothing," Audrey says over her shoulder, with a smug smile as the guard pulls her away. "That bitch deserved to die. Ask Felix. Head Case. He'll tell you."

"Tell me what?" I yank out of Alacata's grip and run back to Audrey.

She leans into me and whispers, "Who killed Bree."

CHAPTER 13

ALACATA YANKS MY ARMS BEHIND MY BACK and slaps handcuffs on me. She pulls me through the gate and down the hall. Another guard drags Audrey in the opposite direction.

"Wait! Audrey!" I yell. "Who murdered Bree?"

"Mind your business, or you'll never get out of here." Alacata shoots Audrey a fierce look, then turns her attention back to me. "Beckwith! Shut your yap." She tightens her hold on me and pulls. "Beckwith, you wanna go to court, or the hole?"

"Court?" I study Alacata's face. "Am I getting out today?"

"No, dimwit, it means you're going to the beauty parlor." She drags me down the hallway like the building's on fire. "Get your ass in gear, lickety split. Bus is waitin'."

I plant my feet. The handcuffs tear at my wrists.

"I need one second to speak to Audrey."

"When hell freezes over." Alacata continues down the hall.

"It's life or death," I say.

I don't want to miss my day in court, but I have to find out what Audrey knows.

"Your momma's right. You really are a troublemaker."

"You spoke to my mother?"

I can't believe this. I mean, I know my mother has connections in all kinds of places, but why would she speak to Alacata?

"Saw her on TV last night. Don't expect her to bail ya out. Said it's time you learn a lesson."

Mom on TV? She promised me she wouldn't speak to the

120

press. A wave of melancholy washes over me.

I take a deep breath. Oh well. It kind of figures. Now that I think about it, she didn't really promise me anything. But I can't imagine my mother saying anything like that. Alacata probably made it up.

"Listen," I say, keeping my voice steady. "Audrey, that girl with the red hair—she's an important witness in a, um...a murder investigation."

Alacata continues pulling me along, toward the staircase.

"Said you hit the bottle real hard after your dad and mom split up," Alacata said. "Got into drugs. Promiscuity. I know your type."

"My type? What the hell? I got straight A's. I was a cheerleader!" I screech like the brakes of a rusty bicycle. "My *mom* left my *dad*."

Alacata completely ignores me. "Said you ran away from home. Barely finished college. Husband dumped you." She yanks me to a stop. "Watch it. Steps coming up."

I trip. Alacata rights me.

"I went to Berkeley, for God's sake. I almost got my master's. Okay, maybe I didn't almost get my master's. But I did take some classes in France after college."

The slick, concrete stairs come up fast as Alacata drags me down the stairs. I stumble and lean into her to stop myself from falling.

"Run away? I went skiing with my best friend and forgot to leave my parents a note," I say.

Why did my mother lie about me on TV? Why isn't she defending me?

Oh my God. It hits me. She's mounting my defense. *Troubled woman from a broken home murders ex-husband's new wife.* My mother thinks I'm guilty. *Distraught mother pleads for mercy for her lunatic daughter.* She actually thinks I murdered Bree Martin.

"Women like you are a dime a dozen inside." At the bottom of the stairs, Alacata stops and looks at me. "Money don't make you special, Beckwith."

I feel numb. I start to defend myself, but what's the point.

Alacata pulls me into a room that looks like a big office. There are several small cubicles equipped with tables, chairs, and phones. A couple of holding cells line the back wall.

Breathing deeply, I look at Alacata directly in her eyes.

"Deputy Alacata," I say with as much confidence and authority as I can muster. "You need to listen to me. There is an inmate here in this jail that has information that may be material to the murder of Bree Martin, and I need to speak with her."

"Keep talking like that, girl, and you'll be back upstairs in isolation so fast your head'll spin." She pulls me over to one of the cells, opens the door, and unlocks my cuffs. She pushes me inside the miserable space and slams the door. Then she turns and walks away.

I rub circulation back into my bruised wrists. They're raw and swollen.

"You can lock me up and throw away the key, but my spirit is free," I yell with gusto. "My soul is free."

For one fleeting moment, I feel proud and confident. But when I look around, my spirits sink. The cell smells like dirty socks. Its small space and thick metal bars add to a feeling of claustrophobia.

I read a graffiti quote on the cell wall: "If a person *thinks* they're free, then they're *free*. Emerson said that in case you didn't know."

"What the hell?" Alacata stops and turns around. "Shut your yap, or you'll be sorry."

"It's a dereliction of duty for you to ignore the information I'm giving you," I say, improvising. "You're, you're, um... obstructing justice!"

"Say what?" Alacata stares at me. Her face is bright red. She steps back toward my cell.

"I would hate to report this incident to the Board of Corrections," I say. "Let me be clear, I'm putting you on notice."

My heart is hammering against my chest. God, I'm such an

idiot. I can't believe I just said that. What am I putting her on notice for? I don't even know what dereliction of duty exactly means.

"Whoa. I'm shaking in my boots," Alacata says.

But her forehead starts to knit into a frown. I think I got to her.

She starts to walk away but turns back to looks at me.

"Let *me* be clear, Beckwith. Inmates like you and Audrey are born liars. With a record like yours, no one'll believe a word you say."

Alacata turns on her heels and walks away.

I sit on the cement bench and wrap my arms around my chest. Audrey, a liar? I never even considered that she might not be telling the truth. Gut instinct tells me that Audrey may be a liar, but she's not lying about knowing Bree. I mean, why would she lie about something like that?

Somewhere, a phone rings. I look up and see a guard walk over to Alacata, who is at one of the desks, filling out paperwork. The deputy whispers something in Alacata's ear. Alacata looks at me. She's annoyed. The deputy shrugs and wanders into one of the cubicles.

Alacata pushes away from the desk and walks toward me. Her face is expressionless now, which is scarier than when she looked angry. Panic squeezes my chest. God, what now?

She pulls out a set of keys and unlocks the door.

I hold my breath. Bite my lower lip.

"Time to go, Beckwith."

"Court?" I say in a weak voice.

"Not court."

My confidence drains.

"You've been bailed out."

"Bailed out?"

I never seriously considered the possibility that anyone would post bail. I mean, not after all that I've done. It's probably my mom.

No. It's likely my dad.

Maybe he flew out to California last night when he heard what happened to me. I mean, he likes to act all tough-love to me, but I know he hates that I'm in jail. It's really bad for his reputation. I mean, who's going to hire a hedge fund manager whose daughter is a jailbird?

"Are you deaf?" Alacata says. "Move it!"

Then again, it could be my mom who put up the money to get me out of here.

I follow Alacata to a desk, where she has me sign a release form. Someone named Saintly Samuelsen bailed me out. Obviously, the bail bondman's name. Who called him? My mom. Bailing me out is right up her alley. She'll probably have a handkerchief clutched to her teary eyes, hoping to catch the attention of the waiting press as we leave jail.

I guess I knew my family would come through for me, so it doesn't really matter whether it was my mom or dad who hired Saintly Samuelsen. I mean, when the chips are down, I can always count on my parents to step up. But the thought of disappointing my parents again makes me feel weak in the knees.

I don't know if I can bear seeing the sadness, and yes, anger in their eyes. Their only daughter has screwed up. Again. But this time, I really didn't do anything wrong. I was home on a Friday night, getting organized.

I'm innocent. I shouldn't have been in jail in the first place. A surge of well-being fills me. I'm going home. But underneath that sense of well-being, something niggles me—something isn't right.

I push the thought into a deeper part of my mind and look up to see Alacata staring at me.

"You really are a brainless twit." An unnerving look of disdain and malice darkens her eyes. "You think you're home free? Leaving your troubles behind you? This, little girl, is only the beginning."

CHAPTER 14

IT'S 5:00 P.M. I'M IN THE BATHROOM AT THE JAIL when I finally pull on my dirty jeans and sweater and slip into my scruffy flats. With pleasure, I drop my shabby prison garb into the designated laundry bin, then wash my hands and face with icy water, and dry off with a paper towel.

I look up to a graffiti-etched wall, where a mirror should be, and repeat, *I am a vicar, not a victim.* I mean, victor. Victor. God, I'm losing my mind.

I band my hair into a ponytail and remind myself that I met someone in jail who knows who murdered Bree. Which is one thing to be grateful for.

I step out of the bathroom, into the large waiting room. Concrete walls, one-way glass, and people who refuse to make eye contact greet me. I hate this place. I swear if I have to beg, steal, lie, or cheat, I'm never coming back here again. I think Scarlet O'Hara said something like that. I'm never coming back to this place again. Ever.

I suddenly remember Audrey. I'll come back here to speak to Audrey. Wild goose chase or not, Audrey knows something.

I look around, hoping to see my mom or dad. I don't recognize a soul. Maybe one of them is outside, waiting for me.

Before I step through the exit, my phone vibrates with a text message. I can't believe it still has a charge. I dig around in my purse and look down at the screen. Kim.

We need 2 talk. Where r u?

Before I can answer back, I hear my name.

"Amanda Beckwith?" a throaty newscaster-like voice calls from behind me.

My heart bangs against my chest. I toss my phone into my purse, then clutch it to my chest. A man who looks like an NFL linebacker, wearing a beautifully tailored Armani-type suit and a Hermès tie, steps in front of me.

"Girl, you're as white as a ghost." He grabs my empty hand and shakes it like we've just been introduced. "Saintly Samuelson at your service."

The words come out in a quick concise sentence, like the beginning of a limerick.

"You, um...did Dad send you?"

I'm completely confused. Who is this guy? I mean, my father's associates look like members of the chess club, not the NFL.

"My mom?"

He places his arm around my shoulder and pulls me close. Leads me toward an exit door.

"We've got lots of time to talk. There's a mob outside. Just follow my lead. I'm using my bump-and-run defense when we get outside. I'll bump. You run."

If my dad or mom didn't send him, who?

Saintly Samuelson's hand is on the metal lever of the door, ready to bump and run. On the sidewalk fifty feet away, I can see hordes of bystanders, and the press with microphones and booms.

"Get close. Hold on to my waist. When I say run, you run."

I have butterflies in my stomach. My knees feel weak.

"Do I have to?" I push away from him.

I have no idea what I'm doing, where I'm going, or who I'm going with.

"Listen up." Saintly takes me by the shoulders with his big hands and looks at me. His deep-brown eyes are sincere. "We're fourth down and goal to go. The press is between us and a touchdown. We stumble and go down; it could get ugly."

Honestly, I don't know what the hell he's talking about, but I decide to go with it. I mean, what other options do I have? I can't go back to jail.

I put my arm around Saintly's girth and grab hold of his coat.

I hug my body close to his. "Let's do it."

Saintly pushes the door open. Loud, impatient voices hit me first. Lights blind us.

"Run!" Saintly says.

My feet barely hit the pavement. Saintly is practically carrying me. My face is buried in his beefy shoulder. People shout my name. I look up. See Danny Starr in the mix. Figures. I really do hate him. For a brief second, our eyes meet. His are impossible to read.

Saintly and I reach the curb in seconds. A black stretch limo with smoky tinted windows pulls up alongside of us. Saintly opens the door and gives me a gentle shove. I break my fall with my hands on cushy leather seats. My hair falls over my face. I brush it aside and look up. Lynette.

"What took you so long?" she says.

"Lynette!" I'm both thrilled to see her and confused. "Did my, um..."

"Don't thank me. Just get in the car so we can get the hell out of here."

Saintly eases his large frame into the seat across from us and slams the door. He slaps the glass partition between the front and back seat, and the car speeds away. I turn and look out the back window. We've got company. The press didn't waste any time. They're on our tail.

"Hi, angel." Saintly flashes Lynette a magnificent toothy smile. "Hate to keep my girl waiting."

"I'm not your *girl*. I'm your wife. There's a difference," Lynette barks, then pats Saintly's leg affectionately.

I can tell from her expression that she likes the sound of it.

"Don't call me angel."

Saintly laughs. "Whatever you say, angel. Whatever you

say." He leans over, squeezes Lynette's hand, and gives her a big, affectionate kiss.

Lynette looks happy.

"Lynette. Saintly's your husband," I say. "Saintly! So happy to meet you. Finally."

Lynette yanks her hand away and gives Saintly a playful shove. He sits back in his seat and smiles.

"Stay on your side of the car, you big lug." She crosses her legs and smiles at him.

"Wish we met under different circumstances." Saintly winks at me and pulls his briefcase onto his lap.

He pats it like it's full of thousand-dollar bills.

"Girl, the good news is you haven't been charged with murder," he continues. "A couple other things we'll get to later, but not murder—yet."

"It's bad, isn't it?" I say.

"*Bad* is a relative term," he says. "Bad is punting on the fifty-yard line."

"Am I on a yard line?" I say.

"Listen. There's no percentage in speculating. We're not looking back. We're focusing on the endgame. Right now, I'm the quarterback, you're the wide receiver. I'll call the plays, but how you take the ball down the field is up to you. Our only focus is winning the game. Got it?"

Too bad for me that I never paid attention at Cal's football games. I was more into the tailgate parties and the frat parties after the game.

"Truthfully, I need a translation."

"Amanda! Did you leave your brain back in jail?" Lynette says. "Saintly is a lawyer. He has agreed to represent you in all your legal matters. Which are many. He will run interference between you and the press, the police, and the district attorney's office."

"We're the first team, see," Saintly says. "You, me, and my baby, sitting next to you."

Lynette crosses her legs the other way and roots in her purse for a licorice stick as she shoots him an annoyed look.

"If the DA decides to prosecute, we'll need to hire additional criminal defense lawyers. I've got a couple associates. Excellent lawyers. They're on the team if we need them. Until then, you and I are the players. Lynette is the cheerleader."

"Saintly, how dare you say such a thing." Lynette sits up straight and narrows her eyes at Saintly, then raises an eyebrow and looks at me. "I'm nobody's cheerleader. I'm the coach, the manager, owner—anything but a ridiculous cheerleader."

"Okay, coach. Together, we're going to figure out who murdered Bree Martin, and end this thing. This is the Super Bowl, Amanda. I may be the quarterback, but you're going to make the touchdown and win the game. It's all up to you. Understand?"

The limo makes a couple of quick turns, and when I look out the back window, I notice that the press seems to have completely disappeared.

"Um, yes," I say. "My parents—"

Lynette starts to say something, but Saintly puts up his hand to quiet her. Which is shocking because I've never, ever known anyone who's been able to quiet Lynette.

"I spoke to your mother and father," he says. "Separately, of course."

"They're furious at me. They're completely done with me. That's why they didn't bail me out. Right?"

I'm choked up. Tears brim in my eyes.

"No offense. Your parents are idiots." Lynette opens her purse and starts rummaging around for something. She looks up at me. "You should disown both of them."

Saintly shakes his head and pats Lynette's leg.

He turns back to me. "They're not angry." He pauses and looks at some papers in his briefcase, then looks up at me and studies me for a moment. "Nice folks. Intense, but solid."

"Why aren't they here?" I say.

"They're on the team, Amanda, but just not in the starting lineup," Saintly says. "I've asked your mother not to appear on anymore TV shows or talk to reporters. She agreed. She's tough, loves the limelight, thought she was helping. Your father knows better. Trust me, he's on the team. Never underestimate what your daddy brings to the team. One of the reasons the DA hasn't charged you yet is because your father has more connections than the man upstairs. The Ventura DA's office is like a Pop Warner team compared to your father. You'll be arraigned in a few days for minor charges, but 1 can assure you that those charges will be dropped. There'll be no rush to judgment, as long as your father's on our team."

"My parents think I'm guilty," 1 say, as the limo glides around a turn and up a freeway on-ramp, heading north to Santa Barbara.

They're obviously not taking me home.

"Right?"

"Your parents don't spend much time thinking about anybody but themselves," Lynette blurts out.

"Lynette, baby. You don't have to be the cheerleader, but you just gotta act like the cheerleader. Come on now, honey. Let's be positive."

"Mom's mounting my defense. That's why she went on TV. 1 know her." 1 twist the bottom of my sweater into a knot. "That's why Dad isn't here."

"Everybody thinks you're guilty except me and Saintly. And maybe your parents."

"1 knew it." Tears spill down my cheeks.

"For God's sake, you need to get control of yourself. Saintly, talk to her."

"Amanda, look at me." He leans forward and takes my hand away from my sweater, and gives it a reassuring squeeze. In a steady, calm voice, he says "You gotta start acting like an innocent woman. You're running for a touchdown at the Super Bowl, not to the lady's room for a hanky. It doesn't matter how many times you've been knocked down. It's getting up and scoring that counts. Suck it up, girl. Get tough. Fight."

I sniffle and wipe my eyes with the cuff of my sweater and sit up straight.

"Okay. You're right. I know you're right, but how am I going to pay you? I'm going to run out of money. Truthfully, who's going to want to work with an accused murderer. My clients are going to drop me. I have a little savings, but it's hardly enough to cover your retainer, let alone a legal battle."

"I'm representing you pro bono," Saintly says. "As far as finances are concerned, you have nothing to worry about. Your parents will help out when, and if, they need to. We win the Super Bowl, it'll all be water under the bridge."

Lynette says, "I want exclusive rights to book deals, TV spots, etcetera."

Book deals? TV? I have no idea what she's talking about.

"What if I lose?" My hands are pulling at my sweater again.

I drop the balled-up hem and force my hands into my lap. I notice that Lynette is sitting quietly in her seat. The limo exits the freeway at Olive Mill Road and glides up the road into the Montecito hills.

"Losing, see, is not an option. You're not guilty," Saintly says matter-of-factly. "Here's the game plan. I help you prove your innocence. No formal charges, no court, no trial. It all goes away like a bad dream. Lynette gets a piece of the action. Win-win."

If I've learned anything in my thirty-two years, I've learned that there's no such thing as *win-win*. The only person who believes it's a win-win situation is the person who actually wins. Someone always loses.

"Am I selling my soul with these book deals and TV stuff? I'm not guilty. I haven't done anything. What is the real cost to me? What about my reputation?"

"Amanda. Please don't insult us with your insipid questions." Lynette digs through her purse. "I hope you're not implying that Saintly and I are taking advantage of you. We're here to help you restore your reputation."

"Lynette, honey, settle down." Saintly closes the file, puts it in his briefcase, and snaps it shut.

"Honestly, this is my life we're talking about. Will someone please just tell me what's going on? I'm really confused."

The limo slows almost to a stop. Wherever we're going, I think we're here.

"Oh, for Christ's sake, Amanda, stop being so dramatic." Lynette looks out the window and then back at me like she's struggling to find the right words. "The truth is, I've found myself in an unfortunate situation. Lord help me, but I actually need you right now, maybe more than you need me."

CHAPTER 15

LYNETTE NEEDS ME MORE THAN I NEED HER? I sit up straight in my seat and look at her.

"Are you giving me my job back?"

"Please, Amanda. For the time being, you are no longer employed by the *Tribune*."

"You just said you need me? Why?"

Seriously. I'm a suspect in a murder investigation, just sprung from jail, dogged by the media, on the verge of a breakdown. What do I bring the table?

"Quite frankly, I'm in trouble. The *Tribune* is in trouble." Lynette fumbles in her purse for a box of Red Vines.

She rips open the box to pinch a couple Red Vines out, and mindlessly starts eating them.

Saintly quietly takes the box from Lynette and slips it in his briefcase.

"That's your second box in what? The last couple hours?"

"Christ," Lynette fires back. "It's my one and only vice."

"Promised I would help you with...let's call it moderation." Saintly pats his briefcase, then turns his attention back to me.

"Truthfully, I'd do anything for you, Lynette, really," I say. "I mean, within the limits of the law."

The irony, given my situation, is completely Holden Caulfieldish.

The limo creeps up the road to massive gates that open automatically. I look out the back window for any lingering reporters. The street is empty. Thank goodness.

Lynette gave me a job when I didn't have a lot of options. She and Saintly bailed me out of jail. She's my friend.

"Of course, I'll help you. You name it."

"Good," Lynette says in a stiff tone, her voice full of impatience.

She shifts positions on the seat. Fluffs her hair and squares her shoulders.

"We'll get into more detail later. I appreciate that you are taking a leap of faith."

Saintly leans over and squeezes Lynette's hand. I know how hard it must be for her to ask anyone for a favor, let alone a subordinate like me.

"Give me a brief play-by- play of the last twenty-four hours," Saintly says to me as he gently places Lynette's hand on her lap, then digs in his briefcase for a legal pad and pen. "Just an overview."

"I've learned a ton in the last couple days. The first thing we need to do is speak to Audrey and her cousin Felix." I look from Lynette to Saintly. "Mike Young. He's the Ventura sheriff who was the first responder the night Bree was murdered. He and Bree were having an affair."

"Time out," Lynette throws her hands up and looks at Saintly.

"Who in God's name is Audrey?"

"We met in jail. She sat next to me at breakfast. Anyway, Audrey's old man was also having an affair with Bree. I mean, Bree was, you know, romantically involved with Audrey's boyfriend or husband, or whatever. She said Felix knows who murdered Bree."

"Who?" Lynette looks at Saintly with a wide-eyed look of complete exasperation. "What the hell is she talking about?"

"That's the point. I don't know who murdered Bree, because Audrey never got a chance to tell me. I need to go back to jail and speak to her."

"Listen up." Saintly reaches across the car and takes my hand. He looks me square in the eyes. "In the twenty years that

I've been practicing criminal law, I've never met anyone on the inside who wouldn't lie to save their own neck, get favors, or just make themselves seem important."

I remember Alacata saying the same thing.

"Still, shouldn't I check it out?" I look from Saintly back to Lynette.

I gently pull my hand out of Saintly's and sit back in my seat.

"At the very least, we need to follow-up with Audrey, if only to eliminate her as a witness, right?"

"Let me work on it, Amanda. I have some connections inside. I'll find out what's what." Saintly takes a pen and a notepad out of his pocket. "Audrey who?"

"You mean, what's her last name?"

Darn it. I try to remember. I'm not sure. I mean, it's a common name, like Smith or Brown. I can't remember. Maybe she never told me her last name.

"You can't be serious!" Saintly says. "You don't know her last name? For God's sake."

"Please don't bully me. A woman is dead. I'm about to be charged with murder for a crime I didn't commit. I need peace. A quiet place where I can think." I grab my purse. "I want to go home."

Saintly frowns at Lynette and shakes his head. He takes my hand away from the door and pulls me back into my seat.

"Chill, girl."

I look at him. His eyes are apologetic.

"We're here to help."

"Please just tell me what you need."

"It's quite simple." Lynette takes Saintly's hand. "I want an exclusive on your story. Period. It's not for me. It's for the *Tribune*. Advertisers love murder mayhem. Believe or not, Amanda, bad news sells papers."

"Advertisers? Game plans? Exclusives?" I choke. "Saving a stupid newspaper? I'm talking about saving my life, finding out who killed Bree. I get the whole football metaphor thing. I just don't know if I want to play."

Lynette scoots forward in her seat. She takes a deep breath and levels that cat-like stare at me before her eyes go soft.

"Amanda, dear, we may not be communicating, but we're talking about the same thing—saving your life and the life of my newspaper. This stupid paper is the heart and soul of Santa Barbara. In a small way, it's symbolic of everything that's right about our city, our country. Freedom of the press. This stupid paper gives everyone a voice—from our most humble constituents to our most powerful detractors. It's the very foundation of our Constitution. It's the one thing that keeps people connected and keeps them honest, for Christ's sake. People may hate me, but they love my paper. They trust it." Lynette's voice chokes. "The *Tribune*, my paper, is on the verge of bankruptcy. I know it's a sign of the times. Papers larger than mine are folding to give way to big conglomerates, cable news, and the fucking Internet. I'll be damned if I'll let some corporate giant like the *LA Times* run me out of business. Believe it or not, the *Tribune* is your ace in the hole."

Saintly reaches over and hugs Lynette. "She's got a way about her, don't she?"

He whispers something in her ear. She smiles.

Saintly says, "You gotta listen to her, Amanda. She knows what she's talking about. You need to tell your story."

"Like the pen is mightier than the sword?" I say.

"Exactly." Lynette shrugs out of Saintly's arms and gives him an affectionate little shove.

It's hard to stay mad at her.

Truth is, I need Lynette a lot more than she needs me. If I'm going to be tried in the court of public opinion, I'd prefer Lynette's reporters to Danny Starr.

"Before I agree to be on the team, I need to speak to my father. I mean, I need to hear it from him that the, um...game plan is a go. Okay?"

"No problem. You call your daddy," Saintly says. "A girl needs her daddy."

I dig out my phone and see that Kim has texted me a couple

times. I text her that I'll call her back ASAP, then punch in my father's cell number. Lynette's face is set in a stony glare. She folds her hands tight in her lap.

Five rings later, my father's wife, Kit Kat, as she likes to be called, answers the phone.

"Amanda. Where are you? Are you finally out of jail? You know you've put us through hell. Your poor father is completely overwrought."

Why did I call? I should've known my dad would turn me over to his nightmare wife. After all the years that they've been married, I can't believe I still let Kit Kat get to me.

"May I speak to my dad, please?"

"Not possible. He needs his rest. He has a very busy day tomorrow. He's playing golf in the morning. Business lunch afterward. Then we have a couple's massage and mani-pedi at the Ritz ..."

Kit Kat rambles on. I can't listen.

"Please let my dad know I called." I hang up before she can add anything else.

"Don't be disappointed," Lynette says in an I-told-you-so voice. "Truth is, most men, with the exception of my Saintly, are emotionally deplete. They really don't like strong women. That's a compliment, Amanda. Your father is exactly like my ex. God rest his soul."

Suck it up. Get tough. Fight.

"So, when you say *exclusive*, you mean like don't-talk-to-any-other-reporters exclusive?"

"Like, don't-talk-to-anyone exclusive," Lynette says, her voice even and businesslike. "Say one word to the wrong person, and they'll throw you under a bus for their fifteen minutes of fame and a couple hundred bucks. The press are junkies for this nonsense. They'll destroy you and your family. They'll hunt down uncles, aunts, cousins, and big-mouthed friends you haven't seen since grammar school. If they can't find a lead, they'll make one up."

I think about Danny Starr. "The *LA Times* is guilty of defamation."

"Look what the so-called mainstream media did to me over firing a half-dozen lousy reporters and staffers."

"But Lynette, won't you be breaching some kind of journalistic ethics or conflict of interest if Saintly represents me, and you serialize my story?"

"Legally speaking, I'm representing a former *Tribune* blogger," Saintly says. "I am the *Tribune's* attorney of record."

"Since when did ethics and conflict of interest ever have anything to do with journalism?" Lynette says. "The answer is no—there is no conflict of interest. You don't work for me anymore." She smooths a wrinkle out of her skirt with her long, graceful hands, and looks up at me with a raised eyebrow. "This is business, and I'm in the business of selling newspapers."

Saintly says, "Amanda, remember, you're the running back. When it's all said and done, you're the one who's going to make the touchdown."

"I know. I remember. You said that." I look at Lynette. "Could you translate, please?"

"You write the story. A first-person account of everything that happened to you from the moment you called the police, until the moment you were thrown in jail, and everything afterward. Let the readers decide whether they believe you or not." Lynette's voice is as blunt as a dull knife. "The only caveat is that the *Tribune* gets the exclusive. No communication with anyone until this is over. The beat reporter covering this story for the *Tribune* is going to call it the way she sees it. Megan Borrow. She's good. She'll be fair, but I'm not going to interfere with her reporting. Your story is separate, serialized, and independent."

"No talking to the detectives, my mom, my best friend, Kim? Seriously, I really do need to go home." I look out the window at a rolling lawn and big, shady oak trees.

"As far as the detectives go," Saintly says, "we can't exclude them from having access to you. When they do come calling, I'll be right by your side." He winks.

"Home is the last place on earth you want to be." Lynette

leans forward and looks me squarely in my eyes. "Did you not hear a word I just said? Your house is ground zero for every scumbag reporter from New York to California."

"I could sneak in."

I imagine Judge Jeanine and her entourage of photographers snapping photos of me groveling in the bushes under one of the big picture windows in front of my house. Maybe I don't need to go home.

The limo slows to a stop. I scoot up in my seat and look out the window to a classic Santa-Barbara-style house surrounded by a wide stone patio and huge pots of white roses.

"I don't have my toothbrush or anything. I need clean clothes. My pajamas."

Lynette looks annoyed and starts digging around in her purse. Probably looking for a cigarette.

"I built my baby a closet bigger than an airplane hangar." Saintly laughs. "You need something to wear? You go shopping in baby's closet. You'll find something."

I have a fleeting image of myself in one of Lynette's Chanel suits or Diane Von Furstenberg dresses. I mean, Lynette dresses like Julianne Moore, and I, um...dress like...I don't really know who I dress like, but my clothes are kind of like a security blanket to me.

"Whose house is this? Does it, um, have a good security system?"

"Ours. Ain't it grand?" Saintly scoots up in his seat. "It's built like Fort Knox."

"Let's just say that when Saintly left the New Orleans Saints, he had a lot of female fans." Lynette clearly smitten by Saintly.

"And some anti-fans as well," he says. "Some people think I deliberately threw my last playoff game. Lots of rumors. It got ugly. It would take a SWAT team to break into this place."

"Let's move the party inside." Lynette scoots around me and out the door. "I'm starving."

I clutch my purse to my chest as the driver offers me his hand and helps me out of the car. Saintly is right behind me. I have no idea what's going to happen next, but I have to focus on the positive. I mean, I'm out of jail, I haven't been charged with murder, I actually have my own attorney, which is huge, and a safe place to stay until I can figure things out or win the Super Bowl. Whichever comes first.

Saintly leads the way through the front door of the house, into an enormous entry with eighteen-foot ceilings. He and Lynette head down a wide hall to a great room with a high-beamed ceiling and two rustic chandeliers. The room opens to a gleaming stainless steel and Carrara marble kitchen.

Little flecks of dust swirl in the fading light like glitter. It's a beautiful room, all windows and open spaces. Creamy-white linen sofas and chairs complement the rustic walnut dining table and neoclassic Welsh cupboard. The entire room looks as if it were created for *Elle Decor* magazine. If I didn't have so much on my mind, I'd give in to my impulse to walk over and take a closer look at the dishes in the cupboard and the paintings on the wall.

With Saintly's urging, I sink into one of the slip-covered linen parson's chairs resting in front of massive glass coffee table. I drop my purse on the wood floor next to me. The memory of Mike Young's big fat rear positioned on my couch at home snaps me out of my reverie. I remember Mike winking at Geoff at the sheriff's department, and the smug, sinister way that Jack O'Brien looked me over—like he knew something that I didn't.

"I'm being set up for Bree's murder." The words pop out of my mouth before I can stop myself. "There's no other explanation. I just wish I knew why."

Lynette lands on the sofa across from me. Saintly continues into the kitchen.

"We'll get to all of that," he says over his shoulder, as he opens the ultra-deluxe Sub-Zero stainless-steel refrigerator. "We all have questions that need answers. But right now, we're eating. Hungry?"

Saintly shuts the fridge with his rear and walks over to the counter and starts arranging cheese and crackers on a large wooden cutting board. He carries the board over to the coffee table and sets it down, then heads back into the kitchen. He grabs a dishtowel out of a drawer and wipes his large hands— he was obviously born to catch and throw a football. He walks back into the great room and sits on the arm of the sofa next to Lynette. She pats his leg and smiles up at him.

"I don't think I can eat." A sense of doom washes over me. The strain of the last twenty-four hours is getting to me. I'm overwhelmed.

"I know it probably feels like there's a conspiracy going on. Everybody's against you. Like a quarterback with lousy offensive support on the field, facing a three-hundred-pound linebacker. Girl, I've been there."

"I don't feel like everyone's against me." I look from Saintly to Lynette.

A restless urge to leave and go home nudges me. I look out one of the big picture windows to the backyard, now shrouded in deep shadows. It's dusk, and I feel the weight of another long night ahead.

"I'm not imagining this stuff. I really believe that Geoff had something to do with Bree's murder. I think his best friend and attorney might be in on it, too. There may be other people involved."

"We need facts," Lynette says. "Not theory."

"How do we know that Bree's death isn't connected to a cold case. I read about a rape and maybe a murder that happened around here. It's worth looking into, right?"

I search their faces for validation, but there isn't any.

"Try telling that to the DA," Lynette says. "We need—"

Saintly puts his hand up to shush Lynette. Amazingly, Lynette clamps her lips.

"Everything is on the table," he says. "Cold cases. Your friend in jail. Geoff and Bree's friends and associates. Go ahead, girl. Tell us what you got. We're open. You got evidence—a theory— lay it out. We can eat later."

Lay it out? I can barely talk, let alone forward a coherent theory on how and why I'm being set up. My brain feels like a big messy overstuffed closet in desperate need of organizing.

I bite my lower lip and fold my hands into my lap.

"Thing is, Amanda," Lynette says, "investigators recovered a lot of evidence from in and around your house. They've matched your hair and fiber samples to the hair and fiber they found on Bree's body."

"How's that possible?"

My body feels like it's on fire. My heart is pounding. I feel like I'm having an out-of-body experience.

"I wasn't anywhere near Bree on the night she was murdered. Why is this happening?"

"It gets worse." Saintly carries over the wooden board laden with a variety of delicious-looking charcuterie, cheeses, crackers, olives, and nuts.

I'm suddenly starving.

He sets it on the massive glass coffee table, along with small white plates and linen napkins.

He sits next to Lynette. "The police recovered what they think is the murder weapon."

"That's a good thing, right?"

I'm trying to be positive. I mean, finding the murder weapon will obviously exonerate me.

"Good and bad," Saintly says.

Lynette is uncharacteristically quiet. She lifts her hand to her mouth.

From the depth of my soul, I know that what's coming next isn't going to be good. I feel cold. I've lost my appetite again.

Lynette drops her hand from her mouth. She shifts her position on the couch and leans toward me. Her gaze zeroes in on mine.

"Amanda, your fingerprints and Bree's blood and DNA are all over the murder weapon."

CHAPTER 16

I'M SO RELIEVED.

"The thing is I don't even own a murder weapon," I say, "so it's impossible that my prints are on it."

Suddenly, I'm starving. I pick up a plate and help myself to crackers and delicious-looking white creamy cheese and salami. I spread cheese on the cracker and shove it in my mouth. Delicious.

Saintly walks back to the kitchen and returns holding a bottle of wine and three glasses. God, I could really use a glass of wine right now. I know it would be the worst thing I could do.

Before I can say *no, thank you*, he hands me a glass of wine, then gives Lynette hers.

"Clos des Papes Châteauneuf-du-Pape, 2005," she says. "Beautiful year for French wine."

"Let's toast to winning the Super Bowl," Saintly says.

We stand. Saintly clinks Lynette's glass, then mine.

"Here's to us. Cin-cin."

I take a big swallow of the wine without really thinking about it. A warm sensation courses through my body. I wipe my mouth with the back of my arm. One night in jail, and my manners are atrocious. My mother would be appalled if she saw me now. I can't help myself. I feel like one of those people rescued after being lost at sea. I jam another cracker into my mouth, then take another big sip of wine.

"See? I mean, doesn't the evidence prove that I'm being framed?" I mumble through a mouthful of food. "Right?"

"Do you own a Cal Berkeley umbrella?" Lynette sits up, rests her arm over the back of the couch and levels a you-better-tell-the-truth look at me.

"I *had* a Cal umbrella." I take another sip from my glass. The wine has an almost medicinal effect on me. I sigh. I should stop drinking now, but I don't.

"I must have left it behind, along with a bunch of other stuff, when I moved out of Geoff's house. The detectives asked me about an umbrella. I told them I didn't own one, which is the truth. This is delicious wine, Saintly. Thanks."

"Had?" Lynette raises an eyebrow with what seems like great difficulty.

She lifts her wine glass and gives it a swirl, then holds it up to the light and finally takes a delicate sip.

"Amanda," she says. "The police recovered the umbrella from your next-door neighbor's trash."

"Jean? Why would Jean have my umbrella?"

My neck feels itchy. I pull my hair into a knot on my head and switch positions on the chair.

Saintly looks at me like a lawyer, not a coach.

"The detectives are connecting dots. That's what they do. If you didn't put the umbrella in your neighbor's trash can, who do you think did?"

"I haven't seen that umbrella in years. It's a golf umbrella. Geoff used it when he played golf on drizzly days. Ask him. He'll tell you. Truth is, anyone could've taken my umbrella."

I untuck my feet and plant them on the floor. My hands feel damp. I wipe them on my jeans and look up to see both Saintly and Lynette staring at me.

"Can you prove that? Geoff has a solid alibi." Lynette crosses her legs and folds her hands in her lap.

Geoff may have an alibi, but what about Jack. He was down on the beach on Friday night. More importantly, Kim didn't just see Jack. She saw Jack *and* Bree. At least, she thought she saw them.

"Okay. Suppose Bree had the umbrella," I say. "It was

raining on and off on Friday. For whatever reason, she was on Hollywood Beach on Friday night. Maybe she had a prearranged meeting with someone. Someone who wanted Bree dead."

Lynette is nodding, but with little enthusiasm.

"Okay. Then what?"

"That person uses my umbrella to bash Bree on the head, then plants the umbrella in my neighbor's trash. Maybe he thought he was tossing it in my trash can. Think about it—it's a perfect setup."

Saintly starts to say something, but I interrupt him.

"The other thing I almost forgot to tell you is too crazy for even me to believe, but it's important." I push myself up from my seat and walk around so I'm facing Lynette and Saintly head on. "On Friday night, when I called the police, Officer Michael Young showed up. He was the first responder. The weird thing was he knew me. We had one date. It was awful. But that's not the crazy part. He knew Bree, too. She was his massage therapist."

Lynette perks up. "What are you saying?"

"Bree was cheating on Geoff with Mike Young. Bree was planning to leave Geoff for him, or so he said. They were lovers."

Saintly stands and goes to his briefcase to retrieve a legal pad and pen.

"Okay. This is important. Mike Young is connected to you and Bree. That's no coincidence. We need to depose him. He's on our witness list. Who told you about his relationship with Bree?"

"He did. He's scary. Dangerous."

Lynette leans in. Saintly's writing.

"On the night before I was arrested, I called the police again. There was a mix-up and I thought someone had broken into my house. It's long story, but the point is that Mike Young showed up again. This time, he's wearing street clothes, not his uniform. I think he was drunk. He blathered on about his relationship with Bree, what he thought of Geoff, all kinds of crazy stuff."

Saintly stops writing. "Do you know why he wanted you to know about his relationship with Bree? That information could potentially put him on the suspect list."

"I know, right? The thing is, Mike Young wasn't worried about implicating himself, because he seemed convinced that I murdered Bree. He was angry. He went after me. Thank God Lynch and Lee arrested me."

"Are you accusing a sheriff of assaulting you?" Lynette is losing patience with me.

"Yes. But the point is, if I killed Bree, why would I leave the murder weapon, with my fingerprints on it, in Jean's trash can and then call the police and report an intruder? Talk about stupid!"

Saintly sets his pad on the coffee table. Lynette sets her glass down.

"You're right about one thing," he says. "None of this makes sense. Lynch and Lee claim they have evidence that points to you. But there are big gaps in their evidence. There are too many unknowns. Here's what I think. If the police had as much evidence as they claim to have, the DA would have charged you with murder, not obstruction of justice. They're having trouble filling the gaps."

Lynette says, "Let's start from the beginning."

"Okay." I stifle a yawn and lean toward her, with my glass. "I think Geoff did it. I don't know how he got back to Las Vegas from Ventura that night. But if there was a way, I'm sure Geoff was able to figure it out. He must have been wearing gloves when he killed Bree. That's why his prints weren't on the umbrella."

"Amanda. Let's stipulate that Geoff has a confirmed alibi," Saintly says. "We need to focus on eliminating you as a suspect. Tell me about that umbrella and where you last saw it."

Saintly is back taking notes, which is reassuring.

"I think that the person I saw on the night Bree was killed was holding something. It could've been an umbrella." I try hard to picture the guy running across my back patio. "But truthfully, I can't remember."

"Our challenge is to prove that the Cal umbrella wasn't in your possession when you moved from Geoff's house," Saintly says. "It's a tall order."

Maybe proving my innocence is going to be more difficult than I thought.

I step behind the couch and then walk over to the massive windows that look out to the backyard. It's dark out, but the iceberg roses and lavender are illuminated by low-voltage lightening. The sycamores are accented with hanging globes of light. Gorgeous landscape.

I'm absolutely sure that Geoff, Jack O'Brien, Mike Young, and even Audrey, are all connected to Bree's death. I just need to figure out how everything fits together.

"For God's sake, sit down," Lynette says. "You're making me a nervous wreck."

I walk back to the couch across from Lynette. I think my innocence depends on Kim. She has information that's important, that could lead to Bree's killer and exonerate me.

"There's something else you should know. My best friend, Kim, saw, um—"

"Hold that thought." Saintly pads out of the room and returns in a few seconds, wheeling one of those big whiteboards that coaches use to strategize game plans.

Using the black marker, he writes the date and the heading: *Amanda's Beckwith's Offense/Defense Strategy*.

"What did you say about your friend?"

Suddenly, my better angels get the best of me. Or maybe it's the wine. I spoke too soon. I can't break my promise to Kim. I need to speak to her before I say anything to Saintly and Lynette.

"I, um...I'm sorry, I lost my train of thought. I meant to say that I'm, um, very lucky to have a best friend like Kim."

"Please." Lynette's voice is edgy with sarcasm. "What does she have to do with anything?"

Lynette sits up in her seat and grabs her wine glass. She takes a big gulp.

"That woman is a menace, and no friend of yours. I told you she called looking for you on Friday. In the name of being a *good friend*, she told me how awful Bree was to you, and that you had every right to hate her and kill her."

"She didn't mean that. No way. Kim and I have been friends forever. She's known for putting her foot in her mouth."

It's true. Sometimes I wonder how we've remained friends for all these years, but Kim would never do anything purposely to hurt me. Would she? Never. I mean, nobody's perfect. Seriously, I'm in no position to judge anyone.

"She says stupid things. I mean, don't we all. But she's not malicious. At least, not on purpose."

"My ass." Lynette lifts her wine glass and feigns a toast, then takes a big swallow of her wine.

Saintly gives her a wide-eyed look that tells me that this wine is meant to be sipped.

He turns to me. "Girl, let's get back to the basics." He stands and walks over to the whiteboard and picks up a black marker and poises it in his hand. "I want to know everything that you know, as it relates to Bree."

I take another sip of wine. *Hiccup.*

"Sorry. What haven't I already told you?"

"The absolute truth," Lynette says. "What? You think the police weren't going to find out that you weren't where you said you were on the night Bree was murdered?"

I swallow hard. "I didn't intend to lie to you. Okay, I'm going to be completely honest. I lied because I hate public speaking and I thought you'd be mad at me for canceling. My meeting wasn't with Rob Lowe on Friday. It was with his assistant on Thursday. Seriously, I'd rather dig ditches than speak in front of a group. I'm sorry I lied to you."

"I'm your employer, not your mother," Lynette takes the bottle of wine and pours herself another glass. "I don't get mad."

I look at the antique clock above the fireplace. It's after 10:00.

"I need sleep. Maybe I can be more, um...helpful in the morning."

"Before we call it a night," Saintly says, "I'd like you to read the article from the *Times* and tell me your version of what happened Friday night. So far, all we have to work with is your statement to us, the police report, and this." He reaches behind him for a newspaper and drops it on the table in front of me.

"You need to read it," Lynette says. "Everyone else has."

The paper is dated December 19, the day after Bree was murdered. It's the issue featuring Danny Starr's article—the one I never read. I completely forgot about it.

The article isn't buried in the California section of the paper like I was hoping it was. It's on the front page. My picture is truly dreadful. The photo was snapped on the night the police found Bree's body. The full-color shot shows me with a deer-in-the-headlights look that makes me look guilty of something. Every flaw in my skin stands out. Dark circles shadow my eyes. I look like the mug shot of the lady astronaut who got caught stalking her boyfriend. My roots look black against the blonde streaks in my hair.

Worse, my boxed picture is next to a professional one of Bree and Geoff on their wedding day, taken on the front steps outside the home that Geoff and I lived in when we were first married. Geoff and Bree look like movie stars. Bree was truly a beautiful bride.

My stomach quakes. I lean into the sofa. Drop the article on my lap, then wipe my sweaty hands on my pants and focus on the headline. I take a deep breath and read on.

WOMAN FOUND DEAD ON HOLLYWOOD BEACH— FOUL PLAY SUSPECTED.

By Danny Starr, Times Staff Writer

Ventura, CA: A well-known businesswoman and wife of a renowned Santa Barbara chiropractor and owner of The Center in Montecito, CA, was found dead on Hollywood Beach in Ventura, late Friday night, authorities said.

A Ventura County sheriff discovered 30-year-old Bree Martin's body concealed between the sand dunes on a popular beach known for its mild weather, small harbor, and low crime rate.

Martin is the wife of chiropractor to the stars and nutrition guru Geoff Martin.

In a surprising twist, Amanda Beckwith, Geoff Martin's former wife and Santa Barbara Tribune blogger, reported the crime.

Beckwith allegedly saw someone leaving the beach minutes before police discovered Martin's body. The body was found less than 100 feet from Beckwith's home.

Beckwith could not be reached for comment.

The story goes on to detail Bree's *high-profile* job at The Center in Montecito. It gives a bio on Geoff and Bree that Danny clearly ripped off from a gushy press release from The Center's press kit. The article shows a Google map of the area where the police found Bree's body, and a close-up of my house, with its whitewashed shingles and bright white trim.

Ventura County coroner, Sam Chin, refused to comment on the cause of death, pending an autopsy report. Sources on the scene said the victim was killed by blunt-force trauma. It is unclear if the victim was lured to the beach and died there, or elsewhere. A murder weapon was not recovered.

No suspects have been apprehended.

Anyone with information about this case is asked to call the Ventura County Sheriff's Department at (805) 463-8976.

Bree's death changes everything. Nothing in my life is ever going to be the same. *This isn't going to go away.*

Saintly stands and moves to a seat directly in front of me.

"If we're going to prove your innocence, you can't be fudging facts."

"Saintly is correct," Lynette says.

I reach for my glass of wine, but Lynette takes it out of my hand and sets it at the end of the table, far away from my reach.

"You're immature, egocentric, and self-indulgent. But from where I sit, this unfortunate situation is a blip. You've got plenty of time to figure out your life. Turn things around. For now, you have to cut the bullshit and come clean."

I feel numb. *Guilty.* I really am self-indulgent, and I suddenly realize, I've had too much to drink.

"We all need to be on the same page." Lynette looks over at me.

I give her an affirmative nod. I mean seriously, I'm not in any position to disagree with her.

"Saintly is paid by the hour. Let's not waste his time. Pay attention."

"Okay, let's scrimmage." Saintly stands and claps. Returns to the whiteboard and picks up the pen. "On first glance, the DA has a strong case. Bree's body was found on the beach behind your house. Her hair and blood were found on the murder weapon, along with your partial fingerprints. And the murder weapon was found very close to your house. I've written out a list of what the police consider incriminating evidence."

Saintly positions the whiteboard to give us a better view. There are three columns in his list of police evidence:

Lying to the police about whereabouts on the night of the murder.

Hair/fiber found on the victim match Beckwith's hair/fiber samples.

The alleged murder weapon was found at the home adjacent to Beckwith's, with Beckwith's partial fingerprints on it.

A witness overheard Bree and Beckwith arguing at Wendy Foster's in Montecito.

Beckwith's police record, that includes assault and a DUI.

Bree's body was found on the beach behind Beckwith's house.

"The DA hasn't discussed motive, but I'd bet money that revenge for Geoff's infidelity with Bree is his starting place." Saintly points the marker at me. "The upside is that all of the DA's evidence is circumstantial. Which is likely the reason why he hasn't filed charges or impaneled a grand jury. He's not rushing to judgement. He's collecting more evidence. Oh, I forgot to mention—Bree's Range Rover was found in her garage in Montecito."

Lynette reaches for the wine and tops off her glass. Raises it to her lips and takes a sip.

She looks up at Saintly. "Does the DA believe that Amanda somehow lured Bree to her house? If so, how did Bree get there? Uber? Lyft? That's traceable. Maybe he thinks Amanda picked Bree up somewhere and brought her to Hollywood Beach? That would be a stretch." Lynette turns to me. "You haven't seen Bree since September, at the gallery, right?"

I untuck my legs, plant them on the floor, and sit straight on the couch.

"That's not entirely true. I did see Bree. Last week." I clear my throat. "Geoff used to take me shopping at Wendy Foster's, then to lunch. It was kind of a special place for us."

Lynette shoots Saintly a look. He calmly raises his finger to his lips to stop Lynette from verbally reacting.

"You need to focus," Saintly tosses his pen back and forth in his hands like a football. "We were talking about your interaction with Bree before she was murdered, not your life story, girl."

"Right. This is going to probably sound worse than it really is. We kind of had a run-in when I saw her last week. Truthfully, it was no big deal. But I think I forgot to tell the cops what happened that day."

"Really." Lynette sets her glass on the table. "Saintly, darling, I'd like another glass of wine. No. Whiskey. The Pappy Van Winkle."

"Good call, baby." Saintly goes to a cabinet and takes out a bottle, then reaches for a glass and pours her a shot.

He walks over to Lynette and hands her the glass, then moves to the whiteboard.

"We're on the right track," he says. "For better or worse, you gotta be completely honest with us, even if you think it makes you look bad."

"I completely forgot about it." I hiccup.

I straighten up in my seat and pull my sweater down over my hands. I'm cold.

Saintly picks up the marker. "Okay, Amanda. Tell us when and what happened the last few times you saw Bree."

His voice sounds tired. All the fun and banter are gone.

"Everything is important, no matter how small or insignificant."

I try to remember exactly how many times I've seen Bree in the last six months. It seems like a year ago since Detectives Lee and Lynch asked me the same questions.

"I saw her once in September, at the Wild Coyote Gallery in Montecito. And twice in October, once in November, and as I mentioned, last week."

"Good." Saintly makes notes on the yellow pad. "Let's talk about last week."

"Remind me again," Lynette says. "Where did you have the confrontation?"

"Seriously, I wouldn't even call it a confrontation. I mean, after the show, I tried on this really, really fabulous Marc Jacobs sweater, and I barely set it down, when Bree grabbed it from me. No. I'm completely wrong. I had just tried on this darling Trina Turk black knit dress. Perfect winter dress. When I came out of the dressing room, Bree literally grabbed it out of my hands. No, wait...I handed Bree the dress. Told her it wasn't my style."

Saintly reaches into his briefcase and pulls out a file. He reads down to what looks like a list.

"Black knit, long sleeves, ruffle at the neck and wrists?"

"Exactly! How'd you know?"

Saintly holds up a form that must be the evidence report.

"Sounds like the dress Bree was wearing on the night she was murdered."

"Did the salesgirls, or anyone else, see you hand the dress to Bree?" Lynette says.

I try to remember how everything unfolded that afternoon.

"Yes. Lilly. I mean Lillian Roth, the manager, rung up Bree's sale. Lilly gave me one of those looks like, um...she felt my pain. Lilly will back me up. I'm absolutely sure."

"Fabulous," Lynette says. "That may explain why the police found your hair and fibers on Bree's body. This is good."

Relief sweeps over me like a cool breeze. I stand and walk over to where Lynette set my wine glass. I reach for it, but she grabs my hand, which is absolutely the best thing. I don't need another drink.

Anyway, I knew there had to be a logical explanation for all the evidence against me.

I suddenly feel so tired I could sleep for a year.

"Could we finish up in the morning? I'm, um, really starting to fade."

"Just a couple more questions." Saintly stands and adds the meeting at Wendy Foster's to what looks like supporting evidence for the defense.

He notes the information about the black dress and Lillian Roth.

"Lynette's right," he says. "This is good news. That happened last week."

"Any other *chance* meetings besides those you've already told us about?" Lynette says. "Think, Amanda."

I hate to bring this up, but I promised I'd be completely honest.

I stifle a yawn. "On Thanksgiving, I had a really meaningless little argument with Bree. It was so stupid."

Lynette rolls her eyes. "Right."

"Where did that argument take place?" Saintly says.

I explain to Lynette and Saintly that Thanksgiving had been

one of those really awful misty kinds of days. Dark. Gloomy. Depressing. I was feeling melancholy and went over to my old house—Bree and Geoff's house, now—to see if I could pick up a tablecloth that I had left behind when Geoff and I split up.

"I knew it was a mistake to go there."

"An understatement in the extreme." Lynette sounds totally exasperated.

"Lynette? Baby? I don't want to bring up a sore subject, but didn't you get in trouble for stalking your ex?"

"Me? Fuck you, Saintly. That was completely different." Lynette stomps over to the cabinet and pours herself another shot of whisky.

"You were saying, Amanda." Saintly walks over and sits on the couch opposite me.

"All I wanted was to pick up a tablecloth that my mother gave me at my wedding shower. See, I left Geoff with basically the clothes on my back. I left everything behind, including my shower, wedding gifts, and that stupid umbrella. Maybe in some weird Freudian way, I left my stuff there so I'd have a reason to go back to my old house and see Geoff."

Lynette looks over at Saintly. "I didn't stalk my ex-husband. We were suing each other. It's called opposition research, not stalking, for God's sake."

I take a deep breath and wipe my eyes. I can't believe I'm actually tearing up after all these years.

"Anyway, Bree came to the door and invited me into the house. The entry opens to the dining room, and there was my tablecloth on my dining room table, all set for Thanksgiving dinner. I sort of freaked out."

Lynette rubs her forehead. "Please tell me there weren't any witnesses."

"Bree's housekeeper was in the next room," I say reluctantly. "But I don't think she saw anything. I think I called Bree a slut and a husband stealer. And she called me a loser and a bitch."

"Shit." Lynette starts to pace. "How can we help you if you continue to act so recklessly?"

"Did you physically harm her?" Saintly says in a quiet voice.

"I don't know what you mean."

Lynette leans forward. "Did. You. Fucking. Hit. Her?"

"No. No way. The argument only lasted a couple minutes, I swear."

"Okay," Saintly says. "Besides the entire contents of your wardrobe, which the police are using to match hair and fiber samples, they also took your laptop. They're going through your bills, bank statements, and phone records."

"You mean, the police took *all* of my clothes."

I remember how messy my closet was on Friday night. I never got the chance to finish organizing it.

"Everything?"

Saintly hands me an official-looking document. I read down the list of my personal belongings.

"Shoes. Purses. Accessories. Everything."

"Which means that the police are digging deep. Not just taking clothes. They're compiling a list of everyone that you've spoken to, emailed, or communicated with on Instagram, Facebook, LinkedIn, Twitter, Pinterest. If there's anything you want to tell us, now's the time."

"I haven't used Facebook in years. I don't really have that many friends anymore."

"I'll drink to that." Lynette raises her glass in a toast. "Best news I've heard tonight."

I can't believe my clothes are gone. I feel like there's been a death. I mean, another death.

Saintly walks over and picks up his notes and starts writing.

"Are you sure that the last time you spoke to Bree was the night before the murder?"

I wrap my arms around my shoulders. "Yes. Positive."

"Between you, me, and Saintly, did you find Bree's body? Is that why you called the police?"

"No. Absolutely not. I didn't even know there was a body until long after the police arrived."

l tuck my feet underneath me. The linen fabric feels cold against my bare legs.

"Let's get back to the murder weapon," Saintly says. "Your partial prints are the only ones found on what the police contend is the murder weapon. Whoever used that umbrella to murder Bree, wore gloves. How did your prints get on the umbrella?"

"I don't know. But it's weird that only my prints were on the umbrella. Doesn't make sense. If we could only find the gloves and the person wearing them, I'd be home free."

"Home free? Not exactly." Saintly goes over and picks up the whiteboard marker and starts writing.

He steps back. "But if the glove doesn't fit, you must acquit!"

"Ha-ha," l say.

Lovely. My entire defense depends on a cliché used to exonerate an ex-football player who everybody believed killed his wife.

CHAPTER 17

I WAKE UP IN SAINTLY AND LYNETTE'S GUEST ROOM, dressed in Lynette's leopard-print PJ's, snuggling under a cool Egyptian cotton duvet and a cashmere blanket. My head is throbbing and fuzzy. Too much wine.

It actually hurts to think. *I'm never drinking again, as long as I live.*

I roll over onto my stomach and thrust my arm under the cool down pillow. How many times have I promised myself that? I roll over onto my other side and pull the blanket up under my chin.

This is only day four of my nightmare. I can't believe it.

In only *four days,* my ex-husband's wife was murdered practically in my backyard, I was fired from my job, went to jail, and am currently the focus of a murder investigation. My parents have basically thrown me under the bus. And my best friend, who thinks she may have seen witnesses that might help exonerate me, refuses to help me because she doesn't want her husband to find out about her so-called friendship with her daughter's teacher.

At least, according to Saintly, all of the evidence against me is circumstantial. But as far as I know, the detectives are only focused on me.

On the upside, I haven't been charged with murder, and Saintly and Lynette sound confident that they can have the obstruction charge dismissed. Still, I feel like my window of opportunity is getting smaller and smaller with every passing day.

One problem is that Detectives Lynch and Lee haven't really listened to my side of the story. I mean, they've listened to my story—actually, like, a million times. They just don't believe it. Plus, they don't know the whole story. They know nothing about Mike Young, Audrey, or Kim's version of what happened on the night Bree was murdered.

Saintly and Lynette don't seem to buy into my theory that Geoff, Jack O'Brien, Officer Mike Young, and Audrey are involved. Maybe I have *too* many theories. Each one of my theories is high on drama and short on facts.

Maybe mounting a winning defense is really like drafting a winning football team. Your team needs depth, plays, and practice. Thing is, I don't have a clear vision or plan of action, or a playbook.

Saintly's game plan seems like it's going to take forever. Forever is too long. I think about all the famous criminals arrested for one thing or another. Guilty or innocent, it takes years to convict or acquit. Years living in limbo. I shiver under the blanket and take a deep breath.

And what about Lynette's plan to use me to save the *Tribune?* It's crazy. But no crazier than anything else that's happened in the last four days.

Bottom line is I need to get out of my head and into action. I've got some solid leads. But the clock is ticking. It's been four days. Four days for whoever murdered Bree to cover their tracks.

I work myself into a sitting position and stretch my arms over my head and look around. It's amazing how everything feels and looks so different after a good night's sleep. The bedroom has that crisp, sunshiny feeling of a five-star hotel.

For no good reason, I feel optimistic. Like any second, I'm going to remember something important, and this entire ordeal will make sense in some really bizarre way.

But I'm smart enough to realize that I'm going to need more than just gut instinct to move me off the suspect list.

I need hard evidence. Facts, eyewitnesses—any witnesses—documentation, security camera photos, a confession.

I wrench myself out of bed and walk over to the window. Behind the white, gauzy drapes, I behold a beautiful blue morning. Beneath the clear sky, the wide green lawn is littered with sycamore leaves and glistening dewdrops. This is truly a magical place. I wish I could stay forever.

After a long, hot shower, I wrap myself in a thick white towel, brush my teeth, and blow-dry my hair. I fold my pajamas and make my bed, then walk into the closet to take Lynette up on her offer to lend me one of her outfits until I can figure out how to get my clothes out of jail.

Lynette's closet is a dream. There are cute little shoe cubbies, built-in drawers, and neat sections for all Lynette's fabulous accessories. Perfect, except that Lynette color-codes her clothes by beginning at the end of the color spectrum.

Beautiful shades of plum and eggplant are arranged to the left of the closet, and bleed into shades of pumpkin and pomegranate, which is completely wrong. I wonder if Lynette realizes what's she's done? How could she? I mean, I took a course called The Physics of the Color Wheel. It fulfilled one of my science electives in college. I got an A.

Lynette probably doesn't even know about color theory, or that Sir Isaac Newton invented the color wheel, which is a wonderful tool for organizing your closet.

I grab a handful of hangers, and am ready to rearrange everything correctly, when I stop myself.

Get a grip. I can't let my obsessive-compulsive side get the best of me.

I put everything back and strum through the wooden hangers, focusing on Lynette's choice of top fashioner designers instead of how the designers are organized in the closet. There's Stella McCartney, Yves Saint Laurent, Chanel, Dolce & Gabbana.

Saintly is right. Lynette really does have enough clothes to fill a small department at Neiman Marcus, and this is just her extra stuff.

I pull out a beautifully tailored navy wool jumper. It's perfect. Conservative but stylish, not trendy or fussy. Simple. It looks brand-new.

I fish around inside the garment and find the price tag: $695.00. *Theory*—very apropos. I'm grateful that Lynette and I are basically the same size.

I turn toward the full-length mirror and hold the dress up in front of me. I fluff my hair and tilt my head. All I need is a turtleneck, navy tights, brown boots, a little makeup, and I'm good to go.

Suddenly, a voice in my head rattles me. Tattered, torn, and beaten up as they are, my clothes are mine, and I have to get used to wearing them, for better or for worse.

It takes all my willpower not to drop my towel and put on the wool jumper. I reluctantly place the dress in its place in the closet and walk back into the bedroom, where my tattered jeans, dirt-smeared sweater, bra and panties sit folded on the dresser.

I look at them and suddenly feel as worn-out as my clothes. I swallow hard. I really need to go home. The detectives must have left something behind.

I pull on my undies, yank the sweater over my head, step into my jeans, then slip on my shoes. I feel good. I mean, good enough. I don't even need to look in the mirror. Maybe I'm completely over the trappings of fancy clothes and trying to look perfect all the time.

I pick up my purse and dig out my pad and a pencil. I go over to the big black varnished retro-modern desk and sit. I write, *Monday, December 22. To Do: Follow-up on SUSPECTS and run down LEADS.* That pretty much sums it up.

The one thing I really need to figure out is the motive for Bree's murder. What did she have that someone wanted? Did she push someone beyond the point of no return? Did they do it out of greed? Revenge? Lust?

From my own experience, I know that Bree could go from normal to bitch in two seconds.

I think back on my recent run-ins with Bree at the gallery, Wendy Foster's, and the day or two before Thanksgiving. She was awful. But would that be reason enough for someone to bash her head in, leave her alone to die on a desolate beach, on freezing rainy night?

Bree's killer had to be someone she knew and trusted. *Probably someone I know and trust.* That sort of undermines my cold-case theory.

One of the most shocking things about Bree's death is that she allowed herself to be in such a vulnerable position. She seemed street-smart, and always in a don't-fuck-with-me mode.

The Bree I knew was more victimizer than victim. She had an agenda. *Social climber* wouldn't be the term I'd use to describe Bree, but it was something like that. Ambitious, cunning, power hungry, duplicitous—yes. But there was something more— something that I can't quite put my finger on. Based on what I learned in jail, and from Mike Young, about Bree, homewrecking was her favorite sport.

It was more than that.

Predator. Exactly the word I was looking for. Bree went after what she wanted. If you had it, she wanted it.

I think about the incident at Wendy Foster's. Bree grabbed that dress out of my hand because I wanted it. And if I wanted it, she had to have it.

Just like she did with Geoff. Bree could have had anyone she wanted. She was beautiful. She could be charming. She only wanted Geoff because he was someone else's husband.

When she joined Geoff's staff as his massage therapist, everything changed. Bree called the shots from her first day on the job. Now that I think about it, Geoff had to have encouraged her. She wielded the power at The Center. She let everyone who worked with Geoff, including me, know it.

She went from employee to vice president overnight. Or it seemed like it. Dumb me, I didn't see her moving in on Geoff until it was too late.

Maybe Bree pushed someone too far.

I pick up my pen and write, *Suspects: Geoff Martin, Jack O'Brien, Mike Young, Audrey's husband/boyfriend, someone from Bree's past—former boyfriends, coworkers, relatives, someone from Bree's life in Southern California. Nevada? Somewhere else?* I add a big question mark.

The most obvious suspect is Geoff. Why? Infidelity. Bree was cheating on Geoff with Jack and Mike Young. Maybe Audrey's husband. Did Geoff find out? Maybe Geoff wanted a divorce, and Bree wouldn't give it to him.

But a divorce would mean some kind of property and money settlement. Geoff murdered Bree because he didn't want to give her any money. Maybe Bree wanted half of Geoff's business. Geoff had to make Bree sign a prenup—he made me sign one.

I was never a threat to Geoff. I didn't cheat on him, and idiotically, I stood on principal and didn't ask for anything.

Like me, Bree was only married to Geoff for a couple years. There wasn't much in it for her, either. Did Geoff give Bree a percentage of his business?

Never. Not in a million years would Geoff do that.

Maybe Geoff believed that another divorce would ruin his reputation as the natural health guru, with his mind-body-spirit crap.

I mean, his stupid seminars are all about achieving a life of perfect harmony and happiness through his private-label supplements, chiropractic therapy, and wellness center. The motto on his business card is *Serenity Not Insanity.* Two divorces and splitting the business with Bree could mean serious disaster for Geoff.

So, Geoff murders Bree and makes it look like I killed her as revenge for breaking up my marriage. Seems like an obvious setup. The problem with that scenario is Geoff's an alibi. He met the detectives at the airport when he got off the plane from Las Vegas. Seems rock solid.

Maybe he has friends in the DA's office. That doesn't make sense. No one is going to be a co-conspirator in a high-profile murder, or any murder.

But what if Geoff really was in Las Vegas when Bree was murdered? Maybe he hired Jack O'Brien to kill Bree. That would explain Kim spotting Jack on the beach near my house.

I write Jack O'Brien's name on the left side of the page. Next to it, I write: *Geoff's best friend and lawyer? Homewrecker? Patsy? Homicidal maniac?*

I need to find out.

I write down, *LEADS: Kim, Audrey, Felix.*

I'll start with Jack O'Brien. I'll go to Jack's office and totally disarm him with the element of surprise. I'm the last person he'd expect to see on his doorstep. Maybe I'll ask him to be my lawyer in my criminal defense. I could see him being flattered by the idea that I chose him to defend me. On the other hand, I could be putting myself in real danger.

There must be a safer way to find out what Jack was up to.

Under Jack's name, I write, *Kim.* She's the person I really need to speak with. She may know more than she thinks she does.

After Jack, I'll go back to the jail and see if I can visit Audrey. I don't even know her last name. I'll cross that bridge when I come to it. The good news is that I have a plan—a starting place.

I close my calendar and return it to my purse, then sling it over my shoulder and tiptoe downstairs, where I find Lynette and Saintly sitting at the kitchen table, reading the paper. Lynette drops the paper and gives me a what-the-hell look when she sees me dressed in my dirty clothes. Saintly folds his section of the paper and sets it on the table.

"You look suited up and ready to go?" He frowns. "Girl, it's way too early to be calling plays on your own."

Saintly's wearing navy Lacoste warmups and multicolored Nikes. The only thing missing is a whistle around his neck. He looks like he just finished his morning workout.

Lynette is dressed in a navy Lululemon workout outfit. Her hair is brushed smooth and gleaming, away from her face. She is tight-lipped and stern.

I look up at the clock. It's not even 7:00 a.m.

"I've made some decisions."

———

An hour later, I'm outside, standing with Saintly next to the front door. It's freezing out.

"I hope you know what you're doing," he says.

"Lynette...is she—"

"She's fine. She's still on the team, and so are you. Nothing's changed."

I squeeze his hand and give him a hug.

"Thank you for everything. *Everything.* I just need, um...a couple days."

Saintly wraps an arm around my shoulder and leads me down the stone path toward the garage. Inside is a black Range Rover with tinted windows.

"Sure, I can't talk you out of this?" Saintly hands me the car keys and frowns. "This isn't fantasy football we're playing. It's the real McCoy. No instant replays. A fumble could mean losing the game—maybe your life."

Truthfully, I wish Saintly could talk me out this. I'm scared for a million different reasons.

"I'll be okay. Really."

He digs into his pocket and pulls out what looks like a small aerosol can with a chain hanging from it and fastens it to his key chain. I look up at him. Hair spray? I know I look like a wreck, but is this necessary?

"It's from Lynette. What?" Saintly lifts his eyebrow. "Never seen one of these? It's a rape escape. Every college girl on campus has one. *Pepper spray.* I'm surprised you never had one in college. My baby's worried about you, girl." He puts the keys in my hand and squeezes. "I hope you never have to use this."

I look up at his big, worried eyes and force a smile.

"Thank her. I won't let her down. I won't let you down. Our exclusive agreement still stands. Promise."

MURDER ON HOLLYWOOD BEACH

Saintly hands me a piece of paper with a phone number on it.

"Remember what we talked about. You're living in a post-Bree world. Err on the side of caution. Your iPhone's GPS is synched with mine with Find My iPhone. Leave your phone on and in your pocket at all times. If you're in trouble, I'll know where to find you. I'm on your Favorites list. Touch my name and we're connected, then dial nine-one-one. For whatever reason, you get separated from your phone, that's my number."

Saintly turns, takes my chin in his hand, and tilts my face so I'm looking up at him. His eyes are serious.

"Don't trust anyone."

I shudder.

"Girl, can't imagine what you're planning to do when you leave here. It could get dangerous. What'd you call it? *Chasing down leads*? Detectives do that in *Law and Order*, not in real life." Saintly opens the car door. "Two days? Don't seem long enough to figure nothing out, but it's plenty of time to get yourself killed."

CHAPTER 18

SOMEONE IS FOLLOWING ME. I see the black Jeep, sans its front license plate, at about the same time that Cold Springs Road becomes Sycamore Canyon and winds into Hot Springs.

Now, on Route 101, the SUV is two cars back and shadowing me. Every time I switch lanes, it switches lanes. It looks familiar. *Who do I know that owns a Jeep?* Can't think of anyone.

I look in the rearview mirror again. The car is closing the distance. Any second, the older-model Jeep's going to be right on my bumper. *Shit.*

I look again. *It's Danny Starr.* Figures. Seriously, if I'm the best story he's got going for him, his career is really in trouble.

But Bree's murder is a newsmaker, and he's the reporter that broke the case. It isn't going to go away just because I've been out of the limelight for the last twenty-four hours.

I reach into my bag, take out my phone and start to press Saintly's number, then change my mind. Fifteen minutes on my own, and already things are falling apart. I'm not calling Saintly unless it's a real emergency.

Truth is, I'm actually relieved it's Danny. Even a hack reporter like Danny Starr could pose a big threat to someone out to get me. But there's also this weird queasy feeling I get every time I run into Danny. Not queasy. Butterflies? Do I have a crush on him? Ridiculous. I can't stand the sight of him. He's caused me nothing but grief.

I look in the rearview mirror. He's getting closer.

Ignore him. I push my mirror up so I'm not tempted to look in it again and focus on the road ahead. Once I'm home, I'm safe. The good news is that my street is permit parking only, so there's nothing he can do but hang out in the county lot a couple blocks from my house and wait for me to get home.

Or he could break into my house like he did the other night. His phony claim that my door was open doesn't hold water. I'm not that stupid. I absolutely locked it when I left the house on Saturday morning.

I should just call him, see what he wants. Maybe he knows something about the investigation that I don't.

I pull my purse on my lap and dig in a side pocket for the card Danny gave me on the night that Bree was murdered. I tap his number on the keypad and wait for Bluetooth to kick in. A couple rings later, he picks up.

"Dan," he says in an impatient tone, like he's on deadline.

"Is it Dan or Danny?"

"Mister Starr."

"Funny. Stalking is illegal." I look over and see that Danny has moved into the lane next to me. "You're going to cause an accident."

"You're a horrible driver."

He rolls down his window and smiles. But even from this distance, I can see something sad behind his grin. I shoot him my best dirty look. A car horn honks. I swerve and step on the gas. I'm going to get myself killed if I don't pay attention.

"Look who's talking," I yell.

"I'm trying to help you," Danny says. "Check your messages."

"Right," I say.

It's obvious he's on a deadline. I mean, it's 7:30 a.m., and he's chasing me down for a lead.

The signal light in front of me turns yellow, and before I can really think through this lame-brain maneuver, I gun the engine and make a sharp left turn in front of a white Mercedes in the lane next to me, and race down the street, away from Danny Starr.

I look in the mirror. The driver in the Mercedes lowers his

window and shows me his middle finger. I leave Danny stuck at the red light, behind the Mercedes.

"Nice move, Andretti," he says. "So your point in nearly getting us killed is...?"

"I'm not allowed to speak to you."

"Hey, *you* called *me*."

He's got a point.

The light changes, and he's now a few car lengths behind me. Before I know it, he's in the lane next to me.

"*You* called me *first*." I hang up.

Danny looks over at me and shakes his head. What does that mean?

We cruise along the 101 for the next twenty minutes in silence. I exit at School House Road and head home. Danny's right behind me as I get off the freeway.

In another ten minutes, I slowly pass the county parking lot up the street from my house. It looks like every available space is occupied by media van or vehicle. People are leaning against their trucks and loitering at the curb at the entrance to my street.

Out of the corner of my eye, I see my neighbor Jean standing next to a KTLA Channel 5 van, smoking a cigarette and talking it up with some big-breasted redhead with a notebook. I thought Jean left her house to stay with family in the Valley. Apparently not.

Even KBS 2TV is here. It's the Korean entertainment channel, according to the logo on the van.

Wow. *Slow news week.*

Before turning left onto my street, I dig into my purse for my Tom Fords. Thank God the Jackie O look is still in. The frames cover half my face.

In Saintly's black Range Rover, with its tinted windows, nobody notices me. I spin the steering wheel left, drive past my house, and park in the driveway of one of the vacant cottages a few houses away. I shift the car into park, turn off the ignition. Danny parks further down the street.

I dial his number and wait for him to pick up.

"What'd you want?"

"To give you the good news."

I can't tell if he's joking or serious. But he must think I'm really dumb to believe he could ever be the bearer of good news for me.

It's a hook. All reporters use that kiss-up routine to disarm their sources.

"Really? Great. Let's have it. I can always use good news."

"That's an understatement," he says.

"Get to the point."

I'm trying to ignore the flutters in my stomach at the sound of Danny's voice.

"Give me five minutes," he says. "You won't regret it. But we can't do it on the phone."

"I'd rather..." I almost say *die*, but clamp my lips. "Lynette warned me about you."

"Lynette Jones? Your employer? Warned you about me? That's rich. She doesn't even know me, except maybe by reputation."

"Exactly." I look in the rearview mirror and pinch some color into my checks. "Thing is, I'm not going to meet you."

"If you knew what I had to tell you, you'd change your mind."

"Stop playing games and just tell me." I pull my hair into a knot on my head and recline my seat. "You're really starting to bug me."

"I really am trying to help you."

"Wanna help me? Get me into my house without the entire LA paparazzi finding out I'm here. I want to go home."

"I can do that."

"Fat chance."

"I'll create a diversion. You slip into the house through a back door."

"Think it'll work?"

"Can't hurt to try. Can't stay in your car forever."

"Hey, how'd you know I was driving a Range Rover?"

"That, I can't tell you. I do have my sources." Danny laughs. "Truth is, anyone who knows anything about sports, knows Saintly Samuelson. He a football legend. I followed the limo to the house and came back early this morning about the same time you left in the Range Rover. Lucky."

"Clever." Hope he knows I'm being sarcastic.

I sit up and look out the window. Danny smiles and waves.

"Okay. What's your plan?" It better be good.

"I'm formulating it as we speak. What about this? I'll get back in my car and head to the parking lot, and roll down my window and yell something like, *I see her*. Then I'll drive toward the freeway like I'm following you."

I bite my lower lip to stop myself from telling Danny that it sounds like a stupid plan. But I could use Danny's help.

Who knows—his plan might work.

"Not so fast," I say. "I thought you had something important to tell me? In person."

I can't believe I'm actually going to speak to Danny and break my promise to Lynette and Saintly.

"I do," he replies. "We can meet later. At the public parking lot—the media staging site. The one next to the Mandalay Bay hotel. Wait until the reporters clear out. Around seven. Don't get out of your car. Keep the doors locked. I'll find you."

"It's a date." I instantly regret the reference.

Danny says, "Hold on a second. This can't wait. I have bad news, too."

I hold my breath and will it not to be too horrible.

"Some weird shit is going down with the murder investigation."

"Weird like what?"

How can anything possibly get weirder than what's happened in the last four days?

"Watch your back, Amanda. I'm serious. Can't talk about it on the phone. Be careful. Don't trust anyone."

My heart is pounding. It almost hurts to breath.

"You're scaring me."

I look out the window. Danny's looking at me, but his attention suddenly shifts to the street in front of the parking lot.

"Good. I'm glad you're afraid," he says. "You should be afraid."

Danny is suddenly quiet. I lift my glasses up and look at him. What's going on? The silence drags on.

"Amanda. Change of plans. Listen to me carefully. Do what I say. I'm not kidding. Hide your face as best you can. Turn on your car. Don't go home. You can't. You need to get out of here. Now."

"Why?" I'm suddenly freezing.

I push the ignition button and rev the engine.

"Slowly now. Put the car in reverse and drive out of your neighborhood. Slowly."

I do exactly what Danny tells me to do. I sink down a little in my seat. Turn and look out the back window, over my shoulder to make a three-point turn. Slowly drive down my street and exit to the main drag. I drive slow and steady while stifling an urge to gun the engine and speed away. A black-and-white passes me as I head off my street.

"Remember that police officer, Michael Young?" Danny says. "I just saw him. He's the cop car that just passed you."

"What about him?"

I buckle my seatbelt and turn left on the street heading toward downtown Ventura, a few miles away. I don't know where else to go or what to do.

"He's stalking you," Danny says.

I look into my mirror and see Danny slowly driving toward the exit to the parking lot.

"He's part of the murder investigation," I say. "He's, um... investigating."

"He's tracking you. Not part of the investigation. I don't think Lynch and Lee know what he's up to. I spoke to Lynch. Asked him a couple questions about Young's involvement in the case. He dismissed me. I think Young is tracking you. Probably through your cell. I'm not sure. You need to be careful."

"Why?"

"Because you know something."

"No, I don't."

I look back and see that Danny's blocked Mike Young's exit from my street with his Jeep. God love Danny. He really is trying to help me.

"You know something, Amanda. Whatever you think you don't know may have gotten Bree Martin murdered."

What the hell does that mean? I start to say something, but Danny has cut the connection.

To my horror, I hear a crash and the sound of screeching tires a couple blocks away. I look in the rearview mirror and see a black-and-white speeding in reverse around Danny's Jeep. It jumps the curb and barrels down the street, toward me.

I slam down on the gas and make a quick right onto a quiet residential street. Make a quick left and turn to look at the street behind me.

Nothing. Thank God.

I look in the review mirror again, and sure enough, Mike Young's squad car is closing the distance. Its lights are off. No siren. He really isn't part of the investigation.

Shit. I have to do something. Fast.

I make another right turn and see a shopping center a couple blocks away. I look in my side mirror. Mike Young is still behind me, but not on my tail.

I barely make the green light and ease into traffic on the main drag in downtown Ventura. Traffic is slow, which is good, because I can see that Mike's car is stuck in traffic behind me.

Up ahead, I spot a Vons market. I pull into the parking lot behind a huge trash truck and follow it around to the alley behind the store. I park Saintly's Range Rover behind a row of mostly empty dumpsters.

What am I going to do now? For a moment, I stare, transfixed as the truck's metal arms lift one of the dumpsters and empties its contents into the back of the truck.

I realize I forgot to shut off my phone. Mike Young has followed me here. I can't hide. He'll find me.

I grab my purse and cell phone and scoot out of the car. My hands are shaking so bad I can barely push the key fob to lock the car.

I look around, and it's just me and the trash collector, who is donning big fat earphones to protect his ears from the truck's grinding engine noise. He is oblivious to my presence.

The truck passes me on its way out. I toss my cell phone into the back of the trash truck seconds before it rounds the corner onto the street behind the alley.

Before I can think of what to do next, I squeeze behind a huge wall of stacked cardboard boxes at exactly the same time that I see Mike Young's cop car out of the corner of my eye. It creeps around the corner of the building and into the alley.

God, I'm trapped. Mike obviously followed my phone's signal, and it led him here. All he has to do is get out of his car and look around the boxes, and he'll find me. If he drives through the alley, he'll find the Range Rover. This was an incredibly stupid idea. What was I thinking?

I'm going end up dead like Bree. Mike will dump my lifeless body in a place where no one will ever find me. I'll be just another cold case.

I'd rather be a suspect than a cold case.

I hold my breath. I want to close my eyes, but I force myself to look. I can see slivers of images out of the tiny spaces between the boxes. I hear Mike's car tires crunching gravel as it inches toward me.

The car stops directly in front of where I'm hiding. I can see Mike's profile through the half-inch space between the boxes. He's looking down at his phone. Slowly, he turns his head toward me. He's looking right at me—or it seems like he is. His forehead knits together. He looks angry. I dig my nails into my hands. Bite my lower lip to keep from gasping.

For no apparent reason, Mike Young backs up the squad car.

The gravel turns under the car's wheels as it creeps back, turns, and speeds away.

I can't believe it. I wait for what seems like an hour, but it's only been a few minutes. I take a deep breath, then ease out from behind the boxes. I look down the alley toward the street. Mike Young is gone. *Really gone.*

A feeling of total triumph bubbles up in me. Thank you, God. Thank you, Saint Anthony. Mike Young fell for my stupid trick and followed my cell phone in the trash truck. I mean, that trick has been done a million times before—no doubt. But Mike Young fell for it. He's tracking my phone away from me, all the way to the county dump or wherever. He's gone, that's all I care about.

I dig in my pocket for Saintly's car keys and open the Range Rover door. But before placing them under the floor mat, I unlatch the pepper spray and drop it my purse.

Unfortunately, Saintly's car is no longer safe to drive. I grab my purse off the seat, quietly shut the car door, and head out of the alley. The only thing I need to worry about now is staying alive for the next couple hours, until I meet Danny Starr.

CHAPTER 19

THIRTY HELLISH MINUTES after running into Danny Starr, and my near miss with Mike Young, I'm still a wreck. I've been hiding out at a Starbucks inside an Albertsons grocery store a couple miles from my house, trying to plot my next move.

The problem is that I don't have a next move. I can't go home. I don't have a cell phone, so I can't really call anyone. I only have a small amount of cash, and I can't use my credit cards because they can be traced. I'm not ready to call Saintly. I've been a failure all my silly life, but I'm not going to call it quits yet.

Walking to Albertsons was a nightmare. Every police car I saw—and it seemed like there was one on every corner—looked like it was driven by Mike Young.

While the list of suspects seems to be growing, my opportunity to exonerate myself is shrinking. Mike Young thinks I know something. I do. I know that Mike and Bree were having an affair.

Did Mike kill Bree? Maybe they planned to meet on Hollywood Beach. That was Mike's beat. That's why he was the first responder. Maybe Bree met with Jack O'Brien earlier that night, when Kim thought she saw them.

When Bree finally hooked up with Mike, he was already angry. Maybe she was late for their meeting. They got in a fight over their breakup, or because she wouldn't leave Geoff. He lost his temper and smashed the umbrella over her head, then dumped it in Jean's trash can. Maybe he didn't even know he killed her.

I picture him on the night Bree was murdered, when he spoke to the press. He had a deer-in-the-headlights look that could be interpreted as guilt. But it could have also been shock.

It's hard to remember all of the details of that night. I called the police, and Mike Young showed up. The dispatcher sent him, right? The dispatcher said that she would send an officer that was in the area. Mike Young was in the area.

But I can't imagine Mike Young having the brainpower to mastermind Bree's murder. Her death must have been an accident. He's seriously the biggest idiot I've ever met. For all I know, he's still following the trash truck all over Ventura.

How did Danny find out that Mike Young is after me? He's a reporter—they know stuff like that. I bet Danny has one of those apps that connects to the police dispatcher. That's probably how he ended up on Hollywood Beach on the night Bree was murdered.

I have so many questions. I mean, how does Danny know that Mike isn't part of the investigation? Who is his source? Somebody told Danny that I know something. Something that might have led to Bree's death.

Who told him that?

There's something I'm missing—something relevant to Bree's murder that happened a long time ago. Maybe while I was married to Geoff. Or after the divorce, when he first got together with Bree. It could be a million different things, but nothing stands out.

Why was Bree murdered the Friday before Christmas? Is the day significant? It had to be an accident. It had to be Michael Young. He had motive, means, opportunity, and one thing that Geoff didn't have—nothing to lose.

Thoughts whirl in my mind. Danny knows more than he was able to tell me on the phone.

I need to make sure I meet with him.

At 2:45 p.m., there are surprisingly few shoppers at Albertsons. I borrow some change from a woman who looks like I was taking her last two bucks. She hands the change to me, eyeing me with sad, empathetic eyes, like she understands my dilemma from first-hand experience.

I call Saintly from a pay phone that took me forever to find. It costs $1.75 to make a call from a public phone. I had no idea. I tell him where he can find his car and brief him on Mike Young. He wants to pick me up and bring me back to his house.

"Are you fucking out of your mind!" Lynette rages. "You need to get your ass back here, now." She obviously grabbed the phone out of Saintly's hand. "No. Stay where you are. We'll pick you up."

"No," I say.

I need to meet Danny, but I can't tell her that.

"Girl, don't go acting like a free agent, now," Saintly says. "I'm not cutting you loose. Hear me?"

He promises to keep his eyes and ears open for any new information and fallout. I assure him that I'm okay and not in any danger. I don't think he believes me.

"You've got twenty-four hours before I bring you home. That's the deal on the table."

"I never break my promises." *I mean, I never break my promises on purpose*, I want to say, but instead end our conversation with some lame football metaphor.

Then I dig around the bottom of my purse and come up with just enough change to call my mother.

"I need to borrow some money," I say, without going into the details.

I don't want to tell her that I can't use my ATM or credit cards, let alone why.

"I just had to borrow six quarters from a stranger to call you."

"Oh, for God's sake, Amanda," my mother says, her voice strident and hard, like I just got caught for some junior high school prank. "You need to stay with me."

After spending a few minutes talking her out of me coming with her to the family home, she agrees to *rendezvous* at an off-the-beaten-path doughnut shop near the liquor store where I'm making my calls.

Keeping my head down, I walk past a couple joggers and a mom strolling her baby, until I see the doughnut shop. I wait for my mother outside, praying that she won't offer to treat me to a coffee so we can have a little *chat*.

Finally, after about a half-hour, my mother drives up and parks her new white Tesla along the curb in front of me. It's a beautiful car. She climbs out from behind the wheel and walks around the front to the sidewalk where I'm waiting.

She's wearing a dove-gray and slate-blue Eileen Fisher outfit with a pale blue, fringed cashmere scarf that complements her perfectly coiffed silver hair.

"You look beautiful, Mother. I love those Uggs." I give her a hug. "You know I hate to ask, but I need to borrow some money and your Platinum card. I promise to pay you back as soon as possible."

"We need a chat." She moves toward the coffee shop. "Let's find a nice little corner inside."

I take her hand and squeeze. Our eyes lock. I hope she knows this is serious.

"I really don't have time. Rain check?"

She tilts her head and looks me up and down like she's buying a Christmas tree. She takes a deep breath and shakes her head.

"What is that outfit you're wearing? Some kind of grunge look? Have you gone Goth? It's dreadful. With all of the money that you spend on your clothes, and with the press at your heels, you'd think you'd make an effort to fix yourself up."

I am seconds away from losing it with her. But I really can't afford a fallout with my mother right now. I simply breathe in and out quietly through my nose and tune her out. *I'm okay. My mother is doing the best that she can.*

After a short lecture on making better choices and

being more responsible—which seems like a complete understatement, given that I'm the prime suspect in a murder investigation, and on the lam from a rogue cop—my mom finally agrees to authorize my use of her Platinum card, but only after I promise her that I haven't broken any laws recently, and that the two of us will appear together on Kathi Lee and Judge Jeanine. So much for my agreement with Lynette and Saintly about speaking to the press.

"Let's walk." I don't think standing in one place for too long is a good idea.

I link my arm through my mom's and guide her down the street. We settle in front of an Enterprise Rent-A-Car storefront.

"Mandi. We need the press on our side. I'm thinking about hiring a publicist to field press offers. Pricey, but surely worth the money."

Apparently, reps from those shows have continued to pester my mother until she promised to confirm a date for an in-studio interview with the two of us.

"Just give me a date, and I'll be there." *There's no way in hell I'm going on TV with my mother or anyone else.* "I need another favor. Big one. I need you to rent me a car."

"Absolutely not." She shakes her head.

"Okay. Then can I borrow your car?"

My mom gasps.

"I just need a car for a few days, maybe a week. Remember to add an extra driver to the contract."

Mom looks over at the car rental sign and gives me a suspicious look.

"Thing is, my name and pictures are all over the news," I say.

I don't want to tell my mom about Mike Young. Knowing her, she'd call the police station and file a complaint, or tell Judge Jeanine that we need to defund the police. She'll hold a fundraiser.

"I don't want anyone to recognize me. I just need a few days to get things squared away. Please, Mom, this is important."

I squeeze her hand gently. It's life-or-death important, but I don't want to say that. It'll scare her. It scares me.

"You promise you'll go on TV with me?"

"Yes. But I need a little time."

After retrieving her proof of insurance and filling out the paperwork necessary to rent a car, my mom walks out of the rental agency.

"I rented you a white Ford Escape. It's parked in a lot behind the building, in parking space eleven. Be careful. You've never been a very good driver."

"Thanks for this. You're a lifesaver."

"What happened with that Saintly person and that awful woman you work for?" Mother says. "I thought they were helping you."

"You mean Lynette Jones?"

I've worked for Lynette for something like four years, and my mother chooses to never remember her name.

"You shouldn't be working for that disreputable paper and its owner. You should be married and having my grandchildren. And you definitely should not be going to jail."

"Saintly and Lynette are, um...scoring one for the home team. They're running interference for me." I give her another hug. "I'll be fine, okay?"

"I have absolutely no idea what you're talking about," she says, but hugs me anyway.

My mom pulls away and searches my eyes. She squeezes an envelope into my hand, and the keys to a white Ford Escape.

"Please don't do anything that'll make me worry about you."

I hug her. "I love you, Mom. Thank you for everything."

After my mother leaves, I look in the envelope. Besides her Platinum card, there are thirty crisp hundred-dollar bills. I knew my mom would come through for me.

I have another epiphany. Mothers, in general, are completely underappreciated. I mean, seriously. The only time most kids are grateful for their mothers is when they need something.

With the help of my mother's card—*thank you, Mom*—I score a pay-as-you-go disposable cell phone at a CVS. The good news is that nobody even flinched when I gave them my mom's credit card. Neither my mother's name nor mine sent up any red flags. My middle name is Elizabeth, just like my mom's. Not that anyone asked to see my ID.

Still, I have to be careful. I can't take it for granted that no one will recognize me or my mother's name and put two and two together.

After a few quiet moments and a double latte at another out-of-the-way Starbucks, I calm down long enough to come up with a plan.

I buckle up behind the wheel of the Escape, lock the doors, and head toward the ocean.

First, I need connect with Audrey's cousin Felix, at Head Case, to find out what he knows about Bree and Audrey. At the same time, I'm going to get a makeover. A disguise.

Then I need to have a face-to-face with Kim. She needs to come clean.

After I meet with Kim, I'll have just enough time to make my date with Danny.

Head Case, in Ventura, is a posh, hip salon frequented mostly by LA women who can afford its outrageous prices for haircuts, extensions, facials, Botox, Restylane injections. It's a full-service boutique salon and spa—a kind of one-stop shop for women around my age who have unlimited funds and plenty of time to spend it.

I remember that it was Bree's go-to spot for her quick fixes. Figured that out from Bree's constant selfie postings on Facebook and Instagram.

When I told Saintly and Lynette that I haven't been on social media sites in years, it was kind of true. What I meant to say is that I haven't posted on Facebook and Instagram in years. I'm on those sites all the time to keep up with what my friends are doing. Oddly enough, Bree friended me on Facebook and Instagram. Like the idiot I am, I friended her back.

Bree visited Head Case at least once a week and posted tons of pictures during her visits.

I've blogged about the salon, but I've never been here. Truth is, I can't afford it.

I park my car between two silver Range Rovers, apparently the car of choice for suburban housewives. I walk through tall, stainless-steel doors, into a world of Carrara marble everything. I mean, the floors, the counters, and even the accent tables seem to be made from the gray and white stone.

I walk up to the front desk.

"Hi," I say over Beyoncé's crooning in the background. "I, um, don't have an appointment. Is it possible to do a cut and color? Is Felix available?"

The young woman looks up at me from her magazine. She has short, chunky burgundy hair, brownish-red lipstick, and skin so pale you can almost see through it. Her expression is somewhere between bored and sleep. She runs her polished, blue-tipped fingernails down an iPad to look for any openings.

"You're in luck." She picks up a walkie-talkie and says, "Felix. Cut n' color."

I look around while the receptionist is typing into the iPad. There's not a ray of natural light in the place. I've never been a big fan of fancy salons like this. Halfway through an appointment, I'm ready to bolt—I get antsy sitting in one spot for too long.

"Name and phone number?" The girl looks up at me with her droopy brown eyes.

The question startles me. "My name?"

The girl rolls her eyes and waits.

"Jayne." I smile. "Austin. Jayne is spelled with a *y,* and Austin with an *i,* not an *e.*"

"Whatever," the girl says.

I give her my new cell number. Then she hands me a key with a number on it.

"The lounge is all the way to the back, through the metal doors. There are robes and a locker to store your clothes. Felix will meet you outside the lounge."

Felix is a dream. He's short, tightly built, with a to-die-for olive complexion, and a white toothy smile that would make George Clooney jealous. He is wearing a perfectly fitted pair of Rock & Republic jeans, a black Royal Underground shirt with leather cuffs, and black Doc Martens. His bedside manner, for lack of a better way of putting it, should be packaged and sold. He almost makes me forget the serious situation I'm in.

The only reason Felix is available is because, and I kid you not, Oprah had to fly back to Chicago for an emergency meeting with former president Obama and canceled at the last minute.

"I promised Oprah I wouldn't tell a soul. Our secret." Felix winks as he turns the imaginary key on his lips and tosses it away.

I'm sitting in a gray leather barber-type chair in front of a big mirror, draped in a steel-gray, crisply laundered smock. Felix is studying me. He knits his brows knit together and folds his arms across his chest. He's holding a comb in one hand, and scissors in the other. He asks me a bunch of questions about my job, recreational activities, and family.

"Brain surgeon?" he says. "Hmm. Serious job. You need a serious cut and color. A blonde with two inches of regrowth isn't going to take a scalpel to my head. No way."

Felix lifts up a lock of my hair and studies the texture. Then he probes my roots with a rat-tailed comb. He steps back and turns my chair to face him.

"You look familiar. Been here before?"

"First time." I look straight ahead. "Everyone thinks I look like someone they know. I must have a twin somewhere, right?"

"Okay, Jayne, here's what we're going to do. You're a beautiful woman." Felix takes my chin in his hand and turns my face from side to side. "You have perfect bone structure and fabulous skin. Beautiful blue eyes. This current...how should I say it...*look* does nothing for you. You are here in California, alone. Single. Doctor. All of your family is in, where did you say? Vermont. You're at what hospital?"

"Saint Johns. Santa Monica."

"Right. Santa Monica. It's hip, it's happening. You need to

have a little fun. Instead, you work day after day. Fixing people's brains. No wonder you look like this." Felix steps back and smiles. "Not a problem. I'll fix you up." He claps, and a young man in a starched white shirt and black apron is by Felix's side in seconds. "Shampoo. Use my voodoo repairing formula."

Back at Felix's station, after a luxurious shampoo, sipping a double espresso, I'm waiting for a gap in his snipping to ask him about Bree.

Finally, he pauses to change scissors. I seize the opportunity.

"Can you believe what happened to Bree Martin?" I scoot up in the chair a little. "You must be devastated. Heard she was your client."

Felix looks around to make sure no one is paying attention to us.

"Not mine," he whispers, and points his scissors at another stylist. "Bernard's client. No one in this salon was devastated. Nada. Especially Bernard. *Chiquita*, she made his life hell."

I look over to see Bernard's hands tangled in the hair of a woman who looks surprisingly like Catherine Zeta-Jones.

"How?" I say. "I mean, Bree couldn't have been that bad? I'm, um, interested for purely clinical reasons."

Felix runs a wide-toothed comb through my hair, then tugs the ends on each side of my face to make sure the lengths are even. He waits until Bernard leads Zeta-Jones into the shampoo room, then leans down and rests his face next to mine like he's trying to get a better view of his handiwork.

In my ear, he says, "Swear to God you won't say anything to anyone."

I zip two fingers across my lips and raise my right hand.

"Swear to God, my lips are sealed."

"She was a bitch. God rest her soul. Extremely high maintenance. Missus Martin, she made Madonna look like Mother Teresa."

This is old news to me.

"I mean, how bad could she be?"

"Very bad." Felix walks over and grabs a rolling stool, sits

185

and scoots it across the floor, and comes to a stop next to me. "There's lots of talk. Some people here," he looks around at the other stylists and clients in the rear of the salon, "say the Mafia did it."

"What? You're joking, right?"

The Mafia is so far off my radar it's in another planet's atmosphere.

"The Mafia killed Bree?"

"I don't know specifically, but here's the deal. Bree paid Bernard in cash."

"So?" I turn in my seat to look at Felix.

I'm going to pay Felix in cash. Big deal.

I shift my position in the seat. I can feel myself getting impatient. This is going nowhere. It's a total wild goose chase.

"No one pays in cash anymore," Felix says so softly I almost don't hear him. "It's not just the cash. Bree pays us in dirty, greasy small bills. Wrinkled tens, twenties. Even five-dollar bills. She was here at least once or twice a week," he says, holding my gaze for a beat then rolling his eyes upward and shaking his head. "One time, I filled in for Bernard. Missus Martin, she came in for a blowout. She had one of those big, Luis Vuitton bowling bag purses. When she opened her bag to pay me, swear on my dear mother's grave, the purse was filled with money. Drug money."

"Seriously?" I think about the envelope of crisp hundred-dollar bills that my mother gave me. "You believe that?"

Felix shrugs. "I have my opinions. I—"

"When was the last time that you saw Bree?"

"The day before she passed." Felix rubs a glob of hair product between his palms, then smooths the goo into my hair before absentmindedly massaging it into my scalp. "She was witchy-bitchy that day. Much more than usual."

"What was that about?" I say, keeping my voice low, casual.

"She had some crazy meeting the next day. She was all hyper over it."

"On the day she was killed?"

Felix steps back from the chair and looks at me. "*Sí.*"

"Wow. You know everything." I feign gossipy interest. "Did she say who she was meeting?"

He scrutinizes my hair, leaning over to smooth a stray strand back into place.

"Aren't we curious."

"Aren't *you*?" I stare at Felix's surprised eyes in the reflection of the mirror. "Seriously. Of course, I'm interested. I'm a brain surgeon, for God's sake. I've devoted my life to studying people's, um...brains. My interest is purely professional. I mean, Bree died from a head injury."

Felix looks at me and blinks. "She did?"

"There's speculation, in the, um, medical community that she died from a blow on the head," I say in my most professional voice. "I also read something about it in the paper."

But I can't remember if Detectives Lynch and Lee publicly confirmed that Bree died from a blunt-force injury or not. I mean, that information might be the kind of thing that the police hold back. Maybe it's the killer's MO or something.

For the next twenty minutes, Felix blows all the curl out of my hair. He finally turns off the dryer and looks at me with a critical eye.

"Better," he says.

"Ever heard Bree talk about a guy named Mike Young? Or, um...Audrey?" I look up at Felix. "You think she was hooked up with either of them?"

Felix looks at me with a funny expression.

He frowns. "Are you really a doctor?"

God, I'm busted.

"Excuse me," I say in my most indignant voice. "That's insulting. It's the blonde hair, right? You're a blonde-o-phobe. I can't be a real doctor because I have blonde hair. Is that it? I've fought this kind of prejudice all of my life. I'm part of the Me Too movement, except it's the one fighting for equal rights for blondes."

"Shhh!" Felix darts his gaze at the dozen or more blondes

throughout the salon and hushes me with a finger to my lips. "Prejudice, *Chica*?" he whispers. "Me? Never."

"You said something about Bree meeting an old friend," I say. "No name, just an old friend. She must have mentioned a name."

Felix gives a non-committal shrug.

"What about Bree's husband? Think he killed her?"

"Doctor Martin?" Felix gently brushes my hair back away from my face and gives it a shot of hair spray. "Never. The man's a saint."

I pull away from Felix's fussing and look him square in the eye. I'm completely disgusted.

Did Audrey lie to me about Felix. She said he knew who killed Bree. Were Saintly and Alacata right about Audrey?

"So, Felix, what's your theory? Who murdered Bree? You can't be serious about the Mafia."

"Could be the Mafia, *Chiquita*." Felix twists a couple curls back into my hair. "But take my word for it—I think the ex-wife did it. But you didn't hear that from me."

CHAPTER 20

I LEAVE HEAD CASE FEELING LIKE A NEW WOMAN, but more confused than ever.

Bree, a Mafia drug dealer? Sounds incredibly farfetched, even though I'd seriously love for it to be true.

One reason it seems like such a crazy idea is because, if Bree is in the Mafia, then so are Geoff and Jack O'Brien. Maybe even Mike Young.

Does the Mafia even exist anymore?

Felix, and everyone else, think that the safe bet is on the ex-wife—me.

As I approach the Escape, I catch my reflection in the window. I hardly recognize myself. My long, wild blonde curls are cut short in a style that's somewhere between Victoria Beckham and Jennifer Aniston from her first couple seasons on *Friends*. My hair is silky smooth and the color of Jack Daniels whiskey.

Is this a brain surgeon's haircut?

I run my fingers through the glossy strands and take one more look at myself. Definitely. *Brain surgeon/hooker.* I like it.

I hop into the Escape, adjust the rearview mirror, and back out of the parking lot. Make a left turn, heading away from the beach, toward Kim's house, about twenty minutes from here.

It's 4:45. I have a little more than two hours before my meeting with Danny Starr.

My mind is spinning in a thousand directions. I need to collect my thoughts before I speak to Kim. I have to convince her that it's in her best interest to contact Lynch and Lee. The problem is that nobody can force Kim to do anything.

It's not because she's stubborn. Kim just needs to be in charge. If you don't play by Kim's rules, you don't play. Somehow, I have to make Kim think that it's her idea to go to the police, not mine.

Easier said than done.

After about four or five miles, I spot a Target, pull into the parking lot, and maneuver the Escape into an empty spot near the front of the store. After turning off the engine, I adjust the seat back to give me more room, then dig in my purse and pull out a pencil and my notebook.

Starting with a clean page, I write the date and time, then number the page from one to ten. Starting with one, I write: *Bree is not in the Mafia.* I continue down the page, finishing with number ten: *Kim needs to come clean.*

I reread my ten points.

Surrendering to common sense, I conclude that Bree isn't in the Mafia, but is possibly involved in some illegal activity that requires her to launder lots of cash. Maybe her clients at The Center tip her in cash, and she was trying to avoid paying taxes. That makes sense.

How much money are we talking about? Petty cash or big bucks? Do clients tip Geoff, too? Doubtful.

The Center is a multi-million-dollar operation. A lot of money passes through that business. Cash money?

What if Bree, Geoff, Jack, and Mike Young are all in on the laundering. Taxes are outrageously high in California. Personally, I hate paying taxes.

I think back to when Geoff and I were married. He gave me a monthly *allowance*, all in cash, and told me not to put it in the bank. I kept it in a drawer and never asked him why I had to do that. Silly me.

I rest my head against the seat and close my eyes for a second. Is paying for things in cash really a major crime? I open my eyes and pick up my pad. I write the word *CASH* and add a big question mark.

But where is the cash coming from? I underscore the question with a heavy dark line. I mean, as Felix said, nobody uses cash anymore. The Center's clients must pay by credit card, like they would at a hotel. I mean, Geoff makes a ton of money, but I don't remember his business generating a lot of cash-paying customers. At least, he never mentioned it.

Even if some of his customers are paying in cash, is it enough money to motivate Geoff and Bree to break the law?

On Thursday, the day before Bree is murdered, Felix overhears her telling Bernard that she has a meeting with a *friend* the next day—Friday.

Did Bree miss her appointment to meet her *friend* because she was dead? Is Bree's *friend* her killer? If Bree missed the appointment on the day she was murdered, wouldn't the *friend* have reported it to the police? Maybe she met with the friend. But wouldn't the friend have reported the meeting to the police?

I'm going in circles.

What if Bree's *friend* was innocent of the murder, but guilty of working with Bree in some kind of illegal business? The *friend* might not want to mention the meeting to the police.

On the evening of the murder, I saw Kim driving away from Hollywood Beach. I try to remember what time it was when I left my house, on my way to Target to pick up more wooden hangers and shoe cubbies to finish organizing my closet. I think it was around six. I make a note to dig out my receipt for the hangers and boxes to prove to Detective Lynch that I didn't make up the story about my closet.

I got back to Hollywood Beach around 6:30 or 7:00, which is around the same time I ran into Kim.

I wonder why I didn't see Kim's teacher friend. Or Jack or Bree, for that matter. Probably because I wasn't looking for them. I mean, for all I know, Jack drove right past me and waved. He was completely off my radar. That last time I saw Jack was at the police station, four days ago.

Truth is, I didn't see anyone on Hollywood Beach Road on Friday night but Kim. The others had already left. Except maybe Bree.

Okay, so sometime before or after Kim met with Sophia's teacher, she sees someone who looks like Jack O'Brien, who's with someone who looks like Bree, on the beach near my house. Did she see Jack and Bree while she was with her friend? Or from her car, when she was coming or going? I wonder if Jack and Bree saw Kim.

It's a lucky break for me that Kim opted to meet her friend on Hollywood Beach on Friday night. At least it's one witness who can place someone other than me at the scene of the crime.

Was Jack the so-called friend that Bree was meeting? I mean, it seems like an amazing coincidence that Jack would be sighted in my neighborhood on the same night that Bree was murdered, especially if Jack wasn't the friend that Bree was supposedly meeting.

I'm confusing myself. I cross out the last half of the question and move on.

Since I don't believe in coincidences, I assume that Jack is Bree's friend, and they plan to meet earlier in the evening to discuss what? Business? Her job? Jack's job? Their affair?

Maybe. Or maybe they broke up and were resuming their affair. They meet on Hollywood Beach because it's far enough away from Montecito not to arouse any suspicion if someone sees them together. That makes sense.

They part ways when it starts raining, and Bree falls victim to a random act of violence. I write, *Cold Cases,* and underline it a couple times. I need to research local unsolved crimes, if for no other reason than to check it off my list.

Could Bree have been involved in other criminal activities besides tax fraud? Was Mike Young a dirty cop covering up for Bree, or paid protection for Bree's operation?

It makes total sense that Mike would've risked his job for Bree. He was madly in love with her. But she dumped him! Could Mike, Bree's scorned lover, be in cahoots with Geoff and

Jack to get rid of Bree? I underscore the question.

Was Bree's other criminal activity selling drugs? Maybe she got back into hooking, like Audrey alluded to. Makes sense.

I didn't have a clue that Bree was a hooker in Las Vegas. Maybe Geoff didn't know either, and when he found out, he killed her.

No. Bree hooking and selling drugs seriously doesn't add up. I mean, under Geoff's brand, Bree operated one of Southern California's largest natural healing and supplement businesses. She had become the face of The Center. She was a celebrity in Santa Barbara. She and Geoff hob-knobbed with Santa Barbara's old-money families. Bree hooking and selling drugs like she did in Las Vegas doesn't fit.

Seriously, the company's mission is to attain perfect harmony and balance by ridding the body of toxic chemicals through exercise, supplementation, and chiropractic healing.

Geoff, a drug dealer? I don't think so.

Would Bree risk a prestigious, moneymaking career and prominent reputation in the community to sell drugs or work as a prostitute? I mean, where would she find the time?

Back to Friday night. Where was Geoff all this time?

According to the detectives, Geoff left for Las Vegas on Friday, on an early morning flight. The police also determined that the time of Bree's death was somewhere between 6:00 p.m., when she was last seen at The Center, and around 1:00 a.m., when the police found her body. Knowing Geoff, he made sure that countless people could vouch for his whereabouts on the day that Bree was murdered. But it doesn't make him innocent if he orchestrated her death.

I flip the page and write Mike Young's name at the top.

Mike was the first officer on the scene after I called 911. He told me he had a partner with him, but I never met him. Detectives Lynch and Lee obviously have no idea that Mike and Bree were lovers. If they knew, Mike Young would have probably been placed on leave, pending an investigation.

Mike Young is still on force, which must mean that

Detectives Lynch and Lee, like Danny said, aren't aware of Mike's connection with Bree.

I underscore it a couple times and look up from my pad to see families leaving Target. Kids dressed in soccer uniforms and play clothes, skipping along next to their parents, on their way home for dinner. It's a Norman Rockwell moment. Sort of. I wonder if I'll ever have another husband—or children.

I set the pencil down, shake out my hands, rub them together, and blow into my palms. I'm getting cold sitting here in the car. I pick up my cell and look at the time. It's twenty minutes after four. Time really flies when you're solving a crime.

I pick up my pencil and continue down the page.

Maybe I'm being naive. I mean, maybe Bree really was selling drugs or doing something behind Geoff's back. Bree worked as a hooker in her former life. Or at least that's what Audrey said. Maybe she also sold drugs. Maybe that's how Audrey is involved.

Old habits die hard.

When I think about it, it kind of makes sense. Geoff's weight-loss program is one of the biggest draws to his health center. Losing weight is hard. The success of Geoff's business depends on demonstrated results.

Maybe Bree was supplying her customers with illegal diet pills that she bought from Audrey. That could be a huge moneymaking business, and a perk to Geoff's supplement pharmacy sales. Geoff sells his *legal* weight-loss supplements that promise great results. But his pills are a sham. Geoff's diet supplements don't get any better results than if customers just ate less and exercised more. I know this for a fact, because I tried Geoff's stupid natural diet pills. *They don't work.*

Enter Bree. She sells Geoff's weight-loss supplements, but promises results only if taken with her *boost formula.* Bree's customers get amazing results. She seduces Mike Young to run interference for her with the police. I mean, I saw *The Godfather*—the Mafia always has police on its payroll.

Maybe Bree pays Mike Young with sex. Unfortunately,

Mike's so stupid he thinks the sex is Bree's demonstration of true love.

Geoff—the saint that everyone thinks he is—has no idea what's going on behind his back. He really believes his diet supplements are getting results. Maybe he reformulated them and thinks that has something to do with the uptick in new customers and sales.

When Geoff finds out what Bree is up to, he gets Jack O'Brien to murder her and dump her body in front of my house.

Mike Young feels betrayed by Bree, decides to help Geoff and Jack. Maybe he helps Jack move Bree's body or acts as the lookout guy.

I wonder if Kim saw his police car in the area? I write it down and underline.

When I call the police, Mike is the first responder, because Hollywood Beach is his beat. Geoff and Jack aren't expecting me to report the crime, but it doesn't really matter who reports finding Bree's body. Maybe they're hoping that nobody will report the murder until the next morning. Or days later, given how rainy and cold it's been. That way, Geoff will be well on his way to establishing his alibi in Las Vegas.

I quickly reread my notes. God, I think I've got the framework for how the murder went down. I mean, this is only speculation, but it sounds true. There are still a lot of gaps, but I think I've seriously cracked the case. All I need is Kim to confirm her story about seeing Jack on the beach, and the rest is just connecting the dots.

I can't think anymore. I need a break.

I spend the next half-hour picking up essentials from Target to tide me over until Detectives Lynch and Lee return my clothes. Two or three weeks, they said. But the truth is, I may never get them back. That's okay. I mean, less is more.

As I walk down the aisles, I feel the new me settling in. I don't need a lot of stuff anymore. But shopping has an incredibly calming effect on me. Seriously, that's why people call shopping *retail therapy*. I love walking through the shoe department at Neiman Marcus and Bloomingdale's. But my best therapy sessions happen walking the aisles at Target.

The idea to leave Geoff came to me in Target's housewares department.

I stop in front of a rack of black Mossimo sweaters, find my size, and move my cart to the jean section. I add a pair of black jeans, a cute wool plum car coat for $39.95, a moss-green pencil skirt, and a cute cashmere scarf in the same green as my skirt. Next, I stroll over to the shoe section and add a pair of leopard-print ballet flats, short black boots, and a pair of tall brown boots that will go with everything.

I grab a rolling overnight bag, a week's worth of undies, black and brown tights, a couple pairs of socks, two pairs of pj's, sundries, makeup from Boots, and a bottle of Pellegrino.

I'm set.

Before getting into the Escape, I dig in one of the plastic Target bags and take out the coat and scarf. I carefully remove the price tags and snuggle into the coat, one arm at a time, then wrap the scarf around my neck. I stash my other purchases in the overnight bag and place everything in the trunk.

Back inside the car, I scoot my seat forward, turn on the engine, and head out of the parking lot, toward Kim's house in Seabridge by the Beach, a few miles away.

Kim lives in a lovely white Cape-Cod–style home with a white picket fence and rose vines entwined in an arbor. The home is situated on an inlet on Harbor Island. She and her husband moved from a tiny cottage on the edge of Montecito, to this enormous house on the water, about the same time that I moved from Montecito to my grandmother's house on Hollywood Beach.

I park next to Kim's silver Range Rover on the street. Her husband Brad's white Tesla is parked in the driveway. I lock my car and head up the driveway, to the front door.

I press the doorbell. The chimes are loud enough to alert the entire neighborhood that I've arrived.

Sophia, Kim's eight-year-old daughter, answers the door.

When she sees me, her eyes show no reaction. She doesn't recognize me.

"Hi. May I help you?" she says, like a small adult dressed in a kid's soccer uniform.

"Sophia, it's me. Amanda."

"OMG!" Her eyes grow as big as saucers. "You look hot."

Hot? I give Sophia a hug. "Thanks. Is your mom home?"

Sophia leans into the staircase. "Mom! Amanda's here."

A few minutes later, Kim looks down from the top of the stairs. She's wearing her usual get-up: top-to-bottom Lululemon workout outfit, and Nikes. She hurries down and gives me a quizzical look, then turns to Sophia.

"Go upstairs and help your sister with her homework."

Kim eyes me but doesn't invite me in or comment on my new look, which is amazing because I've worn my hair the same way since sixth grade.

She looks awful. She seriously looks like she's dropped another five pounds.

"Hi," Kim says, drawing out *hi* as if there's an *e* at the end of the word—like, hieeee.

The look on her face tells me that I'm the last person on earth that she wants to see.

She gives me a weak hug, then pulls away and frowns. Her expression morphs from surprise to concern.

"You okay? Everybody at the gym is asking about you."

This is code for, *we're all gossiping about you and need more dirt.*

Kim keeps looking over her shoulder, to the top of the stairs. She's nervous about something.

"Is Brad home?" I look around to get a sense of who else is there.

I can hear Sophia and Lindsay upstairs fooling around.

"We really need to talk. Here or outside?"

"Shh!" Kim places a finger against her lips, looking frantic and irritated.

She grabs a jacket off a hook near the front door.

"Outside. Let's take a walk."

Kim eases the door shut behind us. She takes my arm and pulls me away from her house, toward a bridge that expands across the channel to shops and restaurants.

"I need to ask you about the night that you saw Jack O'Brien near my house," I say, as we walk away from her house. "Why Hollywood Beach to meet you-know-who? Just curious."

"I already told you everything." Kim stops on the street and looks at me.

"Why Hollywood Beach?"

Kim glares at me. "Is this an inquisition?"

"What is up with you?" I stare at Kim under the glare of the streetlight.

She looks sick.

"You've lost a lot of weight. Are you okay? Maybe you should see a doctor."

"Why? So, I can look like you?" Kim barks. "You don't care if you're fat."

I feel like I've been slapped. "Sorry I said anything. You look great. It's just that you've been acting kind of, um...different lately. I never see you anymore."

Kim turns and starts walking away from me, toward the neighborhood rec center.

"That's not my fault. Hey, it's you that went underground, not me."

I pick up my pace to keep up with her.

"So, on the night you saw Jack, were you in your car, coming or going? Or on foot on the beach? Did, um, Sophia's teacher see Jack?"

"You're always blaming me for everything," Kim stops and turns. She folds her arms across her chest and glares at me. "You're not perfect either, Amanda. Look at all the things you've done. You have DUIs. You're divorced. You don't speak to your father. I tell everyone that it's not your fault that Bree was murdered. I'm on your side. I'm the one who's sticking up for you."

"What the hell?" I'm seriously dumbstruck.

She's totally turning this whole situation back on me. I can't believe it.

I straighten up and pull my coat around me. I'm not going to let Kim bully me.

"Did Jack see you? Did you say anything to him?"

"No," Kim says in a flat voice. "No! How many ways do I need to say it? I'm not even sure it was Jack and Bree. I told you that. It could have been anyone. I was in the car, driving by. I thought I saw them through the empty space between the houses. It was dark. I wish I never told you anything."

"Please don't get upset," I say.

"I have nothing more to say. Stop harassing me."

"I promise to leave you alone after you go to the police and tell them exactly what you just told me. It'll take you five minutes. It's your civic duty to report what you saw. It's evidence."

So much for convincing Kim to think it's her idea to go to the police.

"I don't have to do anything." Kim turns her back on me and keeps walking. "Stop acting like little Miss Goodie-Goodie. If the tables were turned, you wouldn't say a word to the police."

"Well, um, that's because I've had really bad experiences with the police."

But Kim's right. A week ago, had I been in Kim's shoes, I might not have mentioned a word about seeing Jack. I can't imagine doing that now.

"I need you. It's a life-or-death situation. I could end up going to jail forever."

"Don't you have anyone else who can help you?"

"All I have is you and some woman I met in jail. Audrey."

At the mention of Audrey's name, Kim goes quiet. Under streetlight, her face looks ghostly white.

I dig in my purse to pull out Detective Lee's card, and hand it to Kim.

"You'll like him. He's cute. All you have to do is go in and make a statement."

"You've just wasted your time," Kim says, her voice smug, like when someone one-ups you. "I already spoke to the police. I told them that I was on Hollywood Beach, meeting with Sophia's teacher. He confirmed it. She needs extra help with math. I told them that the only person I saw when I was down there was you."

"You lied to me about seeing Jack and Bree?"

I can't believe what I'm hearing. Kim was my last hope. The tragic part about this charade is that I know Kim is lying. The cover-up is worse than the crime. Her lie not only confirms that she saw Jack and Bree, but she knows a lot more than she's willing to tell me.

"Why?" I say.

"I was trying to help you. I assumed it was Jack and Bree, okay? It was my imagination. Period."

"Come on, it's getting cold." I turn toward Kim's house and pick up my pace.

She lags behind me.

I'm tired of Kim and her antics. It's getting late, and I don't want to miss my meeting with Danny Starr.

Outside Kim's house, I stop and let her catch up.

I whisper, "Seriously, Kim, I wouldn't want to get involved either. But that's not a good thing. This whole experience has kind of changed me. I feel like I've grown up a lot. Going to the police was the responsible thing to do. The only thing that you should have done was tell the truth."

"Easy for you to say now." Kim zips up her Lululemon jacket and turns to look at me. "You don't have a choice."

"You're right. But a woman was murdered. You have an obligation to tell the truth."

Kim is silent.

I nod at Detective Lee's card in Kim's hand.

"Call him. It'll do your soul good, to be honest. So, help me God, if you don't go to the police and tell them what you saw Friday night, I'm going to tell them."

Kim's face is still white. Her mouth set in a hard line.

"You think they'll believe your story over mine?" she says.

"Maybe."

"Let me think about it."

I can see the wheels turning behind her eyes.

"I'll call you after carpool and Pilates," she says.

"No. I'll call you tomorrow, around eleven."

I take my new cell out of my coat pocket and look at the screen. It's twenty minutes after seven. I'm late for my appointment with Danny.

"You're not being fair." Kim folds her arms across her chest. "I have a family. All you have to worry about is you."

"Tell me about it," I say, trying to sound empathetic.

"Maybe we can meet at the gym," Kim says absently, her mind clearly on other things. "In the parking lot. Noon. Oh yeah, I changed gyms. I'm working out at The Center."

Geoff's club. "All the way in Montecito?"

It's like hearing fingernails drag across a chalkboard. I can't believe Kim's working out at my ex's gym. *Traitor*, I want to say, but bite my lower lip.

"Let's keep this between the two of us, okay?" she says. "This whole thing is embarrassing."

"Embarrassing? We've been friends forever. I'm not trying to embarrass you or be mean."

I can barely get the words out. Tears burn my eyes.

I gulp the cold air. "I don't think you understand how serious the situation is. Jack O'Brien might have seen *you*."

Kim looks around and shrugs. "So?"

"So, you could be his next victim."

CHAPTER 21

I ZOOM AWAY FROM KIM'S HOUSE, hitting a speed bump at forty miles per hour. The Escape scrapes its underside. Sparks fly. I'm almost a half-hour late for my meeting with Danny Starr.

Crap! I overshot the street leaving the neighborhood, slam on my brakes. The car skids into a spin on the damp street. I steer out of it. The car shudders to a stop. I yank the gear shift into reverse and back up. Step on the gas pedal and speed past one of Kim's neighbors, who gives me a *children-live-here* look that makes me cringe.

Don't panic. Seriously, chances are, Danny won't even be in the parking lot when I get there.

I ease my foot off the gas and slow the Escape to thirty miles per hour. He said he'd wait for me.

But when I think about it, I don't really need Danny. Not only that, I promised Saintly and Lynette I wouldn't speak to *anyone*, especially a reporter. Especially Danny. *Helping* me is another one of his stupid ploys to get me to talk.

Anyway, I need to focus on Kim. I'll pick her up at The Center and drag her, if necessary, to the police station. Until she turns over what she knows, I'm still in big trouble, and we both may be in the killer's crosshairs.

My cell rings. My heart skips. I grab my purse, pull it into my lap and fish around for my phone while trying to keep my eyes on the road.

"Hello?" I say in a tentative voice.

I make a quick left and head toward my house.

A voice I don't recognize says, "Jayne?"

"Sorry, you must have—"

"*Chiquita*, it's Felix. Your stylist. I've been trying to reach you." There's urgency in his voice.

The night is cold, clear, and dark. The road flanked by acres and acres of wide-open fields, and no streetlights.

"You scared me to death. I mean, I don't get many calls, um...on this phone."

"You asked about Audrey?" Felix whispers.

I push my foot down hard on the gas and career around a slow-moving Buick, just in time to make the yellow light before it turns red.

"Audrey!" I say. "Yes. Is she a customer?"

There's commotion in the background on the other end of the phone. Felix barks some orders in Spanish to someone at the salon.

"Listen, I couldn't talk before," Felix says in a voice so low I can barely hear him. "These walls have ears."

"Could you speak up a little?"

"*Un momento.*"

I hear a door shut, and the background noise disappears.

"Audrey Hernandez. Bree's assistant. My cousin. You mentioned her name."

"Bree's assistant? No fucking way!"

I can't believe I just said that. I never say the f-word. Hardly ever.

"Not officially," Felix says. "You know, behind the scenes, under the table."

Wow! Touchdown. Score one for the home team.

I speed through the intersection.

Audrey worked for Bree. Even if it was behind the scenes, that's the link. It makes sense. Bree and Audrey were Las Vegas hookers, and probably involved in all kinds of illegal stuff. So Audrey, Bree's assistant, brokers the illegal diet pills, and the rest is history. I have my hypothesis, but I need supporting facts.

Seriously, this could be my big break. But Audrey is a

common name. It could be anyone. I mean, maybe we're not talking about the same person.

"Is your Audrey tall, red hair, nose ring, pink rose tattoo?" I try to keep my voice calm.

"Diamond stud, *Chiquita*. She has mile-long legs. Gorgeous auburn hair. We had our tattoos done at the same time. My rose is red."

"She really does have beautiful hair." I turn right at the next street.

The parking lot is only a couple blocks away. If Danny's still there, then it's a sign, and I'll talk to him. If he's not there, I'll know he was on deadline and just using me for a scoop.

I hope he waited.

In my mind, I conjure up an image of Audrey sitting across from me in the jail cafeteria.

"Color is my thing, *Chiquita*," Felix says.

I can almost feel his smile radiating through the phone.

"Audrey is my client, too. I take care of my family."

"Audrey is in jail." I've reached the parking lot, but the night is so dark it's hard to tell if one of the half-dozen cars that are parked here is Danny's. "She's nobody's client right now."

"Not anymore," Felix whispers. "She's home." He pauses like he's waiting for someone to leave his station. "She needs help. She's been acting crazy since Bree's death. Scared to death. You're a head doctor. You can help her, no?"

"Help her?" *Oops.* "Right. I'm a doctor. When? Where?"

I don't see Danny's Jeep. He didn't wait for me. Typical. I mean, I didn't really expect him to. But disappointment weighs on me.

The good news is I don't see Mike Young's squad car either. That's a relief.

Felix says, "I'll text you her contact info. Be an angel. Go to her. Talk her out of the trees. You can write her a script, no?"

"Script?" I pull into the lot.

"Prescription. You know, *Chiquita*. Meds. Ativan, Valium, Xanax."

"No problemo!" I pull the Escape into a dark corner in the back of the lot, just like Danny told me to do. "Of course I can do that. That's why I became a doctor. To help people."

Felix messages me Audrey's contact info and promises not to give her a heads-up that I'm planning to visit her. I tell Felix that I'd like to surprise her. If she's jumpy and anxious, Audrey may be too afraid to see anyone.

"I'll run by Audrey's house first thing in the morning, after I, um...check on my other patients."

"Forgot to ask you," Felix says. "How do you know my cousin?"

"We met in jail," I say before I can check myself.

"*Como?* Jail?"

"I'm, um...a volunteer." I can't think. "A doctor volunteer. I visit inmates to, um...prescribe scripts. Xanax, and stuff like that, to the prisoners."

The other end of the line is quiet.

God, I'm such an idiot. I hope I didn't blow it with Felix. I mean, I'm obviously in crisis mode. In the trenches, on the forty-yard line, down, with goal to go—or however Saintly would say it. I can't sweat the small stuff. Jeez, I'm mixing metaphors and thinking in clichés. I'm losing it.

"*Muchas gracias*, Jayne." Felix's voice is choked with emotion. "I'll give you a deep condition treatment next time you come in. On me."

Before Felix can put two-and-two together, I say, "Why was Audrey in jail?"

"Drugs," Felix says, matter-of-factly. "Illegal drugs."

"Diet pills?"

"*Chiquita*, no. Crack. It's not her fault. Bad childhood."

"Bummer. Hey, I totally relate. I mean, seriously, Felix, crap happens."

Before signing off, I assure him once again that I'll check in on Audrey first thing in the morning.

I adjust the rearview mirror and peek at myself before getting out of the car. With the tip of my finger, I wipe off a little mascara that's smudged under my eyes and pinch my checks to raise the color in them.

Maybe Danny is late and will show up any second. Maybe I should give him a few more minutes. Maybe he had to file a story. Or maybe his car ran out of gas.

Seriously, who am I kidding? This isn't a date. I'm not being stood up. It was an appointment, and I was late—I mean really late—and he left. Can't blame him. I wouldn't wait for me, either.

Maybe I should just call him and tell him I'm here.

My stomach flutters. Do I have a crush on Danny Starr? Impossible. I push the thought out of my mind and get out of the car. Danny Starr and me? No way.

Once outside, I look around to make sure that nobody has followed me into the lot.

My chest heaves. I'm all alone. I feel like crying. My feelings about Danny are proof that I've completely lost perspective. I'm so needy, bordering on desperate.

Maybe I have Stockholm Syndrome or something. Post-traumatic stress disorder. It's possible, right?

So now what? Truth is, I can't stand out here forever. But what am I going to do? I could go to a hotel, or back to Saintly and Lynette's house. But I really don't want to face Lynette. I could throw caution to the wind and go home.

Not a good idea.

It's damp and cold. I'm freezing. I grab my purse and sling it over my shoulder and across my body, then close the car door quietly. I'm exhausted. Screw it, I'm going home.

I can't drive home because I don't have a parking sticker on the Escape. My car will get towed. I can't park in my garage because it's a staging area for my work. What am I going to do?

My house is only few blocks away. It's no big deal. One night back home by myself isn't going to hurt.

Using the trees and bushes along the perimeter of the lot as cover, I hurry away from my car, toward Hollywood Beach Road. Every step I take echoes in the quiet night.

Once on the street, I feel completely exposed. Streetlamps dot the road. I look over my shoulder. Nothing. I keep my eyes forward and my head down. I pick up my pace.

I cross the street and make a quick decision to take the beach instead of the road, just in case there are lingering reporters hiding out near my house.

When I reach the beach, I take off my shoes and jam them into my purse. My feet are numb from the cold, but I don't have far to go.

It's inky black out, which makes it hard to navigate through the dunes. If there's a moon, it's behind the clouds. It's darker than I've ever seen it out here. The homes in the distance are shadowy blotches, dark and uninhabited. On my right is the ocean, a black void that seems to go on forever.

God, I wish Danny had waited.

Did Bree walk this same path with Jack? If Kim's original story is true, then Jack could've killed Bree somewhere else and dumped her body here, after dark. But maybe Jack murdered Bree somewhere along the shore and dragged her along the sand until he neared my house, where he dumped her body, covered his tracks, and dropped my old umbrella in Jean's trash can.

I look around. The truth is, in the fall and winter months, Hollywood Beach is a perfect place to murder someone. The beach is completely deserted, and most of the homes are vacant.

Somewhere behind me, I hear a noise. I look around. Nothing. I'm imagining it.

Picking up my pace, I dig my toes into the sand as I jog in the direction of my house. My heart is pounding. *Keep going.* I'm only ten or so houses away.

Somewhere behind me, I hear footfalls. Someone is running between the dunes behind me. A chill travels up my spine. This is bad.

I turn to look behind me and lose my footing. Stumble and fall. I break my fall with my hands and roll on to my back. Push myself into a sitting position.

I see Mike Young walking toward me. I struggle to stand.

He's maybe twenty feet away. He looks angry. I could run. I mean, I know the area. He doesn't. If I can make it to my house, maybe I'll have time to call 911.

I decide that turning my back on Mike is a risk I can't take.

Mike trudges closer. He's dressed in dark clothes, not his green sheriff's uniform. He's wearing leather gloves.

"Stop!" I say loud enough to alert someone nearby.

But there's nobody nearby to alert.

I take a step back and lose my footing and fall. Fear consumes me.

Mike stops. He squints and looks confused. He seriously doesn't recognize me. His forehead puckers between his brows. His mouth slacks open. Slowly, his face changes. He knows it's me.

"Bitch," Mike spits out, and takes several wide strides forward. "Thought you and your boyfriend could make me look like a fucking idiot? Hope it was worth it."

"Boyfriend?"

I stand. Steady myself. My body is shaking. My legs feel weak. My heart is beating so hard I think I might be having some kind of attack.

"Danny Starr? No. He's not my boyfriend. He's an *LA Times* reporter. I told him all about you and Bree. He's probably writing about your affair as we speak."

Mike closes the distance between us. I'm in the grip of fear. I can't move.

"I told you to stop!" I scream. "I mean it. Detectives Lynch and Lee are on their way here. They know all about you, too."

"What?" Mike seethes, but he stops for a second. "Know about *me*? What's that supposed to mean? We work together."

I dig in my purse for the pepper spray. It's gone. I look down. I see that my shoes have fallen out of my bag. Not far away, a glint of metal peeks out of the sand.

I drop to my knees and dig my hand in the sand for the pepper spray.

"What the hell are you doing?" Mike lunges for me.

He grabs me by the hair and tries to yank me up.

I start to scream, but Mike jams his fist into my mouth. He pushes me to the ground and straddles me. I can hardly breathe. I grab a handful of sand and throw it in his face.

He lightens his grip. Sits up a little and wipes the sand out of his mouth and eyes. I flip over on my stomach and dig around in the sand for the pepper spray.

I feel something. It's the spray. I drag it out of the sand and hold it tight by my side.

"You're going to pay for that." Mike flips me onto my back.

He unzips my jeans and tries to pull them down with one hand. The weight of his body is suffocating me. I'm going to pass out.

"You're going to wish you never met me." Mike unzips his pants.

Mike Young is going to rape me! I turn the can of pepper spray in my hand until I feel the safety. I break off the lock with my thumb. Squeeze my eyes shut and spray at Mike's eyes.

He screams and sits up and covers his face with his hands.

With my other hand, I grab Mike's balls and squeeze. He groans and rolls off me. Writhes on the ground.

I struggle to stand, but Mike grabs the back of my coat and pulls me down. Tries to drag me toward him. I squirm as far away as I can while yanking my arms out of the jacket, one at a time.

I stand. Mike looks up at me, his face contorted with rage. His eyes are red and oozing. He's blinking hard to keep them open.

With all my might, I kick Mike Young in the face. His mouth spurts blood. He spits out a tooth. Gets to his knees, then lunges for me and pulls me down.

I point the pepper spray at Mike's and push down on the nozzle. Yank myself away from him, drag my purse into my stomach, stand, and run.

Mike screams behind me. I hear him moving, but I don't turn to look.

I run between two houses. I need to get off the beach and find help.

When I reach a gate, I jam down on the latch with the heel of my hand, but the gate doesn't budge. I notice the lock. God. Now what? I can't go back on the beach.

I drag a squatty clay planter near the gate close to the fence and step up on it. Grab the top of the fence and pull myself up. I hear footfalls on the beach behind me. I inch up the fence. Splinters tear into my bare feet.

I see Mike Young come around the corner and into the yard. He's forty feet from me. He sees me and breaks into a sprint.

I throw my purse over the gate, then drag one leg over the fence and struggle to get the other over. I don't look at Mike—I just hear him coming.

Finally, I pull my entire body over the gate and drop to the stone walkway on the other side of the fence. I'm on the street.

Mike crashes into the gate. It holds.

I don't wait around to see what happens. I grab my purse and run.

CHAPTER 22

I FEEL LIKE MARATHON RUNNER Abebe Bikila. Running like the wind. Or, um, with the wind...or something like that. *Free.* My feet have wings. Even though I'm barefoot, they don't hurt. I'm not afraid. I'm energized. Exhilarated. I just bested a two-hundred-pound brute who intended to hurt me.

Rape me. Maybe kill me.

I feel damn good. Empowered. Ready for anything.

I bolt down an alley, then turn onto a street that I think will take me back to my car. I pass a quiet, dark storefront that sells vacuum cleaners. I fly by a shoe repair business. A car whips by me, and I realize I'm on the main street that borders the beach and the harbor. Besides that, I must look like a crazy person on a rampage, I'm sure this is the street that Mike Young will take to leave Hollywood Beach and look for me.

I jump off the curb and cut across the street, and head down one of the ancillary roads that'll hopefully take me back to my car.

I can't go home. Mike may be waiting for me there.

I can't call the police. I don't trust them. The don't trust me. Mike's a cop. He has radio access to phone transmissions. This is his beat.

Plus, I'm the prime suspect in a murder investigation. I just assaulted a police officer. Left him with a missing tooth, black eyes, and swollen balls.

An image of Mike after I kicked him pops into my mind. There was blood all over his face. I could have broken his nose or seriously hurt him. Maybe he suffered a concussion. He could be on his way to the hospital.

He's not going to call for an ambulance. No way. He's not even going to report the incident. This is on the down low. Way down low.

But even if Mike does report it, who's going to believe my side of the story? Mike's a respected cop. One look at his bloodied face, and I'm screwed.

I dash left to another alley, close to a block of industrial-type buildings. I slow my pace. The parking lot's around here somewhere.

I slow down to a walk but keep moving. I'm starting to lose steam. I stop and bend over, bracing myself with my hands on my knees. I need a second to catch my breath. Even in the freezing night, I'm drenched with sweat.

My heart is still hammering against my chest. At the same time, I feel lightheaded. My feet are tingling. I'm shaking. I feel nauseated.

I stagger over to a nearby bush, bend at the waist, and throw up. I wipe my mouth with the back of my sleeve, take a deep breath, and keep walking.

I step into the middle of the road and look around. I'm totally alone. I'm on a service road. There are tall stalks of bamboo and sand dunes on one side of me, and miles of dark wetland on my other side.

I spin around. The industrial buildings I just left are black blotches in the distance. In front of me, miles away, I can see the twinkling lights of downtown Ventura.

I search for street signs. There are none. I'm all turned around.

Nothing looks familiar. I'm lost.

This is crazy! I've got to get out of here.

I'm calling Saintly. He and I will go meet Audrey together. That makes so much more sense than my crazy plan.

I thrust my hand in my purse and dig around for my phone. Push aside my wallet, keys, a lipstick, a pencil and notepad. Look in the purse pockets. The phone is gone. It's back on the beach, with my shoes and pepper spray, buried somewhere in the sand.

Tears slide down my checks, run over my lips and into my mouth. I rub my face and snivel. My chest heaves. I step over to the side of the road and sit in the dirt next to a large scrappy bush next to a deep ditch. I let out a noisy sob as the tears start to flow.

For no good reason, I think about my mom and dad, my brothers, and our weird, fractured family that looks totally normal on the outside, but is a complete train wreck on the inside. I actually miss my dad, even though we barely speak. What I really miss is my family as a unit. I don't think I'll ever get over my parent's divorce.

I touch my mouth. My fingers are bloody.

I think about my friendship with Kim, and how fake and disappointing it is. I imagine her at Geoff's gym palling around with Bree—at least, when Bree was alive—chatting it up with Geoff about optimal body fat ratios and where to get the best, most holistic boob job. I think about Saintly and Lynette and how much in love they are...

I hear tires crunching gravel. Headlights bobbing somewhere on the other side of the bamboo and shrubs. My heart slams against my chest. I clutch my purse and scramble down into the ditch and try make myself as small as possible. I slow my breath and listen.

A car rolls by. I'm paralyzed with fear. I close my eyes and wait...

And wait. Seriously, I have no clue how long I've been hiding out in the ditch. Long enough for Mike to give up looking for me and move along?

I listen for the slightest noise. Anything out of the ordinary, whatever that means. It's quiet now.

I take a few deep breaths, just like I was taught in the one yoga class I went to. Close my eyes and try to get into a Zen state. I feel a little better.

A sense of calm takes over. Okay, maybe it's not exactly

Nirvana, but I'm calm enough to get a grip and figure out where I am and where I left my car.

I push myself up from the ditch and look through the bamboo, to the road. Nothing. I'm getting the hell out of here. Now.

I take a moment to orient myself. The dunes are on one side of me. The fields and wetlands on the other. I stagger through the bamboo and peer toward the dunes. They're such an ordinary part of the Ventura landscape, I almost forget they exist.

If the dunes are on the west side where the ocean is, and the fields are east, then my car must be somewhere in the middle. It seems so obvious now. How could I have screwed up so badly?

I look up at the dark moonless sky to get a sense of what direction I should take. I mean, that's how people did it before someone invented GPS.

But even looking up in the sky and imagining a full moon and twinkling stars, I still have no clue how to navigate my way out of here, using some kind of celestial directional system. I just have to guess. Backtrack.

My car is somewhere nearby. Thank God Mike Young has no idea what kind of car I'm driving. He's looking for Saintly's black Range Rover.

Using the edge of the bamboo hedge as camouflage, I head toward the water and Hollywood Beach. I hope.

Half an hour later, I'm back on Hollywood Beach. I see that the hotels and public parking lot is in the close distance.

Not far away, I see the Ford Escape. It's not the only car in the lot. There are a half-dozen cars now. There are probably press on the lookout for me, but I don't care. If Mike didn't recognize me at first, the press won't either.

On the beach, a bunch of teenagers are congregating around a sputtering campfire. Could one of the cars be Mike Young's?

Before leaving the protection of the bamboo and tall shrubs, I search the area for Mike Young. I don't even know what I'm looking for. His sheriff's vehicle in the lot. He could be hiding out somewhere.

I can't stand here shivering all night. I dig in my purse for the keys and hold them in my fist. Then I say a silent prayer.

Without looking around again, I dash to my car and press the key fob. Open the door, jump in, press the lock button, jam down on the brake, and press the ignition button.

The sound of the engine revving is like hearing Handel's *Messiah*. Hallelujah!

I put the car in drive, make one wide turn, and leave the lot.

To hell with everything. I'm going to the Four Seasons Biltmore Hotel in Santa Barbara. I'm going to take a long, hot bath, then call room service. Thank God I left my overnighter in my car. At least I have new PJs, a toothbrush, and change of clothes. After breakfast in my room, I'll arrange for a massage and a mani-pedi. After that, I'll call Kim and meet with Audrey.

Once I'm a few blocks off Hollywood Beach, I take a look in the rearview mirror to change lanes and notice that a black SUV-style car is following me. *Perfect.* I swear I'm living proof that Murphy's Law is as real as Newton's Law.

I speed up and change lanes. The car is on my rear. The glare of the headlights makes it impossible to see who's driving, or the make of the car. Damn it.

Thing is, I'm not afraid. I'm in my car. The doors are locked. I have a full tank of gas. I mean, if it's Mike Young, bring him on. I'll just drive to the Biltmore and let the valets deal with him. I'm going to be okay.

But I'm not okay. My hands are shaking.

I step down hard on the gas, and the Escape shoots forward. I'm going eighty-five in a forty-five-mile-an-hour zone. The car behind me matches my speed. God, what should I do? Maybe I shouldn't get on the freeway. Maybe I should just drive into downtown and stop my car as soon as I see people and scream for help.

If it's Mike Young, what's he going to do? Shoot me? Beat me up? Kidnap me? Arrest me. There'll be witnesses.

I press down on the gas and swerve around an SUV and cross the double yellow lines. Oncoming headlights blind me before I jerk the steering wheel and merge back into my lane. I could be arrested for driving like a maniac. Not a good idea.

I slow to a normal speed. My hands are so sweaty I can barely grip the steering wheel. I wipe my palms on my filthy jeans and ease up on the gas.

I realize that the car behind me isn't just tailing me, its honking its horn. Maybe it's not Mike Young, after all. Maybe it's just a person on the road who notices that there's something wrong with my car.

I let my foot off the gas a little, slow down, and start moving toward the shoulder so the car can pass me. I look in the side mirror. The car's coming up fast alongside me. I move the Escape onto the shoulder. The car is right next to me.

It's Danny Starr in his black Jeep. He's motioning to me to get off the road.

I pull my car into a twenty-four-hour Walgreens and step down on the brake. My car comes to a sudden stop. Danny pulls his Jeep in front of me and parks. He gets out and moves toward me. I push the window button and the glass slides down.

I feel an overwhelming swell of emotion. But I don't know whether I'm overjoyed to see Danny, or angry that he didn't wait for me. I mean, if he had stuck it out a little bit longer in the parking lot, none the stuff with Mike Young would've happened.

My heart rate goes up. I look out the window to see Danny heading toward my car. I'm seriously overjoyed to see him.

I open the car door and step outside in my bare feet. Danny steps in front of me. He's quiet, but the look on his face scares me. He's stricken.

Oh my God. Something bad has happened.

My hand goes to my mouth, then clutches his jacket sleeve. "What?" I can barely get the word out.

Danny takes off his jacket and wraps it around me. He pulls me close to his chest and wraps his arms around me. I lay my head down on his shoulder. I feel his heart beat next to mine.

He pulls away and looks at me. His eyes are full of pain and worry.

"Everything is fine." Danny strokes my back.

He takes my chin in his hand and turns my face up toward his.

"Except you. Who did this to you?"

"I'm okay. Seriously," I say. "How'd you find me?"

"I'll tell you later. Here, put this on." Danny takes one of my arms and slips it into the sleeve of his jacket.

He wraps it around my back and guides my other arm into the sleeve.

"You need to go a hospital. We can leave your car here overnight. Pick it up in the morning."

"No!" I picture Mike Young waiting in the ER, with a missing tooth and bloody nose. "I know I look like death, but I'm okay. Honestly. I'm staying at a hotel tonight. I, um, have a reservation. I need to go."

"We can't stand out here in the cold and argue." Danny takes my hands in his and rubs warmth into them.

His voice is strong but reassuring.

"You're freezing. You're gonna get sick. Come with me. I'll drive you wherever you want to go. You shouldn't be behind the wheel of a car right now."

I'm so tempted to go with him, I almost ache inside. I want someone else to take over. The law of diminishing returns has set in. I want to surrender to the moment, but I can't.

"I have an appointment in the morning," I say.

"I'll bring you back to your car first thing tomorrow. Promise." Danny touches my cheek with his warm hand and brushes aside one of the short strands of hair that Felix styled. "Please, Amanda. Let's get out of here."

CHAPTER 23

I HAVE NO IDEA HOW LONG IT TAKES DANNY to drive from Walgreens to the hills above downtown Ventura. He's quiet during the ride.

My mind whirls. Should I tell Danny about Mike Young? Should I report my assault to Lynch and Lee? Tell them what Mike Young did to me—or attempted to do to me?

Will they believe me? Doubtful. Let's face it, I've lied to them more times than I can count. Why should anyone believe me, especially Lynch and Lee?

Now that I think about it, reporting Mike could actually hurt me. He might have tried to kill me tonight because he believes I had something to do with Bree's death—which is exactly what Lynch and Lee believe.

But maybe Mike had other reasons for attacking me. Maybe Mike murdered Bree, and he wanted to silence me because I know about his affair with her. God, I'm so confused.

But if I don't report Mike, he's free to come after me. He will. I know it. I'm seriously screwed, whether I report him or not.

Saintly. I need to call him. I really do need his help.

I look over at Danny. His gaze drifts from the road over to me. He gives me a half-smile and shakes his head like he doesn't know what to do with me. He reaches for my hand and gives it a reassuring squeeze. A shiver goes up my spine. In a good way.

I think I'm starting to like him. Is that possible? He's so irritating. A couple days ago, I couldn't stand the sight of him.

It starts to rain. Heavy drops hit the windshield and beat a soft rhythm on the car's roof. Danny shifts into low gear as he winds up the road. The action forces me back into my seat and sets off aches and pains everywhere in my body.

I lean my head back on the seat and let my thoughts wander to Kim, Audrey, Geoff, Jack, and Mike Young.

Kim. Audrey. Geoff. Jack. Mike Young. What do they all have in common?

They're witnesses. They have information that could turn the tide of this investigation. But no one is talking. Why? Are they somehow working together? Farfetched. Impossible. Kim involved in Bree's murder. Conspiring with Geoff and Jack. No way. I seriously don't believe in conspiracies.

"Occam's razor," I blurt out, and turn to Danny.

Pain jets through my shoulders and neck. My head starts to throb again.

"Um, right?" I say.

Danny peers into the rearview mirror and frowns.

"Where are you going with this?"

The side mirror shows headlights bouncing off the wet asphalt a couple hundred feet behind us. Is someone following us?

"You know, the simple solution." My voice squeaks.

I look in the mirror again. The car is gone. A sigh escapes my lips. I take a deep breath and press my fingers to my forehead to ease the onset of a pounding headache. I look at my fingers. They're tinged with blood. My nails are broken. The rubbing opened one of the scratches on my forehead.

"There is nothing simple about you, Amanda. Or your situation."

"I know."

Thing is, I'm ignoring the obvious. Kim is the tipping point. She can place Jack O'Brien, or someone who looked like him, at the scene of the crime. I had a reason for being on Hollywood Beach. I live there. I called the police. No one was expecting me to do that. I should have been sound asleep by midnight, when all of this probably came down.

What was Audrey's role in Bree's murder?

I start to say something, but Danny looks over at me and pats my leg.

"Hold your thoughts. We're almost home."

I lean my head back and stifle a yawn. I can barely think. I remind myself that this will all be over soon. When Lynch and Lee finally arrest Bree's murderer, they'll apologize for putting me through hell. Lynette will serialize my story. Danny will write a blistering exposé about police brutality and their rush to judgment. Saintly will sue everyone—the Ventura County Sheriff's Department, the State of California, Geoff, all the major networks. I'll get an amazing settlement and move a million miles away from here, to some other beautiful place.

Case closed.

But the case won't be closed until I speak to Audrey, and Kim shares what she knows with Lynch and Lee. Until then, I'm going to have to lay low. As Saintly said, I need evidence, not just talk. Kim, and maybe Audrey, may be my only hope.

Saintly will know—

"We're here," Danny says.

I jump at the sound of his voice. Sit straight. Look around. We pull into the driveway of a post-and-beam house that looks more like glass than post-and-beam. A blanket of clouds floats north to reveal a half-moon and a scattering of stars. Frost covers the lawn in front of Danny's house.

I scoot over and reach for the door.

Danny gently holds my arm. "Don't move."

He rushes around to my side and opens the door. Takes my arm and helps me out of the car. I step onto the driveway. The flagstone feels like ice, burning and stinging my bare feet. Every part of my body aches, even the tips of my fingers. I swear my hair hurts when I move my head.

"Lean on me." Danny reaches over the seat and grabs my purse and overnight bag.

He moves his arm around my waist and guides me across a patch of grass, to the stone walkway. Native plants flank the pathway that stops at the front door of his house.

"Thanks." I'm savoring the feeling of Danny's warm body so close to mine.

Inside the house, I catch my reflection in a mirror behind the dining room table. My $400 haircut is one big knot. My face is sickly white and marked with dirt and scratches. My lips are swollen and cut. I quickly turn away.

Danny leads me to the couch and helps me sit. He grabs a furry throw and wraps it around me, then tucks it under my feet. He turns on a lamp next to the couch. Soft light fills the room with deep shadows. He goes to the fireplace, grabs a pack of matches and a rolled-up newspaper. Strikes the match against the stone hearth and lights the paper, then shoves it between the logs. The fire comes to life.

"I'll be right back," he says.

I close my eyes. I feel myself drifting off.

Danny nudges me. I open my eyes to see him standing above me, holding a tray laden with a tea kettle, mugs, bottled water, and a bag of cookies. There's also what looks like a first aid kit on the tray.

I suppress another yawn and rearrange myself on the sofa. The pain in my body has dulled to a constant throb. I smile up at him, which starts my bottom lip bleeding again. I wipe my mouth with my dirty sleeve.

Danny sets the tray down on the coffee table, then sits on the couch next to me. He takes a paper napkin and wets it with the bottled water, then gently wipes the blood off my lip.

"I'm a coffee drinker myself. But this stuff, topped off with a little brandy, will warm you right up," he whispers, as if a louder voice might further injure me. "Actually, Meredith, our health editor, swears by it."

"Hold the brandy." I've seriously sworn off alcohol for life.

"Here, take these. Ibuprofen." He drops a couple capsules into my palm and hands me the bottled water.

"Thanks."

Danny's no more than a foot away. I want him to move

closer, wrap his arms around me, hold me close. I push the thought out of my mind.

Danny lifts his Dopp Kit off the tray and takes out a small bottle of peroxide and some cotton balls.

"These scratches could get infected." He brushes the hair away from my face and secures it behind my ear. "This is going to hurt me more than it's going to hurt you." He dabs the cotton ball on cuts and scratches on my forehead.

"Ouch!" My eyes tear up from the peroxide, and I take Danny's hand away from my face. "That stings. What I'd really love is a hot bath."

"A few more seconds," Danny says.

While he's working on me, he explains that when I didn't show up for our meeting, he left the parking lot and went to get something to eat.

"I was only gone about twenty minutes. I came back and waited for you. I was looking for your black Range Rover. When I finally saw you, you took off like a bat out of hell in a white Ford. What happened to you?"

"I don't want to talk about it."

He sits back and looks at me. Cradles my chin in his hand and turns my face from side to side to make sure he didn't miss any scratches.

"You need to go to the hospital. Report this. If you don't, I will."

"No! Really. I'm okay." I pull away from him.

The action shoots pain through my body. I bite my lower lip and wait for the pain to fade.

"Please don't," I say.

"Talk to me, Amanda." Danny places the peroxide back into the Dopp Kit. "This is getting out of control."

I look at my bloodied hands. I don't know how to respond. Things *are* getting out of control, but I have a plan. I just can't tell Danny about it.

He zips up the Dopp Kit and hands me the mug.

"Drink your tea. Meredith claims it's a cure-all."

Meredith? A picture of Meredith Armstrong pops in my mind. She worked at the *Tribune* when I started there. I heard she left for a better job. Maybe Lynette fired her. I remember her jet-black hair, ostrich-long legs, and beautiful smile.

"Meredith Armstrong? Right? Tall, kind of heavy, about our age, wears big flowy clothes?" I sip the tea and shiver.

It tastes like poison, but it warms me right down to my toes.

"She used to write a New Age column for the *Tribune*," I say. "I know her. We worked out at the same gym."

Geoff's gym. I wonder if Danny's dating Meredith. My stomach churns. I take another sip from the mug. It's green tea with a hint of honey, lemon, and something else. The hot liquid courses through my body. The effect is seriously medicinal.

"Must be a different Meredith Armstrong." Danny brushes a loose strand of hair off my forehead and studies my face. His brows knit together. "She worked at the *Tribune,* but she isn't heavy. She's super fit. Listen, that doesn't really matter. I don't know how to say this, but...forget it."

Danny is silent.

"What?" I take another sip of tea.

My heart thumps against my chest. What is Danny trying to say? That Meredith is his girlfriend? Please don't let that be it. The last time a man said something like that to me, it was Geoff, when he confirmed that he and Bree were having an affair.

"Nothing," Danny says. "Really. Let's talk in the morning."

He stands, picks up the tray, and heads toward the kitchen.

He turns back and looks at me. "I'll get you some fresh towels. The bathroom's down the hall. The sheets on the bed in the extra room are clean, so don't worry. I'm pretty tidy, myself. Nothing compared to you, but I like everything in its place. I'll get you another blanket. It gets cold at night with all these windows."

"Wait. Come on. Tell me what you were going to say. You wanted to meet me—you had something you wanted to tell me? You said it was important. I mean, it's not like you want to take my picture or interview me, right?"

Danny disappears into the kitchen, then walks back into the room. He sits back down on the couch and takes my hand in his. His face is serious.

"Well, yeah," he says. "Since you brought it up. The interview can wait until the morning, but I should get some shots of you now. Document what's happened to you."

"Shots? Like photographs? Of me? Now?" I pull my hand out of his.

I'm appalled. All of his kindness and attention are nothing more than ploys to score a scoop for the *Times*. He's been on the job this entire time. That's why he didn't insist on taking me to the hospital or calling the cops. It would have blown his chance for a front-page story.

I set the cup on the table. My chest feels like someone's stepping on it. Tears burn my eyes, but I quickly blink them back. I've totally misread every nice thing that Danny's done to help me. I feel like such a fool.

I stand up and fold the blanket.

"What are you doing?" Danny stands and takes the blanket out of my hand and tosses it on the couch.

"I'm leaving." I try to keep my voice steady and devoid of the anger and betrayal I'm feeling. "You're such a mercenary. I don't know what I was thinking. You're a reporter. I get it. I guess if I worked for the *LA Times*, I'd do the same thing. I mean, I can't really blame you. Can I use your phone to call an Uber?"

"Let me finish what I was going to say." Danny takes me by my shoulders. "Would you just sit down and hear me out? It's important."

I stare at him. Before I can stop myself, I say, in a voice that sounds shrill in the quiet room, "Just tell me the truth. Is Meredith your girlfriend?"

"Take it easy. She's a friend." Danny narrows his eyes at me. "We hung out a couple times. Big deal. What does Meredith have to do with anything."

"Nothing." My voice is stiff.

Hung out is probably code for *hook up*. Perfect. He's hooking up with Meredith, the heavy girl who's now model-thin. She works out at Geoff's gym. She's probably enrolled in one of his stupid weight-loss programs.

"Hey," I say, as Danny starts to walk out of the room.

He stops and turns back to me.

"So, what was so important that you wanted to tell me? Or was it just some BS story you made up to get me to talk to you?"

"Can you please sit down?" he says.

"No. I like standing." I pull my arms out of Danny's jacket and set it on the couch.

"You're stubborn."

I want to fire back that he's annoying but fold my arms across my chest and stare at him.

"Fine," he says. "There is some crazy shit going down. You were right about one thing. Those women who were raped around here? There were two women, not one. The attacks occurred about eight months ago on Silver Strand Beach. The one next to Hollywood Beach. Based on DNA found on the bodies, they were connected. The perp is still at large. I wish I knew more, but I've hit a wall."

I wasn't imagining the story I read about the women who were raped around here.

"I also know that you need to stay out of Michael Young's way. He works security for your ex. I don't know why yet, but he's out to get you."

A chill runs up my spin. I remember Mike winking at Geoff at the police station. He tried to kill me tonight. Did Geoff put him up to it?

"Who told you that?" I say.

Danny steps closer to me. Our eyes lock. He's hesitating to tell me.

"Listen to me. You need to watch out for him."

"Thanks for the heads up," I say.

He won't reveal his source. He doesn't trust me.

"But it's too little, too late," I say.

"I'm trying to help you."

It hits me. Maybe Meredith is the one who told Danny about Mike working for Geoff. Maybe Meredith is in Geoff's weight-loss program, and she met Mike when he worked security at one of The Center's events.

Maybe Meredith uses Bree's illegal diet pills—if that's what Bree was doing. That's why she's so thin. Which makes me think of Kim. Maybe Kim is enrolled in Geoff's program, too. I mean, I've never seen her look so thin. Or so sick.

Maybe Meredith and Kim joined Geoff's gym for the diet pills. I have no idea what it all means. Is it possible that Kim's involved in Bree's death? I saw Kim on the beach the night Bree was murdered. I didn't see Jack. Maybe Kim lied to me about seeing Jack on the beach. If Kim had anything to do with Bree's murder, she would have never gone to the police.

For all I know, Bree had nothing to do with selling illegal diet pills, and I'm thinking about a different Meredith. Kim couldn't possibly be involved in any of this. I'm losing it.

I need to figure out if there's even a shred of truth to my harebrained theory.

I need to get my hands on a list of customers enrolled in Geoff's weight-loss program. I'll call everyone on the list and ask them about their results. The only way to get a list is to sneak into the admin office at The Center. *Tonight.*

I look at Danny's watch. It's a few minutes after nine. The Center closes at midnight. I've got to get a move on.

"Could you drive me to my car? I need to go."

Danny walks over to me and tries to take my hand.

"Come on. Don't be like this. It's late. Stay. Please. I want your picture to document what's happened to you, not to use it in the paper."

"Right." I try to bite back the sarcasm. "Changing subjects. Did Meredith ever tell you how she lost so much weight?"

"We're back on Meredith?" Danny says. "I don't get you. You're the subject of a murder investigation, and all you're interested in is how a girl I dated lost weight?"

I scan the room for my overnighter and my purse. It's on the floor next to the front door. I walk over and dig a pair of socks and the short boots out of the overnighter. Rip the tags off the socks and toss them in the bag. Slip the socks on my freezing feet and relish the instant warmth. Pull on the boots and yank up the zippers.

"It seems like she lost a lot of weight really fast."

Danny's brows knit together, and his mouth opens like he wants to say something but can't find the words.

He shakes his head. "Meredith has nothing to do with any of this. This is about you. You need help."

"Thanks for the advice," I say.

I don't expect Danny to know anything about Meredith's weight loss. I mean, I'd rather die than talk to a guy about my weight.

Maybe Bree was selling illegal diet pills behind Geoff's back. Maybe that's why she got away with it for as long as she did.

I pick up my purse and excuse myself to go to the bathroom. The mirror reflects someone I barely recognize, and not because of my new haircut and color.

I pull a couple tissues from the dispenser on the sink and soak them under the faucet.

I do need help, but not from Danny. And certainly not from the cops.

I gently wipe away traces of blood from my mouth and cheeks and toss the tissue into the toilet and flush. I dig into my purse for my powder and lipstick. Quickly apply it and look in the mirror. Marginally better. I reach back in my purse for a comb. It's gone. It must have fallen out at the beach. I pull open a drawer under the sink and find a brush with a pink plastic handle, obviously left behind by a former or current girlfriend.

Why does the idea of Danny having a girlfriend bug me so much? I don't even know Danny Starr. I feel like such an idiot.

When all of this mess is behind me, I'm going back into therapy.

I leave the bathroom and walk down the short hall to the great room, where Danny is standing near the couch, waiting for me. I sling my purse over my shoulder and lift my overnighter.

"Thanks for everything. I really need to go."

Looking a little shaken, Danny goes into the kitchen and grabs his keys from the kitchen table, then walks back into the living room and takes my hand.

"You're wrong about me. I think you should calm down and think about what I've told you. It's important."

I'm barely listening to Danny.

I head for the door. I need to get out of here and back to my car. If Danny won't take me, I'll walk. I mean, how long can it take me to get to my car? It's all downhill from here.

"Come on. I'll drive you." Danny's on my heels.

He takes my arm and turns me toward him. His fingers bite into my shoulders. He looks like he wants to kiss me or slap me. His eyes search mine.

"You're going from the frying pan to the fire. Be careful."

CHAPTER 24

INSIDE THE ESCAPE, I FASTEN MY SEATBELT, press on the ignition, and crank up the heater. It's 9:15 p.m. Geoff's center closes in a few hours. I don't have a lot of time.

I remind myself that everything takes longer than you think it will.

I have to sneak into Geoff's office, steal some files, check into the Four Seasons Biltmore, get a good night's sleep, make phone calls in the morning, meet with Audrey, then swing by and pick up Kim so she can meet with Detectives Lynch and Lee and tell them what she knows.

This whole nightmare will be over soon.

I'm feeling a little more focused and less shaky than I did before I left Danny's house. The ibuprofen he gave me is kicking in. My head has finally stopped throbbing. I'm feeling almost normal. I'm wide awake and ready to execute my plan.

I yank the car in gear and roll out of the Walgreen's parking lot. I look in the rearview mirror and see Danny sitting in his car. I turn the corner, heading toward the freeway. I look in the mirror again, and he's gone.

My well-being fades. I've never felt so lonely in my life.

It takes me less than thirty minutes to drive to Montecito. I can't stop thinking about Danny and how stupid I always act when I'm around him. I mean, I can't believe I asked him if Meredith was his girlfriend. Dumb.

He looked at me like I was crazy. Even worse, I can't believe how stupid I was to believe, even for a minute, that he actually cared about me. That he sincerely wanted to help me. I swear, the events of the last few days have been a complete setback.

Danny wanted a scoop. He wanted to take my picture. I fell for it. God, I'm such a dope.

But I can't discount his warning about Mike Young. He works for Geoff! I knew they were somehow connected. I have to figure out how deep that connection is.

It's one thing to work part-time security at The Center. It's another thing to run interference for Geoff's illegal activities, if that's what he was doing.

Did Geoff pay Mike to kill Bree and attack me? Kill me?

I exit the freeway at San Ysidro Ranch Road and follow the street over the 101 Freeway, to South Jameson Lane. In the distance, I can see Geoff's new wellness center, set in the location of the old Miramar Hotel, an oceanfront Montecito landmark. He built the new Center building after we divorced. I've never been here.

The property stood vacant for years until Geoff bought it. With the help of some really high-paid lawyers and consultants, Geoff successfully argued that building his center would promote the public interest while creating a lucrative revenue stream for the city and county. As a trade-off to appease the California Coastal Commission, Geoff had to give up twenty acres of the one-hundred-acre parcel for public amenities, including a meditation garden, protected open space, and trails down to the beach. Truth is, Geoff probably paid off the Coastal Commission and county supervisors to win approval to build his center.

I turn toward the beach and guide the Ford slowly down Harmony Lane, which used to be Miramar Road. It's now a private lane marked with low-voltage lighting and symmetrically placed giant bamboo, plumeria, ginger, and palms. I round a bend, and Geoff's new facility looms in front of me. It's a far cry from his old wellness center, which had been housed in a 1960s medical building in the upper east section of Santa Barbara.

The new building is an architectural blend of neo-pagoda

and Eichler. All very Zen, with its natural stone and smooth wood textures and walls of glass. It's beautiful.

I pull my car into the parking lot, driving past a white Mercedes GLC SUV with personalized license plates that read *BABE1*. Figures. There are only a few cars in the lot. Geoff's Range Rover is not one of them.

Is Geoff hurting for business? The place looks dead. To be fair, it's a Monday, just a few days before Christmas.

I drive as far back in the lot as I can until I see a small service road that leads me around to the rear of the building. I pull the Ford behind a tall bamboo hedge that conceals two large metal dumpsters. My favorite place to park.

Before getting out of the car, I angle the mirror above the dash toward me to make sure I won't scare anyone with the way I look. I finger-comb my hair to smooth out the knots, the way Felix did at the salon. I pull my sweater down over my hand and wipe away the smudges under my eyes with the edge of the fabric. I look back in the mirror. My lips are bruised, and the scratches look red, but I don't look hideous. I look like I'm healing from a facelift. Geoff's clients are right at home with that look. Perfect.

I open the car door and step out onto the gravel path. Crunch my way toward the front door of the building. The sound of my boots grate against the decomposed granite and remind me of my run-in with Mike Young. I cringe and look behind me. My heart pounds. I'm alone. But for how long? I start to sweat, even though it's freezing.

I pick up my pace. This might not have been the best idea in the world.

The path meanders and ends at a wide stone entry. Water bubbles over a massive ultra-modern fountain and snakes between flagstone, into a larger stream that disappears into the bamboo. I walk up to the front door and take a deep breath. *Stay calm. Walk in like you own the place. Grab the files and get out.*

Nobody's going to recognize me. I hope.

With a slight push, the massive chrome door whooshes

open to a softly lit lobby and reception area. The first thing I see is a discreetly placed sign that tells me the winter hours for the wellness center and spa: 8:00 a.m. to 8:00 p.m. The gym is open from 6:00 a.m. to 10:00 p.m.

I'm screwed.

I have maybe fifteen minutes to find the office, grab the files, and get out before The Center closes. What the hell am I going to do? I'm not going to make it! I don't even know where to go once I get inside the guts of the building.

I stand in the middle of the lobby and stare at the sign, paralyzed, willing it to change back to summer hours: 5:00 a.m. to midnight.

I hear footsteps heading toward me. I take a deep breath and continue moving toward the sound. *Act like a member and pray that nobody recognizes you.*

I mean, I used to be a member of Geoff's club.

I draw my shoulders back, hold my head up, and walk through the lobby, forcing a casual and confident rhythm to my stride.

Rob Lowe, the actor, my client—who I've never met—smiles and brushes past me on his way out. Everyone's going to be leaving. *Move!*

I head toward where Rob Lowe came from and find myself in a circular indoor atrium with several tall passageways feeding in and out of it. To my right, a passageway is marked with an inconspicuous brass sign that says *Wellness Center and Spa*. I head in the opposite direction.

"We're closing soon," a woman's soft voice says, from behind me.

I literally jump. Let out a yelp.

I look over my shoulder to see that the reception kiosk is tucked into an inconspicuous alcove and is staffed by a young woman.

"Are you doing okay?" The woman frowns at me.

She's wearing a low-cut, garish-red kimono with her name embroidered in yellow across a top pocket. *Jasmine.*

Geoff may have good taste in architectural design, but he has horrible taste in uniforms. Maybe Bree chose the attire.

"I'm good," I reply. "Forgot something. I'll be quick."

The girl shrugs.

I hurry out of the atrium and down a curved hallway. I have no idea where the hell I'm going. The office at Geoff's old center was in the back of the building. But this stupid place is all circles and intersecting walls. I'm lost.

I hear footsteps and hurry toward the sound. Two women carrying gym bags stroll toward me on their way out of the building. They probably came together in the Mercedes SUV, which means that the other car in the lot must belong to Jasmine.

"Hey." I nod at them.

"Hey," they say in unison.

They barely notice me.

I turn back toward them. "Excuse me. Where's the business office?"

The tall blonde points with her water bottle. "It's confusing, right? Keep walking. Follow the signs. It's up ahead on the left."

I give her a thumbs-up, then hurry along the hall until I find a sign that says *Employees Only*. This has got to be it.

I pull my sweater over my hand to prevent leaving fingerprints and grab the handle and pull down. Locked. On the left of the door is a card key swipe mechanism just like the ones used in hotels.

Damn it. Now what?

A female voice echoes through hidden speakers. "Closing in five minutes. Please exit The Center immediately. Thank you."

I run around the hall until I find what I'm looking for. A fire alarm. This is crazy. I have no idea what I'm doing! I think I saw this done in a movie.

I cover my hand with my sweater, then break the glass with the attached hammer and pull the release. An ear-shattering, pulsating horn breaks the silence.

I charge toward the reception area. I see the back of Jasmine's kimono as she runs out toward the front of the building. I hurry behind the reception kiosk and search for Jasmine's purse. I open a deep drawer. A brown leather satchel is sitting there. I empty her purse out on the counter. The key card's not there. *Crap.*

I open another drawer. Jasmine's wallet is there. I snap it open and find the key card in one of the slots opposite her driver's license. *Thank God.*

I pocket the card and drop the wallet back in the drawer. Hurry out of the kiosk and run down the long hallway toward the offices.

The alarm is deafening. I can barely think. I swipe the card and try the door. It opens to a brightly lit hall that feeds into one large room—which is less Zen and more office industrial. The key card must have triggered the lights. On the wall next to the door is a modern-looking wall switch with an *All Off* button. *Good.* I press the button and the room goes dark.

The room is divided into cubicles, each fitted with a metal desk, black office chair, computer, phone, and filing cabinet. It reminds me of a newer version of the inmate intake department of the Ventura County Jail.

I take one second to try to remember where the accountant in the Geoff's old office kept her desk. I close my eyes and imagine the room. *By a window.*

I run to the cubicles that face a bank of floor-to-ceiling windows. In the distance, in between the pulse of the screaming alarm, I hear a fire engine and a police car with the siren running. *Shit!*

I step back and look at the row of desks. There's a computer with tons of yellow Post-its stuck around the monitor. *Molly! The accountant!* She's been with Geoff since he started.

The sounds of the fire engine and police escort are getting closer. Geoff is probably right behind them.

Molly's cabinets are rows of wide metal doors that lift up and push back to reveal hundreds of files. I run my hand across them. This was a dumb idea. I'm going to get caught and thrown back in jail. I'll be there forever.

I take a deep breath to settle my pounding heart and try to focus. I run my gaze down the labeled sections. Nothing. I open another door and push it back. It's there: Zen 2 Slim, Geoff's weight-loss program.

I move my gaze to a section marked *active* and immediately look for the W's. I finger through the charts until I find what I'm looking for—*Wilder, Kimberly Barrett*. I open the file to the first page, where I see a before-and-after shots of Kim.

I'm blown away. In the *before* shot, Kim looks pretty good in her skimpy tank top and spandex leggings. Okay, maybe she could lose a few pounds. But *healthy* is the word that comes to mind when I look at her in the picture. Now, a year later, the *after* picture shows a smiling Kim looking like she hasn't eaten in a year. She is skin and bones. Her cheeks are shallow. Bones are showing on her chest.

In the *after* photo, taken a year later, Kim is wearing a black crop top and bun-hugging shorts that show off her stomach and hips. She's smiling, but dark circles smudge the skin under her eyes. She looks old. Her checks are sunken. Her stomach is flat, but her ribs and hip bones are showing in an unflattering way. She's at least fifteen pounds underweight.

No wonder Kim looks sick. She's suffering from malnutrition.

I close Kim's chart and jam it under my sweater. I go back to the A's. Flip through the tabs until I find *Armstrong, Meredith*. I pull out her file. God, this is so bad. I feel like I'm spying on Danny's private life by checking out the intimate details of a woman he's dating.

I peek at the first page. Meredith Armstrong stares back at me from her before-and-after pictures. Her transformation is truly remarkable. She could be the poster child for Geoff's products and Zen 2 Slim program.

I don't need to know any more about her. I slip the file back where it belongs and grab two or three files from each section of the alphabet. I straighten up the remaining charts, hoping Molly won't notice the missing files for a couple days, then shut the cabinet door.

I cram the files under my sweater, next to Kim's file, and tuck my sweater into my jeans. Stash Jasmine's key card in the back of one of Molly's desk drawers, just as I hear the wonk-wonk of the sirens as the fire truck and police cars pull into the parking lot.

I run to the office door that exits to the hall and open the door. The lights instantly come on. I press the *All Off*. The room goes dark. I leave the office and run back into the hallway. Search for a window, door, or exit sign.

The fire alarm goes silent. The quiet is terrifying. Because the quiet means the firemen are inside the building.

CHAPTER 25

I START DOWN THE HALLWAY, in the opposite direction of the reception room, praying I'm not going in circles. I imagine the firefighters and police officers closing in on me. Mike Young is leading the charge, with Geoff at his heels. I'm running out of time.

Finally, I see a sign marked *EXIT*. I pad as quietly as I can on the stone floors. Round another curved wall. The exit is no more than fifty feet away. In the close distance, I hear footsteps closing in behind me. There's nowhere to hide.

Forget trying to leave quietly. It's now or never.

I bolt to the door, my boots slapping the stone floor and echoing in the hallway. I shove the metal bar to release the lock, and step outside to a frigid blast of air. I take a second to let my eyes adjust to the inky night. I hurry past an employee table and chairs set on a thick concrete slab. Trip over the chair but catch myself and run for the parking lot, hoping I'm going the right way.

No more than a hundred feet away, I see headlights bounce off the trees and bushes as a couple cars speed down the road.

Crap. Reinforcements.

I hide behind a large banana tree to catch my breath, hugging the stolen files under my sweater. God, I hope there's another way out of here besides Harmony Lane.

I hurry through the lush foliage and try not to think about what will happen to me if I get caught. Christmas in jail is just the tip of the iceberg.

Up ahead, I see the bamboo hedge where I parked my car. *Run. Don't look back. Just get the hell out of here.*

Twigs snap under my boots as I dash toward my car. I dig in my pocket for my key, yank it out and push the fob. I accidentally hit the fob twice, and it chirps open and its headlights blink through the dense shrubbery. I might as well just have shined a strobe light on my location. If someone missed the sound when I opened the car, they're bound to see the flash of my headlights.

I step around the bamboo. My heart feels like it's in a vice. The Escape is sitting right where I left it. Honestly, what did I expect? The car sitting on the back of a tow truck?

Relief fills me. I look around. I'm alone. I open the car door, grab the steering wheel and pull myself into the seat. Reach under my sweater to pull out the files and cram them into the Target bag. I jam my foot down on the brake and push in the ignition. The engine roars to life. I cringe.

With the headlights off, I put the car in drive and creep in the opposite direction of Harmony Lane. I bump and weave around trees and shrubs until I see what looks like a street.

I made it. *Thank God.*

I ease the Ford over a tiny berm and hit the pavement with a thud. I turn on the headlights, fasten my seatbelt, and head up the street, toward the Four Seasons Biltmore. I heave a sigh of relief.

In just a few minutes, I enter the heart of Montecito. All the shops and restaurants on Coast Village Road are blanketed in white Christmas lights.

It's beautiful.

I make a left turn onto Olive Mill Road and head toward the beach. The Four Seasons is a few blocks away, across the street from Butterfly Beach.

There are no big hotel signs, just a small bronze placard that says *The Four Seasons Biltmore.* I maneuver the Escape into the circular drive and park in front of the valet sign. Like the town, the hotel is completely decked out with white twinkling lights and poinsettias everywhere. It looks like a fairyland.

For no good reason, I feel happy, almost giddy.

I get out of my car and grab my purse, Target bag, and overnighter. Before handing my keys over to the valet, I look behind me at the dark street, and beyond that, at the dark void that is the ocean. The only light comes from the festively lit oil platforms out at sea.

It dawns on me that Mike Young could have somehow followed me to Walgreens, watched me go with Danny, then waited near my car until Danny dropped me back off, and followed me to The Center. From there, he could have followed me here.

I'm psyching myself out. It's not logical. A chill wracks my body. *Nothing about this situation is logical.*

I walk back to the street and search the road for headlights. Nothing. I cross the street. Not a car or person in sight.

The valet hands me a parking stub. I dig into my bag for the envelope of hundred-dollar bills that my mother gave me, and hand him one.

"Could you keep my car parked up front just in case I have to, um, leave...quickly."

"Dude!" the valet says.

I take it as a yes.

I lug my stuff into the beautifully appointed lobby. I have no idea what time it is, but I'm the only guest checking in. Nobody is expecting me.

Like the front entry, the hotel's interior is all dolled up for the holidays. Swags of fragrant cedar garland adorn the fireplace mantle, gold ribbon and sparkly baubles drip from all the fixtures. A huge lighted Christmas tree is positioned in the middle of the lobby. "Have Yourself a Merry Little Christmas" is playing in the background. My favorite Christmas song. A huge lump forms in my throat.

Oh well. If I don't wind up in jail, next year will be different.

I love this place. Even though I've stayed here many times with Geoff when we were married and attended countless charity events with my friends—when I actually used to have friends—walking into the main lobby now is like seeing it for the first time. It's beautiful.

It was built in the 1920s, and through all its different owners, it has never lost its style and grace. I can't help myself from gaping at the twenty-foot ceilings with rough-hewn beams, terra cotta floors, original mosaic murals, and tall archways accented with art deco sconces and chandeliers.

At the front desk, two wide-eyed clerks dressed in unisex navy suits blink at me. They look nervous.

"Do you need help?" the woman says, in a British accent.

She doesn't say, *May I help you?* but *Do you need help?* I get the distinction.

"You, uh, have something in your hair," she says.

I feel around on the top of my head and pull out a twig with a couple leaves on it.

"Thanks." I smile.

The male clerk's hand is resting on the phone as if he's ready to call security. His name is Bob, which makes me think about a stupid, sick joke about a guy named Bob swimming in a pool or something, and I feel a completely inappropriate laughing jag coming on. I bite my lip hard.

"I'd like a room." I try to sound nonchalant.

I dig out my mother's Platinum card. "Two nights. Your best cottage, if it's available."

"Have you been a guest here before?" the woman clicks the keyboard and studies the screen in front of her.

The male clerk hands me a pen and a registration card to fill out. I give my mother's name, which thankfully is the same as mine—Amanda Elizabeth Beckwith—except my mother uses our middle name as her first name. I write down her address instead of my Hollywood Beach address to avoid any reference to the scene of the crime.

It's close to midnight when I finally walk into my $2,850-a-night oceanfront cottage, toting my overnighter and the Target bag laden with stolen Zen 2 Slim files.

After three attempts with the plastic card key, the green

light flashes, and I open the door. Inside the room, I feel the wall for the light and flip it on. The room brightens. I shut the door behind me and drop my purse and Target bag on the floor, then lock the door and engage the privacy chain.

The one-bedroom cottage is beautiful—worth every penny I paid. The good news is I have my whole life to pay my mother back for the money I borrowed.

Stripping off my clothes right where I'm standing, I kick them away and walk into the bathroom. I avoid looking at myself in the mirror. I just can't go there right now. I can deal with my cuts and bruises after my bath.

A bath sounds wonderful, but it's a luxury I can't afford right now. Instead, I turn on the shower to hot and stick my hand under the water until it warms up. After stepping in, I let the water run over my body, unwrap the soap and rub it between my hands. I slide the bar over my body until it's cover with luxurious suds. I'm in heaven. I feel around for the shampoo and lather it into my hair. Steam fills the room. I feel like I'm floating. My body is finally beginning to relax.

When my hands start to prune, I turn the faucet off and step out of the shower. Wrap a towel around my head, grab another one off the rack and gently dry myself off. Drop the towels in a wicker basket next to the sink, then take the white terry robe off the hanger on the back of the door and snuggle into it.

With the robe's sleeve, I wipe the condensation off the mirror and really look at myself for the first time since my encounter with Mike Young.

Before the mirror fogs up again, I see a dark bruise on my cheek, and tiny scrapes on my forehead. There's a scratch across my cheek. All healable. There won't be any scars. At least, not on my skin. I'm not in as bad shape as I expected.

My lips are Mick-Jagger-big, which probably means that Mike Young punched me in the mouth. I seriously don't remember much about what happened to me. There's a small cut on my chin that I didn't notice before. It's already starting to heal, but the cut looks deep enough to leave a scar. Oh well. It'll be one of the character marks that I can tell my grandchildren about someday. I hope.

I sweep my sleeve across the mirror again and pull my robe down to see if there's any damage to the rest of my upper body. My shoulders and arms are one expansive black-and-blue mark. It could be just my imagination, but I think I can actually see what looks like a handprint on my neck. I look down and see that a gash on my knee has opened. I grab a handful of facial tissue and place it over the cut. No wonder Danny wanted to take me to the hospital, and the hotel staff acted like they did.

I feel woozy. I need to sit down. Eat something.

I stagger into the sitting room and turn the fireplace on by pushing a button next to the hearth. It lights up immediately. I step over to the French doors and pull back the drapes. The doors lead out to a balcony that can't be more than fifteen feet above the ground, and completely exposed to the street that runs between the hotel and the ocean.

After closing the drapes, I turn my thoughts to the stolen files and pray that I'll find something in them that could mean that this nightmare will soon be over.

First, I need to eat. I find the list of hotel services in a book next to the phone on the desk and cuddle up with it in a big cushy chair next to the fireplace. I stretch my legs out on the ottoman.

A thick leather-bound folder reveals my dinner choices: lamb chops finished in a rosemary apricot reduction sauce, served with grilled asparagus and wild rice; wild sockeye salmon with grilled hearts of romaine; prime rib of beef with root vegetables and garlic mashed potatoes.

I close the book and set it back on the table. It all sounds delicious, but too much. I'll raid the mini bar instead.

I push myself out of the chair and walk over to the armoire that hides a small fridge stocked with an entire array of alcoholic beverages, soda, bottled water, and every gourmet snack imaginable. I eye an airport-sized vodka bottle and feel a nudge.

I mean, if ever I deserved a drink, now is certainly the time.

I feel another nudge. Reach for the bottle. One drink, that's all. It'll calm my nerves.

No way. I can't keep kidding myself that I can drink like a normal person. Alcohol is poison to me. Alcohol has been the basis for almost every bad decision I've ever made.

I grab a bottle of Pellegrino, and everything else that looks like food, and arrange it on the chair-side table. Olives, a small wedge of French brie, poppy seed water crackers, a small jar of almonds, and shortbread cookies—it's a feast.

For the next twenty minutes, I eat like I haven't had a meal in a year. I take a last swig from the Pellegrino bottle, then collect all the cans, jars, and wrappers and toss them into the trash.

I quickly change into my new PJs, then step over to the bed and fold back the spread. Walk back to where I dropped the Target bag and lug it to the bed and drop it. Sit on the soft white duvet, pick up the files and drop them on the bed. I fan the files out over comforter.

Search through the files until I find Kim's.

I start at the beginning, with the basics, scrutinizing every word, every date, every nuance. Nothing stands out. I seriously don't know what I'm looking for. I thought something would jump out at me. But there's nothing. I mean, all I really find are your average medical-type spreadsheets that show accounts payable, and whether or not Kim is current with her monthly fees.

I sink back into a pile of pillows and try to focus on what I'm looking for, like hard evidence.

Hard evidence of what?

I turn to the next page and start at the top, using my finger to make sure I don't miss a line. I reread each entry.

Kim signed up for Geoff's program right after Geoff and I split up about two years ago. I had no idea Kim had enrolled in Geoff's weight-loss program. She's never had a weight problem.

I mean, maybe when we were in middle school, but not in her adult life.

I'm amazed that she kept something like that from me for such a long time. I mean, if Kim really wanted to lose weight, why go to my ex? There are tons of great nutritionists in the area besides Geoff.

But Geoff is sort of a celebrity in our little town. It's kind of a status symbol to belong to his fitness center. I think Oprah started with Geoff but dropped out of his program when she didn't lose weight. Other celebs signed up, too, and Kim loves being in the middle of everything. She's kind of the go-to person for the latest scoop on everyone, from friends to celebrities.

The Center has become a rumor mill, so it makes sense that she joined The Center. But I'm surprised that she wouldn't have told me.

When Geoff dumped me, rumors spread like wildfire. I stopped speaking to everyone about my situation, except Kim. But cutting off my old friends didn't stop the gossip. All the stupid, he-said-she-said drama about my broken marriage finally got to me. So when my grandmother offered me her home, I decided to leave town and move to Hollywood Beach. The gossip only got worse.

That was then. This is now.

I page through Kim's file and stare at her picture. In the last year, Kim's gotten progressively thinner and more hyper. It's hard to be around her. Truth is, I haven't really spent time with her.

This is a wild goose chase. There's no damning evidence in Kim's file to prove my theory that Bree is selling illegal drugs.

I set Kim's file aside and organize the files in alphabetical order. Then I open Jane Andersen's file. I stare at the before-and-after shots on the second page. Unlike Kim, Jane really did need to lose weight.

She's a beautiful woman, even with the extra pounds. She looks healthy. But after twelve weeks in Zen 2 Slim, the transformation is stunning. Jane in her *before* photo is packing at least forty extra pounds, and wearing a loose-fitting, frumpy pair of faded pink sweats. In the *after* shot, she's wearing Lululemon leggings and a matching jacket, sporting a new haircut, and a wide, seductive grin.

She could be a model. *An America's Got Talent* winner. Wow. But the most amazing thing is that Jane is still listed as *active*, not *maintenance*, which must mean that she's still trying to lose weight.

Is she still trying to lose weight, or is she addicted to Bree's diet pills?

My heart races with excitement. Maybe I really am on to something. Maybe I'm actually going to discover a link between Geoff's Zen 2 Slim weight-loss program, and the reason why Bree was murdered. Maybe she really was selling illegal diet pills.

I flip through the next couple pages in Jane's chart, then turn back to the first page, which, like in Kim's file, is devoted to general information—emergency contact info, phone numbers, address, date of birth. I yawn, rub my eyes, and stretch my arms over my head. I'm exhausted.

The next page is the client's medical history. I peruse the sheet, word by word, line by line. I reread it, searching for a clue or code. Nothing stands out.

The next section includes the client's personal food diary, exercise log, and short- and long-term weight-loss goals. It's all fairly benign. Three meals a day. No snacks. No carbs. It all makes sense. The kind of stuff you'd find in every diet book on the shelf.

The last section is a spreadsheet documenting the payment schedule. It's doctor's-office boring. Each line records the date of the visit and a payment. The first visit is $2,500. Follow-up appointments cost $525. Jeez, that's a lot of money just to be weighed in.

I flip back through the chart to see what the initial visit and follow-up appointments include. Basic stuff. Counseling, weight and body mass assessment, a visit with The Center's fitness trainer. It also includes Geoff's Zen 2 Slim weight-loss supplements, which, if I remember correctly, are made up mostly of caffeine and some other harmless natural ingredients. There's nothing in the chart to indicate that customers are getting any additional supplements or prescription-type medication.

I read every word once, twice, three times. I flip through the pages and reread the entire chart. Set it aside and repeat the drill with several more charts.

After setting aside the *F*'s, I sink back in to the pillows, scoot my feet under the duvet, careful not to upset the files. I tuck the covers up under my chin.

What am I missing? Maybe if I speak with these women directly, I'll find out what I'm looking for.

Bree, a drug dealer? Illegal diet pills? It's a story I made up in my head. I felt like I was on a roll. Now, I just feel defeated. I've wasted all this time running down a rabbit hole. There's nothing here.

Exhaustion is getting the best of me.

I close my eyes and try to recap what I've learned in the last several days. I don't want to fall asleep. Can't fall asleep. But I'm running out of steam.

Did Mike Young murder Bree? He had the means, motive, and opportunity. But Mike thought I killed Bree. At least, that's what he led me to believe. He's a sociopath who would've raped and murdered me if he had caught me.

I remember the look of surprise and angst on Mike's face the night Bree's body was found. It seemed genuine.

Maybe Geoff did pay Mike to murder Bree on Friday night. Maybe he chickened out and only tried to scare her but ended up killing her by accident. He meets her in the bar at the Mandalay Bay Hotel, not far from my house. They go outside to talk. Maybe they take a walk. She has my umbrella. They argue. One thing leads to another. He bashes in her head. Drags her body down to the beach, not realizing that he has left Bree near my house.

No, that's too coincidental. Geoff told Mike where I lived. He leaves the beach between my house and my neighbor's house. Drops the umbrella in the trash. I hear Jean's dog, Daisy, and call the police. He's the cop in the area, so when I call the police, Mike Young is dispatched because it's his beat.

Mike is in his police uniform when he shows up at my house.

Would Mike plan to meet Bree at a public place when he's in uniform and on duty?

It doesn't fit. Too easy for someone to identify him.

Maybe he's in street clothes when he meets up with Bree.

Maybe Mike stalks Bree, like he stalked me.

Maybe, on the night Bree was murdered, she was meeting someone else at one of the restaurants or hotels. Mike's not worried about being seen in his uniform because he's supposed to be in the area on Friday night.

So, who was Bree meeting? Not Geoff. Geoff was in Las Vegas when Bree was murdered. Maybe she meets Jack O'Brien.

Bree leaves Jack O'Brien at the hotel bar and walks out to the parking lot alone. Mike Young knows she's having an affair with Jack and confronts her. They fight. He hits her in the head with the butt of his gun and drags her body down to the beach, where he leaves her in front of my house.

But Kim didn't see Mike Young on the beach. She saw Jack O'Brien.

Mike Young loves Bree. He thinks I murdered her. Mike is somehow involved, but he didn't murder Bree.

How does Kim fit into this scheme? She sees Jack O'Brien on the beach where Bree is found dead. She doesn't want to go to the police because she's afraid her husband will find out that she's having an affair, putting her marriage and the well-being of her family at risk.

That's why Kim is on the beach. It's a good place to go if you don't want anyone you know to see you. Which is important if you're contemplating an affair with your daughter's teacher. I get it. But the timing seems odd. Not just the timing and her behavior that night, but also her resistance to reporting her encounter to Lynch and Lee.

Back to Geoff. Maybe he murdered Bree because she was ripping him off and undermining his business with her illegal activities. Forget that I still haven't found evidence of illegal activity. I'm just going to stipulate that Bree's nefarious activities are a fact of my investigation. The details will follow.

Geoff kills Bree before going to Las Vegas, and has Jack dump her body in front of my house at the same time that Kim sees him.

It's the simplest explanation. But it doesn't jibe with the coroner's timeline, which determined that Bree was murdered sometime between 6:00 p.m. and midnight. Also, Kim thought she saw Bree alive, not dead.

I turn on my side and let my mind wander back to my life with Geoff. Did he ever love me? I don't think he did. Did I really love Geoff? No. I try to remember why we got married in the first place.

I married Geoff because he asked me, and my mother loved the idea of me finally getting married and marrying a successful doctor. Geoff married me because I was pretty enough, and I came from a semi-famous family.

I try to recall what happened when I confronted Geoff about his affair with Bree. He was mad at me. Furious. Why? Because I blew his peace-harmony-love image. Was Bree about to destroy Geoff's image? Blow the lid off his sleazy business? Expose that his Zen 2 Slim supplements are nothing but a sham?

I close my eyes and start to drift off. In my mind, I see Audrey with her beautiful red hair flowing over her shoulders, and her obvious contempt for Bree. Audrey tells me that she knows who murdered Bree and why. That's a relief.

She's sitting next to me at a big round table in jail. Bree is sitting across from us. I'm so happy she's actually not dead.

Bree is all dressed up in the black Trina Turk dress that we fought over that day at Wendy Foster's. I wonder how she got it.

Maybe she ordered it online or something. The dress looks great on Bree, but she's wearing a pair of Havaiana flip-flops, which are cool, but way too casual for the dress.

All of a sudden, I realize we're on the beach, so I guess it's okay.

The wind is blowing. It's freezing out, but I don't feel cold. Bree's skin deathly pale. Her blonde hair is cascading over her shoulders. She seems angry at Audrey. I want to ask her who murdered her, but I can't find my voice. I mouth the words, but my voice doesn't work, and she's not looking at me.

I realize that Bree's not mad at Audrey. She's trying to tell her something. But Audrey keeps looking behind Bree like she sees someone coming. What is Bree trying to say?

The answer to the question is the key. The key to what? Weird.

I try to hear what Bree is saying, but I can't. Her voice is muffled by the pounding waves. The sound is close and loud. Pounding over and over again, against the shore.

Hallow and haunting.

Not waves. My mind is trying to register what's happening. Someone wants in. I open my eyes. Someone is beating on the door of my cottage.

CHAPTER 26

I UNTANGLE MYSELF FROM THE BLANKETS and push myself up in bed. My heart is racing. I'm sweaty and disoriented. The room is dark. I must have turned the lights off in my sleep.

I step on the carpet and stand, holding the edge of the bed to keep my balance. I stumble over to the drapes and pull them back. It's cloudy, but I can see a ray of sunshine peeking through the gloom.

The glare burns my eyes. I let the drapes fall back in place. Look at the clock next to the bed. The illuminated numbers tell me that it's after 10:00. How long did I sleep?

Another thud against the door tells me someone wants in.

I trip over something on the way to the door. I'm scared. It could be the police. Mike Young. Danny Starr.

No. Danny could've followed me here, but he didn't. That's telling.

I can't think about Danny. Have to focus.

With my ear to the door, I listen.

"Housekeeping."

I jump back. She must have heard me breathing.

Housekeeping. That's what all the crooks say when they want to get into a hotel room.

"I'm good. Mind coming back?"

Flipping on the wall switch, I lean against the door. Sigh with relief. I'm a wreck.

I look at the bed. Files are everywhere. Some on the bed, but most are lying open on the floor.

One by one, I organize the papers into the proper files and set them back on the bed with the others.

What's Kim's role in all of this. I'm stunned that she's mixed up in Geoff's weight-loss program. I feel betrayed and hurt. I move out of town, and she moves in on all my friends and my ex-husband and his wife. I wish I could be honest with her and tell her how I feel, but knowing Kim, she'd turn it around on me and then gossip about it.

Sitting down, I try to sort through the jumble of thoughts in my head. Geoff and I split up. Geoff marries Bree. And around that time, Kim joins Geoff's gym and signs up for his weight-loss program. She stays in the program, even after she's lost a ton of weight.

On the evening Bree is found murdered, Kim chooses to go down to Hollywood Beach to meet with Sophia's teacher. Maybe the teacher moonlighted at The Center to make extra money. Considering how poorly teachers are paid, it kind of makes sense.

As Kim leaves the beach, she sees Jack O'Brien and maybe Bree. Kim won't go to the police with the information because...

...the police will find out that she's having an affair. An affair would probably end Kim's marriage. But maybe the *affair* is just a cover for something else.

Exactly. Something else.

What?

The point is that Kim was down on Hollywood Beach on the evening Bree was found murdered. Affair or not, she is seriously doing an end run around the quarterback. I don't really know what that means, but it sounds right.

Kim obviously wasn't planning on running into me on the night Bree was murdered. She needed a quick cover for why she was on Hollywood Beach, so she lied about meeting Sophia's teacher.

Cover for what? Maybe Kim was on the beach to meet Bree. Score more pills. Yes. A drug deal gone south.

But that doesn't make sense. Kim had been using Bree's pills for a long time. She didn't need to go all the way to Hollywood Beach, on a cold drizzly night, to buy more. Anyway, there's no hard evidence that the pills that Kim uses are illegal diet pills. All Geoff's clients are using is his stupid Zen 2 Slim supplements that never worked for me or Oprah.

I'm tap dancing in the end zone. All I seriously have to go on are some crazy theories, a few *maybe* witness who aren't talking, and a bunch of stolen files.

But what if Geoff has changed his supplement formula to get better results? What if *Bree* changed Geoff's formula to include illegal substances—substances not listed in the formula's ingredients? I'm pretty sure that supplements don't require FDA approval. There's no oversight or regulation for supplements.

Not only do Bree's supplements get excellent results, but the addictive nature of the new formula also creates a significant demand and increased sales. No wonder Geoff's business is skyrocketing.

But diet pills are dangerous. I wonder if any of Geoff's clients have gotten sick or overdosed from taking Zen 2 Slim supplements.

After gathering up the rest of the files, with Kim's on top, I walk over to the chair, turn on the lamp, and sit. I straighten all the files into a neat stack and reorganize them by dates: files that were active before Bree's death, and the ones that are active now.

I go back to Kim's file. Start at the top of the page and move down the chart, line by line, one more time. In the first year, Kim only loses a few pounds. But this is probably true for everyone who signed up for Geoff's weight-loss program before Bree found her source for diet pills.

When Geoff's diet program failed to get results, I'm guessing that Bree reached out to Audrey, knowing she has connections in the drug world. Bree entices Audrey to move to California with the opportunity to work at The Center. She hires Audrey as her behind-the-scenes assistant, according to Felix. This is the one bit of evidence that I actually know for a fact to be true.

Once Bree starts selling her new *boosted formula*, the Zen 2 Slim program really takes off. Bree's customer base doubles. She and Geoff are making big money now.

I read down the chart. In the next year, Kim really starts to lose weight. I flip through the pages and find an entry that has Kim currently registered in the program's maintenance phase. Missed that the first time I went through the file.

Maintenance? Ha. *Addicted phase* is more like it.

Bree has a captive, and growing, customer base.

I turn to the payment schedule to see if I can distinguish club membership, services, products from the payments for Bree's pills.

Everything is recorded by product name, SKU number, and price. Geoff's natural supplement business is huge. Under his private label, Geoff sells hundreds of supplements—pills for everything from sleeping disorders to regulating blood sugar to mood enhancers.

I moved my finger down the spreadsheet and stop at *Zen 2 Slim weight-loss supplements*. There's regular and extra-strength. But no one's buying the regular Zen 2 Slim supplements.

Seems to me that Bree is too cunning and greedy to let Geoff share in the profits of her extra-strength supplement sales. Maybe her customers pay cash for her boosted pills. Maybe Audrey manages the books for Bree's diet pill sales. Maybe all sales must be paid in cash. I think about what Felix said about Bree paying for everything in cash. Audrey will know.

Sitting back in the chair, I recap everything that I've learned. The bummer is that I don't actually have any hard evidence. Just what I've extrapolated from Kim, Lynch and Lee, Mike, Danny, and stolen files. The files prove nothing.

I pick up Kim's file one last time and open it to the first page. I really had zero clue that Kim had signed up for Geoff's Zen 2 Slim program. She didn't tell me, and I never asked why she was losing so much weight. For all I knew, she could have been sick with some serious illness. I guess I was too consumed with *me* to worry about *her*. Not good. If I get through this nightmare, I swear I'm going to be a better friend, daughter, sister, person.

I continue down the page and focus on the dates recorded every time Kim visits The Center. According to Kim's chart, she weighed in at The Center on the day Bree was murdered.

Interesting. But I'm not sure why.

Starting at the top of the first page, I reread each entry in the file. I notice a little box marked *Program Concierge*. Beneath it are the initials *BDM*. Bree Daniels Martin. I flip through the pages and notice that every subsequent visit is also initialed by the program concierge—BDM.

I grab another file from the table next to me and replace it with Kim's file. I wonder who else serves as program concierge?

Shuffling through pages in the new files, I find the program concierge's initials. BDM. Zen 2 Slim was obviously Bree's baby. Smart. She had full control over the program, which meant that no one questioned her client's rapid weight loss except her. Geoff is making money, so he's oblivious, and the customers are getting great results, so they're not complaining.

Bree was the perfect little moneymaking machine.

How does it all fall apart? Maybe Audrey tips Geoff off to what Bree is up to. Maybe Kim discovers that Bree is cheating Geoff out of a ton of money and tells him. Maybe Kim's hoping that Geoff will dump Bree and go back to me. Maybe Geoff hears something through the grapevine from one of his patients. Maybe one of Geoff's Zen 2 Slim clients dies from a bad reaction to Bree's diet pills. It could be anything.

I bet Audrey knows what really happened. That's why she's so afraid.

I retrieve another file and open it to the first page. Beth Jenkins. Doesn't ring a bell. I skip through the next couple pages until I come to the last time Beth checked in with her program concierge—three days *before* Bree's murder.

Bree initials the visit. I go through several more files. I'm not sure what I'm looking for.

I pick up Lynn Taylor's chart. Go to the page noting Lynn's

last weigh-in. Yesterday. Two days *after* Bree is murdered. I read the initials.

Shit! This is the last thing I expected to see.

KB. Kim Barrett.

Is Kim The Center's new program concierge? Is Kim in charge of Zen 2 Slim?

I grab the charts that I had set aside and go through each one until I find another enrollee's visit dated after Bree's death.

KB.

Is Kim having an affair with Geoff? I know this is a leap, but maybe it's Geoff that Kim meets on Hollywood Beach the evening Bree is murdered, not her daughter's teacher. Maybe Kim demands that Geoff leaves Bree. He refuses. He can't afford another failed marriage. It would be horrible for his reputation.

After Geoff leaves the beach, Kim talks Bree into meeting her. They fight. Maybe Kim doesn't kill Bree on purpose. Maybe it's an accident. She's strung out on diet pills. She's not thinking straight. Bree ends up dead.

When Kim leaves the beach, she unexpectedly runs into me. Her cover is blown. She makes up a story about an affair and seeing Jack O'Brien on the beach near my house. Of course, she refuses go to the police with her story. In fact, she freaks out when I mention the police, because why?

Kim murdered Bree? That's crazy. There's no way. I've known her since middle school. She can be conniving and manipulative, but she would never physically hurt anyone. She's no more dangerous than I am. I don't know if Lynch or Lee would agree, but it's true.

God, I really don't know what the truth is anymore. I don't know what's real or what's imaginary.

Suddenly, it dawns on me that I told Kim that Audrey knows who murdered Bree. I need to warn Audrey. Even if Kim isn't the culprit, she might have told Geoff.

Audrey's in danger.

I grab my bag and dig in it for the piece of paper that Felix gave me with Audrey's phone number and address. I can barely read the numbers my hand is shaking so hard. I sit on the bed next to the nightstand and the phone. I take a couple of deep breaths to calm myself before picking up the receiver and punching in Audrey's number. The phone goes directly to voicemail. *Shit.*

As soon as I leave here, I'm getting another cell phone.

I call Lynette at the *Tribune.* I'm told that she's at a meeting. I leave her a voicemail message to contact Saintly and the police. I give her Audrey's address.

I call my mother. Voicemail. Today's probably her spa day.

All my other numbers, including my father's and Saintly's, are in my phone buried on Hollywood Beach.

I hang up and dig in my purse for Detective Lynch's card. I punch in his number and wait.

I look at the clock as I pace the floor. It's after 11:00.

"Ventura Sheriff's Department. Can I help you?" a woman says, in an indifferent voice.

"Detective Lynch. It's an emergency!" I scream into the phone.

"If this is a real emergency, hang up and dial 911."

"I need to speak with Detective Lynch."

"Detective Lynch is in the field. I'll put you through to our desk sergeant. Hold, please."

Hold, please? Is she crazy? I twist the phone cord in my fingers and force myself to breathe slowly so I don't start hyperventilating.

Several rings later, the line picks up.

"Officer Mike Young—"

I hang up and dial 911.

"State your emergency."

For the next couple minutes, I try to calmly explain my emergency, but the only coherent thing I can manage is Audrey's address. Everything else sounds like a crazy person talking.

I hang up when she asks me my name. Once the dispatcher hears my name, she'll send it to the Ventura sheriff, and Mike

Young will intercept it. She'll direct him to the location of the call.

I need to get out of here.

I dash over to the overnighter and dump the contents on the floor. Rip off my pajamas, then tear off all the tags on my new clothes. Tug on my undies, bra, jeans, and sweater. Reach for my socks and boots and pull them on. I put Kim's file on top of the others and cram them all into the Target bag. Place the *Do Not Disturb* sign on the door before I shut it and hurry down the hall, to the valet.

As I'm running, I fish around in my purse for the parking stub and the envelope full of hundred-dollar bills. I find both just as the attendant approaches me on the curb outside the hotel. I hand him another one of the bills, with the stub.

"Thanks." He's smiling like I just gave him a Christmas present. "Want change?"

"I'm good."

As promised, the Escape is parked up front. I pull myself into the car, jam it into gear, and step on the gas. The wheels spin on the damp pavement. I smell smoke.

Fishtailing out of the driveway, I make a sharp left turn and head toward Highway 101. I'm only vaguely familiar with the location of Audrey's apartment. I'm pretty sure she lives in a sketchy part of Santa Barbara.

When I hit Montecito's lower village, I come to a dead stop. Cars start to move, but at a snail's pace. I'm stuck in traffic behind a guy in a silver Bentley who's searching for a parking space.

Damn it!

I'm operating on instinct and adrenaline. I jam my hand down on the horn as I edge the Escape as close to the Bentley's bumper as I can get without hitting it. The driver moves to the left to give me some room, and politely waves me around. I put the car in reverse, back up a little, then yank the steering wheel to the right and speed around the Bentley, almost hitting a couple of women out for a morning stroll. They jump out of my way, grabbing each other protectively.

Before leaving Montecito Village, I park at a CVS to get another untraceable phone and run into the store. I'm out in less than five minutes.

Instead of taking the freeway, I jerk the steering wheel to the right and turn my car onto Old Coast Highway. I step on the gas while digging into my bag for Audrey's address.

Punta Gorda Street. It's only a few miles away.

As Old Coast Highway forks, I make a left toward the beach, into a residential neighborhood, and slow the car. This area of Santa Barbara feels a bit like a shantytown. Most of the homes and apartments are dilapidated. Some look abandoned. There are old cars parked along the street that look inoperable. Some are missing tires.

It's hard to believe that I'm still in Santa Barbara.

Thunder rumbles in the distance. Rain patters on the windshield.

Mixed into the homes are random businesses and storefronts. I pass a tire store, a tattoo parlor, a metal-surplus recycling center, and a liquor store before I spot Punta Gorda and turn right.

Two blocks later, I locate Audrey's address. It's a standalone two-story building on the corner that looks like it used to be an auto repair shop.

This can't be right. Is Felix messing with me? I read the address again while I drive past the building and make a U-turn. I edge the Escape toward the curb and park across the street. I gawk at the building.

It looks abandoned. One side of the building is fenced off with chain links and razor wire and looks like it serves as some kind of storage area for cars and equipment.

I crane my neck to get a better view of the back of the building, but it's no use. I'm going to have get closer on foot.

I pull away from the curb, drive around the corner, and park. Step out of the car. Press the key fob and stride toward the abandoned tire store. Raindrops splatter the pavement. I put my head down and hurry across the street. When I reach the corner, I look back over my shoulder. I'm alone. I mean, really alone. This part of town is dead quiet.

I continue down the block until I'm in front of the address that Felix gave me. I walk around and find what looks like a residential unit in the back of the main building. I search the street for Kim's black Range Rover or Geoff's red Ferrari. There are a handful of older-model cars, but none look familiar.

From the sidewalk, I can hear music coming from the apartment. Etta James's deep, soulful voice is belting out her rendition of "At Last." Next to the front entrance is a metal mailbox. I take a deep breath and walk up a couple concrete steps and open the lid of the box. The hinges screech. I reach inside and pull out a couple envelopes. Audrey's name is printed on the front of one of the bills. This is it.

I gently knock on the door, step back, and wait like I'm selling Girl Scout cookies or something. Maybe I can talk Audrey into coming back to the Biltmore with me. She can pack up some stuff and stay with me until we can go to meet with Detectives Lynch and Lee and tell them everything she knows. They'll place her in a witness protection program. She'll start a new life.

I knock harder on the door again. No answer. Audrey didn't pick up her phone. Maybe she isn't home.

There's a window next to the door, above a planter of dead scrubs. I step over and wipe away the grime with the edge of my sweater and look into what looks like a makeshift living room. There's a worn-out-looking sofa sitting on a cement floor, and a couple chairs. An old-school TV set is propped on cinderblocks and a wood homemade shelf.

Audrey's lifestyle and Bree's couldn't be more different.

I step around to the front door and try the handle. The door opens under my touch.

I take a deep breath and step inside. The room is dingy and smells damp and musty. Inside, the music is blasting. Maybe

Audrey's in the shower, and that's why she didn't answer the door.

I take several steps into the room, which opens to what looks like a breakfast nook, kitchen, and hallway.

"Audrey?" I say above the music.

My voice sounds uncomfortably loud.

I hear steps coming my way. I hold my breath.

Kim. She looks stricken. Confused to see me. Her face is white. Dark circles shadow her eyes. She's afraid.

"Where's Audrey…"

Even in the dim light, I see blood on Kim's hands. The front of her white sweatshirt is smeared in red.

My hand goes to my mouth to stifle a scream. I want to run, but I need to find out what's happened to Audrey.

"It's not what you think." Kim's gaze darts around the room. She steps toward me. "You need to leave."

"It's too late for that." I hear Geoff's voice before I see him.

He walks out of the shadows and follows Kim into the hall. He takes a position behind her. He's dressed in a black OJ Simpson knit cap, turtleneck, and pants like some kind of Ninja assassin.

He's wearing the same black leather gloves he wore the day I saw him at the police station. In one of his gloved hands, he's gripping a large hunting knife.

"Jagged Edge," I blurt out for no good reason. My voice squeaks.

My knees are trembling. I want to run, but if I turn my back on Geoff, I'm dead.

"Your knife. It's just like the one in *Jagged Edge,* the movie."

"What the hell did you do to your hair?" Geoff frowns at me. "It looks like shit."

"Thanks." I can't let Geoff know how afraid I am. "You're always such a breath of fresh air."

I turn to Kim. "Where's Audrey?" I choke, staring at her hands and sweatshirt.

"I like your hair long," Geoff says, his voice strident. "You butchered it."

"You murdered Bree," I say to Kim.

I know I should keep my mouth shut and figure a way out of here, but I can't help myself. Kim murdered Bree and tried to frame me for her death.

"You set me up."

"No." Kim's lips are trembling. She's shivering. Her china blue eyes grow huge; her pupils look like pinpoints. This isn't deer in the headlights – it's deer before the hunter pulls the trigger of his gun.

She eyes Geoff and nods at him to indicate that Geoff's the one who killed Bree. He grabs Kim by the hair and yanks her close. Tears run down her cheeks.

It was Geoff all along.

"You think this dimwit killed Bree?" Geoff blusters as he twists his fingers in Kim's hair, hurting her.

She crumbles under his grip, but Geoff pulls her up to her feet.

"You're joking. Kim and Bree thought they could go into business for themselves. They tried to screw me." Geoff yanks her head back. "You think I wasn't going to find out?"

"Let her go," I say, in an even tone.

I look Geoff square in the eye. I'm not afraid of him. I'm fed up with him.

I step toward Kim and reach out to her.

"Kim, come with me."

"You're as stupid as this bitch and Bree. Playing detective." Geoff gives me a condescending smile.

It's a look I remember too well. He used it every time he lied to me and tried to make me feel like everything was my fault.

"How's that workin' out for you?" But the bravado in Geoff's eyes is gone.

He's sweating, even though it's cold outside. He looks almost as pale as Kim. He's losing control. His world is falling apart.

"You're still angry that I left you." I scan the room, looking for a way out. "Bree was planning to leave you, too. That's what this is all about, isn't it? Leave you and take all of your money."

Unless I can buy some time, I'm going to end up like Bree. If the police get here, I might have a chance. I have to keep Geoff talking.

"Amanda, you've always been a very short-sighted, selfish woman. No staying power. If you hadn't jumped ship when times got tough, Bree might still be alive."

"You're blaming me for Bree's death?"

"Don't look so surprised. Had we stayed married, none of this would've happened."

"You cheated on me." Anger bubbles up inside me.

"Had you been a better wife, I wouldn't have had to."

Geoff takes a step toward me, dragging Kim with him. Her gaze darts back and forth like a rabbit caught in the mouth of a mountain lion. She's searching for an escape.

She's looking everywhere but at me. Kim won't make eye contact with me. I'm speechless.

"I provided for you, gave you a beautiful home to live in. It wasn't enough, was it?" Geoff seethes.

Kim starts to say something, but Geoff yanks her head back.

"Now look at the mess you've created. You're going to go to jail. It won't just be for murdering Bree. All the evidence will lead to you. No more Neiman Marcus or Wendy Foster's."

"You're delusional." I take a step back toward the door.

If I can just get outside, I can scream for help.

"And fat. Really fat. You've gained weight. Not really getting good results from Zen 2 Slim, are you?"

An uncontrollable giggle escapes my lips. I feel giddy at the irony of it all.

"Fuck you, Amanda." Geoff sucks in his stomach. "You should've let the detectives handle this. Bree had a nasty temper. Everyone knew she hated you. A good lawyer could've made a case for justifiable homicide. You cop a plea and spend a couple years in jail. It'd be like going to rehab."

Like going to rehab? It's an insulting dig, but I'm unfazed. I struck a nerve in Geoff. Which, while uplifting in some weird, perverse way, is not good.

He's going to kill us. He has no choice. We are witnesses. Knowing Geoff, he'll get away with it.

I stare at him. He's diabolical. He used to be handsome and confident. He looks pudgy and nervous. His depravity has aged him. I don't know what I ever saw in him.

"The entire time we were together, I faked it."

Geoff becomes very still. "Faked what."

"S-e-x." I spell it like Mike Young did on the night I met him.

Time is running out. I have to move. There's no escape as long as Geoff has the knife trained on us. *Do something.*

Geoff takes a step toward me.

"Hey, Geoff." I force a smile. "Your fly's down."

When he looks down at his zipper, I hurl my body into Geoff and Kim. Geoff grunts like I knocked the air out of him. Kim screams. We all go down.

Out of the corner of my eye, I see the knife fly out of his hand. I reach for his balls like I did with Mike Young, and squeeze.

Crap. He's wearing some kind of large cup with wadding. Like a padded bra.

I go for his eyes, digging my fingers into the sockets, deep and hard. Geoff screams as he struggles to grab me.

Next to me, Kim is wriggling out of his grasp. He can't hold on to both of us.

He lets go of Kim, grabs my hair, and yanks. Tears burn my eyes.

I turn my head and bite down on his exposed wrist until I taste blood. He makes a horrible groaning sound, like a wounded dog might make. He jerks his hand away and let's go of my hair. I push myself away and reach for Kim. Drag her away from Geoff and give her a firm shove.

"Go!" I yell.

She stands and stumbles out of the house.

I scramble on my hands and knees and grab the knife. I can hear Geoff moving behind me.

I stand and point the blade at him. He struggles to get up. His knit cap is on the ground. Deep scratches mark his face and skin around his eyes. He's bleeding. He's gonna need plastic surgery. Those scars aren't going away on their own.

Geoff is gulping air. I look around for an escape.

The front door's behind me. If I turn and run, it's over. He's only a few yards away from me. He looks shaken, which gives me satisfaction. But more than anything, he looks furious.

What am I going to do now? Stab him?

"What are you gonna do? Stab me?" Geoff hisses in a mocking voice and takes a step toward me.

His hand goes to his face. He looks at his gloved hand. It's wet with blood.

He reaches in his pant pocket and takes out a white handkerchief, wipes the smear of blood off his cheek, then wraps the cloth around his bloodied wrist. His gaze bores into mine. Pure evil.

Geoff takes another step toward me.

He looks worried. I have the knife.

The sound of fire trucks, ambulances, and police cars drone over Etta James's lusty version of "Stormy Weather." Any second, they'll be here.

Geoff lifts his chin toward the sound.

"You're so stupid," Geoff says. "I can't believe I ever married such a moron."

"I was thinking the same thing about you," I choke. "You'll never get away with this."

"Really?" Geoff smiles. "Whose prints are on the knife?"

He turns and walks out of the house, through a back door, just as the police sirens close in.

CHAPTER 27

MY PRINTS ARE ON THE KNIFE, but Geoff's hair is in his cap sitting on the floor. Not very smart of him to leave it behind. Plus, Kim has gone for help and will be able to vouch for my innocence.

After wiping my fingerprints off the knife with the bottom of my sweater, I set it on the floor next to the cap like it's infected with a deadly disease.

The sirens blow right by the house, on their way to someone else's emergency.

Where are the police that I called almost an hour ago?

Audrey is somewhere in the house. I pick up my purse and head toward the music playing somewhere nearby.

At the end of a short hall, I find two closed doors. Loud music is coming from the one on the right. I take a deep breath and open the door on my left. I need to clear the room. Make sure no one is hiding out there.

Audrey obviously uses this room for storage. Cardboard boxes are stacked on every square inch of floor space. Clothes are piled on a chair, desk, and bench. An old toaster, microwave, and TV are among Audrey's stuff. Even *my* organizational skills couldn't sort out this mess.

I go to one of boxes: 2020. I tear off the lid and grab one of the files. *June*. It's a thick profit–loss spreadsheet from Bree's pill sales. Bree was making a ton of illegal money, and obviously cutting Geoff out of everything. With Bree's cunning and Kim's business sense and drive, it wouldn't be long before they could take over Geoff's entire Center.

I wonder if The Center's new building was in Bree's name? It wouldn't surprise me if Geoff underestimated Bree's ambition and smarts and put the building in her name to skirt taxes or hide profits.

Bree had other plans for the building. But I can't deal with this now. I have to get out of here.

I cram the file in my bag and head out of the room, to the other bedroom door. I grab the doorknob. It feels sticky. I look at my hand. Blood. *Shit!*

Blood smears the casing around the door.

My heart slams inside my chest.

I push the door open and look inside. It's a bedroom. Dingy white eyelet curtains cover a window. Green mottled walls are desperate for paint. A faded flower print bedspread and worn sheets are tangled at the foot of the bed. An old boom box sitting on a rickety end table shrieks, "*Great Balls of Fire.*"

I walk over and press the off button.

The room goes quiet. I still hear the sirens, but they're fading fast.

A chill racks my body. Geoff will be coming back for me. I have to find Audrey, see if she's alive, and get us the hell out of here.

I hurry around the bed. Audrey's on the floor. There's a dark, wet-looking splotch on her black sweater. I touch it and pull my hand away. *Blood.*

I carefully put my hand to her neck and feel for a pulse. A faint *bump-bump* pulses against my fingers.

She's alive. *Thank God.*

I pull the hair away from her face. An ugly gash mars her forehead, but the bleeding has stopped. She might need stitches, but it doesn't look fatal. She has a black eye and bloodied lips. Blood cakes her nostrils. Her nose looks broken. Geoff roughed her up, bad enough to maybe kill her.

"Audrey," I say, in a firm voice, and give her a gentle shake. "We've got to get out of here."

She groans and struggles to open her eyes. One eye is swollen shut. She stares at me through her better eye. She's terrified. She has no idea who I am.

"Felix sent me. You're safe. But we need to get out of here." I take Audrey's hand in mine and reach around her back for support. I try pull her up. Her body is limp. I can't move her. *I shouldn't move her.*

I yank a blanket off the bed and wrap it around her.

"You'll be okay. I'm getting help."

I pull out my phone and punch in 911.

"There's a badly injured woman here. I called you more than an hour ago with the address."

I don't wait for an answer. I make a quick decision to leave the house through the front door. Geoff went out the back, but he could be hiding out, waiting for me to leave.

For whatever reason, I feel less vulnerable on the street.

I hurry down the hall to the living room. Wrench open the front door. A flood of light pours into the room. I step over the threshold, into the cold air. It feels good. Low, thick clouds cloak the sky. It's raining.

I hurry down the stoop and jog down Punta Gorda and around the corner, to the Escape. Even though it's only late afternoon, the streetlights are on and reflecting off the wet pavement. It's still quiet and lifeless, but it feels good to be away from Audrey's building and on my way to safety.

I jerk my purse up to my hip and dig around for the key fob. I feel the smooth, oval-shaped fob and push the open button with my thumb. The usual squawk breaks the silence and sets my heart into a crazy *thump-thump* against my chest. I need to get out of here.

I yank the door open, throw my purse onto the passenger seat, bury the phone in my pocket, then pull myself up behind the steering. I start to draw the door shut, but a firm hand stops me. I gasp.

It's Jack O'Brien.

I'm seriously living in hell.

Where did he come from? Geoff sent him to clean up his mess. Finish off Audrey. Find me and Kim.

I hope Kim got away and went for help.

"Hey," I say, like I'm greeting a guest for a dinner party.

Jack is pointing a gun at me. I look away from the gun to his eyes.

Pretend you didn't see it. Stay calm. Be strong. Don't show him how terrified you are. I mean, he's not going to shoot me in broad daylight. Is he?

"Long time no see."

"Get out of the car." Jack waves the gun barrel at me. "Now! Don't make any funny moves. This isn't a game, Amanda."

Even with the gun pointing at me, Jack looks weak and deflated. He's dressed in a pair of limp-looking khakis, a snugly fitted polo that shows off his gut, and a gray windbreaker that looks like it's from his Little League Baseball days. Beads of sweat dot his forehead. He's nervous.

For no logical reason, I'm not afraid of him. I feel sorry for him.

I step out of the car and shut the door behind me.

"Let's go." He jabs his gun toward me.

"No way, Jack." I stand my ground. "I'm not going anywhere with you. Put the gun down."

"Think I'm kidding, don't you?" Jack snaps, but his bottom lip quivers.

He's falling apart.

"You have no idea how serious this is. How you ruined everything."

"Aren't you tired of doing Geoff's dirty work? Seriously, Jack. What's in it for you?"

"You have no idea what you're talking about." He brandishes the gun at me. "I work for myself."

"Don't take the fall for Geoff."

I search his eyes and try to remember what I know about Jack O'Brien. He and Geoff have been friends since grade school.

Even though they kind of look alike, Jack's the nerd. Geoff's the jock. Nothing's really changed.

"It's not fair."

"Your little buddy Kim tried to get away." Jack has the gun at his side instead of pointing at me. "Didn't get very far. She's not doing so well."

"Come on, Jack." I take a step toward him. "Take me to Kim. You're a successful lawyer. You don't need to do this."

"Shut up," Jack barks.

He yanks my arm and shoves me toward Punta Gorda and Audrey's house.

"Move!"

"I know a great lawyer. He'll help you. Seriously. He's a famous criminal defense lawyer." I touch his arm. "He helped me with my arrest."

"Move!" He yanks away from me and opens Audrey's front door before, then pushes me through.

I stumble into the living room. Jack jabs me with the gun and nods toward the kitchen.

"You haven't done anything wrong yet." I sit on one of the rickety kitchen chairs and search the room for a weapon. "Geoff's setting you up, just like he tried to do to me."

"Stop talking, or you'll be sorry." Jack yanks me up from the chair and kicks open the kitchen door.

He shoves me out toward a late-model white Lexus that's hidden from the street, behind a metal lean-to.

Suddenly, the sky turns dark, rain starts falling in huge drops.

He unlocks the car manually and opens the door.

"Get in."

"Listen to me. I told you I'm not going with you." I search the area for some sign of life.

We're hidden from view. No one can see us.

Don't get in his car. I'll have a much better chance of surviving if I stay where I am.

"Your girlfriend didn't want to get in the car, either. Want to know what happened to her?"

"Kim? Jack, please. Don't be an idiot. You're the one who'll go to jail for this, not Geoff."

"Idiot? You think I'm an idiot? Get in the car, Amanda, or so help me God, I'll kill you right here," he spits, and pushes me forward. "Behind the wheel. You're driving."

Jack shoves me against the driver's side. I hit the door with a *thud*.

"Ouch!" I scream and rub my leg.

I'm totally drenched and freezing. My leg throbs.

"Why'd you do that? What have I ever done to you?"

"You never gave me the time of day." He grabs my arm and jabs the gun in my side. "Now you're on my side? Don't make me laugh. Shut up and get in the car."

I remember when Geoff first introduced me to Jack. I remember wondering why Geoff hung out with him. With his skintight jeans and geeky polos, he really didn't fit in with the cool crowd that Geoff and I surrounded ourselves with.

But Jack's right about one thing. I didn't give him the time of day.

"I was awful. I'm sorry." I reach over and touch his arm. "I really am."

"Yeah?" Jack shakes off my hand as he reaches around me for the car door.

He's still a dork. A dangerous dork.

He opens the door and shoves me inside. I sit behind the steering wheel. Jack hands me the keys and moves into the passenger seat.

"When you leave the yard, go left. Keep going until you hit Coast Highway. Get on the freeway heading south. One wrong move, and I'll shoot you."

Jack's eyes look like they're spinning in his head. His lips are twitching. He's on something. Crack? Pills?

My heart is beating so hard I can barely breathe. Jack's going to kill me.

Okay. I can live with that. Everyone eventually dies, right?

A bubble of laughter escapes me. I'm clearly losing it, too. Which is good because I suddenly realize that the worst thing that Jack can do to me is shoot me. Not the best outcome, but accepting the worst-case scenario is kind of empowering. Every alternative outcome is a plus.

Jack jabs the gun in my side. "Quiet!"

I stifle a laugh, insert the old-school key into the ignition, and rev the engine. Rain splashes the windshield. I turn on the wipers.

"Where are we going?"

"Hollywood Beach. You know the way."

CHAPTER 28

JACK IS RANTING. *Bree. Kim. Geoff.* They've all *screwed* him. His work *sucks*. He's going on and on.

"Geoff changed after you dumped him. It ruined him. Everything that's happened is your fault."

Jack obviously doesn't even know who he's talking to. Maybe he's having a psychotic break. It sounds more like he's talking to Bree than to me. He knows that Geoff dumped me—he helped Geoff with the divorce.

Going to Hollywood Beach can only mean one thing. Jack is taking me to Geoff.

Geoff killed Bree. I don't know how he managed it, but he did. He'll have no problem killing Kim and me.

How am I going to prove it? Detectives Lynch and Lee confirmed he was in Las Vegas the night Bree was murdered.

Thoughts are spinning in my head. I can barely think.

I shift into drive and angle the Lexus out of the yard. Take surface streets for several blocks until I come to the freeway. I'm driving like a sixteen-year-old being tested for her driver's license. Every turn, stop, and acceleration is deliberate and well-orchestrated. I'm buying time.

I see the Coast Highway on-ramp and make a quick decision to drive past it.

"Oops."

"One more move like that, and it's over."

"Sorry." I look over at Jack and shrug.

He shoves the gun in my side.

Jack may not have the balls to kill me, but if he keeps shoving that gun in my side, it's going to go off by accident.

I make a quick U-turn and drive up the on-ramp onto the freeway headed toward Hollywood Beach. My heart is pounding. I don't have a plan, but I'm sure that Jack has one—a plan completely masterminded by Geoff.

"Jack, there's something you need to know."

He looks at me and rolls his eyes. He's clutching the gun in his lap instead of jabbing it my ribs.

"Keep it to yourself," he says.

"It's about Bree." I stay focused on the road.

I feel his eyes on me. He's quiet. Waiting.

"I heard, um, through the grapevine that Bree was in love with you." I keep the steering wheel steady, and my eyes straight ahead. "She was planning to leave Geoff."

"You're crazy. No way."

I take my eyes off the road for a second to look at his face. I can see that I'm piquing his interest.

"Seriously. You were in love with her. You dated her first, right? You met her in Las Vegas. You introduced her to Geoff."

I'm making this up.

Traffic on the 101 seems light for a Thursday evening. School is out for Christmas vacation. Maybe families are taking advantage of the holiday to go on vacation.

"Shut up." Jack's expression is grim.

"I heard that from a couple people." I grip the steering wheel.

"Who? Who told you that?" Jack's voice is wary, but he shifts his body in his seat and turns toward me. "Don't mess with me."

"Mike Young." I exit the freeway at Victoria and head toward Hollywood Beach. "He's a friend. He told me that she was in love with you."

"Mike Young told you that?" Jack frowns. "How does he know Bree? He worked security for The Center a couple times. I don't believe you."

"Bree met Mike at The Center. She was his massage

therapist. Which is almost like being his shrink, right?"

I make a left at the next street. The rain has let up a little. I turn off the wipers.

"Get to the point."

Jack is getting impatient. I've got to wrap this up soon.

"The point is..." *Crap. What was my point?* "Bree told Mike everything. But if you don't believe Mike, you should ask Kim. Kim was, um...kind of Bree's confidante."

"Keep driving." Jack waves the gun at me.

I'm losing him.

"I wouldn't believe a word Kim says. You should hear the stuff she says about you."

"Can we stipulate that Geoff murdered Bree?" I say matter-of-factly, channeling Saintly. "You and Bree could have had a life together. You haven't hurt anyone. You haven't done anything wrong. You're a good person, Jack. Don't let Geoff take you down."

"Shut up and keep driving. When you get to the stop sign, turn into the parking lot behind the warehouse up ahead."

I make the turn and slowly drive down a gravel ancillary road, then turn into a deserted parking lot that's hidden behind a shuttered warehouse, a wide swath of wetlands, and tall bamboo. I stop the car and put it in park.

"We'll wait here," Jack says.

This place looks familiar. I look around.

This is where I hid from Mike Young last night, after he attacked me. Maybe this is where Geoff murdered Bree, then somehow moved her body to the beach behind my house.

For what seems like forever, we wait in the car without speaking.

"Jack," I beg, finally. "Let's leave before it's too late."

"Time to go. Get out of the car. Now!"

I've lost Jack. I had him for a minute. Now I'm finished.

I open the door and stagger out of the car. The day is fading into night. That's what Jack was waiting for.

He jabs me with the gun.

With Jack's hand clamped around my waist, and his gun digging into my ribs, we walk across the gravel road and move through the tall bamboo hedge. We run across the highway, to the beach.

It hits me.

"Hold on a second. *You* went to Las Vegas. Not Geoff. You used a fake ID with Geoff's name on it to get through airport security and register at the hotel. When you flew home, Geoff was the one who greeted the detectives at the luggage pick-up. The detectives probably never even saw you."

Jacks shoves me toward the beach. It's pitch-black out.

"You didn't even know Geoff was planning to murder Bree, did you?"

Jack stops. He stares at me. His body is rigid. He's on high alert. Something I said is clicking in his mind. I see it in his eyes.

"Geoff convinced you that I murdered Bree." I search his eyes.

"I liked going to Vegas for Geoff," Jack mumbles, almost to himself. "When Geoff told you he was at one of his Vegas seminars, he was in Hawaii, the Virgin Islands. He even went to Italy with one of his girlfriends. You didn't have a clue, did you?"

I look at Jack but can't find the words to respond. I had no idea.

I think back on all the times that Geoff went to *Las Vegas*. He never invited me to go with him. He told me that he was working, and that I'd be bored.

I wonder what would've happened if I had showed up to surprise him? I can't even think about that right now. Geoff probably had a backup plan.

"You were right. I introduced Bree to Geoff," Jack says, but his voice has lost momentum.

He nudges the gun in my back and gives me another push. I start walking toward the dunes.

"Move."

God, I've got to come up with a plan to get out of here.

It's so dark I can barely see. My feet dig into the damp sand as I struggle to get up to the top of one of the dunes.

Just beyond the crest of the sand, I see a lifeguard tower.

Jack gives me another shove. I lose my balance and tumble.

I dig my hands into the sand to stop myself from rolling all the way to the bottom of the dune.

I push myself into a sitting position. Try to get my bearings.

I look behind me. Jack is laboring in the sand nearby. He's wielding the gun.

I rub the sand from my eyes and focus on Jack. He's crying. Even in the dark, I can make out tears sliding down his cheeks.

I quickly look away. Jack's losing it. I don't want him to know that I know.

My heart pounds. He may not have the nerve to kill me in cold blood, but he may not even realize what he's doing. Which is almost worse.

I've got to do something. It's now or never.

I slide to the bottom of the dune and push myself into a standing position but make no effort to run. Where am I going to go? I'll never make it to the hotel or my house. They're both too far away. If I turn and run, Jack will shoot me in the back. If I don't run, I'm dead anyway.

I look over at Jack. He looks disoriented. His face is tear streaked. I don't think he's even aware that he's crying.

Move. Now! I turn away from Jack and run. It's hard getting traction in the soft sand, but I keep going.

Gunfire erupts. A scream erupts from my throat. Sand explodes next to my feet. I stop for the briefest second.

Move. I scramble up another dune on my hands and knees.

"Geoff!" I hear Jack yell, his voice rising above the wind. "Geoff! Where the hell are you!"

Cresting the dune, I look back to see Jack only about fifty feet away, but he isn't looking at me. I turn my back on him, roll over the top of the dune, steady myself with my hands, and slide the rest of the way. At the bottom, I start toward the lifeguard tower.

At the base of tower, I lean back against the ladder to catch my breath. Jack is nowhere in sight. I push away from the tower and jog toward the shoreline and firm sand.

Gun fire explodes behind me. A hot blast of air soars past my cheek. The sand in front of me jumps. I hold my hands over my face.

Behind me, I hear a door squeak open. I drop my hands and look toward the lifeguard tower. Geoff is standing on deck, looking at me, a large gun trained on me.

Jack scuffles over the top of the dune and slides down.

"Amanda almost got away," Geoff barks.

He turns and steps down the ladder to the sand and looks from me to Jack and back to me again.

"Can you believe this loser?" Geoff says to me, then turns to Jack. "You almost botched the whole plan! What took you so long to get here?"

Jack is pointing the gun at me, but his hand is shaking.

"I, uh...we, uh..."

"Are you fucking crying?" Geoff's says. "Give me the gun."

I step toward Jack. "Leave him alone, Geoff. Stop your bullying."

"No." Jack holds the gun steady with both hands and points it at Geoff. "No."

The next few seconds are a blur.

Geoff lunges for Jack. They fall on the ground. Sand kicks up and hits me in the face. I start to run toward the hotel, but I remember Kim.

I scramble up the lifeguard tower stairs and push the door open. Kim is lying on the wood floor. Blood cakes her forehead. Her hands are crusted in blood. I feel for a pulse. She's not dead. Yet.

The silence is broken by a deafening *pop, pop, pop!*

Jack's gun? Geoff's?

I look out one of the windows. I can't see anything.

I step out on the deck of the tower. Wind whips my face. Geoff is at the bottom of the stairs.

He's pointing his gun at me.

CHAPTER 29

GEOFF OPENS FIRE. Splinters fly off the rail next to me. I don't wait to see what Geoff's next move is. I run around to the back of the tower, climb over the rail, and jump. I try to run up the dunes toward the parking lot, but the heavy, damp sand is like running in oatmeal.

Bang! Gunfire explodes. Sprays of sand erupt around me.

When I reach the top of the dunes, I hear another *pop!* Sand kicks up near my feet. I keep running. I trip and fall down the slope, into the sand. I stay still and listen. Waves pound the shore. The wind roars in my ears.

I need to go back for Kim.

Lying flat on the sand, I drag myself up to the crest of the mound. It's getting darker by the minute, but my eyes are adjusting.

I peek over the edge. Jack is on his back. His arms and legs are splayed crookedly. Not far away is Geoff. He's on his knees, slumped against the lifeguard tower stairs. One hand is clinging to the stair rail. He's hanging on for dear life. His other hand is clutching his side. He's been hit. The pistol is on the sand near him. He doesn't have the strength to get it.

I stand and run down the hill. Kick the gun far away from Geoff, then run to Jack and feel his neck for a pulse. There is none—at least, not to my touch.

I dig my phone out of the pocket of my jeans. Dial 911. This time, when I speak to the dispatcher, there's no ambiguity.

"My name is Amanda Beckwith."

I explain where I am and what has happened. I give the woman Audrey's address and describe her injuries. I tell her that they are life-threatening.

The dispatcher asks if the perpetrator has left the scene.

"Yes," I say, in a steady, clear voice. "I'm on Hollywood Beach, south of the Mandalay Bay Hotel in Ventura. I'm on the sand next to Tower Eighteen. The perpetrator is here. He may be dead. There are two other people here with major injuries."

I end the call and phone my mother. Of course, she screens the call when she doesn't recognize the number.

I leave her a message to please call Detectives Lynch and Lee. I tell her where I am.

"I'm okay," I say. "Mother, this is a real emergency."

I pocket the phone and head toward the dunes. I pass by Geoff and Jack. Their lifeless bodies are just ten feet apart. There's nothing I can do for them now.

I struggle up the sand to the top of the dune, willing my legs to take one more step. They feel like rubber. I sit on the cold, wet sand. From here, I have a great view of the twinkling lights on the oil platforms to the north. My eyes adjust to the black night, and I can make out the Lexus in the parking lot. Somewhere north is the hotel.

I punch in the after-hours number for the *Tribune* and ask for Lynette. I know she's not there, but the operator will page her. Lynette is always available for breaking news.

I give the operator my name. "It's an emergency. Can you connect me?"

Seconds later, the phone rings.

"Where the hell are you," Lynette says.

I hear her chomping on something. Probably Red Vines. She sounds nervous.

"We're worried sick!"

I give her directions to where she can find me.

"You've got your story," I say.

I stretch my sweater over my knees and down to my ankles to keep warm while I wait for the police to arrive.

CHAPTER 30

IT'S CHRISTMAS EVE. Close to midnight. I'm finally back at my house on Hollywood Beach. I'm standing outside my closet, looking at the mess on the floor. Detective Lynch returned my clothes a few days ago. It was like a Christmas present. They're heaped in cardboard boxes on the closet floor. I'm in no hurry to get organized. I'm off the clock, taking a break from organizing anything—including myself.

I reach down and grab a cozy, cream cable knit sweater off the top of one of the boxes, pull it over my head, and snuggle into it. I turn on my heels and head downstairs.

Surprisingly, I feel relaxed, centered. Chill, as Danny says.

Wood crackles in the fireplace. And even though I never found time to buy a Christmas tree, I'm embracing the holiday spirit.

In the weirdest and happiest way, I'm looking at life from another altitude.

I sit on the sofa and rest my feet on the coffee table. I look up to see Danny Starr. He walks out of the kitchen and hands me a Champagne glass filled with sparkling cider.

Danny's drinking Champagne. He sits next to me and picks up the remote control in one hand, his Champagne glass in the other. He smiles, raises his glass to me. I lift my glass to him. Our eyes meet. We touch glasses.

"Here's to the future," Danny says. "The best is yet to be."

I bite my lip. *God, I hope so.*

"Ready?" Danny sets his glass on the table.

He gives my hand a reassuring squeeze and leans over and kisses me. His lips are warm. The taste of Champagne lingers in his mouth.

I pull away and look at him.

"I'm kind of scared." My stomach flip-flops.

"Here we go." Danny presses a button on the remote.

The flat screen comes to life. It's Andersen Cooper on CNN, leading a recorded segment titled, "Murder on Hollywood Beach: a California Nightmare."

His panel includes my mother and Lynette—who both look absolutely radiant in the limelight—Dr. Phil, Saintly Samuelson, me, and David Lee.

Lee left the Ventura County Sheriff's Department to finish law school. He's planning to practice criminal defense law after he passes the State Bar Exam.

I'm sitting between Saintly and David, looking rested and at peace. The dark circles under my eyes have faded. The scratches on my face are hidden by makeup.

I look happy. My hair looks fabulous, thanks to Felix, who also styled my mother and Lynette's hair for the segment.

Felix forgave me for lying to him about being a brain surgeon, because I saved his cousin Audrey's life. Even though Audrey is probably facing jail time for her role in Bree's illegal Zen 2 Slim drug sales, she's healing and positive about her future.

The show begins with Andersen Cooper giving an overview of Bree's death and the ongoing Ventura County District Attorney's investigation.

He asks former detective David Lee about Kim's status. By the grace of God, he reports, she pulled through but is still in the hospital, recuperating from multiple injuries. She also faces charges for participating in illegal drug sales, but was not charged in relation to Bree's death. Yet.

I still have a lot of unanswered questions regarding Kim's involvement. I drove to LA to visit her at Cedar Sinai, but she refused to see me. Maybe I'll never know the whole truth.

Jack survived. A medical miracle, according to his doctors. He was airlifted to Cedars-Sinai Medical Center in Los Angeles, where he remains in intensive care. I've been told that he's hanging on by a thread. If he lives, according to David Lee, he's facing the possibility of life in prison for aiding and abetting Geoff for Bree's murder.

Saintly and Lynette, my champions and friends for life, award me with one of Saintly's signed Super Bowl footballs. He hands it to me, along with a bear hug.

"Girl, you went goal to goal and won the game. I knew you had it in you."

My mother is uncharacteristically silent during the entire segment.

Andersen Cooper finally brings up Geoff—wellness guru to the stars.

"Doctor Geoff Martin. Great chiropractor. I actually went to him once. Hard to believe he masterminded his wife's murder. As we know, he wasn't as lucky as Jack O'Brien. He died in the ambulance on the way to the hospital."

Mike Young, the report continues, is suspended without pay, pending the outcome of the investigation for various criminal offenses, including his assault on me. Mike's DNA also matched the cold cases involving two women who were raped six months ago. It's suspected that those women are only the tip of the iceberg.

The Center is permanently closed. The beautiful neoclassic Montecito building that housed Zen 2 Slim is shuttered. The building's marquee is gone, but the outline of the letters are still there. A huge *For Sale* sign stands in front of the building.

"Any news about the Zen 2 Slim site?" I ask Danny, as he switches off the TV. "I heard Oprah bought it and is building a retreat center."

Danny lifts his glass and takes a sip.

"Don't think so. It's sited for a luxury hotel."

I start to say something, but Danny wraps his arms around me and pulls me close.

"Shhh." He places his finger on my lips. "Did you hear that?"
I wiggle out of his embrace and walk to the window that looks out to the beach. It's a beautiful star-studded night. A crescent moon shines on the water. A thousand diamonds on the ocean sparkle back at me. The beach is quiet.

"No," I reply.

I see something move in the distance between the dunes. Looks like teenagers.

I pull down the blinds and turn back to Danny.

"Didn't hear a thing."

ABOUT THE AUTHOR

CAROL FINIZZA has had a passion for storytelling since crafting articles for her college newspaper. She was a former sportswriter for the Orange County Register and a regular contributor to Orange Coast Magazine. She continued her writing career in advertising, where she wrote ad copy for some of Orange County's most successful companies and non-profit organizations.

Carol served as Director of Marketing for The Strand at Headlands, a historic property located on California's Gold Coast. Her creative and inspired approach to marketing, her deep connection to the community and her team spirit helped to position The Strand as one of California's most coveted residential communities and storied destinations.

Carol resides in Dana Point. She is the author of *The Surf-Vival Handbook for Land and Sea*, a girl's guide to life at the beach. *Murder on Hollywood Beach* is Carol's debut novel in *The Messy Girl Murder Series*.

Connect with Carol at
www.carolfinizzaauthor.com

CPSIA information can be obtained
at www.ICGtesting.com
Printed in the USA
LVHW101926150522
718656LV00003B/14

9 781611 534320